"Gazara! Wendo Ty Ureh! Magri! Magri!"

Clouds began to form over the shadowed kingdom, dark ones that did not remind Kentril so much of Heaven as of that other realm. Arms stretched toward the ruins, Quov Tsin continued shouting the spell. *"Lucin Ahn! Lucin—"*

"In the name of the Balance," someone broke in, "I charge you to cease this effort before you cause great calamity!"

Tsin faltered. The mercenaries turned as one, some reaching for blades.

A slim figure clad completely in black eyed them all with the arrogance reserved for those who did not just believe themselves superior in all ways but *knew* it to be truth. Plain of face and younger than the captain by more than a few years, the intruder would not have disturbed Kentril if not for two things. One had to do with the slanted eyes, so unearthly a gray color that they seized the attention of all who looked into them. Yet almost immediately those same eyes repelled, for in them Kentril sensed his own mortality, something no mercenary desired to come to know.

The man was a necromancer, the most feared of spellcasters . . .

DIABLO®

THE KINGDOM OF SHADOW

Richard A. Knaak

ISBN: 978-1-945683-16-9

First Pocket Books printing November 2004
First Blizzard Entertainment printing October 2018

10   9   8   7   6   5   4   3   2   1

Cover art by Bill Petras

Printed in China

for Chris Metzen and Marco Palmieri

†HE KINGDOM
OF
SHADOW

Oпe

The horrific scream came from the direction of the river.

Kentril Dumon cursed as he shouted orders to the others. He had warned his men to avoid the waterways as much as possible, but in the dense, steamy jungles of Kehjistan, it sometimes became difficult to keep track of the myriad wanderings of the rivers and streams. Some of the other mercenaries also had a tendency to forget orders when cool water lay just yards away.

The fool who had screamed had just learned the danger of growing complacent—not that he would likely live long enough to appreciate that lesson.

The slim, sunburnt captain battled his way through the lush foliage, following the pleading call. Ahead of him, he saw Gorst, his second, the giant, shirtless fighter ripping through the vines and branches as if they had no substance at all. While most of the other mercenaries, natives of cooler, highland regions in the Western Kingdoms, suffered badly from the heat, bronzed Gorst ever took all in stride. The scraggy mop of hair, dark black compared with Kentril's own light brown, made the giant look like a fleeing lion as he disappeared toward the river.

Following his friend's trail, Captain Dumon made better time. The screaming continued, bringing back graphic memories of the other three men the party had lost since entering the vast jungle that covered most of this land. The second had died a most horrible death, snared in the web of a horde of monstrous spiders, his body so injected with poison that it had become bloated and distorted.

Kentril had ordered torches used against the web and its hungry denizens, carefully burning out the creatures. It had not saved his man, but it had avenged the death somewhat.

The third hapless fighter had never been found. He had simply vanished during an arduous trek through an area filled with soft soil that pulled one's boots down with each step. Having nearly sunken to his knees at one point, the weary captain suspected he knew the fate of the lost soldier. The mud could be quick and efficient in its work.

And as he considered the death of the very first mercenary lost to Kehjistan's fearsome jungles, Kentril stepped out into a scene almost identical to that disaster.

A huge, serpentine form rose well above the riverbank, long reptilian orbs narrowed at the small figures below who sought in vain to pry free the struggling form in its tremendous maw. Even with its jaws clamped tight on the frantic mercenary whose screams had alerted Kentril and the others, it somehow managed to hiss furiously at the humans. A lance stuck out of its side, but the strike had evidently been a shallow one, for the behemoth appeared in no way even annoyed by it.

Someone loosed an arrow toward the head, likely aiming for the terrible eyes, but the shaft flew high, bouncing off the scaly hide. The tentacle beast—the name their esteemed employer, Quov Tsin, had used for such horrors—swung its prey around and around, giving Kentril at last a glimpse of whom it had seized.

Hargo. Of course, it would be Hargo. The bearded idiot had been much a disappointment on this journey, having shirked many of his duties since their arrival on this side of the Twin Seas. Still, even Hargo deserved no such fate as this, whatever his shortcomings.

"Get rope ready!" Kentril shouted at his men. The creatures had twin curved horns toward the backs of their heads, the one place on their snakelike bodies that the mercenaries might be able to use to their advantage. "Keep him from returning to deep water!"

As the others followed his instructions, Captain Dumon counted them. Sixteen, including himself and the unfortunate Hargo. That accounted for everyone—except Quov Tsin.

Where was the damned Vizjerei this time? He had a very annoying habit of wandering ahead of the band he had hired, leaving the mercenaries to guess half the time what he wanted of them. Kentril regretted ever taking this offer, but the talk of treasure had been so insistent, so beguiling . . .

He shook such thoughts from his head. Hargo still had a slim chance for life. The tentacle beast could have easily bitten him in two, but they just as often preferred to drag their prey under and let the water do their work for them. Made their meals soft and manageable, too, so the cursed sorcerer had said with scholarly indifference.

The men had the ropes ready. Kentril ordered them in place. Others still harassed the gargantuan serpent, making it forget that it could have long finished this encounter just by backing away. If the mercenaries could rely on its simple animal mind a little longer—

Gorst had a line set to toss. He did not wait for Kentril to give the order, already understanding what the captain wanted. The giant threw the loop with unerring accuracy, snagging the rope on the right horn.

"Oskal! Try to throw Hargo a line! Benjin! Get that rope on the other horn! You two—give Gorst a hand with that now!"

Stout Oskal tossed his rope toward the weakening, blood-soaked figure in the behemoth's maw. Hargo tried in vain to grab it, but it fell short. The tentacle beast hissed again and tried to retreat, only to have the line held by Gorst and the other two men keep it from getting very far.

"Benjin! The other horn, damn you!"

"Tell 'im to quit wigglin', and I will, captain!"

Oskal threw the rope again, and this time Hargo managed to grab it. With what strength he had, he looped it around him.

The entire tableau reminded Kentril of some macabre game. Again he cursed himself for accepting this contract, and he cursed Quov Tsin for having offered it in the first place.

Where *was* the foul sorcerer? Why had he not come running with the rest? Could he be dead?

The captain doubted his luck could be that good. Whatever the Vizjerei's present circumstances, they would have no effect on the desperate situation here. Everything rested on Kentril's already burdened shoulders.

A few of the fighters continued to try to wound the serpentine monster in any way they could. Unfortunately, the tough hide of the tentacle beast prevented those with lances and swords from doing any harm, and the two archers still at work had to watch out for fear of slaying the very man they hoped to save.

A rope caught the left horn. Captain Dumon fought back the swell of hope he felt; it had been one thing to catch the monster, but now they had to bring it in.

"Everyone who can, grab onto the lines! Bring that thing onto shore! It'll be more clumsy, more vulnerable on land!"

He joined with the others, pulling on the line Benjin had tossed. The tentacle beast hissed loudly, and although it clearly understood at some level the danger it faced, it still did not release its captive. Kentril could generally admire such tenacity in any living creature, but not when the life of one of his men was also at stake.

"Pull!" the captain shouted, sweat from the effort making his brown shirt cling to his body. His leather boots—his fine leather boots that he had bought with the pay from his last contract—sank into the muddy ground near the river. Despite four men on each rope, it took all they could give just to inch the aquatic horror onto the shore.

Yet inch it they did, and as the bulk of the beast came onto land, the mercenaries' efforts redoubled. A little more, and surely they could then free their comrade.

With the target much closer, one of the archers took aim.

"Hold your—" was all Kentril got out before the shaft buried itself in the left eye.

The serpentine monster reared back in agony. It opened its mouth, but not enough to enable the gravely-injured Hargo to fall free, even with two men pulling from the ground. Despite having no appreciable limbs, the tentacle beast writhed back and forth so much that it began dragging all of its adversaries toward the dark waters.

One of the men behind Gorst slipped, sending another there also falling. The imbalance threw the rest of the mercenaries off. Benjin lost his grip, nearly stumbling into his captain in the process.

One orb a mass of ichor, the tentacle beast pulled back into the river.

"Hold him! Hold him!" Kentril shouted uselessly. Between the two ropes snaring the horns remained only five men. Gorst, his huge form a mass of taut muscle, made up for the fact that he had only one other mercenary with him, but in the end even his prodigious strength proved ineffective.

The back half of the gigantic reptile vanished under the water.

They had lost the battle; the captain knew that. In no way could they regain enough momentum to turn the tide.

And Hargo, somehow madly clinging onto life and consciousness, obviously knew that as well as Kentril Dumon did. His face a bloody mess, he shouted out hoarse pleas to all.

Kentril would not let this man go the same way the first one had. "Benjin! Grab the line again!"

"It's too late, captain! There's nothin'—"

"Grab hold of it, I said!"

The moment the other fighter had obeyed, Kentril ran over to the nearest archer. The bowman stood transfixed, watching the unfolding fate of his unfortunate companion with a slack jaw and skin as pale as bone.

"Your bow! Give it to me!"

"Captain?"

"The bow, damn you!" Kentril ripped it out of the uncomprehending archer's hands. Captain Dumon had trained long and hard with the bow himself, and among his motley crew he could still count himself as the second or third best shot.

For what he intended now, Kentril prayed he would have the eye of the best.

Without hesitation, the wiry commander raised the bow, sighting his target as he did. Hargo stared back at him, and the pleas suddenly faltered. A look in the dying man's eyes begged the captain to fire quickly.

Kentril did.

The wooden bolt caught Hargo in the upper chest, burying itself deep.

Hargo slumped in the beast's jaws, dead instantly.

The act caught the other mercenaries completely by surprise. Gorst lost his grip. The others belatedly released theirs, not wanting to be pulled in by accident.

In sullen silence, the survivors watched as the wounded monster sank swiftly into the river, still hissing its rage and pain even as its head vanished below the surface. Hargo's arms briefly floated above the innocent-looking water—then suddenly, they, too, disappeared below.

Letting the bow drop, Kentril turned and started away from the area.

The other fighters nervously gathered their things and followed, keeping much closer to one another. They had grown complacent after the third death, and now one of them had paid for that. Kentril blamed himself most of all, for, as company captain, he should have kept a better watch on his men. Only once before had he ever been forced to resort to slaying one of his own in order to alleviate suffering, and that had been on a good, solid battlefield, not in some insufferable madhouse of a jungle. That first man had been lying on the ground with a belly wound so massive that Captain Dumon had been amazed any life lingered. It had been a simple thing then to put the mortally wounded soldier to rest.

This . . . this had felt barbaric.

"Kentril," came Gorst's quiet voice. For someone so massive, the tanned giant could speak very softly when he chose. "Kentril. Hargo—"

"Quiet, Gorst."

"Kentril—"

"Enough." Of all those under his command through the past ten years, only Gorst ever called him by his first name. Captain Dumon had never offered that choice; the simplistic titan had just decided to do so. Perhaps that had been why they had become the best of friends, the only true friends among all those who had fought under Kentril for money.

Now only fifteen men remained. Fewer with whom to divide the supposed treasure the Vizjerei had offered, but fewer also to defend the party in case of trouble. Kentril would have dearly loved to have brought more, but he had been able to find no more takers of the offer. The seventeen hardened fighters accompanying him and Gorst had been all who would accept this arduous journey. The coins Quov Tsin had given him had barely paid them enough as it was.

And speaking of Tsin—*where* was he?

"Tsin, damn you!" the scarred captain shouted to the jungle. "Unless you've been eaten, I want you to show yourself right now!"

No answer.

Peering through the dense jungle, Kentril searched for the diminutive spellcaster, but nowhere did he see Quov Tsin's bald head.

"Tsin! Show yourself, or I'll have the men start dumping your precious equipment into the river! Then you can go and talk to the beasts if you want to do any more of your incessant calculations!" Since the beginning of this trek, the Vizjerei had demanded pause after pause in order to set up instruments, draw patterns, and cast minor spells—all supposedly to guide them to their destination. Tsin seemed to know where he headed, but up until now none of the others, not even Kentril, could have said the same.

A high-pitched, rather nasal voice called from the distance. Neither he nor Gorst could make out the words, but both readily recognized their employer's condescending tones.

"That way," the giant said, pointing ahead and slightly to the right of the party.

Knowing that the sorcerer had not only survived but had utterly ignored Hargo's fate ignited a fire within Kentril. Even as he proceeded, his hand slipped to the hilt of his sword. Just because the Vizjerei had purchased their services did not mean in any way that he could be forgiven for not lending his dubious talent with magic to the desperate hope of rescuing the ill-fated mercenary.

Yes, Kentril would have more than words with Quov Tsin . . .

"Where are you?" he called out.

"Here, of course!" snapped Tsin from somewhere behind the thick foliage. "Do hurry now! We've wasted so much valuable time!"

Wasted it? Captain Dumon's fury grew. *Wasted it?* As a hired fighter and treasure hunter, he knew that his livelihood meant risking death every day, but Kentril had always prided himself on knowing the value of life nonetheless. It had always been those with the gold, those who offered riches, who least appreciated the cost the mercenary captain and his men suffered.

He drew the sword slowly from the scabbard. With each passing day, this trek had begun to seem more and more like a wild chase. Kentril had had enough. It was time to break the contract.

"That's not good," Gorst murmured. "You should put it back, Kentril."

"Just mind your place." No one, not even Gorst, would deter him.

"Kentril—"

At that moment, the object of the slim captain's ire burst through the jungle foliage. To Kentril, who stood just over six feet in height, Gorst had always seemed an astonishing sight, but as tall as the giant appeared in comparison with his commander, so, too, did Dumon loom over the Vizjerei.

Legend had always made the race of sorcerers seem more than men, tall, hooded figures clad in rune-covered, red-orange cloaks called *Turinnash,* or "spirit mantles." The small silver runes covering much of the voluminous garment supposedly protected the mage from lesser magical threats and even, to a limited degree, some demonic powers. The Vizjerei wore the Turinnash proudly, almost like a badge of office, a mark of superiority. However, although Quov Tsin, too, had such a cloak, on his barely five-foot frame it did little to enhance any image of mystical power. The slight, wrinkled figure with the long gray beard reminded Kentril of nothing more than his elderly grandfather—without any of the sympathetic nature of the latter.

Tsin's slanted, silver-gray eyes peered over his aquiline nose in obvious disdain. The diminutive mage had no patience whatsoever and clearly did not see that his own life hung by a thread. Of course, as a Vizjerei, he not only had spells with which to likely defend himself, but the staff he held in his right hand also carried protective magicks designed for countless circumstances.

One quick strike, though, Kentril thought to himself. *One quick strike, and I can put an end to this sanctimonious little toad . . .*

"It's about time!" snapped the mercenary's employer. He shook one end of the staff in the captain's face.

"What took you so long? You know I'm running out of time!"

More than you think, you babbling cur . . . "While you were wandering off, Master Tsin, I was trying to save a man from one of those water serpents. We could've used your help."

"Yes, well, enough of this babble!" Quov Tsin returned, his gaze slipping back to the jungle behind him. Likely he had not even heard what Kentril had just said. "Come! Come quickly! You must see!"

As the Vizjerei turned away, Captain Dumon's hand rose, the sword at the ready.

Gorst put his own hand on his friend's arm. "Let's go see, Kentril."

The giant casually stepped in front of the captain, effectively coming between Kentril and Tsin's unprotected back. The first two moved on, Kentril reluctantly following them.

He could wait a few moments longer.

First Quov Tsin, then Gorst, vanished among the plants. Kentril soon found himself needing to hack his way through, but he took some pleasure in imagining each dismembered branch or vine as the spellcaster's neck.

Then, without any warning, the jungle gave way. The early evening sun lit up the landscape before him as it had not done in two weeks. Kentril found himself staring at a series of high, jagged peaks, the beginnings of the vast chain running up and down the length of Kehjistan and heading even farther east for as far as the eye could see.

And in the distance, just above the eastern base of a particularly tall and ugly peak at the very southern tip of this particular chain, lay the weatherworn, jumbled remains of a once mighty city. The fragments of a great stone wall encircling the entire eastern side could still be made out. A few hardy structures maintained precarious stances within the city itself. One, possibly the home of the lost kingdom's ruler, stood perched atop a vast ledge, no doubt having once enabled the master of the realm to gaze down upon his entire domain.

Although the jungle had surrendered in part to this region, lush plants still covered much of the landscape and had, over time, invaded the ruins themselves. What they had not already covered, the elements had battered well. Erosion had ripped away part of the northern section of the wall and taken with it a good portion of the city. Further in, a sizable chunk of the mountain had collapsed onto the interior of the city.

Kentril could not imagine that there would be much left intact anywhere inside. Time had taken its toll on this ancient place.

"That should assuage your anger a bit, Captain Dumon," Quov Tsin suddenly remarked, eyes fixed on the sight before them. "Quite a bit."

"What do you mean?" Lowering his sword, Kentril eyed the ruins with some discomfort. He felt as if he had just intruded upon a place where even ghosts moved with trepidation. "Is that it? Is that—"

" 'The Light among Lights'? The most pure of realms in all the history of the world, built upon the very slope of the towering mountain called Nymyr? Aye, captain, there it stands—and, for our needs, just in time, if my calculations hold true!"

Gasps came from behind Kentril. The other men had finally caught up, just in time to hear the sorcerer's words. They all knew the legends of the realm called the Light among Lights by the ancients, a place fabled to be the one kingdom where the darkness of Hell had feared to intrude. They all knew of its story, even as far away as the Western Kingdoms.

Here had been a city revered by those who followed the light. Here had stood a marvel, ruled by regal and kind lords who had guided the souls of all toward Heaven.

Here had been a kingdom so pure, stories had it that it had at last risen whole above the mortal plane, its inhabitants transcending mortal limitations, rising to join the angels.

"You see a sight worthy of the loss of your men, captain," the Vizjerei whispered, extending one bony hand toward the ruins. "For now you are one of the few fortunate ever to cast your eyes upon one of the wonders of the past—fabulous, lost *Ureh!*"

Two

She had alabaster skin devoid of even the slightest imperfection, long chestnut-red hair that fell well below her perfectly rounded shoulders, and eyes of the deepest emerald green. If not for the eastern cast of her facial features, he might have taken her for one of the tempestuous maidens of his own highland home.

She was beautiful, everything a weary, war-bitten adventurer like Kentril had dreamed of each night during the innocence of his youth—and still did to this very day.

A pity she had been dead for several hundred years.

Fingering the ancient brooch he had almost literally stumbled upon, Kentril surreptitiously studied his nearby companions. They continued their back-breaking labor in complete ignorance of his find, searching among the crumbled, foliage-enshrouded ruins for anything of value. So far, the treasure hunt had been an utter failure as far as Kentril had been concerned. Here they worked, fifteen men strong, in the midst of the remains of one of the most fabled cities of all, and the sum total for three days of hard effort had been a small sack of rusted, bent, and mostly broken items of dubious value. The intricately detailed brooch represented the greatest find yet, and even it would not pay for more than a fraction of their arduous journey to this bug-infested necropolis.

No one looked his way. Deciding that he had earned at least this one token, Kentril slipped the artifact into his belt pouch. As leader of the mercenaries, he would have been entitled to an extra share of all treasure anyway, so the scarred commander felt no qualms about what he did.

"Kentril?"

The captain bit back his startlement. Turning, he faced the one who had so stealthily approached him. Somehow, Gorst could always manage to move in silence when he chose to, despite his oxlike appearance.

Running one hand through his hair, Kentril tried to pretend that he had done nothing wrong. "Gorst! I thought you'd been helping our esteemed employer with his tools and calculating devices! What brings you here?"

"The magic man . . . he wants to see you, Kentril." Gorst had a smile on his round face. Magic fascinated him as it did many small children, and while so far the Vizjerei sorcerer had shown little in the way of spells, the brutish mercenary seemed to enjoy the incomprehensible and enigmatic devices and objects Quov Tsin had brought with him.

"Tell him I'll be along in a little bit."

"He wants to see you now," the bronzed figure returned, his tone that of one who could not understand why someone would not want to rush over immediately to find out what the Vizjerei desired. Gorst clearly believed that some wondrous spectacle of sorcery had to be imminent and any delay by his friend in returning to Tsin would only mean prolonging the waiting.

Knowing the futility of holding off and realizing suddenly that he had reason to talk to the Vizjerei, Captain Dumon shrugged. "All right. We'll go see the magic man."

As he started past Gorst, the giant abruptly asked, "Can I see it, Kentril?"

"See what?"

"What you found."

Kentril almost denied having found anything, but Gorst knew him better than anyone. With a slight grimace, he carefully withdrew the brooch and held it in his palm so that only the other mercenary could see he had anything at all.

Gorst gave him a wide grin. "Pretty."

"Listen—" Kentril began.

But the massive fighter had already started past him, leaving the captain to feel foolish about his attempted subterfuge. He never knew completely what Gorst thought, but it seemed that to his friend the matter of the brooch had been satisfied, and now they needed to move on. Gorst's "magic man" awaited them, obviously a far more interesting subject to the mercenary leader's companion than any picture of a centuries-dead female.

They found Tsin impatiently scurrying around a display of stones, alchemaic devices, and other tools of his disreputable trade. Every now and then, the balding sorcerer would scribble notes on a parchment atop the makeshift desk his hired crew had put together early on. He seemed especially interested this day in peering through an eyeglass pointed at the very tip of Nymyr, then consulting a tattered scroll. As they approached, Kentril heard him chuckle with glee, then resort to the scroll again.

The Vizjerei reached for a device that most resembled to the mercenary a sextant, save that the sorcerer had clearly made some changes in the design. As his bony fingers touched the object, Quov Tsin noticed the pair.

"Ah! Dumon! About time! And has your latest day's labor born any more fruit than the previous?"

"No . . . it's just as you said. So far, we've found little more than junk." Kentril chose not to mention the brooch. With his luck, Tsin would have found some relevance in the artifact and therefore confiscated it.

"No matter, no matter! I let you and your band search mostly to keep you out of my way until the final readings could be made. Of course, had you found anything, that would have been a plus, but in the long run, I am not bothered by the lack of success."

Perhaps the sorcerer had not been, but the mercenaries

certainly grumbled. Kentril had promised his companions much based on the words of the Vizjerei, and the
failure would hang more around his neck than even
Tsin's.

"Listen, sorcerer," he muttered. "You paid us enough to
get this madness underway, but you also made promises of
a lot more. Myself, I could go home right now and be
happy just to be out of this place, but the others expect
much. You said that we'd find treasure—ample amounts of
it—in this ancient ruin, but so far we've—"

"Yes, yes, yes! I've explained it all before! It is just not
the proper time! Soon, though, soon!"

Kentril looked to Gorst, who shrugged. Turning his gaze
back to the slight mage, Captain Dumon snarled, "You've
told me some wild things, Vizjerei, and they keep getting
wilder the longer this goes on! Why don't you explain once
more to Gorst and me what you've got in mind, eh? And
make it clear for once."

"That would be a waste of my time," the diminutive sorcerer grated. Seeing Kentril's expression darken further, he
sighed in exasperation. "Very well, but this is the last I'll
speak of it! You already know the legends of the piousness
of those who lived in the city, so I'll not bother with
retelling that. I'll go straight to the time of troubles—will
that do?"

Propping himself against a large chunk of rubble once
forming part of the great wall, Kentril folded his arms,
then nodded. "Go from there. That's when your story
starts getting a little too fantastic for my tastes."

"The mercenary's a critic." Nonetheless, Quov Tsin
paused in his tasks and began the tale that Captain Dumon
suspected he could hear a hundred times and still not completely fathom. "It began during a time . . . a time known to
those of us versed in the arts and the battle between light
and darkness . . . a time known as the *Sin War*."

Hardened as he had become over the years, Kentril
could not help but shudder whenever the short Vizjerei

muttered those last two words. Until he had met Tsin, he had never even heard such legends, but something about the mythic war of which his employer spoke filled the mercenary's head with visions of diabolic demons seeking to guide the mortal world down the path of corruption, leading all to Hell.

The Sin War had not been fought as normal wars, for it had been fought by Heaven and Hell themselves. True, the archangels and demons stood opposing one another like two armies, but the battles most often took place behind the scenes, behind the eyes of mortals. The supposed war had also stretched hundreds of years—for what were years to immortal beings? Kingdoms had risen and fallen, fiends such as Bartuc, the Warlord of Blood, had come to power, then been defeated—and still the war had pressed on.

And early on in this struggle, wondrous Ureh had become a central battleground.

"All knew of Ureh's greatness in those days," the bald sorcerer went on. "A fount of light, the guiding force of good in those troubled days—which, of course, meant that it drew the attention not only of the archangels but of the lords of Hell themselves, the *Prime Evils.*"

The Prime Evils. Whatever land one had been born in, whether in the jungles of Kehjistan or the cooler, rockier realms of the Western Kingdoms, all knew of the Prime Evils, the three brothers who ruled Hell. Mephisto, Lord of Hatred, master of undead. Baal, Lord of Destruction, bringer of chaos.

Diablo.

Diablo, perhaps the most feared, the ultimate manifestation of terror, the nightmare not only of children but of veteran warriors who had already seen the horrors men themselves could produce. Diablo it had been who had gazed most at bright Ureh from his monstrous domain, who had most been offended by its glorious existence. Order could be brought forth from the chaos created by Baal, and the hatred of Mephisto could be mastered by any man with strength, but to have no fear of fear itself—such a thing Diablo could not believe and would not stand.

"The lands around Ureh grew darker with each passing year, Captain Dumon. Creatures twisted by evil or born not of this world harried those who would journey to and from the city walls. Sinister magicks insinuated themselves where they could, barely driven back by the sorcerers of the kingdom."

And with each defeat by the peoples of Ureh, the Vizjerei added, Diablo grew more determined. He would bring down the wondrous city and make its inhabitants the slaves of Hell. All would see that no power on the mortal plane could withstand the most foul of the Prime Evils.

"It came to the point when no one dared travel to the city and few could escape it. It is said that then the lord of the realm, the just and kind Juris Khan, gathered his greatest priests and mages and decreed that they would do what they had to in order to save their people once and for all. Legend has it that Juris Khan had been granted a vision by an archangel, one who had declared to him that the powers above had seen the trials of their most honored followers and had felt moved to grant them the greatest of havens, so long as the humans put it upon themselves to reach it." Quov Tsin had an almost enraptured expression on his wizened face. "He offered the people of Ureh the very safety of Heaven itself."

Gorst grunted, his way of expressing his outright awe at these words. Kentril held his peace, but he had trouble imagining such an offer. The archangel had opened the very gates of Heaven to the mortals of Ureh, opened to them a place where not even all three Prime Evils combined could have made the slightest incursion. All the people of Ureh had to do was find their way there.

"Some gesture," the mercenary captain interjected, not without some sarcasm. " 'Here we are, but you can find your own good way to get to us.' "

"You asked for the story, Dumon—do you want it or

not? I've far more important things to do than entertain you."

"Go ahead, sorcerer. I'll try to keep my awe reined in."

With a disdainful sniff, Tsin said, "The archangel came twice more in Juris Khan's dreams, each time with the same promise and each time with some clues as to how this miracle could come to be . . ."

Guided by his visions, Lord Khan urged the sorcerers and priests to efforts such as none had ever conjectured before. The archangel had left what hints he could of what needed to be done, but the restrictions by which he existed forbade him from granting the mortals any more than that. Still, with the faith of Heaven behind them, Ureh dedicated its efforts to achieving this wondrous task. They knew what they had been offered, and they knew what fate likely would befall them if they failed.

"What little we know of that period comes from Gregus Mazi, the only inhabitant of Ureh to be found afterward. One of the circle of mages involved in the casting of the great spell, it is assumed by most scholars that at the last moment he must've faltered in his faith, for when the sorcerers and priests finally opened the way to Heaven—how is never said—Gregus Mazi was not taken with the rest."

"Hardly seems fair."

"From him," Quov Tsin went on, utterly ignoring Kentril, "we know that a tremendous red light enshrouded Ureh at that point, covering everything up to and including the very walls surrounding it. As Gregus—still heart-stricken at being left behind—watched, a second city seemed to rise above the first, an exact if ethereal twin of Ureh . . ."

Before the wide, unblinking eyes of the unfortunate sorcerer, the vast, phantasmal display hovered above its mortal shell. Even from where he stood, Gregus Mazi could see torchlight, could even see a few figures standing upon the ghostly battlements. To him, it had been as if the soul of Ureh had left the mortal plane, for when he glanced at the abandoned buildings around him, they had already begun to crumble and collapse, as if all they had been had been sucked from their very substance, leaving only swiftly decaying skeletons.

And as the lone figure looked up once more, he saw the shimmering city grow more insubstantial. The crimson aura flared, growing almost as bright as the sun that had set but moments before. Gregus Mazi had shielded his eyes for just a second—and in that second the glorious vision of a floating Ureh had faded away.

"Gregus Mazi was left a broken man, Captain Dumon. He was found by followers of Rathma, the necromancers of the deep jungle, and they cared for him until his mind had healed enough. He left them, then, an obsession already growing in his heart. He would join his family and friends yet. The sorcerer traveled all over the world in search of what he needed, for although he had been a part of the spellwork that had enabled the people of Ureh to ascend to Heaven, he had not known all of it."

"Get to the point, Tsin, the point of our being here at all."

"Cretin." With a scowl, the robed figure continued. "Twelve years after Ureh, Gregus Mazi returned to his abandoned homeland. In his wake he left scrolls and books, all indications of his studies. He left notes here and there, most of which I've tracked down. Twelve years after Ureh, Gregus Mazi came to the ruins . . . and simply vanished."

Kentril rubbed his mustache. He had a very real answer for the ancient sorcerer's fate. "An animal ate him, or he had an accident."

"I might have thought the same, my dear captain, if I had not early on in my efforts procured this."

Quov Tsin reached into a massive pouch where he kept his most valued notes and withdrew an old scroll. He held it out to Kentril, who reluctantly took it.

Captain Dumon unrolled it as gently as he could. The

parchment was fragile and the script written on it badly faded, but with effort he could make it out. "This was written by a man from Westmarch!"

"Yes . . . the mercenary captain who journeyed with Gregus Mazi. I found it both ironic and perhaps telling that you approached me when I sent news of my offer to those who might be interested. I see it as fate that we two follow the tracks of my predecessor and this man."

"This man" proved to be one Humbart Wessel, a veteran fighter with a thankfully plain manner of writing. Kentril puzzled through the passages, at first finding nothing.

"Toward the bottom," Tsin offered.

The slim mercenary read over that part of the aged scroll, which Humbart Wessel had clearly written years after the fact.

On the seventh day, near dusk, the passage began, *Master Mazi again approached the edge of the ruins. Says I to him, that this quest's seen no good end and we should go, but he says he's certain this time. The shadow will touch at just the right angle. It has to.*

Master Mazi promised much gold to us and another offer none there'd take, however worthy any might think themselves. Fly up to Heaven . . . older now, I still wouldn't have taken it.

The shadow came like he said, Nymyr's hand reaching out for old Ureh. We watched, certain as before that we'd been on a fool's quest.

Aah, what fools we were to believe that!

I recall the shadow. I recall the shimmering. How the ruins suddenly looked alive again. How the lights glowed inside! Swear I still will that I heard the voices of folk, but couldn't see any!

"I'm coming . . ." Those were Master Mazi's last words, but not to us, though. I remember them still, and I remember how we thought we saw the glitter of the gold that he'd told us about again and again—but not one man would enter. Not one man would follow. Master Mazi went it alone.

We camped there, hearing the voices, hearing some of them call to us, it seemed. None of us would go, though. Tomorrow, I says to the others, tomorrow when Master Mazi comes out and shows all's well, we'll go in and get our fill. One night, it won't matter.

And in the morning, all we saw were ruins. No lights. No voices.

No Master Mazi.

Lord Hyram, I writ this down like I agreed and it goes to the Zakarum—

Captain Dumon turned the scroll over, looking for more.

"You'll see nothing. What little was left beyond this passage speaks of other matters and was of no concern to me. Only this page."

"A few scribbled lines by an old warrior? This brought us all the way here?" Kentril felt like tossing the parchment back into Tsin's ugly face.

"Cretin," Quov Tsin repeated. "You see words but cannot read past them. Don't you trust one of your own?" He waved a gnarled hand. "Never mind! That was just to show the one point. Gregus Mazi found a way to the Ureh of old, the Ureh he had lost twelve years before—and we can do the very same!"

Kentril recalled the line about gold, the selfsame gold that had lured him into this foolishness in the first place. However, he also recalled how Humbart Wessel and his men had been too frightened to go after it once the opportunity had finally presented itself. "I've no desire to go to Heaven just yet, sorcerer."

The diminutive Tsin snorted. "Nor have I! Gregus Mazi was welcome to that path, but I seek earthier rewards. Once they had ascended, the people of Ureh would not need the items they had collected in their mortal lives. Any valuables, books of spells, talismans . . . those would have been left behind."

"Then why haven't we found anything?"

"The clues are in the manuscript of Humbart Wessel! For these living mortals to ascend, Juris Khan and his sorcerers had to cast a spell like no other. They had to bridge the gap between this plane and that of Heaven. In doing so, they created a place in between—in the form of this shadow Ureh that Gregus found again years later!"

Captain Dumon tried desperately to follow the mage's reasoning. The gold that he had been promised existed not in these ruins but rather in the floating vision described by the previous mercenary leader, the ghostly city.

He glanced at the rubble, all that remained of physical Ureh. "But how can we possibly reach such a place, even if it does exist? You said it isn't part of our world, but in between ours and—and—"

"And Heaven, yes," finished the Vizjerei. He returned to his devices, peering through one. "It took Gregus Mazi more than a decade to do it, but because of him, my own calculations took but three years once I had the proper information. I know exactly when it will all occur!"

"It's coming back again?"

Tsin's eyes widened, and he gave Kentril an incredulous look. "Of course! Have you not been paying attention to anything I have said?"

"But—"

"I have told you more than enough now, Captain Dumon, and I really must return to my work! Try not to bother me again unless it is absolutely necessary, is that understood?"

Gritting his teeth, Kentril straightened. "You summoned me, Vizjerei."

"Did I? Oh, yes, of course. That's what I wanted to tell you. It is tomorrow evening."

More and more the slim captain began to wonder if he and Quov Tsin actually spoke the same language. "*What's* tomorrow evening, sorcerer?"

"What we were just speaking of, cretin! The shadow comes tomorrow evening, an hour before night!" Tsin glanced again at his notes. "Make that an hour and a quarter to be safe."

"An hour and a quarter . . ." the captain murmured, dumbstruck.

"Exactly so! Run along now!" The bald Vizjerei became enmeshed in his work once more. Watching him, Kentril realized that the slight figure had already completely forgotten the presence of the two fighters. The only thing that mattered to Quov Tsin, the only thing that *existed* for him, was lost, legendary Ureh.

Kentril retreated from the vicinity of the wizened mage, thoughts racing. Now he knew that he had indeed followed a madman. All the talk of gold in the past had made the captain assume that Tsin actually meant that the wealth of the city had been secreted in some cache whose whereabouts could be ascertained only by the direction of the shadows at some point of the day. He had never truly understood that the Vizjerei had literally hunted a ghost realm, a place not of this world.

I've brought us here to chase phantoms . . .

But what if Tsin were right? What if the legend of the city had any grain of truth? Heaven had no need of gold. Perhaps, as the sorcerer had claimed, it had all been left behind, there for the taking.

Yet, Humbart Wessel had been offered the opportunity, and not one man of his had risked the shadowed kingdom.

Kentril Dumon's hand slipped to his belt pouch, removing from it the elegant brooch he had discovered. For the woman it depicted, he would gladly have journeyed into Ureh, but, failing that, some bit of valuable jewelry from her household or that of another wealthy citizen of the fabled realm would satisfy him just as much.

It was not as if any of the owners would still need them.

Zayl watched the band of mercenaries from his position atop the crumbling guard tower with much trepidation. The men below moved about the ruins like a small but determined swarm of ants. They went through every crevice, searched under every boulder, and even though they obviously met with meager success, they pushed on.

Pale of skin and with a studious expression more suited to a clerk in a shipping house than to a well-trained and well-versed necromancer, Zayl had observed the newcomers since their arrival. None of his readings had predicted the coming of these intruders, and at such a critical juncture Zayl felt this no mere coincidence.

Ureh had always been treated most gingerly by the followers of Rathma, who had sensed in it some delicately held balance among the various planes of existence. Zayl knew the legends as well as anyone and knew a little of the true history behind them. Ureh had always drawn him, much to the displeasure and dismay of his mentors. They believed him enchanted by the notion of the astonishing spells utilized and the power one might wield if one learned how to recreate them. After all, the sorcerers of the ancient land had blurred the lines between life and death far more than any necromancer could have ever dreamed. In fact, if the legends spoke true, then the people of Ureh had bypassed death altogether, which went against everything in the teachings of Rathma.

Zayl, however, did not desire to relearn the secrets of those mages—not that he had bothered to tell his teachers that fact. No, the plain-faced necromancer who now watched the mercenaries through almond-shaped eyes of gray desired something entirely different.

Zayl sought to commune with the archangels themselves—and the power behind them.

"Like rats hunting for garbage," mocked a high-pitched voice from his side.

Without looking at the speaker, the necromancer replied, "I was thinking more of ants."

"Rats is what they are, I say . . . and I should know, for didn't they gnaw off my legs and arms, then burrow through my chest for good measure? This bunch has the same look to 'em as those beasts did!"

"They should not be here at this time. They should have stayed away. That would have been common sense."

Zayl's companion laughed, a hollow sound. "I didn't have enough sense even though I knew better!"

"You had no choice. Once so touched by Ureh, you had to come back eventually." The hooded necromancer peered beyond the mercenaries, surveying the region from which their apparent captain had just come. "There is a sorcerer with them. He has not stepped out into the open since he came here, but I can sense him."

"Smells that awful, does he? Wish I still had a nose."

"I sense his power . . . and I know he senses mine, although he may not realize the source." Zayl slipped back a little, then rose. The grave robbers would not be able to see him from their much lower vantage points. "Neither he nor his paid underlings must interfere."

"What do you plan to do?"

The black-clad form did not answer. Instead, he reached for a small array of objects previously positioned by his side. Into a pouch he kept handy at his belt went a dagger carved from ivory, two candles nearly burned down to wax puddles, a small vial containing a thick, crimson liquid—and the human skull, minus jaw, that had been the centerpiece of the display.

"Gently now," mocked the skull. "We're quite a height up! I wouldn't want to be repeating that fall again!"

"Quiet, Humbart." Zayl placed the macabre artifact in the pouch, then strung the latter shut. Finished with his task, he took one last look at the treasure hunters below and pondered their fates.

One way or another, they could not be permitted to be here tomorrow evening—for their sakes as well as his own.

THREE

"Cap'n Dumon . . ."

Kentril rolled over in his sleep, trying to find comfort on the rocky ground beneath his blanket. Only Quov Tsin had a tent, the mercenaries more accustomed to dealing with the elements. Yet the area around the ruins of Ureh seemed the most disturbing, most awkward of places to try to rest even for such hardened fighters. Throughout the camp, the captain's tossing and turning were duplicated by every man save Gorst, who most believed could slumber peacefully on a bed of thorns.

"Cap'n Dumon . . ."

"Mmm? Wha—?" Kentril stirred, pushing himself slowly up on one elbow. "Who's there?"

The nearly full moon shone with such brightness that it took little time for his eyes to adjust to the night. Kentril looked around, noted the snoring forms around the low fires. From the sorcerer's tent, the snoring sounded particularly loud.

"Damned place . . ." The mercenary lowered his head again. He would be glad when they abandoned the ruins. Not even the field of battle left him so on edge.

"Cap'n Dumon . . ."

Kentril rolled off his blanket, hand already on the hilt of the dagger he always wore on his belt. The hair on the back of his neck stiffened, and a cold chill washed over the mercenary leader as he focused on a figure only a few feet to his right, a figure who had not been standing there a second before.

Of itself, that discovery might not have bothered the captain, for he himself could move with the utmost stealth. However, what did unnerve him so very much, even to the point where the dagger nearly fell from his shaking fingers, had to do with the fact that the one who faced him could be none other than the hapless *Hargo*.

Faced might have been an inappropriate and unfortunate choice of terms, for Hargo no longer had a good portion of his. The right side of his head had been ripped away, exposing skull and rotting muscle. One eye had been completely lost, a deep red and black crater all that remained. The mercenary's bedraggled beard framed a mouth curled open to reveal death's grin, and the eye that did remain stared almost accusingly at Kentril.

The rest of Hargo had fared no better. The right arm had been gnawed away just below the shoulder and the chest and stomach torn wide open, revealing ribs, guts, and more. Only tatters of clothes still existed, emphasizing even more the horrific fate of the man.

"*Cap'n Dumon . . .*" rasped the monstrous visitor.

Now the dagger did slip, Kentril's fingers limp. He glanced around, but no one else had been disturbed by this monstrous vision. The others all slumbered away.

"Har-Hargo?" he finally managed.

"*Cap'n Dumon . . .*" The corpse shambled forward a couple of steps, water from the river still dripping from the half-devoured form. "*You shouldn't be here . . .*"

As far as Kentril had suddenly become concerned, he should have been back in Westmarch, drinking himself into a stupor at his favorite tavern. Anywhere in the world but where he now stood.

"*You gotta leave, cap'n,*" Hargo continued, ignorant of the fact that his own throat had a gaping hole in the side and therefore should not have let him even speak. "*There's death in this place. It got me, and it'll get you all . . . all of you . . .*"

As he warned Kentril, the ravaged figure raised the one good arm he had left, pointing at his captain. The moon accented the pale, deathly sheen of Hargo's corpse and the rot already taking place even on the otherwise untouched appendage.

"What do you mean?" Dumon managed. "What do you mean?"

But Hargo only repeated his warning. *"It'll kill you all. Just like me, cap'n . . . Take you all dead just like me . . ."*

And with that, the corpse raised his face to the moonlit heaven and let out a blood-chilling cry full of regret and fear.

A brave man, Kentril still broke. He fell to his knees, his hands over his ears in a pathetic attempt to keep the heart-jolting sound out. Tears streamed from his eyes, and he looked earthward, no longer able to face the ghastly sight before him.

The cry came to an abrupt halt.

Still holding his ears, the mercenary captain dared to glance up—

—And awoke.

"Aaah!" Kentril scrambled from his bedroll, tossing aside his blanket and stumbling to his feet. Only as he straightened did he realize that all around him his men acted in similar fashion, shouts of dismay and wild looks abounding. Two men had swords free and now swung them madly about, risking injuring their fellows. One hardy fighter sat still, eyes wide and unblinking, body shivering.

From more than one Kentril heard whispered or shouted a single name . . . the name of *Hargo*.

"I saw 'im!" gasped Oskal. "Standin' before me as big as life!"

"Nuthin' live about him!" snarled another. "Death himself couldn'ta looked worse!"

"It was a warning!" Benjin declared. "He wants us out of here now!" The fighter reached down for his bedroll. "Well, I'm all for that!"

Seeing his men in disarray brought Captain Dumon back to his senses. Whatever fearful message Hargo might or might not have delivered, common sense still dictated certain cautions.

"Hold it right there!" the fair-haired officer shouted. "No one goes anywhere!"

"But cap'n," protested Oskal. "You saw him, too! I can see it plain in your face!"

"Maybe so, but that's no reason to go fleeing into the jungle, the better to end up like Hargo did, eh?"

This bit of truth struck all of them. Oskal dropped his blanket, eyes briefly shifting to the murky landscape to the south. Benjin shivered.

"What do you say, Gorst?" Kentril's second appeared the most calm of the band, although even he had a perturbed expression on his generally cheerful countenance. Still, it did Captain Dumon some good to see that Gorst had not fallen prey to the panic of the others.

"Better here," grunted the massive figure. "Not out there."

"You hear that? Even Gorst wouldn't venture back into the jungle right now! Any of you think you'd survive better?"

He had them back under control now. No one wanted to reenter that hellish place, at least not in the dark. Even the almost full moon would do little to illuminate the many dangers of the jungle.

Kentril nodded. "We'll decide better come morning. Now, sheathe those weapons! Put some order back into this camp, and build up those fires!"

They moved to obey, especially in regard to the last command. Kentril noted them beginning to relax as the familiarity of the routine took hold. He felt certain that the nightmare would soon fade some in the veterans' minds. Men in their line of work often suffered bad dreams. Kentril himself still experienced nightmares of his first campaign, when his commander and nearly all those in the squad had been slaughtered before his very eyes. Only luck had saved him then, but the memories of that terrible time remained clear.

Yet this horrific dream stood out even from those recurring torments, for Kentril had not suffered it alone. Everyone had experienced it at the same time, in the same way. He had no doubt that if he questioned each man, they would all describe the details in more or less the exact manner.

A harsh, cutting sound suddenly brought back vestiges of the fearful vision. Kentril had his hand on the hilt of his dagger before he realized that what he had just heard had been, in reality, the sound of *snoring*.

Quov Tsin's snoring.

The Vizjerei had slept through not only the dream but the panic ensuing afterward. In utter disbelief, Captain Dumon started toward the tent, only to pause at the last moment. What good would it do to look upon the sleeping sorcerer or, for that matter, to wake him? Tsin would only sputter denigrating words at the captain, then demand to know why he had been disturbed.

Kentril backed away. He could imagine the Vizjerei's wrinkled face tightening into an expression of deep contempt once the spellcaster heard the reason. Big, brave mercenaries frightened by a nightmare? Quov Tsin would laugh at such fear, mock Dumon and his men.

No, Kentril would let sleeping sorcerers lie. Tomorrow, however, he would inform their employer that the mercenaries had no intention of waiting for the gold of Ureh to come falling from the sky. Tomorrow morning, Kentril's band would be leaving.

After all, how much gold could dead men spend?

Just into the jungle and well out of sight of the camp, the damp, shambling form of Hargo paused. Branches and leaves stirred up by the night wind fluttered through the ghastly form, unhindered by the rotting flesh and gnawed bone. The lone eye stared sightlessly ahead, and the mouth hung open, revealing a blackened tongue and gums.

From atop a tall, gnarled tree, Zayl looked down upon

the ghoulish shade. In his hand the pale necromancer held a tiny talisman shaped like a dragon around which had been wrapped a piece of torn material.

"Your mission is done," he quietly informed the ghost. "Rest easy now, friend."

Hargo turned his gaze up toward the necromancer— and faded away.

"Not the most talkative fellow," remarked the skull from the branch upon which Zayl had propped it. "Me, I think death needs to have a little life to spice it up, eh?"

"Be quiet, Humbart." The slim necromancer slipped the bit of fabric off the talisman, putting the latter then within the confines of his cloak. The cloth he studied for a moment.

"You think them boys'll get the point?"

"I should hope so. I went through much trouble for this." And, indeed, Zayl had. He had smelled the death of the one mercenary even from his vantage point near the ruins. That had enabled him to track the death to its point of origin, and there Zayl had searched the area around the river for some time for any vestiges of the late, lamented Hargo. The necromancer had been rewarded with this scrap of garment, but only after dodging the hungry senses of the very beast that had taken the man.

A bit of flesh, a few drops of blood . . . those would have served Zayl better, but the cloth had come from the body of the dead, had been worn for so long close to his skin that it had contained link enough to its wearer for the summoning. Zayl had wanted only to touch the sleeping minds of the other mercenaries, use their dead comrade to scare them into leaving Ureh before it became too late. Hargo's shade had performed his task to perfection. The necromancer felt certain that the fighters would flee the area come the first hints of sun.

He had not even bothered to try the spell on the Vizjerei. Not only would it have been a waste of time, but the sorcerer's defensive spells, active even during his sleep, might have warned of Zayl's presence. That could not be condoned.

"He will have to leave if they do," the ebony-clad figure muttered to himself. "He will have to." Living mostly alone, necromancers had a habit of talking much to themselves. Even after finding Humbart Wessel's remains two years before and animating the skull, Zayl had been unable to break his old habit.

Humbart did not care whether the other spoke to himself or to the skull; he answered as he felt, which meant often. "That was a mighty fine piece of work, that was," he interjected. "And maybe that'll send the sorcerer packing, too—but only if the fighters do leave, you know."

"Of course, they will leave. After an omen such as that, experienced by all, they would be fools otherwise."

"But come the morning, my not-so-worldly friend, the sweet murmurs of gold can easily outshout the rasping warnings of a nightmare! Think you I came back for the lovely weather and the playful serpents of the river? Ha! Mark me, Zayl! If they don't leave at daybreak, they won't be leaving at all!" The jawless skull chuckled.

Letting the scrap fall to the jungle floor, the necromancer nodded solemnly. "Let us pray you are wrong, Humbart."

The men readied themselves, lining up for inspection by their captain. Looks of unease still branded the visages of many, unease combined with growing uncertainty. They had all come far, risked their lives for promised gold and jewels. To go back now would mean to go back empty-handed.

But at least they would be able to go back. No one desired Hargo's fate.

Kentril stood determined to lead his men out of here. The others might waver in their decisions, but he knew a true harbinger of danger when he saw it. As he finished his inspection, his hand grazed the pouch in which he carried the brooch. At least he had that more soothing memory to bring back with him.

Quov Tsin exited his tent just as Kentril steeled himself for the confrontation. The short sorcerer blinked as he stepped out into the sunshine, then noticed the officer coming toward him.

"Today is the day, Dumon! The secrets, the riches of Ureh, today they shall be open to us!"

"Tsin—we're leaving."

The silver-gray eyes narrowed even more than normal. "What's that you say?"

"We're leaving. We won't stay in this cursed place." The captain chose not to tell his employer just why.

"Don't be absurd! One, two more days, and you'll be able to leave here all of you as rich as kings!"

This brought a couple of murmurs from the men, who had been watching the two from the distance. Captain Dumon silently cursed. Here he was trying to save all their lives, and already the hint of gold had staked a claim in the hearts of some. How quickly some could forget.

"We're leaving. That's all there is to it."

"You've been paid—"

"Only enough to get you here. We've no more obligation to you, Vizjerei, and you've nothing you could possibly give us."

The sorcerer opened his mouth to speak, then abruptly shut it. Kentril, expecting the usual tirades, found himself slightly disconcerted. Still, perhaps he had convinced Tsin of the uselessness of arguing.

"If that is your choice, so be it." The diminutive figure suddenly turned back to his tent. "If you will excuse your-selves, I've much work to do."

As he watched Quov Tsin vanish again, Kentril frowned. He had successfully faced the sorcerer. His pact with the Vizjerei had been severed. The captain and his men could leave right now if they so chose.

So why did his own feet move with such sluggishness?

We will be leaving! he silently roared at himself. Turning to the others, Kentril shouted, "Get your packs ready! I want us on the path back home within the next few minutes! Understood?"

Under his stern gaze and commanding tone, the mercenaries hurried to break camp. As he gathered his own things, Captain Dumon glanced now and then toward the tent of his soon-to-be former employer. Never once, though, did the Vizjerei poke his bald head out. Kentril wondered whether the sorcerer might be sulking or had simply begun his preparations for the supposed spectacle. It bothered him slightly to leave Tsin alone here, but if the Vizjerei chose to stay even with everyone else abandoning Ureh, the captain would not waste any more time on him. The men came first.

In short order, the mercenaries stood prepared to march. Gorst grinned at Kentril, who opened his mouth to give the order to move out.

A rumble from the south froze the words on his very lips.

He looked over his shoulder to see dark clouds rolling toward them from the direction of the jungle. Black as pitch, the thick, angry clouds roared over the landscape at a phenomenal pace. The wind picked up nearby, growing to near hurricane proportions in the space of a few breaths. Lightning played across the sky. A dust storm arose, turning the camp into chaos.

"Find shelter!" Kentril looked around quickly, saw that, other than the crumbling city, there stood nothing around that could protect him and his men from what would surely be a titanic assault by the elements. With much reluctance, he waved for the others to follow him.

At a section of the outer wall that had some years past collapsed, the mercenary band slipped into ruined Ureh, paying no more mind to the once fabulous architecture than they had during their earlier treasure forays. Kentril quickly spotted a rounded building three stories in height and judged it to be among the most stable in the vicinity.

He led the rest there, and the fighters huddled inside, waiting for the blast to come.

An ocean of rain swamped the area almost as soon as the mercenaries found cover. Jagged bolts shot dangerously close to their location. Rumbles of thunder shook the building as if an army of catapults assaulted it. Dust and bits of masonry dropped from the ceiling.

Seated near the entrance, Kentril fought to turn his mind from the horrendous storm. The thunder and lightning once more brought back the memories of earlier battles and comrades lost. In desperation, he finally slipped the brooch out, holding it hidden in one hand while he stared at the perfect face and dreamed.

One hour passed. Two. Three. Still the dire storm did not let up. Unable to make a fire, the mercenaries sat in small groups, some trying to slumber, others talking among themselves.

More time passed—and then Gorst, blinking, suddenly asked a question that Kentril realized he himself should have asked long, long ago. "Where's the magic man?"

In all their haste, the motley band had not even bothered to think about the Vizjerei. As little as he cared for the man, Kentril could not leave the sorcerer out there. Thrusting the brooch back into its pouch, he surveyed the others, then decided that it remained up to him to find out the truth.

Rising, he looked at his second. "Gorst. You keep the others under control. I'll be back as soon as possible."

The torrential rain showed no sign of letting up as he stood in the doorway. Swearing at his own burdensome sense of decency, Captain Dumon raced out into the storm.

The wind nearly buffeted him back inside. Despite such terrible resistance, though, he struggled through the ruins, finding some meager protection along the way.

At the gap in the outer wall, the captain paused. A bolt of lightning struck the rocky ground just ahead, pelting him with bits of stone and clay. As the earthy shower ended, Kentril took a deep breath and stepped from the relative safety of Ureh.

Squinting through drenched eyes, he searched for the sorcerer's tent.

There it stood, seemingly unaffected whatsoever by the rampaging elements. The flimsy tent looked remarkably untouched, as if not even the slightest wind blew nor a single drop of rain had alighted onto it. Despite his own lamentable situation, Kentril paused again and stared, disbelieving.

Another bolt struck near. Common sense revived, Kentril charged toward the tent, fighting the storm with as much ferocity as he would have any other foe. Twice he slipped, but each time the captain leapt back to his feet. As Kentril reached Quov Tsin's abode, he shouted out the sorcerer's name, but no one answered.

Lightning ravaged the area. Rain and rock assaulting him, Kentril Dumon finally threw himself into the tent—

"And what exactly do you think you're doing?"

Bent over a scroll and seemingly unaffected by the storm raging around him, the wrinkled Vizjerei eyed Kentril as if he had just grown a second head.

"I came . . . to see if you're all right," the soldier lamely replied. Tsin looked as if he had just risen from a long, refreshing nap, while Kentril felt as if he had just swum the entire length of one of the dank jungle rivers.

"Such concern! And why shouldn't I be?"

"Well, the storm—"

The sorcerer's brow furrowed slightly. "What storm?"

"The huge one raging out—" The mercenary captain stopped. In the tent, he could no longer hear the roar of thunder, the howl of the wind. Even the heavy rain left not the slightest patter on the fabric.

"If there's a storm out there," Quov Tsin remarked dryly, "shouldn't you be wet?"

Kentril glanced down and saw that no moisture covered his boots, his pants. He stared at hands devoid of rain, and when he reached up to touch his head, only a few droplets of sweat gave any hint of dampness.

"I was soaked to the bone!"

"The humidity here can be very harsh at times, especially in the jungle, but you look fairly well to me, Dumon."

"But outside—" The captain whirled toward the entrance, thrusting aside the tent flaps so that both could witness the horrific weather beyond.

A sunlit day greeted Kentril's dumbstruck eyes.

"Did you come all the way back here because of this mythical storm, Dumon?" the dwarfish spellcaster asked, his expression guarded.

"We never left camp, Tsin . . . it started just after we'd packed up!"

"So, then, where are the others?"

"Taking . . . protection . . . in the ruins . . ." Even as he said it, Kentril felt his embarrassment growing. More than a dozen veteran fighters now huddled inside a building, for the past several hours trying to shield themselves from—a cloudless sky?

But it *had* stormed . . .

Yet when he looked around for any sign of the deluge, Kentril saw nothing. The rocky ground appeared parched, not a single droplet to be seen. The wind blew strong, but only at a fraction of the velocity that he recalled from earlier. Even his own body betrayed his beliefs, for how to explain the relative dryness of his clothes, his very skin?

"Hmmph."

Captain Dumon turned to find Quov Tsin drawn up to his full height. The sorcerer had his arms crossed, his expression one of growing bemusement.

"Dipping into the rum rations before leaving, Dumon? I'd thought better of you in at least that regard."

"I'm not drunk."

The robed figure waved off his protest. "That's neither

here nor there now, captain. We've a more important matter to discuss. Since you and yours have decided to be here
after all, we should make plans. The hour approaches rapidly . . ."

"The hour—" Realizing what Tsin referred to, Kentril
made a quick calculation. With the time his men had already
lost, they would not get very far. Even if they had started off
as planned, the mercenaries would have barely made what he
considered a safe place to camp by sundown.

Yet if they stayed one more night here, they might be
able to go back with something to show for their misfor-
tunes.

But did they want to stay even one more night in a place
where the dead invaded one's dreams and monstrous rain
storms appeared and vanished in the blink of an eye?

Before Kentril could come to any conclusion of his own,
Tsin made it for him. "Now, run along and gather your
men, Dumon," the sorcerer ordered. "I've a few outside
calculations to make. Come back in a couple of hours, and
I'll inform you of what must be done. We must time this
right, after all . . ."

With that, Quov Tsin turned his back on the tall fighter,
once more becoming engrossed in his curious tasks. Still at
a loss, Kentril blinked, then reluctantly stepped outside.
He took one last look around for any sign of the storm,
then started back to Ureh, hoping all the while that by
deciding to stay a little longer he had not made a terrible
mistake.

Only when Kentril had already reached the broken wall
did it occur to him that the Vizjerei might have been too
calm, too relaxed, when told about the tempest. Only then
did he wonder if perhaps the sorcerer had known more
about it than he had revealed, if perhaps the timeliness of
the storm, not to mention its abrupt end, had been no coincidence.

But Tsin had never shown such power . . . unless everything the fighters had experienced had been nothing more

than illusion. Still, even that would have required great skill, for not one of Captain Dumon's men had seen through it.

A shout came from the building in which he had left Gorst and the others. The huge, shirtless mercenary waved at Kentril, grinning as usual. He seemed not at all bothered by the peculiar finish to the rain.

The captain decided to say nothing about his concerns . . . for now. At the very least, he and the others still had a chance of coming out of this with some profit. Surely, then, one more night in the vicinity of Ureh would not matter.

They could always leave tomorrow . . .

Kentril's quick talk of the possibility of yet garnering some profit from their venture rapidly eradicated any apprehensions caused by the unsettling weather. They all understood, as he did, that a late start into the jungle would not be a good thing, but they understood even more that by waiting the one night, they might leave with their packs filled with treasure. The fears of the previous eve became more and more simply a bad dream, replaced gradually by visions of gold and jewels.

And so, just before the appointed hour, the captain positioned his men as requested and turned to the sorcerer, who had made still more last-minute calculations. The shadow of the mountain Nymyr had already stretched forth its fingers over much of fallen Ureh, but Tsin had informed him again that only when it touched the entire city in just a certain way would they all be rewarded for their waiting.

Finally lifting his head from the scrolls, the Vizjerei announced, "It is time."

Like a plague of black ants, the shadow spread faster and faster. A sense of unease once more enveloped Kentril, but he held his position. Soon, very soon . . .

"*Basara Ty Komi* . . ." chanted Quov Tsin. "*Basara Yn Alli!*"

Kentril's body tingled, as if some powerful force had spread over him. He glanced at the others and saw that they, too, felt it. To their credit, however, none moved from his location.

Together, the party formed a crude, five-sided form, with the sorcerer in the very middle. Both the pattern and the unintelligible words spoken by Tsin had been gleaned from the works of Gregus Mazi, and with them the ancient spellcaster had supposedly reopened the corridor by which he had finally joined the other blessed inhabitants of the city. None now desired to take that same path to its ultimate conclusion, but if enough earthly belongings lay scattered along the trail, so to speak, every man would feel very, very blessed indeed.

"Gazara! Wendo Ty Ureh! Magri! Magri!"

The air felt charged with what could only be described as pure magical energy. Clouds began to form over the shadowed kingdom, dark ones that did not remind Kentril so much of Heaven as of that other realm. Still, if the words had worked once, they surely would work again . . .

Arms stretched toward the ruins, Quov Tsin shouted, *"Lucin Ahn! Lucin—"*

"In the name of the Balance," someone broke in, "I charge you to cease this effort before you cause great calamity!"

Tsin faltered. The mercenaries turned as one, some reaching for blades. Kentril bit back the yelp he had been about to make and glared at the fool who had interrupted at such a crucial moment.

A slim figure clad completely in black eyed them all with the arrogance reserved for those who did not just believe themselves superior in all ways but *knew* it to be truth. Plain of face and younger than the captain by more than a few years, the intruder would not have disturbed Kentril if not for two things. One had to do with the slanted eyes, so unearthly a gray color that they seized the attention of all who looked into them. Yet almost immediately those same eyes repelled, for in them Kentril sensed his own mortality, not something any mercenary desired to come to know.

The second had to do with the garments he wore, for while many folk favored black, the dark robe and cloak of the stranger had upon them tiny patterns, markings of which Captain Dumon had some past knowledge. Each symbol represented an aspect of the afterlife, including those shunned by most.

As the intruder marched toward him, Kentril also caught glimpses of a dagger at the other's belt, one unlike those the mercenaries carried. This dagger had been carved, not forged, and even from where he stood, Kentril could guess that it had been made from the purest ivory.

The man was a necromancer, the most feared of spell-casters . . .

"Take good sense and leave here now!" the black-clad figure cried out. "Only death awaits in those troubled ruins!"

Oskal started to retreat, but a look from the captain put him in his place again.

"*Ques Ty Norgu!*" replied Quov Tsin with a sneer. Ignoring the warnings of the necromancer, he gestured a final time at the remains of the once proud city. "*Protasi! Ureh! Protast!*"

The sky rumbled. The wind swirled and roared, changing direction each second. Kentril saw the necromancer fall to one knee, a hand touching the ivory dagger. Despite the gathering clouds, the shadow that had been enshrouding the fabled realm seemed, if anything, stronger, more distinct.

Lightning flashed . . . lightning from places in the heavens where no clouds yet floated.

"*Ureh!*" screamed the wrinkled Vizjerei. "*Ureh Aproxos!*"

Three bolts shot forth, striking one another simultaneously over the ruins. The men cringed, and one or two even let out gasps.

And when the lightning ceased and the rumbling faded, Kentril stared at last at what Quov Tsin had wrought, stared at the culmination of the weeks of sweat, even of blood. He eyed Ureh, the legendary city, the *Light among Lights*, and finally blurted, *"Well?"*

The ruins had not changed.

FOUR

"I don't understand!" Tsin fairly shrieked. "I don't understand!"

Ureh remained untouched, the same crumbling skeleton that the party had first come across. The clouds, the lightning, the wind—all had died or faded away. Only the immense shadow cast by Nymyr still lay claim to the ancient kingdom, and with each passing second it tightened its grip, sinking Ureh deeper and deeper into darkness.

"Him!" The Vizjerei poked a gnarled finger at the necromancer. "It was him! He caused it all to go astray! He interrupted at the time most crucial!"

"My interruption," responded the studious-looking figure, "did nothing, I regret to say." Despite his dire warnings and his clear attempt to get the others to flee, to Kentril even he seemed a bit disappointed by the lack of any fantastic change in Ureh. "I am as mystified as you."

With no apparent reason remaining for them to stay in position, the mercenaries swarmed around the necromancer. Even Gorst, who found the Vizjerei sorcerer fascinating, studied the other spellcaster with little enthusiasm. All knew how the necromancers trafficked with the dead, blurred the lines between the mortal world and the afterlife.

His own sword drawn, Captain Dumon confronted the arrogant intruder. "Who are you? How long've you been spying on us?"

"My name is Zayl." He stared down the length of Kentril's blade as if unconcerned. "This is my home."

"That doesn't answer my second question . . ." The mercenary leader hesitated, his mind suddenly racing. Necromancers toyed with the dead. Could that mean—

Suddenly certain he knew the truth, Kentril put the tip of his blade just under Zayl's jaw. "It was you! You sent Hargo's ghost into our dreams, didn't you? You sent that warning to get us to leave!"

At this, the other fighters grew incensed. Tsin, standing slightly back, cocked his head, studying his rival spellcaster with more interest.

"I did what had to be done . . . at least, I thought so at the time."

"So!" announced Tsin. "You, too, felt certain that the path opened by Gregus Mazi could be reopened this day! I thought so!"

Kentril heard a slight chuckle, but one that did not seem to come from the direction of any of his men. Zayl's hand slipped momentarily to a large, bulging pouch at his side, which looked as if it contained a melon or some similarly shaped object. When the necromancer noted the captain's interest, he casually pulled his hand away.

"I had my confidence in that fact," Zayl reluctantly agreed. "As unfounded, it seems, as all your research."

"So there's no gold?" Benjin asked mournfully.

Kentril scowled at the other mercenary. "Shut up. As for you"—he tapped Zayl's throat with the sword tip—"I think you know even more than you're saying."

"Undoubtedly true, captain," added Quov Tsin. "It would be best if you kept this creature under guard, even bound, perhaps. Yes, that would be the right course, I think."

For once Kentril found himself in utter agreement with his employer. Everyone knew that necromancers could not be trusted. Zayl might already have a poison or potion just up his sleeve.

In the course of their brief conversation, the shadow of the mountain had continued to stretch forth, so much so that now it even began to blanket the party. A chill wind arose as the shadow settled on them, one that made some of the mercenaries shake. Zayl's cloak began to flutter wildly, and Kentril had to tighten the collar of his shirt.

"Nymyr has a cold touch," the necromancer commented. "If you plan to stay near Ureh, you had best be better dressed."

"What's the point?" Oskal muttered. "Buncha rocks and empty tombs! All this way for nothin' . . ."

"We're gonna need more than cloaks," agreed another fighter. "This gets any darker, we'll even need torches!"

Indeed, the mountain had caused the area to turn almost as black as night, truly a contrast when one saw the sun shining but a few yards farther. Ureh lay in such darkness that one could barely even make out distinct shapes in the city, and the longer the band stood where it was, the more the shadow covering them thickened to the same murkiness.

"Let's withdraw to the camp," Kentril suggested. "And that includes you, too, Master Zayl."

The pale necromancer bowed slightly and, under guard by four of the captain's men, started off. Gorst quickly helped Quov Tsin with his scrolls and talismans, following after the Vizjerei like an obedient puppy. Kentril himself stood his ground until everyone else had departed, then took one last sweeping survey of the vicinity in order to make certain that nothing had been left behind.

His gaze froze as it fell upon the ruins.

A glimmer of *light* flickered in one of the distant towers.

He blinked, thinking the sight simply a momentary trick of his imagination—only then to see *two* lights, the second far to the right in another part of the city.

And as every nerve tingled, and every hair on his neck stood on end, Captain Kentril Dumon watched a dead city blossom with illumination. Light after flickering light burst to life, transforming fabled Ureh before his very eyes.

"Tsin!" he shouted, gaze still fixed on the fantastic display. "*Tsin!*"

Now more visible, the ruined city also proved not so ruined anymore. The gaping hole in the wall had vanished, and what had been a crumbling watchtower again stood proud sentinel. From the top of the battlements, Kentril almost swore he even saw banners fluttering in the ever-increasing wind.

"It's true . . ." muttered a very familiar voice to his side. Kentril glanced down to see the wizened Vizjerei, the latter's expression akin to that of a child who had just received the greatest toy, staring at the wondrous sight. "It's true . . ."

Around Captain Dumon, the rest of the party quickly gathered, many of the veteran mercenaries gazing slack-jawed at Ureh. Even the necromancer Zayl watched the city with something akin to astonishment. That no one at the moment guarded the black-clad spellcaster did not bother Kentril in the least, for clearly Zayl had no intention of flight. As it had done with the rest, the miracle before them had ensnared the necromancer.

"The legends spoke truth," Zayl whispered. "You were right, Humbart."

"What are we waiting for?" Tsin suddenly demanded. "This is why we came so far! Why we struggled so long! Dumon! Your men were promised gold and more! Well? There it is for the taking!"

This finally stirred the mercenaries. "He's right!" laughed Benjin. "Gold! A city full of gold!"

Even Kentril found the lure of treasure enough to push back the anxiety he felt. Ureh had been a kingdom said to be among the wealthiest in the history of the world. Tales had been told of other hunters who had come seeking its riches, but none of those tales had ever left any belief that the searches had been successful. That meant that enough might be found to make each man here as wealthy as any king or sultan . . .

"You cannot be serious," Zayl interjected. "Ureh's riches are for Ureh alone. You rob the dead."

"They're not dead, remember?" Kentril pointed out. "They departed . . . and if that's the case, anything they left behind they surely didn't want. That means that Tsin's right. It's ours."

The necromancer looked as if he wanted to argue further but clearly had little with which to counter the captain's claim. He finally nodded, albeit with much reluctance.

Turning to the Vizjerei, Kentril asked, "Those lights. Does that mean any trouble?"

"Nonsense! The story clearly indicates that the people left the mortal plane in the space of but a few minutes. If we see Ureh as they abandoned it, surely many lamps and torches were left lit. Beyond the mortal plane, time is but a word. Why, we may even find food left in bowls and good ale for your men! What do you say to that?"

The other fighters cheered at this possible bonus. Something about the sorcerer's logic briefly troubled Captain Dumon, but, unable to decide just what, the mercenary officer shrugged off the slight concern. Even he could not help feeling much enthusiasm.

"All right!" he cried to the others. "Get what each of you needs! Bring rope and torches with you, too—I'm not going to trust those lights alone! Don't forget sacks! Hurry!"

With far more eagerness than before, Kentril's men went into action. Quov Tsin also prepared himself, retrieving his magical staff and placing about his neck three amulets he had been carrying in a pouch at his belt. Despite their many disagreements, the captain planned to search alongside Tsin once they entered Ureh. Kentril felt certain that wherever the Vizjerei sought his magical artifacts and tomes they would also find great riches.

To everyone's surprise, when the small troop reassembled, the necromancer stood waiting for them. In their eagerness to ready themselves, the mercenaries had more or less forgotten to guard him, but it seemed that Zayl, too, continued to be drawn by the possible offerings of the magical kingdom. Once more he had one hand on the bulging pouch, but as Kentril approached him, the slim figure let the cloak cover it.

"I will be going with you," he stated firmly.

Kentril did not like that notion, but, to his surprise, Tsin readily agreed.

"Of course you will," the Vizjerei declared. "Your knowledge and expertise will prove most invaluable. You'll come with Captain Dumon and myself, naturally."

Zayl executed his slight bow, his face impassive. "Of course."

While none of the mercenaries protested the necromancer's presence, they kept their distance from him as the band, torches already lit, headed toward Ureh. With the outer wall no longer visibly damaged, Kentril, under Zayl's guidance, led them toward the main gate. Although the fear existed that with the city seemingly whole the gate might also be blocked, they came around to the entrance to discover it open and the drawbridge down as well.

"Almost as if we're invited in," commented Kentril.

Quov Tsin snorted. "Then, by all means, let us not stand around here gaping!"

Weapons drawn and torches held ahead, the group entered.

To the naked eye, it might have seemed as if the inhabitants had just stepped out or even simply gone to sleep. Buildings that on previous visits had been crushed in or at least cracking stood tall and new. Rows of high oil lanterns that had previously been rusted, crumbling wrecks now brightly illuminated the avenues. Other lights boldly shone from towers and structures deeper in the city.

Even the very street upon which the band walked looked as if it had been freshly swept.

Yet not one sound did they hear. No words, no laughter, no crying, not even the calls of birds or insects.

Reborn Ureh itself might seem, but the stillness within reminded all of the stunning fates of the inhabitants.

A short distance in, the main avenue split off into three directions. Kentril studied each in turn before saying, "Gorst! Take four men down the right for about a hundred paces, no more. Albord! You, Benjin, and four more check the left. The rest of you, come with Tsin and me. No one goes farther than I said, and we all meet back here as soon as possible."

He did not include Zayl in any of the groups, especially his own, but the necromancer followed him regardless. Kentril took the point, Oskal and another man flanking him just a step behind. Eyes darting from one side of the street to the other, the captain kept careful count of each step as they proceeded.

Building after building they passed. Light gleamed in some of them, but each time one of the party investigated, they found no sign of any life.

"Check those doors," Kentril commanded Oskal, pointing to what looked to be a business on the left. Lit within more than any of the previous structures, it drew the captain's attention like a moth to the proverbial flame.

Guarded by another mercenary, Oskal tried one of the doors. It swung open with little effort. Leaning in, the veteran surveyed the interior for a moment, then, in a relaxed voice, called back, "A potter's shop, cap'n! Stacks of fancy pieces on the walls. There's one even sittin' on the wheel lookin' freshly shaped." An avaricious look spread over his ugly features. "Think we should check to see if he left any coin in the till?"

"Leave it. It'll still be there when we get around to it—if you even want such meager coin once we've gone through this entire place!"

The mercenaries laughed at this suggestion, and even Tsin cracked a rare smile, but Zayl remained almost devoid of emotion. Kentril noticed that his hand touched the large pouch again.

"What is that you've got in there, necromancer?"

"A keepsake, nothing more."

"I think it's more than—"

A shriek filled the air, echoing time and again through the empty avenues of Ureh.

"That sounds like one of ours!" gasped Oskal.

The captain had already begun to turn back. "It is! Run, you fools!"

The cry did not repeat, but now came the sounds of cursing men, the clatter of arms, and what very briefly might have been the low, sinister rumble of some animal.

Gorst and the rest joined Kentril's men at the original intersection. No one spoke, each breath now saved only for action.

They came across tall, gangly Albord, a white-haired fighter from an area north of Captain Dumon's own, shouting at four other mercenaries, all of whom had hunted looks in their eyes. Near Albord's feet, a torn and ravaged form lay sprawled near the right side of the avenue. It took Kentril a moment to realize by process of elimination that the mangled, bloody mess had once been Benjin.

"What happened?" the captain demanded.

"Something came out, tore him apart, and moved so quick none of us saw it much at all!"

"Was a cat!" insisted another man. His expression turned dumbfounded. "A huge, hellish cat . . ."

"All I saw was a blur!" insisted Albord.

"No blur rips open a man's guts like that!"

Kentril looked to Tsin. "Well?"

The sorcerer raised his staff, drawing a circle in the air. He stared upward for a moment, then said, "Whatever it was, it's not around here anymore, Dumon."

"Can you be certain?" asked Zayl. "Not all things are so easily detected by magic."

"Do you sense anything, cretin?"

Zayl pulled free the ivory dagger Kentril had earlier seen. Before the eyes of the startled mercenaries, he pricked a finger with the tip. As a few droplets of blood coursed down the blade, the necromancer muttered silent words.

The dagger flared bright, then faded to normal again.

"I sense nothing," the pale figure reported. "But that does not mean that there is nothing."

Swearing, Kentril turned to Albord. "Which way did it head after it killed Benjin?"

"Toward that building there on the left . . . I think."

"Nah!" interrupted a fellow mercenary. "It turned and went farther up into the dark!"

"You're daft!" came the one who had identified it as a cat. "It whirled around and darted back the way it came! That's how I saw it fer what it was!"

The rest of the party looked at Albord's group as if all of them had gone mad. One of Gorst's men spat on the building next to which he stood, snarling, "I'm beginnin' to wonder if maybe they killed 'im themselves, eh, captain?"

It would not have been the first time that mercenaries had murdered one another over treasure, but Captain Dumon did not see that as the case this time. Still, it made sense to question those involved further. "Where were each of you when Benjin bought it?"

"Spread out like you've always taught us, captain," Albord replied. "Jodas there, me next to him, Benjin right there where Toko,"—he indicated the man who had accused him of murder—"is—"

And at that moment, a flash of black burst out of the doorway next to Toko, catching him across the chest.

The fighter screamed in much the same way as Benjin had as curled claws a foot in length tore through padded leather and flesh, revealing to his horrified companions wet, red ribs and ravaged organs. Toko actually managed to look down at his horrendous wound before death claimed him and he toppled forward.

A beast that, yes, could vaguely be described as a cat emerged from the building, hissing at the humans. Yet no cat stood seven feet in height and had eyes red and without pupils. In the light of the lamps, its fur looked jagged, almost sharp, and fire black. The hell cat roared once, a blood-curdling sound, and revealed not one but *two* sets of long, feline teeth.

"Pincer pattern!" called Kentril. "Pincer pattern!"

The familiar tone of their captain giving commands brought the rest of the soldiers back to the moment at hand. They quickly formed themselves as he had ordered, working to cut off the monstrous beast's escape.

Barbed tail swishing back and forth, the cat stepped toward its foes. The eyes went from man to man, studying each.

"What's that thing doin'?"

"Maybe it's deciding who to eat next?"

"Silence in the ranks!" Kentril demanded. The beast paused in its study of the others to take special care in viewing him. Captain Dumon met the inhuman gaze and, despite his inner fears, matched it.

At last, it proved to be the creature who looked away first. It slowly backed up, almost as if intending to return to the building from whence it had come.

That could not be allowed. Kentril knew better than to follow any foe back into his lair. Worse, if the cat escaped, it would likely catch them again later, when their guards were down. "Albord! Oskal! You and—"

With another horrific cry, the cat suddenly crouched, then leapt for him.

Kentril had no time to recover. Claws flared from the paws of the monster, the same razor-sharp sickles that had ripped to bloody gobbets two of his men. He saw his own terrible death coming and knew that his reactions would be too slow even to delay the dire event.

Then a form as much a shadow as the beast met the cat in midair. Although smaller, the second hit with such force that both fell directly to the street.

A flash of white appeared at the end of the new figure's limb. Not a claw or talon, as Kentril first believed, but rather a dagger—a dagger made of ivory.

Zayl had sacrificed himself to save the captain.

Never had Kentril seen such agility and speed in any man. Despite still wearing his voluminous cloak, the necromancer danced around the savage claws of the cat. The hellish creature snapped at Zayl, tasting only air. The pale spellcaster leapt atop his gargantuan foe and this time struck true with the ivory dagger.

A flash of emerald-green light flared where the peculiar blade bit in, and although Zayl clearly managed only a shallow wound, the cat howled as if pierced through the heart. It writhed wildly, finally sending the necromancer tumbling to the side.

Kentril dove in, determined that no man should die for his sorry sake. As he attacked, Oskal, Jodas, and two others joined in while another fighter dragged Zayl to momentary safety.

The cat swiped at the necromancer, howling when the claws missed. Kentril thrust, managing only to catch its unwanted attention again.

As one paw reached with lightning swiftness for their leader, Oskal and Jodas attacked from opposing sides. The beast's head turned toward the latter, who stumbled back as quickly as he could. On the other side, Oskal, still undetected, jabbed as hard as possible into the unprotected flank.

His sword went in a foot and more. The cat shrieked, turning upon the mercenary. Withdrawing his blade, Oskal fled from the reach of either the jaws or the curved claws.

The retreat proved a fatal mistake.

With the full force of a footman's mace, the barbed tail swung down hard on the unwary fighter.

The weaponlike appendage crushed the back of the mercenary's skull with an audible crack. Blood splattered the two men nearest Oskal. Eyes still wide, the already dead soldier fell forward, his sword clattering to the ground.

Enraged, Kentril charged again, thrusting with all his might at the cat's throat. The beast turned to meet him, but something distracted it again from the other side. Caught between two directions, the monstrous feline hesitated.

With as much force as he could muster, Captain Dumon drove the full length of his sword into the thick, muscular throat.

The hellish cat pulled back, taking Kentril's weapon with it. Hacking, its life clearly flowing from the great wound, the badly injured beast spat and swiped at everything in sight. Albord barely missed having his head taken from his body. The mercenaries retreated a step, hoping that death would come quick.

But even with such a wound, the cat did not forget Kentril. Still lithe, still quick, it focused on the cause of its agony, the unblinking eyes locked on Kentril's own. In those crimson orbs, the captain saw clearly his death coming.

Then Gorst acted, the barbarian giving a howl worthy of the cat and leaping atop from behind. The monstrous creature tried to twist backward to get the shirtless giant. However, Gorst wrapped his arms around the neck and used the hilt of Kentril's sword as a grip. Not only did he keep his foe from reaching him, but with his prodigious strength he worked the already deep blade around, further tearing at the cat's dripping wound.

At last, the murderous beast stumbled, then fell. It tried to rise but failed. Even then, Gorst held on tight. His muscles strained, seeming almost ready to tear apart, but still he held his position. The barbed tail flew at him once, twice, but, positioned where he was, Gorst remained beyond its limited reach.

"Let's finish it!" Kentril demanded.

Zayl alongside them, the rest of the mercenaries closed in, everyone still avoiding the tail. Seizing Oskal's sword, Kentril joined the others in stabbing the cat time after time. For what seemed an hour but in truth was only a minute, maybe two, they tried to put an end to the murderous creature.

Then, when Kentril had just begun to believe that nothing could completely slay the monster, the cat exhaled once . . . and fell motionless.

Still untrusting, the survivors watched with blades ready as Gorst dismounted. When the hellish beast made no move for Captain Dumon's second, they knew at last that they had slain it.

"Are you well?" asked a much-too-calm voice.

Kentril turned to see Zayl, the necromancer, looking untouched both physically and mentally by the disastrous event. At another time, that might have irritated the mercenary, but Zayl had saved his life, and Kentril would never forget that.

"Thank you, Master Zayl. I would've surely been dead if not for your quick reaction."

This brought a brief ghost of a smile. "I am simply Zayl. One born to the jungle finds it necessary to learn to react even quicker than the animals, captain—or one gets eaten at an early age."

Not certain whether the necromancer had just made a jest or not, Kentril nodded politely, then turned toward the only one in the party who had done nothing to avert the tragedy.

"Tsin! Damn you, Tsin! Where was all your vaunted power? I thought you Vizjerei had all sorts of magical spells! Three men are dead!"

Yet again, the diminutive sorcerer managed somehow to look down his nose at the much taller fighter. "And I stood

ready in case there existed more than one of these beasts—
or did you think your little troop capable of fending off a
second at the same time?"

"Captain," Albord cut in. "Captain, let's leave this place.
No gold's worth this."

"Leave?" snarled another fighter. "I ain't going back
without something!"

"How about your head still on your shoulders, eh?"

Kentril whirled on his men. "Quiet, all of you!"

"Leaving would probably be a wise choice," suggested
Zayl.

Tsin waved the wooden staff at the necromancer.
"Nonsense! So much awaits us in this city! Likely the animal already lived here before the change, and we just
never ran across it. And since no other came to its defense,
I dare say it lived alone after all. There should be nothing
else to fear here. Nothing!"

And at that moment, music began to play.

"Where's that from?" blurted Jodas.

"Sounds like it's comin' from everywhere!" replied one
of his comrades.

Indeed, the music seemed to close in on the band from
all sides. A simple yet haunting tune, not entirely unmerry,
played on what sounded like a single flute. Kentril felt two
urges at once, one to dance to the tune and the other to run
away as fast as he could.

A man's light laughter briefly joined the music.

To Kentril's far right, a figure moved . . . a human
figure.

Albord pointed down the street. "Captain, there's folk
over by that old inn!"

"Horse and rider comin' this way!" shouted another
mercenary.

"That old man! He wasn't there before!"

All around the party, figures that had not been visible
moments before now walked, rode, or simply stood
nearby. They wore free-flowing garments of all shades,

and Kentril identified the old, young, strong, and infirm all in the space of one sweeping glance.

And through each one he could see the buildings beyond . . .

"Not all the riches in the world are enough for this, Tsin!" The captain summoned the men toward him. "We head to the front gate together! No one strays, no one tries to turn off to search for a few trinkets, understand?"

None of the fighters argued. To ransack an abandoned city was one thing, but to be trapped in a city of *ghosts* . . .

"No!" spat the Vizjerei. "We're so close!" Nevertheless, he did not wait behind when the mercenaries and Zayl started off.

Thinking of the necromancer, Kentril asked, "Zayl! You deal with the likes of these. Any suggestions?"

"Your command is the most prudent course, captain."

"Can you do anything about the ghosts?"

The pale figure's brow furrowed. "I can ward them off, I believe, but something about them leaves me uneasy. It would be best if we could escape Ureh without any confrontation."

This warning from the necromancer did not ease Kentril's concerns in the least. If even Zayl found Ureh's ghosts unsettling, then the sooner the band made it through the gates, the better.

So far, though, the phantasmal figures had done nothing, did not even seem to notice the intruders. And while the flute continued to play, its song growing stronger with each passing moment, it, too, had caused the fleeing group no actual harm.

"There's the gate!" Albord shouted. "There's the—"

He got no further. As one, the mercenaries froze, the blood draining from their faces as they beheld the way to safety . . . a way open to them no more.

Yes, there indeed stood the gate, but not as they had left it. Now the drawbridge stood high, and the gate itself had been bolted shut. Worse, a throng had assembled before it, a throng of pale, spectral forms with drawn faces and hollow eyes, the ghostly inhabitants of the shadow-enshrouded kingdom. The hollow eyes turned as one toward the treasure hunters, stared at Kentril and his companions with dreadful intensity.

Above the music, the light laughter of a man continued.

FIVE

Zayl held up the ivory dagger, at the same time muttering something under his breath. The dagger flared bright, and for a moment, the unearthly horde seemed to back away. Then, as if galvanized by some unseen force, they surged forward, moving in determined silence toward the small party.

"That should have worked," muttered the necromancer in an almost clinical tone. "They are ghosts, nothing more . . . I think."

The horrific throng seemed to swell further with each second. They did not stretch forth grasping hands toward the fighters, did not in any visible way show menace, but they kept coming, more and more of them. Their eyes never strayed from Kentril's band, never gave any indication but that they sought to reach those before them.

No one wanted to know what would happen when they did.

One of the mercenaries finally broke, turning and fleeing back the way the group had just come. Captain Dumon swore, yet he could think of no other course of action. Waving his sword high over his head, he ordered the rest back as well.

Weapons clutched tightly—although what use against fleshless horrors blades might be no one could say—the treasure hunters retreated into Ureh in quick fashion. Even Zayl and the Vizjerei ran, Quov Tsin remarkably quick for one of his size and age. Behind them, seeming barely to move yet somehow more than keeping pace, the legion of pale figures followed.

"At the next street, turn left!" Kentril called to the others. If memory served him, that way led to one of the watchtowers. If they could gain entrance to it, then they could use it to climb over the wall. Two of the men still alive carried rope, certainly enough for them to reach the ground outside.

But as they approached the intersection, movement from down the very path Kentril had chosen made the mercenaries pause.

More of Ureh's forgotten inhabitants approached from there, their faces as hollow and wanting as those behind.

"They're comin' from ahead, too!" shouted Albord, pointing.

True enough, more filled the street before them. Kentril glanced right. Only in that direction did no ghastly horde yet confront the party. Only to the right did any hope of escape remain.

Beside him, Zayl murmured, "What other choice do we have?"

With a wave of his hand, Kentril led the way. At every moment, he expected them to be cut off, but, despite his concerns, their path remained clear as they went along.

Not so any of the side avenues. When two of the mercenaries broke away from the rest and tried to take one, spectral figures materialized from the shadows barely inches from the startled men. The fearful pair quickly returned to the group. Curiously, although the new ghosts also gave pursuit, they, like those already behind, neared the fleeing party but never actually came within reach.

The necromancer said it first. "We are being led, captain. We are going exactly where they want us."

Kentril knew what he meant. Even the slightest indication of variance in the party's route summoned forth scores of additional silent, horrific shades, but none that ever actually caught any of their prey. No, so long as the mercenaries continued on the path designated, the ghosts only kept pace.

But what, the captain wondered, awaited the intruders at the end?

Past tall stonework shops they fled. Past narrow, elegant homes with domed roofs and walled entrances the band ran. In many, lamps and torches flickered, and now and then voices could be heard, but the few times Kentril managed a glance into one of the structures, he saw no sign of life.

And throughout their perilous flight, the flute continued to play the same, never-ending tune. The jovial laugh of the unseen man would now and then join in, seeming to mock the efforts of the harried company.

Then the weary mercenaries found the path ahead cut off by more of the ghastly throng. At first, Kentril did not understand why, but then he saw the narrow alley to the left, a dark, uninviting place that went on seemingly forever. The captain quickly surveyed the rest of his surroundings for some other recourse, but only the alley offered any chance.

"That way!" he shouted, pointing with the sword and hoping that he had not just made a terrible mistake.

No unblinking, ghoulish forms materialized to block their way. One by one, the men slipped into the narrow passage. Kentril kept the sword ahead of him at all times, aware of the foolishness of the act but feeling some slight comfort despite that knowledge.

"They're still behind us, cap'n!" shouted the last in line.

"Keep following me! There has to be an end to this! There has to be—"

As if reacting to his very words, the alley abruptly gave way to a vast, open plaza. Kentril paused just beyond the end of the alley, staring at what he could not recall having seen at all during the first few days' scavenging.

"We couldn't have missed this . . ." he whispered. "We couldn't have . . ."

"By the dragon!" gasped Zayl, now behind him. When Kentril glanced at the necromancer, he saw that Zayl's mouth hung open in outright awe, a sight in some manner nearly as startling as what lay before them.

A massive hill—in actuality a huge outcropping of Nymyr itself—rose up in the very midst of Ureh. The hill itself Captain Dumon did recall, of course, and even then he had wondered why the inhabitants would have chosen to build their kingdom to encompass a several-hundred-foot-tall mound of pure, black rock. Yet not only had they chosen to include it in their plans, but someone had successfully carved out an entire stairway leading up to the very top.

And there, looming over all else, stood what had so ensnared the eyes of all. A magnificent stone edifice with three spiral towers and a high wall of its own overlooked not only Ureh but the countryside far beyond. In shape it reminded Kentril more of the castles from back home, tall, jagged, cold. Fierce winged figures guarded the gate through which any had to pass even to reach the outer grounds. Where the black hill upon which it stood melted perfectly into the shadow cast by the mountain, a faint aura seemed to surround the peculiar white marble from which the keep had evidently been built.

Kentril blinked twice, but the hint of light surrounding the regal structure remained. A bad feeling rumbled to life in his stomach.

"The palace of Juris Khan!" whispered Zayl. "But it vanished with him—"

"Juris Khan's palace?" Quov Tsin barged through the stunned group, battering larger, more able fighters with only the staff. He stepped to the front and surveyed it as best he could from his low position. More than a hint of avarice tinged his voice as he muttered, "Yesss . . . what better place to look? What better place to look?"

Kentril suddenly recalled the pursuing phantoms. He glanced over his shoulder, expecting to see them even now emerging from the alley, only to find his party seemingly abandoned by their terrifying companions.

"They have ended the hunt," declared the necromancer, expression guarded. "They have led us to where we must go."

Captain Dumon examined again the high, twisting stairway leading up to the huge, barred gate and the murky, winged forms atop the wall who seemed to stare down at the newcomers. "We go up there?"

"At the moment," Zayl remarked, "it would seem better than returning to our friends. Do not doubt that if we turn back, they will come again . . . and this time, they may do more than follow."

"Of course we should go up!" Tsin nearly spat. He jabbed the staff in the direction of the fabled palace. "In there, Juris Khan's master spellwork was completed by the combined efforts of his priests and wizards! In there, the greatest of the magebooks will be found—and much gold, of course!"

Only the Vizjerei seemed at all interested in the pursuit of power and treasure. Kentril and his surviving men had lost their lust for riches, at least for the moment. Not a soldier there wanted more than to be far from the shadowed kingdom, even if it meant leaving without the smallest coin.

But no choice had been given them. They had been led to this stairway, and the mercenary captain knew that it had indeed not been by accident.

"Up we go," he growled. "Keep those torches well lit."

As they reluctantly began the climb, Kentril noticed that something else had changed with the vanishing of their unearthly pursuers. No longer did he hear the unnerving music or even the laughter. Ureh had fallen as silent as death.

Up they slowly struggled, the stairway so steep, so awkward, that Kentril wondered how anyone could have made the journey often. Here and there, parts of steps had given way, making the trek even more troublesome. The torches helped little to guide them, the flames seeming to be dulled somehow by the intense shade. Kentril had seen pitch-black nights brighter than this day. Why, he wondered, had he not noticed how dark it had been on the previous excursions into the ruins? Why did it seem so different now?

Up and up the band climbed. The stairway seemed twice as long as it should have been. After what felt like a thousand steps, Kentril noted the ragged breathing—his own included—and called for a brief rest. Even Tsin, who so desired to reach the palace, did not argue.

Zayl, looking far less worn than the rest, sat down a few paces above, hand once more on the bulging pouch. Eyes closed, he sniffed the air, as if seeking something.

The necromancer opened his eyes quickly when Kentril approached him. Once more, the hand slipped away, and the cloak obscured the pouch. "Captain Dumon."

"A word with you, Zayl?"

"I am at your service."

Squatting down near the spellcaster, Kentril commented, "You evidently know a lot about this place. You know more even than old Tsin, and he's been obsessed with this region all his life."

"He has been obsessed all *his* life, but I have lived near it all *mine*, captain."

"A point well taken, Zayl. How much *do* you know? When you saw this"—Captain Dumon indicated the palace—"you reacted with some surprise, but not nearly as much as me. This *wasn't* here, necromancer! This hill, yes, but this palace of marble, *it* wasn't!"

"And in a realm with ties to Heaven itself, this surprises you?"

Kentril snorted. "For an earthly Heaven, Ureh's shown me only blood."

Zayl's left eyebrow arched. "You have a very sharp sense, Captain Dumon, and an innate knowledge of the world I suspect would surprise even me."

"I ask you again, necromancer, what do you know about this palace?"

"Only that, as the *Vizjerei* indicated"—the pale figure pronounced the one word with something akin to disgust—"it was the place where the spell unfolded, where the path to Heaven was opened. It does not surprise me to find that the home of Juris Khan would not follow mortal dictates even now. It was touched by forces beyond our ken, and even a few centuries would not lessen their effect upon it."

The words did Kentril little good. He tried a different tack. "I want to know what's in that pouch."

"As I said, a keepsake."

"And for what reason are you keeping it? It seems very precious to you."

Zayl stood, his face unemotional. In a louder voice, he asked, "Is it not time we pushed on, captain? We have a bit of a climb still."

"He's right, Dumon," muttered Tsin from farther down. "Time is wasting."

Zayl started up without another word. Kentril gritted his teeth, then reluctantly nodded to the others to continue the climb. The time would come when the spellcaster told him the truth, the captain swore to himself . . . provided that they survived this madness, of course.

Curiously, from that point on, the remainder of the trek went much swifter. The walled domain of the great and long-absent Juris Khan grew larger and larger with each passing step. Before very long, the high gates finally beckoned to the climbers.

"Ugly beasts," Albord grunted, eyeing the two winged gargoyles. Up close, they had manlike bodies but with leonine tendencies and beaked faces reminiscent of vultures. Their paws ended in curved talons like those of eagles or hawks. Wide, inhuman orbs glared down at any who stood directly before the barred entrance.

"This is the home of the most pious of the pious?" Kentril remarked.

"Gargoyles are often considered the guardians against Hell," Zayl explained. "These obviously impress upon the visitor that only the good of heart will cross into the palace."

"Does that mean we got to wait out here, cap'n?" someone in the rear called.

"We all go in, or none of us goes in." Kentril studied the barred gateway. "If we get in at all."

In answer, Zayl reached forward to check. At the slightest touch of his hand, the massive door swung wide open.

"Shall we enter?" he politely asked the mercenaries.

The captain fought down a shiver. In opening, the ancient gate had been perfectly silent, as if freshly oiled.

Zayl took a step forward, then, when nothing happened, he continued on to the palace grounds. Emboldened by the necromancer's success, Captain Dumon followed him, then signaled his men to come one by one.

Albord crossed next, to be followed by Jodas and the rest. The more nothing happened to the first through, the easier the minds of those following became. One man even jested with the gargoyles, insisting that they reminded him of a former wife. For the first time since the city had awakened, the mood became somewhat relaxed.

Tsin stood back, watching each mercenary enter. When the last had passed through the gate, he tightened his grip on the staff and strode forward with all the arrogance of a conqueror.

From above the entrance, the gargoyles suddenly howled to life.

Wings outspread, the beaked creatures reared up, stony orbs glaring at the Vizjerei. Talons stretched forth. Tsin immediately retreated.

The gargoyles instantly returned to their still positions.

"The guardians are wise-eyed," murmured Zayl from behind Kentril.

Ignoring him, the captain stepped to the gate, looking over each gargoyle in turn. Had he not seen it himself, he would have thought someone had made the incident up over a few mugs of strong ale. Reaching up with his sword, he tapped lightly on one figure, hearing only the sound of metal against solid rock.

"Stand aside, Dumon," the sorcerer abruptly commanded. "I shall deal with these noisy dogs."

Quov Tsin had the tip of his magical staff pointed at the gargoyle to his left. Even as he spoke, his other hand gestured over the wooden rod, causing some of the many runes inscribed in it to glow ominously.

Zayl joined Kentril. "That might not be wise, Captain Dumon."

The mercenary officer had to agree. "Don't do it, Tsin. You'll only make matters worse!"

"This from the man who so demanded my magical aid earlier?" the Vizjerei scoffed. "These beasts will not keep me out!"

Kentril quickly jumped through the entranceway, blocking Tsin. The Vizjerei stepped back but did not lower the staff.

"Get next to me," ordered the captain. "Stay close, and we might be able to avoid unnecessary trouble."

"What do you intend?"

"Just do as I said, Tsin!"

As Kentril started to moved back to the gate, Zayl confronted him. "If you insist upon this, you will need someone other than the Vizjerei to watch the second gargoyle." He held the ivory dagger steady. "I will assist you."

"I don't need any—" the wrinkled spellcaster began.

"Quiet, Tsin!" Sorcerer or not, Captain Dumon had finally had more than enough of his employer. Zayl had been able to step where Tsin could not, and that said much about both men.

With the diminutive figure between them, Kentril and the necromancer moved sideways toward the gate. The gargoyles stood fixed, simple statues of rock. No hint of their previous awakening could be seen.

Placing one foot within the palace grounds, Kentril exhaled slightly. His idea appeared to be working; with the sorcerer hidden between the two taller men, the magical guardians seemed caught unaware.

"Just a step or two more—"

As Tsin's robed form began to cross the threshold, the gargoyle before Kentril leapt to life, wings suddenly flapping, monstrous eyes glaring, and stony mouth opened in a wild, ear-splitting roar.

Behind him, Kentril heard a second, identical cry, proof enough that Zayl also faced a newly revived beast.

The beaked head came forward, snapping at an area just to the left side of the fighter. The captain's sword clanged hard against the marble maw, but the gargoyle at least withdrew. From the necromancer, Kentril heard words of some unfamiliar tongue, then a brief flash of light at the corner of his vision startled him.

The first gargoyle used his surprise to attack again, and again it tried to reach around the mercenary. *It wants Tsin!* Kentril realized. *It's trying to avoid fighting me! It wants only him!*

Fearsome talons swept by his shoulder, snatching at the small sorcerer. The Vizjerei batted at them with the staff, sparks flashing whenever the wooden rod touched stone.

"Tsin!" Kentril shouted. "Now's your chance! Jump—"

At that moment, the flute music began again, seeming to come from everywhere at once. Kentril clamped his mouth shut, wondering what the return of the haunting melody portended.

The music had a startling effect on the gargoyles. The one before the leader of the mercenaries paused in mid-attack, then peered up at the sky. It squawked once, then quickly repositioned itself as the party had first seen it. As Kentril watched, all semblance of life swiftly vanished, the guardian once more simply a sentinel of stone.

"Incredible . . ." he heard Zayl remark. Twisting, Kentril

saw that the necromancer's monstrous foe had also returned to its original state.

There could be no question but that the music had given them this reprieve, and the captain intended to make good use of that sudden luck. "Move it, Tsin!"

The Vizjerei needed no encouragement. Already he had one foot on the inner yard of the ancient palace, and by the time Kentril and Zayl turned to follow, Quov Tsin stood waiting for them some distance inside.

And still the music played . . .

"It comes from inside," insisted the Vizjerei, now very eager to enter. "Follow me!"

A chuckle escaped from the vicinity of Zayl. "Brave man, indeed, I say, to go where he's clearly not wanted!"

Kentril glanced at the necromancer, but Zayl acted as if he had not spoken, and the captain had to admit that the voice had not sounded like his. Nor had it sounded like any of the men under Kentril's command.

No one else seemed to have noticed the voice, though. Albord and the others awaited his orders. Tsin already had a good start on the rest of the party, and for some reason, Kentril did not want the Vizjerei getting too far away. Something told him that he should keep an eye on the short, arrogant figure. The gargoyles had been placed at the entrance for a reason, and they had reacted only to Tsin—not Zayl, as one might have expected. That did not bode well.

Guided by the flute, the party reached the entrance, a high, arched opening with two bronze doors upon which had been sculpted sword-wielding archangels. Curiously, the images looked badly battered while everything else appeared untouched.

With the tip of his staff, Quov Tsin pushed at one of the doors. Like the gate, it swung open in silence. With all the confidence of one returning to his *own* home, the Vizjerei marched inside.

Marble columns three stories tall flanked a magnificent

hall illuminated by a massive chandelier that the captain esti-mated held more than a hundred lit candles. The floor con-sisted entirely of skillfully crafted mosaic patterns of fanciful animals such as dragons and chimaera—something of a con-trast to the archangels, Kentril thought. Between the two series of columns, portraits of imposing figures in robes of state no doubt gave homage to those who had ruled Ureh over the centuries.

At the end of the corridor, another set of doors awaited them. Making their way past the staring visages of lords long dead, the party paused there, everyone quite aware that the music seemed now to be coming from within. Once again, archangels with swords adorned the entrance, and once again, the figures had been battered hard. Tsin reached for the doors, but this time they would not open for him. When Zayl, too, tried, he met with no better suc-cess.

Kentril stepped up next to the two spellcasters. "Maybe there's a lock or a—"

He had been about to touch one of the ruined images when suddenly *both* doors swung wide open. The trio backed away as a rush of cold air swept out from the dark-ened chamber before them.

At first, they saw nothing, but then the music drew their gazes to the very back of the room, where they could faintly make out a dim lamp . . . and, seated next to it in a high-backed chair, an elderly man in robes of white.

He leaned forward, as if not noticing their coming. Kentril's eyes adjusted enough to see that a slim, hooded figure sat upon the floor before the elder, a figure with a flute held up to where the lips would have been.

"More ghosts . . ." Albord muttered.

Although he had spoken only in whispers, the two within reacted as if the chandelier had suddenly fallen whole from the ceiling, loudly smashing to fragments on the marble floor. The hooded form ceased playing, then rose and slipped into the darkness with one graceful movement. The robed patriarch glanced up and, to every-one's surprise, *greeted* them as if having waited all this time for their arrival.

"You have come at last, friends," he announced in a soft voice that yet seemed to carry the strength of an army in it.

Never one to stand on ceremony save where it con-cerned his own magnificence, the Vizjerei tapped the staff once on the floor and declared, "I am Quov Tsin! Sorcerer of the Innermost Circle, Brother of the High Initiate, Master of—"

"I know who you are," the elder responded solemnly. He looked at Kentril and the others, and even though a vast distance stretched between them, the captain felt as if he stood immediately in front of the former, every thought and emotion revealed. "I know who all of you are, my friends."

Zayl pushed ahead of the sorcerer. He wore an intense expression that surprised most of those around him, espe-cially Kentril. All had come to assume that the necromancer had such utter control over his emotions that nothing, not even a ghostly kingdom, could draw much reaction from him. Even the expression he had worn when first seeing the looming palace could not match his present eagerness.

"And am I right, honored sir, am I right in thinking I know you as well?"

This the white-robed figure found almost amusing. He leaned on one arm of the chair, his chin resting on the palm of his hand. "And do you?"

"Are you not—are you not the great *Juris Khan?*"

A frown escaped their host. "Yes . . . yes, I am Juris Khan."

"Saints above!" whispered one mercenary.

"Another ghost!" snapped another.

Kentril silenced the mercenaries with a swift wave of his hand. He looked to Tsin for confirmation, and although the sorcerer did not respond directly, the Vizjerei's covetous expression said it all.

Incredible as it seemed, they had found Juris Khan, he who had been the guiding light of a kingdom considered the most holy of all . . . and a man who should have been as dead as the horrific phantoms that had herded them to this place.

Herded them?

"He did it," Kentril informed the others, advancing on the seated form. "He had them force us here. He's the one who trapped us so that our only path could be to his palace."

If he expected the lord of Ureh to deny the charges, Juris Khan much surprised him. Instead, the regal figure rose quietly from his seat and, arms folded into the voluminous sleeves of his robes, bent his head in what appeared remorse. "Yes. I am responsible. It is through my means that you were forced to come to me . . . but that is because I could not leave here to come to you."

"What sort of nonsense—" But Captain Dumon got no farther, for as he finished speaking, Khan reached down, seized his robe, and raised it just enough to reveal his feet.

Or where they would have been.

Just above the ankles, the lord of Ureh's feet melded perfectly into the front legs of the chair, so much so that one could not tell where the man ended and the wood began.

Juris Khan lowered the robe and, in a most sincere tone, said, "I hope you will forgive me."

Even Tsin found this too extraordinary to ignore. "But what does this mean? What about the path to Heaven? The legends say that—"

"Legends say many things," Zayl interrupted. "And most of them are found false in the end."

"Ours being the falsest of all," murmured a voice from the darkness to their left.

Juris Khan reached his hand forward to that darkness, smiling at the one within. "They are what they seem. It is safe to come forth."

And from the shadows, the flute player emerged,

hooded no more. For the first time, Kentril saw that the flowing garment had hidden a woman, a young and very beautiful woman with smooth skin like alabaster, eyes that gleamed like emeralds even in the faint light of the lamp and his men's torches, cascading red hair even more vivid than that of the women of his homeland, and an eastern cast to her features that spoke true of her birth in this faraway realm.

"My friends . . . my daughter, Atanna."

Atanna. A name that buried itself there and then in the veteran fighter's heart. Atanna, the most beautiful of beautiful women Captain Kentril Dumon had ever beheld. Atanna, an angel among mortals . . .

Atanna . . . the face from the brooch.

Six

"It was betrayal," Juris Khan told them as Atanna passed to each a goblet filled with wine. "Betrayal from one whom all trusted most."

"Gregus Mazi," his daughter interjected, seating herself on the floor near Kentril. Her eyes met the captain's, and for a moment, a brief light seemed to shine in those almond-shaped, emerald orbs, but then the subject at hand doused that light. "Gregus Mazi . . . my father once called him *brother of brothers.*"

"He sat at my left hand, as the good priest Tobio sat at my right." The white-haired lord leaned back, the head of his own goblet cupped in his palms. "To them I gave the glorious task of translating the visions to reality. To them I gave the blessed task to lead us to the sanctuary of Heaven."

The mercenaries and the two spellcasters sat on the floor before the imprisoned monarch, fruit and wine brought to each of them by the graceful and beauteous Atanna. After so much bloodshed, so much fear, the entire party gratefully accepted Lord Khan's hospitality. Besides, many questions needed to be answered, and who better than the legendary ruler of the holy kingdom himself?

Juris Khan fit very much the mold of a leader. Standing, he had been as tall as Kentril and almost as broad. For one of advanced years, Khan had a youthful appearance and personality and little sign of frailty. Although his features had become weathered, his strong jaw, regal nose, and piercing green eyes still gave him a commanding countenance. Even his long silvering hair did not age the ruler so much as mark his years of wisdom.

Thinking over his host's words, Kentril frowned into his wine. "But the legends say that Mazi was left behind by accident, that he spent years trying to join you . . ."

Juris Khan sighed. "Legends tend to be more fiction than fact, my friend."

"So you didn't make it to Heaven?" asked Tsin, already having downed most of his drink. "The spell failed?" To the captain, the Vizjerei appeared more disappointed in the fact that the magic had not worked than in the fates of the hapless citizenry of Ureh.

"No. We found ourselves trapped in limbo, trapped in a timeless passage between the earthly plane and our glorious destination . . . and all because of one man's evil."

"Gregus Mazi," Atanna repeated, her eyes downcast.

A tremendous desire to comfort her arose in Captain Dumon, but he fought down the urge. "What did he do?"

"When the time came for the final casting," the fatherly monarch explained, "Tobio realized that the words did not read right. Their meaning had been reversed, an invitation not to journey to Heaven . . . but to be thrust down into the pits of Hell!"

Kentril glanced at Zayl, who had been listening as intently as any. The necromancer nodded to him. "In many forms of spellwork, to reverse subtlely the meanings of single words is to reverse the effect. A spell of healing can be made to wound further or even to slay."

"Gregus sought to do more than slay us," murmured Juris Khan. "He sought to damn our very souls . . . and nearly succeeded."

The captain thought of the woman next to him cast down into the realm of Diablo and shuddered. Had he been able to, Kentril would have taken the foul Gregus Mazi by the neck and twisted tight until with his eyes the sorcerer would have been able to look down upon his own heels.

"He would have succeeded," Atanna added, blushing slightly under Captain Dumon's gaze, "if not for my father and Tobio."

"We tried to respeak the already spoken incantation, reverse what had been reversed, and so, instead of Heaven, instead of Hell, we ended up in the middle of a vast nothingness, that timeless realm from which we could not escape."

Snorting, Quov Tsin commented, "You should have recast the spell from there! It would've been a simple matter for any well-trained group of Vizjerei, much less—"

"Not so simple, my friend, when the priests and mages were all slain by the selfsame spell." A cold look spread over the generally kind features of the ruler of Ureh. "Gregus planned thoroughly. A single line altered also drained swiftly the life force of each chanting the spell except for Tobio and myself. Our superior strength and knowledge saved us but left us weak. Worse, without the others, we lacked the power to recast it."

If not able to recast the spell, Juris Khan and the head priest were at least able to expel Gregus Mazi in his moment of triumph. The battle cost Tobio his life, but by sending the traitorous sorcerer away, they prevented him from fulfilling his horrific plan to send Ureh to the realm of the Prime Evils.

And so the kingdom and its people had floated in the midst of nothingness, time forever locked—until there came a moment when suddenly the world materialized around them again, the world in deep shadow.

"No one who had lived his life in Ureh would have failed to recognize immediately grand Nymyr and the shade it always cast upon our fair kingdom. With the belief that our curse had abruptly ended, more than twoscore of my people rushed through the front gate without thinking. All they wanted was to feel the sun, feel the soft wind . . ." Khan leaned back, more pale than even the necromancer. "And what they were repaid with was death most horrible."

Out into the sun they had raced and therein sealed their fates. The moment the light touched them, they *burned*. Like chips of mountain ice tossed into a smith's well-heated forge, the hapless inhabitants of Ureh literally melted away, their screams echoing long after they had been reduced to puddles that themselves evaporated in seconds. Some at the edge managed to cross back into the shadow of the mountain, but in doing so they only worsened their agony, for that which had been touched a breath too long still burned away. In the end, those who had managed to halt in time became forced to slay the shrieking, suffering, half-eaten victims.

Atanna poured Kentril more wine, giving him a soft smile. However, at the same time, tears coursed down her cheeks. She took up her own untouched goblet and added to her father's shocking tale. "We had underestimated Gregus Mazi's monstrosity. That vile serpent had left us no longer a true part of the mortal world. Worse, we began to fear that once the shadow vanished and sunlight touched our home, we would all suffer as the first had."

But what would initially be seen as a miracle visited the terrified citizens that next morning, for, as the first glimpse of sunlight came over the horizon . . . the world began to fade away.

Once more, the nothing of limbo welcomed back the city and its people.

Although shocked, all agreed that until a solution could be found, exile remained much preferable to the ghastly deaths some had suffered. All looked to their blessed leader, Juris Khan, certain that he would yet discover a way to freedom. Many even took the escape from the burning sunlight as a sign that Heaven had not forsaken them. Somehow, Ureh would either return to the mortal plane safely or continue on its intended journey to the holy realm.

"And I determined after much study," Atanna's father revealed, "that a way did exist at least to anchor us without danger in the real world, for I had also determined that we would be returning there again at some point. With the aid of my precious daughter"—he smiled lovingly at the young, crimson-tressed woman—"skilled in her own way, I worked hard to fashion two unique and mystical gems."

Juris Khan handed Atanna his goblet and then, before the eyes of his guests, drew with one finger a fiery circle in the air. In the midst of that blazing ring, a pair of images alternated, a pale crystal as glittering as sun-touched ice and its raven-black twin. Never before had there been two such perfect gemstones, and Captain Dumon and his remaining men both admired and coveted them from the first moment.

"The Key to Shadow," Khan uttered, indicating the black one. "The Key to Light," he added, showing again the icy one. "One placed below Ureh, in the deepest of caverns, the other atop Nymyr, there to catch the first rays of day. Together to tie the shadow now over us, keep it in place at *all* times so that we may stay here while we seek our final escape."

And so, when it came to pass that Ureh did again appear on the mortal plane—just as Juris Khan had predicted—the plan was put into motion. Volunteers were asked for, brave men, ten in all. Five were sent to the depths below, there to find the most dark of the dark places, where shadow had its strongest ties. The other five set out to reach the top of Nymyr, to position the other gem at a place their lord had determined would be the prime location. In addition to the Key to Light, the second group also carried a specially designed pair of tongs so as to avoid the threat of sun. Hopes rose to their fullest as the two parties started out, for truly it seemed that the prayers of the people had been answered.

Unfortunately, no one had counted on the return of Gregus Mazi.

It could only be assumed that he had suspected or even detected the presence of those he had so long ago betrayed.

When Ureh reformed in the shadows the next time, the corrupt sorcerer already stood waiting just beyond its borders. He discovered the attempt to save the kingdom and quickly followed those who climbed the mountain. There, with words of power, he shattered the very top of the peak with a bolt of lightning, slaying the five.

That part of his wicked work done, Gregus Mazi then secretly made his way into the palace of his former master. There he caught Khan by surprise.

"I had scarce time to look up before I realized that he had struck. When I moved to confront him, I found that I and the chair had become one, and we, in turn, had become a part of the palace itself. 'I leave you to sit and contemplate your failures forever, my lord,' the foul beast jested to me. 'And now I go to seal your beloved kingdom's fate by seizing the second gem deep below and destroying it as I have the first.'"

The robed figure ran a hand through his silvering hair. A tear slipped from one eye. "Understand, my friends, that I loved Gregus as I would've my own son. There had been a time when I had thought—" He glanced briefly at Atanna, who reddened. Next to her, Kentril experienced an unwarranted pang of jealousy. "But that is nothing. What matters is that he intended to leave me there, unable to pursue, while he went to destroy the final hopes of all those who had depended on me."

Yet Gregus Mazi had underestimated his former master. Weakened, yes. Trapped, surely so. But Khan had another source of strength. He had the people and his love for them. Khan drew from that now, drew from all Ureh. When he struck at the mocking Gregus Mazi, he did so with the raw force of thousands, not a single being.

"I admit it," the weary monarch muttered, eyes closing briefly in remembrance and regret. "I struck with anger, struck with hatred, struck sinfully . . . but I also struck with gladness and determination. Gregus had no chance."

There had been no body of the traitor to bury or burn;

only a few wisps of smoke marked the final moment of he who had cursed the Light among Lights. Unfortunately, although the monster had paid, he had succeeded in again cursing Juris Khan's beloved kingdom to its horrific exile. Without the crystal in place atop Nymyr, Ureh had no permanent hold in the real world. When dawn broke the next morning, the entire city once more found itself cast into limbo, this time with no hope.

"I could not remake the crystals, you see," Khan revealed. "For their formation required elements no longer available to me. Worse, I was now trapped in this chamber, unable to free myself no matter how I tried, depending ever on my loving daughter to care for me."

But even confined as he was, Juris Khan did not give up. He had all books, scrolls, and talismans to be found brought to him. He researched spell after spell, hoping that when his kingdom returned to the mortal plane, some aid might be found. On those rare occasions Ureh did reappear, he used scrying stones to seek out any possible help that might have wandered near.

And so he had this time discovered the presence of Kentril Dumon and the others, already within the very walls of the city.

"You cannot imagine my delight at finding you! Brave explorers in the heart of my own realm! I knew that I could not pass up this chance, this one hope. I had to bring you to me!"

Kentril saw in his mind the legions of ghostly figures guiding his group from street to street. "You could've chosen a better manner . . ."

"My father did what he could, captain," Atanna interjected apologetically. "He could not come to you. He had to do it."

"Those were your people?" Zayl asked in a tone that indicated he required no answer. "They are like the dead . . . and yet they are not."

The master of Ureh nodded grimly. "Being trapped

between Heaven and the mortal plane has taken its toll. We are not quite alive anymore, not quite dead, either. Atanna and I and those others who serve in the palace suffer less so, for the spells that protect and bind this place have helped us, yet even we will eventually turn as they if someone does not help us soon."

"Someone," the fiery-tressed beauty at Kentril's side murmured, gazing at him.

"But what can we do?" the mercenary leader blurted to her.

The smile she gave him seemed to swallow his heart whole. "You can replace the Key to Light."

"Replace the crystal?" snapped Quov Tsin. "You said it was destroyed!"

Khan nodded politely to the Vizjerei. "So we had thought. So Gregus had thought. But one time in the past, when I sought help from such as you, I found instead that the Key to Light had not been shattered with the mountaintop. Instead, it had been cast far from its intended location, thrown down the other side of the mountain by the force of the blast."

The diminutive sorcerer rubbed his bony chin. "And you've not retrieved it? Surely during night, when all is in shadow—"

"But not *the* shadow. That first time when we once again beheld our homeland, the very eve after the victims of the sun, I sent a small band out to get the lay of the land, discover what might have occurred. Under cover of night, that surely would have been no difficult task. All I sought was some little knowledge, some hope of a nearby settlement." He bared his teeth. "The moment the first stepped beyond where Nymyr's shade would have ended, he, too, *burned* to death."

Atanna placed her hand on Kentril's own, her eyes asking for understanding and assistance. "We're well and truly trapped, captain. Our world ends just beyond the walls of the city. Were I to step one inch farther, I would risk the flesh melting from my bones, my bones incinerating to ash."

Against those eyes, that face, Captain Dumon could not struggle. He slipped his hand on top of hers, then faced Juris Khan. "Can we reach the crystal? Can we get it in place in time?"

Hope lit the elder man's expression. "You will do this for us? You will help us? I promise a king's reward for each if you can do this!"

Jodas nearly choked on his wine. The moods of the other fighters brightened. Here seemed a quest harsh but doable and with much gain to be made. At once, each volunteered, leaving only Zayl and Tsin silent.

"We don't all need to go," Kentril told the others. "Gorst, I need you definitely. Jodas, you can climb well. Brek, Orlif, you come with us also. Albord, you're in charge of the rest."

Some of those to be left behind started to complain, but Khan silenced their concerns by stating, "If this miracle is done for us, all shall share in the reward, I promise."

Kentril asked again about the time factor and where the gem might be found. In response to the first question, Juris Khan assured him that if they left within the hour, there would be time enough. A path cut along the mountain centuries past would serve them well in that respect.

In regard to the second question, the lord of Ureh requested that his daughter retrieve a box. Moments later, when Atanna had returned with the small silver container and given it to him, Khan produced for the captain a small stone of brilliant clarity upon whose top had been etched a single rune.

"This is a piece left from the shaping of the original. The rune spell ties it to the other. Hold it before you, and it'll guide your way."

"You should depart now," his daughter informed them. She touched Kentril's hand again. "Go with my blessing."

Zayl confronted him. "Captain Dumon, I would like to

go with you. My skills could be of use, and I know this area well. It would speed matters up some, I believe."

"A sage suggestion," Juris Khan declared. "I thank you."

"Well if he goes, you've no need of me up on that chill mountain," snapped Tsin. "I prefer to wait here."

Their host accepted this decision also. "You would do me a boon by being here, master sorcerer. Perhaps with you to aid me, I can be freed of Gregus's wicked magic. I offer you all the books, scrolls, and other works gathered in my sanctum as a start for your research, and in exchange for my freedom, afterward you may keep any that you wish."

If the talk of gold and riches had stirred the hearts of Kentril's men, the mention of so much magical knowledge did the same for the Vizjerei. "You're—you're *most* generous, my Lord Khan."

"I would give anything to end this nightmare," the elder responded, his gaze turning to Captain Dumon. "Is that not so, Atanna?"

"Anything," she agreed, also looking at Kentril.

The tiny gem glowed bright, an encouraging sign.

Quickly folding his hand so as not to risk losing the small stone, Kentril deposited it in the same pouch in which he also carried the brooch. He had not told Atanna about finding the latter but swore he would return it to her once the Key to Light had been set in its proper place.

Juris Khan had given them explicit instructions about what they needed to do once they had obtained the magical gem. Kentril knew exactly where to place it, not only to make certain that the wind did not blow it off but also so as to catch the very first hint of sun. Only by following the instructions to the letter could he hope to keep Ureh—and Atanna—from vanishing from his life.

The five men struggled their way around the mountain. While the path had been well carved, time had taken its toll. More than once, they had been forced to leap over breaks or climb above rock falls. Orlif had nearly slipped once, but Gorst and Jodas had pulled him back before anything could happen.

Much to the mercenaries' surprise, Zayl proved an excellent guide. He had spoken truth when he said he knew the area well. True, the necromancer had never climbed to the top of Nymyr, but he seemed to have a sense for how the mountain had been shaped.

Torch in hand, Kentril now followed Zayl, which meant that as the fierce, cold wind blew the necromancer's cloak about, the captain had a good look every once in a while at the mysterious pouch. Something about its contents still bothered him; he almost felt that the bag stared back at him. The notion struck Kentril as ludicrous, but still he could not shake off the sensation of being watched.

"There is an outcropping here that we must go over," Zayl informed him.

"Gorst." The brawny fighter, now clad in a simple cloak of his own, slipped ahead with a length of rope. With Kentril's aid, the pair secured the rope, then, one by one, each man worked his way up.

Once over, Kentril called a pause while he checked the tiny stone again. This time, it flared so bright that he almost expected to see the Key to Light sitting on the ledge before them.

"It must be close," he muttered.

"Yes, we are in luck," replied the pale spellcaster. "Juris Khan thought it had fallen much farther away."

"How long do you reckon we still have?"

Zayl peered up at the night sky. It had taken them several hours to reach this point. The shadow of Nymyr had been swallowed by the dark some time ago. "Just enough, if we find the Key soon. This side of the mountain is not so harsh a climb as that which overlooks Ureh."

They moved on, steeling themselves against the cold night. Kentril retrieved the small stone again, correcting their path.

Minutes later, they literally stumbled over the magical gemstone.

Dirt and rock, possibly from Gregus Mazi's murderous spell, had all but buried the artifact. Only when Kentril turned in a circle, trying to find out why it seemed the party should go no farther, did he kick up a few loose pieces of rock and uncover one glittering edge.

Although the only nearby illumination consisted of their meager torches, the Key to Light still shone like a miniature star. Zayl bent down, digging up the gem. It fit in the cup of his hands, a perfectly shaped crystal.

"Must be worth a fortune," grunted bearded Brek. "What do you think we could get for it, captain?"

"From Ureh, more than you could ever get selling it elsewhere," Kentril retorted, glaring at the mercenary. The thought of betraying Atanna filled him with anger.

Zayl quickly played peacemaker. "No one would think to do anything less than what we intended, captain. Now we must hurry; dawn will be too quick in coming."

With the necromancer carrying the artifact, they began their final ascent. Gorst secured all lines for them and acted as a counterweight now and then when they had to swing from place to place. Kentril actually found the way far more easy than he would have expected; the mountains of his homeland would have caused him much more difficulty. If not for the fact that the people of Ureh had been cursed to remain hidden in the shadow of this very peak, they could have easily rectified their own situation.

At last, they neared the top. As the group paused on a large ledge, Zayl handed the Key to Light over to Kentril.

"Say, cap'n?"

"What is it, Jodas?"

"What happens to the rest of the party if we don't get this thing in the right place? They disappear with the rest?"

Kentril's gaze shifted to Zayl, who shrugged and answered, "It is best we do not find out."

After a few moments' more searching, both Captain Dumon and the necromancer came to the same conclusion regarding the most appropriate location. Unfortunately, that location meant a treacherous climb up a dangerous rise some three hundred feet and more. Although only a small part of the tip of Nymyr, both agreed that based on Khan's calculations it would be best.

"I'll do it alone," Kentril informed the others.

Gorst, however, would not hear it. Although he had remained fairly quiet up until now, Kentril's suggestion stirred him to protest. "You need an anchor. We'll tie the end of a rope around our waists. You fall, I'll catch you, honest."

Knowing better than to try to argue at this point, Kentril agreed to let the giant join in the climb. In truth, it made him feel safer knowing Gorst would be there. They had fought side-by-side in many battles and could always depend on each other's aid. If anyone could be trusted up there, it would have to be Gorst.

Kentril gritted his teeth hard as he began. After a fairly simple journey, even a relatively easy search for the artifact, this last bit threatened to rip victory from their grasp. The wind felt a hundred times more fierce, and nowhere could he get a hold that satisfied him. Out of fear that to stop would mean slipping and falling to his death, Kentril pushed faster and faster, praying he would reach the top before his luck ran out.

With the natural skill he seemed to have for everything, Gorst more than kept pace. Kentril imagined his friend gouging handholds out of the rock face. Likely it would have been better if the much larger mercenary had gone up by himself, but then it would have been his captain who would have protested.

Kentril's fingers finally stretched over the upper edge. He had to rebrace himself when ice caused his initial grip to falter, but after that, he managed to pull himself up with little trouble. Peering around, Kentril studied the immediate area. Large enough for four men to stand, it definitely offered the first place on Nymyr to receive the sun's kiss.

With the agility of a mountain goat, Gorst climbed up after him. Thick hair flying in his face, the other mercenary gave Kentril a big grin.

From his belt pouch, Captain Dumon removed the artifact. He looked the vicinity over, not wanting the Key to Light to fall from its perch the moment the climbers had returned to Ureh.

"There?" suggested Gorst.

There proved to be a tiny outcropping shaped somewhat like a bowl turned on its side. It faced the right direction and fit in with Juris Khan's directions but was not quite large enough for the gem to fit.

Taking his dagger, Kentril began chopping at the spot. He only needed to remove a little of the frozen earth below. Then he could securely place the artifact within and be finished with this chill place.

His dagger slowly bit into the icy ground. Chips of rock-hard dirt flew away—

The tip of the blade scratched at something white. Kentril worked at it, trying to remove the obstacle to his success.

He swore. With his dagger, he had unearthed a bone.

There existed little doubt in his head that this bone had belonged once to one of the five unfortunates who had been murdered by Gregus Mazi. Now fate had let the dead sorcerer again hinder the plans to free Ureh from his curse. Try as he might, Kentril could not dig the bone out, and no other spot atop Nymyr would do.

"Let me try." Gorst took Kentril's place, pulling out his own blade. For many men, the giant's dagger would have almost served as a short sword. Gorst chipped away using his prodigious might, making progress where even his captain could not.

Finally, enough of the bone—likely from the forearm—had been exposed that Gorst seized it in his huge hands and began to pull. The massive fighter grunted with strain, the muscles and veins in his neck throbbing. The frozen ground around the area cracked . . .

The bone came free.

With a startled yell, Gorst fell backward, slipping on the icy mountaintop.

He began to slide toward the edge.

Thrusting the artifact into the newly created hole, Kentril wrapped one arm around the outcropping, then braced himself against it. With his other hand, he seized the rope linking him to Gorst and pulled with all his might.

The other mercenary's head and arms went over the side. However, as the rope went taut, he spun sideways, sending one leg over but giving one hand the chance to reach for a hold.

Gasping, Kentril tugged with all his might, fighting exhaustion, gravity, and Gorst's not inconsiderable weight. The arm that held tight to the outcropping shrieked with pain but held.

Gorst lost his first attempt at finding a grip, nearly skidding off into the air in the process. Only Kentril kept him from doing so, the captain throwing his own weight back to counter as best he could that of the larger mercenary.

On his second attempt, the giant managed to grab hold of a small rocky area. With care, Gorst pulled himself to safety, for once gasping from effort.

"The Key," he called to Kentril.

"Where it should be." Barring another sorcerer blasting away what remained of the mountaintop, it would stay there for some time to come. Juris Khan had also indicated that even on days of rain or snow, the artifact would somehow be able to do its duty.

The Key to Light twinkled suddenly, almost as if stirring to life. For a moment, Kentril wondered what inner magic would cause it to do so, but then it occurred to him that not only did the gemstone look brighter, but he could now see his surroundings in better detail.

He looked over his shoulder.

They had cut this even closer than he had thought.

Dawn had come.

The artifact flared like a sun itself, seeming to take in every bit of illumination around it. Kentril watched it a few seconds more, then hurried as best he could across the icy top of Nymyr.

The light of day encroached upon where Ureh had sat protected. In the distance, the jungle seemed to open its green canopy. Nearer, the rocky landscape leading to the fabled realm took on distinct shapes.

And Ureh?

As the captain watched, sunlight hit the city where Atanna prayed for his success. Sunlight touched where shadow had kept her safe.

And in the end, sunlight failed . . . and under the impenetrable and impossible shade of the mountain, the walled city stood triumphant.

SEVEΠ

Music touched the returning party, music full of gaiety and life. Not only did flutes play, but so did horns, lutes, and drums. As Kentril and the others entered, they also heard voices raised in merriment and noted light upon light darting about in the city below.

Deep shadow still covered the kingdom, but hopelessness no longer enshrouded the lost realm.

Atanna met them almost immediately. Her eyes became Kentril's world, and her voice as she thanked him stirred again his heart and soul.

"I want you to see something before we go to my father," she immediately said. Taking him by the hand, she led the captain and the others to a high balcony, from which nearly all the city could be seen. Atanna waved her hand across the vision of Ureh, showing Kentril the fruits of his success.

There were people—*live* people—celebrating in the streets.

They were everywhere. Not the pallid specters of before, but breathing folk in flowing, colorful clothes more like those donned by the desert inhabitants of Lut Gholein rather than the more dour and formal eastern wear normally seen in Kehjistan. They laughed, they danced, they sang, all the things of life.

"Nice," Gorst commented, grinning at the festive activity.

Captain Dumon looked at his hostess, ever a wonderful sight in herself. "I don't understand. The people—"

"It happened the moment the sun failed to touch our

kingdom. Not only did the shadow hold, but all of Ureh seemed to gain earthly substance. We're still not truly yet a part of the world again, but we are nearer to it than ever before!"

The necromancer leaned close. "Magic is a strange and complicated creature, captain. Perhaps the lord of the realm can better explain this miracle."

Kentril nodded. "We shouldn't keep him and the others waiting any longer."

Atanna did not release his hand, and he made no move to force her. They and the rest hurried through the halls of the palace, halls that, like all else, looked different in ways not noticeable at first.

The chandeliers and oil lamps had become brighter, that much Kentril would have readily sworn. In addition, the sense of death and decay that he had experienced on his first entry had been replaced by one of spirit, of rebirth.

And as there had been people of flesh in the streets, there now stood in the halls figures both solid of body and clad in gleaming metal. Armored from toe to neck in chain and plate and wearing open helmets with broad rims in front that stretched a good hand's width ahead, they saluted the mercenaries and Atanna as the group passed. In some ways, their narrow eyes and pale skin reminded Kentril of Zayl, and he wondered if the necromancer's ancestry held some link to Ureh.

More people crossed their path as they neared Juris Khan's chamber. These wore robes of state with blue or red sashes, and each bowed gracefully as Atanna and the captain headed to the doors. Courtiers also paid homage, men going down on one knee and women curtsying. Brek almost paused to make a play for one of the latter, but Gorst batted him lightly on the back of the head, urging the fighter on.

The doors opened—and what had once been a room plunged in darkness even greater than that of the deepest shadow now glittered in gold and jewels.

The very *walls* had been gilded in gold. Scrollwork lined each segment, and reliefs decorated the centers. To accent figures and designs, gemstones of every color, hue, and transparency had been artfully interjected. Likely it had taken years for those who had crafted this astonishing display to complete their work, but their effort had obviously been worth the difficulties and time.

A full honor guard greeted them as they walked inside, a score of armored figures snapping to attention, their lances pointing to the ceiling. At the far end, where the rich crimson rug that started at the doors finally came to its conclusion, a jubilant Juris Khan awaited the new arrivals. Albord and the rest who had been left behind seemed no less pleased at Kentril's return than the lord of Ureh, and why not? The success of the venture meant that all of them would leave the shadowed kingdom laden with as much treasure as they could carry.

Of Tsin, however, there was no sign. Remembering the talk of the Vizjerei aiding their host in escaping his personal curse, Kentril assumed that the bearded sorcerer had already rushed off to peruse Khan's vast library of magical knowledge. So much the better, as far as the captain felt concerned. Not only would Tsin finally do something of value, but he would also be well out of the way.

"My friends!" the gray-haired monarch gladly called. "My good and trusted friends! You have the gratitude of an entire realm! You have given Ureh a chance to be whole again in a manner we never thought possible!" He indicated the room, the guards, even the courtiers beyond the doors. "Already the fruits of your labors ripen. You bring life to a city! The people celebrate not only their renewal, but those who granted it to them."

"Captain Kentril Dumon," Khan continued, resting his arms on his knees and smiling graciously. "You and your men—and you, too, Master Zayl—are the guests of the palace. It will take a few days to formulate your rewards properly, but in the meantime, whatever you desire in Ureh is yours."

Kentril thought of the festival outside. "Are my men free to leave the palace if they so choose?"

"I think my people would demand it!" Juris Khan looked over the other mercenaries. "There are places for you to sleep in the palace, but there's no need for you to stay here otherwise. Outside, I know that wine, food, and other entertainments are available to you, my friends! If you like, go now with my blessing, and when you finally reach your limit, you are welcome back here!"

The captain nodded permission. That was all the news that Albord and the others needed. With much backslapping and cheerful words, they started out of the chamber, each saluting Kentril as they passed.

"You men can go, too," he informed Jodas and those who had journeyed to the mountain.

They quickly joined their fellows. As Gorst started to leave, though, the captain called him over.

"Keep a bit of an eye on them if you can," he asked of his loyal second. "Make certain that they don't wear out our welcome despite everything, eh?"

Gorst gave him his biggest grin yet. "I'll watch, Kentril. I will."

That left only Zayl, and while Captain Dumon felt more comfortable around the necromancer than he had at first, he still desired his pale companion to find some other interest. Atanna still held Kentril's hand, and he hoped that meant that she would not be averse to advances made by him.

As if reading his thoughts, Zayl suddenly announced, "Great Lord of Ureh, with your permission, I think that I shall see if the Vizjerei might need some of my assistance."

"That would be most appreciated, my friend. One of the guards can direct you."

With a sweeping bow, the necromancer backed away, leaving Kentril with Juris Khan's daughter.

Her father smiled at the pair. "Atanna, I'm sure that the captain hungers. See that he is satiated."

"If that is your order," she replied with a slight inclination of her head.

Atanna led Kentril out, guiding him down a hall he had not traversed previously. Not once did she loosen her hold on him, and not once did the veteran fighter struggle to free his hand. In his mind, she could have led him the length and breadth of the kingdom, and he would have willingly followed.

"You've done so much for us, so much for me," she said as they walked alone. "I don't know how to thank you, captain."

"Kentril. My name's Kentril, my lady."

Under thick lashes, she smiled at him. "Kentril. You must call me Atanna in return, of course."

"It'd be my honor." He frowned. "Is Ureh really safe? Have we really beaten Gregus Mazi's spell?"

The smile faltered a bit. "You have secured us to the world. We cannot go beyond the area the shadow forms, but there is hope now that soon we can. Once my father is free of the other spell, he can proceed with some thoughts he has had, possibilities in which the sorcerer and the necromancer would be of much aid."

"You'd better have someone keep an eye on old Tsin. He's not the most honest of his ilk."

"My father knows how to read people, Kentril. You should realize that."

The corridor suddenly felt much too warm. The captain tried to think of another direction of conversation . . . and finally recalled the brooch.

"My lady—Atanna—I've got to confess that when I saw you with Lord Khan, it wasn't the first time I'd seen your face."

She laughed lightly, a musical sound. "And here I thought that I had entranced you with one single glimpse! I noted that you reacted far more than any of your comrades." Atanna cocked her head. "Tell me, then. How do you know of me?"

"Because of this." He pulled forth the brooch.

Atanna gasped when she saw it. She took it from his hand, running her index finger over the image of herself. "So long! So very long since I saw this! Where did you find it?"

"In the ruins, in the midst of the city—"

"He took it," the crimson-tressed young woman said in a tone so dark it actually made Kentril shiver slightly. "Gregus. He took it."

"But why?"

"Because he desired me, Kentril, desired me heart and soul. When he discovered that Ureh would return once the shadow of Nymyr touched this area in just such a way, he came not only to rectify his foul failure but to try to take me as his prize!"

Without his realizing it, the mercenary captain's hand slipped to the hilt of his sword. Atanna, however, noticed his action and blushed.

"You would be my champion, Kentril? If only you would've been there the first time. I know you wouldn't have let him do to Ureh what he did. I know that you would have slain the beast for us . . . for me."

He wanted to throw his arms around her but managed to hold back. Yet Captain Dumon could not help himself from replying, "I would do anything for you."

Her blushing only increased . . . and made her that much more alluring. Atanna put the brooch back into his palm. "Take this back as a gift from me. Let it be a sign of my gratitude and . . . and my favor."

He tried to speak, tried to thank her, but before he could, Juris Khan's daughter stepped up on her toes and kissed him.

All else in the world faded to insignificance.

Zayl felt extremely uncomfortable. He had felt so for quite a long time, almost since he and the others had first met Juris Khan. That no one else might have recognized this discomfort gave credit to the necromancer's mental and physical skills. The training through which he had lived his entire life had granted Zayl virtual control over every aspect of his being. Few things could disturb the balance within him.

But something about Ureh and its inhabitants had. On the surface, the necromancer could see nothing capable of doing so. Khan and his people had been thrown into a most dire predicament, the victims of a spell twisted by a corrupted sorcerer. He as much as Captain Dumon had wanted to help them, although while the mercenary's interests had much to do with the beauteous offspring of Ureh's ruler, Zayl's interest had been in returning to balance that which had been madly left awry. Such a travesty as Gregus Mazi had enacted could have threatened the stability of the world itself, for whenever innocents suffered as the citizens of this kingdom had, it strengthened the cause of Hell.

Gregus Mazi . . .

"Here we are, sir," the guard who had accompanied Zayl remarked.

"Thank you. I have no more need of you."

The pale spellcaster entered. As he had requested, he had been led to the library where Juris Khan had kept Ureh's greatest magical tomes, holy works, scrolls, and artifacts. In the days of the kingdom's glory, a hundred scholars of both the mystical and theological paths would have been in the vast room perusing the ceiling-high shelves for the secrets and truths gathered here over the centuries.

Now only one slight figure hunched over a massive, moldering book almost as large as himself. Even as he entered, Zayl could hear Quov Tsin muttering to himself.

"But if the rune here means the sun's power and this segment refers to the Eye of Hest . . ."

The Vizjerei suddenly looked up, then glanced over his shoulder in the direction of the necromancer.

"Master Tsin," Zayl greeted the other spellcaster.

The short, bearded man snorted at the newcomer, then returned his gaze to the book.

"How goes your research?"

Without looking at Zayl, Quov Tsin testily retorted, "It goes slowly when young cretins constantly interrupt it with their blather!"

"Perhaps a combination of efforts would—"

Now the elderly Vizjerei did look at the necromancer again, but with eyes that burned bright with growing fury. "I am a sorcerer of the first magnitude. There is nothing I could learn from you."

"I only meant—"

"Wait! It occurs to me that there is one thing you can do."

Zayl frowned, suspicious. "What?"

With a venomous tone, the Vizjerei replied, "You can leave this library right now and get as far away from me as possible! You taint the very air I breathe."

The necromancer's gray eyes met Tsin's silver-gray ones. Both the Vizjerei and the servants of Rathma shared some common ancestry, but neither spellcaster would have ever acknowledged such a blood relation. As far as both sides were concerned, a gulf almost as wide as that between Heaven and Hell existed, a gulf neither wished to bridge.

"As you desire," the pale mage responded. "I would not want to put too much distress on one of such senior years. It could prove fatal."

With a snarl, Quov Tsin turned away. Zayl did likewise, leaving the library and marching down a deserted hallway.

He had not meant to get into any confrontation with the Vizjerei, no matter how minor. The necromancer had honestly wanted to help, the better to see Juris Khan free.

However, there were spells and research that Zayl could do on his own, paths of which the more materialistic Tsin would have never approved. Those who followed the

ways of Rathma often found what other spellcasters care-
lessly overlooked. How ironic it would be if Zayl discovered quickly what his counterpart so struggled to find.
Tsin badly wanted the magical tomes and relics Khan had
promised him; it would eat him up inside if Zayl instead
garnered the prizes.

"Zayl, boy! I must speak!"

He planted a hand over the bulky pouch at his side, trying to smother the voice that could not be smothered. Even
though it had hardly spoken above a whisper, to the necromancer it had resounded like thunder in the empty hall.

"Zayl—"

"Quiet, Humbart!" he whispered. Quickly surveying the
area, Zayl noticed the entrance to a balcony. With smooth,
silent movements, the slim, pale man darted outside.

Below, the sounds of merriment continued. Zayl
exhaled; out here, no one would hear him speaking with
the skull.

He pulled what remained of Humbart Wessel out of the
pouch, glaring into the empty eye sockets. "More than
once you have nearly given away yourself, Humbart, and
thereby put me in straits! Trust is not always an easy thing
for one of my kind to attain, but it is a fairly easy thing for
us to lose. Those who do not understand the truth of
Rathma prefer to believe the lies."

"You mean, like raising the dead?"

"What is it you want, Humbart?"

"Gregus Mazi," answered the skull, the eye sockets
almost seeming to narrow.

He had captured Zayl's attention. "What about him?"

"You didn't believe that hogwash about old Gregus, did
you?" mocked Humbart. "Gregus, who wanted so badly to
join his friends in Heaven that he prayed each morning
and eve and cried most of the day through?"

Looking down at the torchlit city, the necromancer
thought over everything that had been said about the
sorcerer. During Juris Khan's revelations, Zayl had more

than once pondered inconsistencies with what Humbart Wessel had told him but had also assumed that the lord of Ureh would certainly know Mazi better. "Sorcerers, especially those like the Vizjerei, can be a treacherous, lying bunch. Mazi simply fooled you, Humbart."

"If he fooled me, lad, then I've got two legs, a pair of arms, and all the bones in between still—and covered in a good wrapping of flesh to boot! Old Gregus, he was a torn man, blaming himself for not being good enough and praying for redemption from day one. He was no monster, no corrupted wizard, mark me!"

"But Juris Khan—"

"Either was fooled or lies through his teeth. I'd swear on my grave, and you know that's one oath I'll hold true to."

Now Zayl truly understood his own earlier anxieties. In the past, he had heard from the skull bits and pieces of the events that had taken place outside the shadowed kingdom, when Humbart Wessel and his men had watched Gregus Mazi rush to the ghostly city, arms raised in praise to Heaven and voice calling out thanks for this second opportunity. Every time Humbart had mentioned the spellcaster, it had always been as a man driven to redeem himself, to prove himself worthy.

Not at all the beast that Khan and his daughter had described.

"And what would you suggest?" the necromancer muttered.

"Find out the truth from the source, of course!"

Zayl gaped. "Gregus Mazi?"

It had never occurred to him to try to raise the specter of the dead mage. In the past, it had seemed impossible, for all trace of the man had been thought to have vanished along with the legendary kingdom, but now Zayl stood within that realm himself.

One problem remained, though. According to Juris Khan, Mazi had been utterly destroyed, his corporeal form incinerated. Without skin, hair, blood, or a sample of well-worn clothes, even a skilled necromancer such as Zayl could hope to accomplish little.

He said as much to the skull, which brought back a harsh and sarcastic response from Humbart. "Am I the only one of us who still has a brain in his head? Think, lad! Gregus was born and raised in Ureh. He lived here all his life until the spell that cast the soul of the city and its people into oblivion, and then he still came back again. More to the point, Zayl, Ureh's been frozen in time, almost unchanging. If old Gregus had a place to call his own here, the betting's good that it still stands."

What Humbart said made such sense that Zayl could not believe that he had not thought it. If a piece of clothing or an item often used could be found among the dead mage's belongings, it might prove enough to summon the shade of the man. Then from Gregus Mazi himself the necromancer could learn the truth—and possibly even the key to Ureh's salvation. If Mazi proved to be the evil that Juris Khan claimed him to be, Zayl could wring the secret of his spellwork from him far faster than Tsin could ever hope to do by thumbing through volume after volume of dusty tomes.

"We must find his home."

"Can't likely just ask, though, can we?"

Eyeing again the city below, where the celebrations continued unabated, Zayl allowed himself the slightest of smiles. "Perhaps we can, Humbart . . . perhaps we can."

A few minutes later, the cloaked spellcaster walked among the citizens of Ureh, a tower of black among the colorful locals dancing, cheering, and singing under the light of torches and oil lamps. It seemed odd to need torches and lamps at what should have been the brightest part of the day, but with the deep shadow of Nymyr also their protection from both exile and horrific death, the inhabitants of Ureh certainly seemed unwilling to complain.

Several men insisted on shaking his hand or slapping his back, while more than one enticing female sought to thank him even more personally. Zayl suffered the slaps and accepted politely the kisses on his cheek, but although he could not help being slightly caught up by the mood around him, the necromancer kept his mind on the task ahead.

"Damn, but I wish I had a body to go with this cracked old skull," came Humbart's voice from the pouch. "Ah, to drink some good ale, to find some bad women—"

"Quiet!" While it seemed unlikely that anyone would hear the skull in the midst of all this festivity, Zayl wanted to take no chances.

One of Kentril Dumon's men came swaggering down the street, a young woman on each arm. The bearded mercenary kissed the one clad in a golden outfit more appropriate for a harem, then noticed the necromancer watching him.

"Enjoyin' yourself, spellcaster?" He grinned and, momentarily releasing his companions, extended his arms to include all of Ureh. "The whole blasted kingdom wants ta celebrate us heroes!"

Zayl recalled the dark-haired fighter's name. Putting a slight smile on his own face, he commented, "A change from the usual mercenary's reward, yes, Brek?"

"You can say that!" Brek placed his arm around the second young woman, a sultry beauty with ample curves whose gossamer dress hid little. The fighter let his fingers dangle a scant inch or two over the uppermost of those curved areas as he paused to kiss her on the throat.

The one in gold began giving Zayl admiring glances. Under shaded eyes, she said, "Are you one of the heroes, too?"

"Careful there!" the mercenary jested. "He's a necromancer, ladies! You know, raise the dead and commune with spirits!"

If Brek thought that this would scare the two, he was

sorely mistaken. In fact, both eyed Zayl with much more interest, so much, in fact, that he felt like a bound mouse set before two hungry cats.

"You raise the dead?" the first breathed. "And spirits, too?"

"Can you show us?" asked the second.

"Here now, ladies! Don't go givin' him any notions about that!"

Zayl shook his head. "It is not something lightly done, anyway, my ladies. Besides, I would not wish to dampen these festivities. After all, the curse of Gregus Mazi has finally been countered."

The one in gold lost all trace of humor. "A terrible, terrible man!"

"Yes, a traitorous person. Ureh would be well rid of all memory of him. Any images, any writings, they should all be destroyed. Even his sanctum should be razed to the ground, the better to forget his evil . . . that is, unless to do so would endanger the homes of others."

"There'd be little enough to burn," replied the curvaceous woman, "built into the mountain as it is."

"The mountain? He lived in a cave? How monstrous!"

"It was part of an old monastery, built before the city," she offered. "But monstrous of him, yes," the woman quickly added. "Monstrous, indeed."

Brek had heard enough such talk. "Now, girls, why don't we let the spellcaster be on his way? I'm sure he's got himself a rendezvous of his own, don't you, sir?"

Zayl recognized the suggestion to leave. With the smile still in place, he said, "Yes, as a matter of fact, there is someone dying to meet me."

The women laughed lightly at this, but the fighter gave Zayl's jest a sour expression in reply. Bowing slightly, the necromancer bid them goodbye, then walked off as if rejoining the celebration.

"Now I know where they got the expression *gallows humor*," Humbart muttered from his pouch.

"I merely wanted them to think I had no purpose but amusement tonight."

"With jests like that? Now, me, I would've said—"

"Quiet." Zayl gave the pouch a slight rap as added emphasis.

He now knew where to find the former abode of the mysterious Gregus Mazi, and, once there, he would surely be able to locate some item with which to summon the man's shade. Then, at last, Zayl would find out the truth, find out whose version of facts fit.

Find out why a reborn Ureh would trouble him so.

Brek stumbled into the home of one of his two companions with lust fully on his besotted mind. Even the necromancer's thankfully brief interruption of his pleasuring had not lessened his desires. Not only did both young women seem willing, but they were far, far more attractive than those with whom he usually found himself. It would be good, for a change, not to find the next morning that he had bedded some one-eyed she-demon with skin more leathery than his boots. Brek felt certain he had it in him to more than satisfy both beauties, and even if it turned out he didn't, at least if they satisfied him, it would all be worth it.

Only a dim light far, far back in the building cast any illumination. The mercenary wended his way toward it, only belatedly realizing that he no longer had an arm around either of his intended treats. At some point near the doorway, both had gone missing.

"Here now, ladies!" he called. "Where've you run off to?"

"Over here . . ." called the voice of the one Brek recalled as wearing the striking golden outfit.

If she wanted to be first, then he would not disappoint her. Brek followed the call, reaching out with his hands as he gradually made his way toward the faint light.

"Almost there . . ." murmured the second, the woman whose shape the fighter had found so appealing.

"So you both want a piece of me at once?" He laughed. "That's fine with me!"

"We're glad you think so," said the first, moving into the light.

Brek screamed.

Under scraps of hair, a husk of a face stared empty-eyed at the mercenary. A mouth shaped into a circle and filled at the edges with sharp, needlelike teeth gaped. Any flesh on what had once been a female face had dried away, leaving skin so taut it barely could hold in the skull.

Bony claws stretched forth, seeking him. Vaguely he noted the tattered remains of the golden dress, then the horror of what he faced finally stirred Brek to action. He reached down for his sword, only to find the scabbard empty.

Where had the weapon gone? He slowly recalled how, at an inn, he had showed the women and some other onlookers how he had helped battle the hellish cat. After that, there had been a round of drinks in honor of his heroism, and then—

He had never retrieved the sword from next to his chair.

Brek fearfully backed away, only to collided with someone. He looked over his shoulder and saw, to his horror, another cadaverous yet hungry face, a mummified shell who could only be the other of his feminine companions.

"We'd all like a piece of you," it said.

And as she spoke, Brek became aware that other figures moved in the dim light, figures with similar outlines, figures all around him, reaching, hungering . . .

He managed one last, short cry before they enveloped him.

Eight

Captain Dumon had always imagined Heaven as a place of light, a place where darkness could never invade. He would have never thought that Heaven could be a realm where shadow preserved and even the light of dawn could mean death.

Of course, Heaven to him was any place where he could be with Atanna.

He had left her some hours before, but still she had his heart and mind. Kentril had only slept lightly since, yet he felt refreshed, more alive than ever in his entire life.

He peered out of the window of the room given to him, to see the city still alive with torches. Although a part of him yearned for some bit of daylight simply in order to mark the passage of time, the captain knew that could not be. Until the people of Ureh could safely stand in the sun, the shadow had to remain fixed over the kingdom.

Atanna felt certain that her father could remedy the situation now that they had some stability on the mortal plane. However, to accomplish anything, he first had to be free, and only through Quov Tsin could that be possible.

Never before had Kentril looked to the Vizjerei for any true magical assistance. He had desired some, yes, during the battle with the demon cat, but had not actually expected much. Now he prayed that Tsin would prove himself the master he claimed to be.

"Kentril."

Gorst stood at the doorway to his chambers, the massive fighter at attention. Kentril blinked, recalling that each morning he generally received a status report from his second. Of course, with their work for Tsin seemingly at an end, the captain had put all such tasks from his mind. Only Khan's daughter concerned him now.

"Yes, Gorst."

"Three missing, Kentril."

"Missing?"

"Seven came back." He grinned. "Drunk. Three didn't."

Captain Dumon shrugged. "Not too surprising, all things considered. Actually, I'm amazed that so many returned."

"Want me to watch for them?"

"Not unless they go missing for a couple days. We're all being treated like kings here, Gorst. They're just reveling in it, that's all."

The black-maned fighter started to turn away, then commented, "She's prettier than on the brooch, Kentril."

"I know. Gorst . . . any word from Tsin on his efforts?" If any of them had kept some track of the Vizjerei's work, it would have been the huge mercenary.

"The magic man thinks he's got something."

That pleased Kentril. "Good. Where can I find him?"

"With the books." When it became clear that his captain did not understand, Gorst grunted. "I'll show you."

Kentril followed him through a maze of halls until they came to what surely had to be one of the largest collections of writings the mercenary had ever either heard of or seen. While he could read and write after a fashion—not something most of his men could do—Kentril could not imagine himself putting together so many words. Moreover, the words in these tomes and scrolls had not only meaning but *power*. These words had magic.

The shelves rose high, each filled with leather-bound volumes or tightly sealed parchments. No direct system of order could be seen, but as a military man, Captain Dumon assumed that there had to be one. Well-worn ladders stood before every other set of shelves, and tables with stools had been set aside for those making use of Ureh's literary treasures.

As a mercenary, Kentril could also appreciate the value of the many writings stored in this vast chamber. Sorcerers like Quov Tsin often paid hefty prices for such books, and he had himself retrieved one or two for good pay. Still, at the moment, all Kentril saw in the library was the means by which Atanna could be free.

No, he saw something else besides. Seated in the midst of the lamplit chamber, Quov Tsin huddled over books and sheets, scribbling notes with a quill and keeping his index finger on one of the pages of one particularly massive tome.

The Vizjerei did not look up as Kentril neared. Under his breath, Tsin muttered incomprehensible things, and the sorcerer had a look upon his wrinkled features that caused the hardened fighter to pause. He had seen the diminutive Vizjerei obsessed before, but now Tsin resembled a man gone completely mad. His eyes never blinked as he worked, and his gaze went only from the book to the sheet upon which he wrote and back again. A grin that the captain had only seen on corpses stretched far across the slight figure's face, giving Tsin a very unsettling expression.

Kentril cleared his throat.

The stooped figure did not look up, instead scrawling new notes over the already heavily covered parchment.

"Tsin."

With what almost seemed a monumental struggle, the avian face turned his way. *"What is it, Dumon?"*

The venom with which the Vizjerei spoke each syllable left both Kentril and Gorst taken aback. The captain realized that his hand had slipped to the hilt of his sword, and he quickly removed it before Tsin could take any further umbrage.

"I came to see how you were progressing with Lord Khan and the city's—"

"I could be progressing much faster without constant and inane

interruptions by the likes of you, cretin!" Quov Tsin slammed his fist on the table, sending ink spreading across the bottom of the parchment and over his hand. He seemed not to notice what he had done, more concerned with spitting barbed words at those before him. *"You come clawing and squeaking and questioning, all of you, when here I sit on the verge of discovery! Can your feeble minds not comprehend the magnitude of what I struggle toward?"*

Releasing the quill, the ink-stained hand reached for the sorcerer's staff. Malice filled Tsin's eyes.

Kentril backed up more, nearly colliding with Gorst. "Easy there, Tsin! Are you insane?"

Knuckles white, the Vizjerei clutched the staff. His silver-gray eyes darted from the two men to the rune-covered rod and back again. For a few dangerous seconds, a struggle between choices clearly unfolded . . . and then at last Quov Tsin put the staff to the side and with much effort turned back to his task.

Without looking at the pair, he whispered, "You had better leave."

"Tsin, I think you need some rest . . . and when's the last time you ate any—"

Both of the spellcaster's bony hands tightened. Eyes still downcast, he said again, *"You had better leave."*

Gorst took Kentril by the shoulder, and the two backed out of the library. They said nothing until several steps down the corridor, where they hoped Tsin could not hear them.

"Was he like that the last time you saw him?" Captain Dumon interrogated his second.

"No . . . not so bad, anyway, Kentril."

"I knew the old mage was ill tempered, but Tsin nearly tried to kill us, you know that, don't you?"

The giant gave him a brooding look. "I know."

"I should go have a talk with Juris Khan. It won't do anyone any good if old Tsin goes violently mad. He might hurt someone."

"Maybe he just needs to take a nap."

Kentril grimaced. "Well, if anyone can make him do it, it'd have to be Khan. You saw how much he listened to me."

"You want me to keep an eye on him?" Gorst asked.

"Only if you keep your distance. Don't do it immediately, though. Let him get lost in his work again for an hour or two first. That might be better."

From somewhere within the palace, a flute began to play. Suddenly, Kentril lost all interest in the damnable Vizjerei's antics. He knew of only one person in Khan's sanctum who played a flute.

"Maybe if I talk to Atanna first, she can better explain it to her father," the captain could not help saying. "That'd probably be the best course of action for me."

The grin returned to Gorst's broad face. "Probably be."

Kentril felt his face flush. He turned to go, but could not help adding at the last, "Just be careful, Gorst."

The grin remained. "You, too."

The flute playing continued, the same haunting melody that he had heard that first fateful time. Captain Dumon followed the music through numerous, winding halls that made it feel to him as if he were repeating his journey to the library. At last, Kentril came not to a balcony or one of the many vast chambers but rather to an open gate leading to, of all things, a vast inner courtyard open to the sky, a courtyard doubling as an extensive garden.

Garden perhaps understated severely the sight. A miniature forest—more a jungle—spread out before the veteran soldier. Exotic trees and plants that seemed like none Kentril had ever encountered, not even on the trek to this distant part of Kehjistan, grew tall and strong. Dark greens, vivid crimsons, bright yellows, and fiery oranges decorated the tableau in arresting fashion. There were hanging vine plants and monstrous flowers, some of the latter larger than his head. One could literally become lost within a garden such as this, of that Kentril had no doubt.

And near the path leading into it, Atanna, seated on a stone bench, played her flute. A billowing, silky dress with a long, thin skirt somehow emphasized rather than hid her slim but curved form. Her long red tresses hung down over the left side of her face, reaching all the way to a most attractive décolletage. She did not notice him at first, but when he started toward her, captivated by the sight of her playing, Atanna suddenly looked up.

Her eyes held such an intensity that they left Kentril at a loss for how to proceed. Atanna, however, took control of the situation by putting down her flute and coming to him.

"Kentril! I hope you slept well."

"Very much. You play beautifully, Atanna."

She gave him a most demure look. "I think not, but my father shares your opinion."

Not certain what to say yet, the captain glanced past her at the garden. "One never knows what to expect next here."

"Do you like it? This is my favorite place. I've spent much of my life here, and much of our exile, too."

"It's . . . unique."

Atanna pulled him toward it. "You must have a closer look!"

Despite the fanciful colors of the flowers and some of the plants, the garden had a rather foreboding look that Kentril did not truly notice until his hostess had led him up to the path running through it. Suddenly the beauty and wonder of it gave way to an uneasiness. Now it reminded him more of the jungle through which he and his men had fought, the same jungle that had claimed four of his party.

"What's the matter?" Juris Khan's daughter asked.

"Nothing." He steeled himself for the walk through. This was not the same stark jungle. This was simply a fanciful garden built for the lord of the realm. What danger could possibly exist within such a confined space?

"I love it here," she murmured. "It takes me away from

the world in which I'm trapped, lets me imagine I'm far away, in another land, about to meet a handsome stranger."

Kentril started to say something but decided he could not trust his tongue not to tie itself up. He could scarcely believe himself. Never in his life had any woman left him feeling so befuddled.

Broad-leafed plants brushed their shoulders, and occasional vines, seeming to drop from nowhere, dangled near their heads. The path at their feet had been made to seem quite natural, a covering of soft dirt and sand over what felt like solid stone.

With each step, though, it grew darker and darker, until at last he could see neither the entrance through which they had come nor the exit far ahead. Now he truly felt as if he had stepped back into the jungle.

His companion noticed his sudden anxiety. "You're shivering!"

"It's nothing, my lady."

"You're supposed to call me Atanna," she responded in mock anger. "Or did this mean so little to you?"

She leaned forward and kissed him. His anxieties concerning his surroundings vanished in an instant. Kentril wrapped his arms around her and returned her passion.

Then he felt something on his neck, a slow but steady movement like that of a worm or a caterpillar. Yet whatever crawled upon his skin did so with appendages as sharp as needles.

Unable to withstand it, Captain Dumon pushed Atanna back and quickly reached for the creature. However, as his hand neared, the thing suddenly pulled away, as if perhaps falling off.

"What is it?" Atanna cautiously asked.

"Something landed on me! It felt as if it walked across my neck with tiny swords at the end of each leg!"

Even in the darkness, he could make out her face well enough. Atanna frowned in consideration, but seemed to have no knowledge to offer. "Shall we leave?"

The pain had faded, and Kentril had no desire to look cowardly and foolish before her, especially over some insect. "No, let's go on as we have."

They moved on a few paces, stopping again to kiss. Atanna then buried her head in his chest, saying, "Father still hopes to complete the journey to Heaven."

He stiffened. "Is that still possible?"

"So he believes. I pray he's wrong."

"But why?"

She put her hand on his cheek. "Because I find the mortal world more to my liking."

"Can you talk him out of it?" The gentle caress of her hand against his skin helped Kentril relax again.

"It would help if I knew that we stood an easier and safer chance of making our tentative hold on the mortal plane a permanent one. If I could convince him that for the sake of all, we would be better off once more among men, then I feel that he'd acquiesce. After all, the threat we fled no longer exists."

She wanted to stay, and he wanted her to stay. Yet Juris Khan wished at last to achieve the holy goal offered to him during those dark years of terror. Not surprising, but certainly not wanted by either here.

"Maybe Tsin would know—" Kentril started before recalling the possession the Vizjerei seemed under. He did not want to try to speak with Tsin, at least not until the sorcerer had been persuaded to rest and eat properly.

"Maybe he could convince Father?" Her tone spoke openly of hope. "The old one seems very skilled, if lacking in common courtesy. Do you think he could do it?"

"I don't—" The captain paused. An idea began to formulate, one that would possibly play on old Tsin's personality.

Atanna appeared to sense his shifting mood. "You've thought of something, haven't you?"

"A possible idea. If Tsin remains constant, it could work to our—your benefit. I need to think about it a little longer, and it would be good if I didn't talk to him just now."

"I have no intention of parting with you just yet, any-way," the young woman responded. "Not at the moment." Atanna stepped up and kissed him again.

Feeling much better about matters, Captain Dumon responded in kind. If the Vizjerei could be persuaded to see his way, then Tsin, in turn, would likely persuade Khan. All Kentril had to do was play on the spellcaster's greed—

He let out a gasp of pain. Something dug at his back as if trying to reach all the way into his heart. He twisted around, felt what seemed one of the vines, and swiftly grabbed it.

What felt like a thousand pins sank into his fingers and palm.

"Kentril!"

Despite his agony, the mercenary kept his hold, then tugged with all his might.

A peculiar and not at all human squeal coursed through the garden. The entire vine tumbled to the path, a dark, sinewy form more than three times the length of a man.

Throwing the end down, Kentril clutched the hand that had held the plant with his other. It felt as if he had stuck the throbbing appendage into an open fire.

"Atanna! Wh-what was—"

"I've no idea! Your hand! Give me your hand!"

Her soft fingers lightly touched his own. The pain receded. Atanna whispered something, then leaned down and let her lips lightly touch his palm.

Fearful of her suffering from whatever plant poison had gotten him, the captain tried to pull away. With surprising strength, however, Juris Khan's daughter held on.

"Please, Kentril! Rest easy. I know what I'm about."

It seemed that she did, for the more she worked at his injury, the less and less it hurt him. Before long, he could even flex the fingers without feeling so much as a twinge.

"What did you do?" he finally asked.

"I am my father's daughter," was her reply. "I am the daughter of the Most Revered Juris Khan."

Meaning that she shared some of his wondrous skills. Caught up in her glory, he had forgotten that she had such talents.

Now that Atanna had dealt with his injury, he recalled what had attacked him in the first place. Squinting, Kentril searched the dark path for the end of the vine.

His companion found it first. "Were you looking for this?"

"Be careful!"

But she looked unaffected by the vile plant. "This could not be what stung you. This is only a *Hakkara* vine. In some parts of the world, they eat the fleshy bottom part. It has much juice and is claimed to be healthy."

"That spiny thing?" He took it from her, only to find it smooth and soft save for a few tiny bumps. Frustrated, Kentril ran his hands along the length of the vine, finding nothing out of the ordinary.

"You must've been bitten by an insect of some sort. Probably the same one that bothered you before," Atanna suggested. "Sometimes some of the jungle insects used to make their way to the city, despite how the mountain causes the air here to be cooler than they like."

"An insect? In Ureh?"

"And why not? You and your friends are here. Why not an insect that happened to be near? The jungle isn't that far from the edge of our kingdom."

Her words made sense, but did not completely mollify him. He looked around the darkened garden, finally saying, "Let's move on."

Only when the first glimmer of light at the other end materialized did Kentril feel any calmer. As they exited, he looked back with barely concealed distaste. Atanna and others in Ureh might find such a grove peaceful and beautiful, but to the soldier, it now seemed more in tune with the nightmarish curse Gregus Mazi had wrought. Had the timeless exile in limbo somehow changed the plants in ways that Khan's daughter did not notice?

"Now that we've got better light," Atanna suddenly said, "let me see your hand again."

He turned it over for both of them to study—and saw little more than a few healing welts. Kentril could scarcely believe it, having felt as if his entire hand should be a bloody, perforated mess.

Running her finger over the remaining marks, the young woman commented, "In a short time, these, too, will vanish."

"It's amazing. Thank you." He had witnessed magic before, but never had any been performed on him. Kentril felt certain that if Atanna had not used her skills, he would have been much worse at this moment.

"It's only a small thing . . . and I feel bad that you suffered because of me. If I hadn't invited you to walk with me—"

"Such things happen. Don't blame yourself."

She looked up at him with imploring eyes. "Will you still talk to Master Tsin about trying to get Father to change his mind?"

"Of course I will!" How could Atanna think otherwise? The captain did this as much for himself as for her. "Old Tsin's consistent. I explain the matter to his liking, he'll be certain to do what he can to make Lord Khan see it right, too."

"I hope so." She kissed him again. "And thinking of my father, I must go to him now. Since he cannot move from the chair, I play for him to help ease his burdens. Perhaps I can even make a mild suggestion already. He's always more agreeable after my music."

With one final kiss, Atanna left him, her slim form disappearing into the garden. Kentril watched her vanish, but although the garden would have likewise been the appropriate route for him, the mercenary did not enter. Instead, he walked around the perimeter, keeping a cautious distance. By the time Kentril reached where Khan's daughter had been playing, both she and the flute had long left.

Alone, Captain Dumon took one last, measured look at the unsettling grove. At first glance, it seemed no more unusual than any patch of jungle or forest, and as a place specifically sculpted by some master gardener, it should have presented an even less intimidating image than either of the former. Yet, the more he studied it, the more Kentril felt that if he had entered alone, it would have been much more difficult to come out.

From behind him, someone cleared his throat. "Captain?"

"Albord." He hoped that the other mercenary had not noticed him jump ever so slightly. "What is it?"

"Sorry to bother you, but a couple of us were wonderin' when we might get our reward from his lordship so we can get goin' home."

"You're already tired of all the acclamation, Albord?"

The plain-faced, white-haired fighter looked a bit uncomfortable. Kentril forgot that despite his experience and skills, Albord was much younger than most of those in the company. That he had often been left in charge when Gorst could not be spared had said much for his abilities. "It's not that— I had as good a time as any, captain—but a few of us want to head back to Westmarch." He shrugged. "Just feel more comfortable at home than here, sir."

The last thing that Kentril wanted was to leave, but he could understand how the others might feel. Gorst would probably stay; he had no family, no kin. The rest, though, had ties to the Western Kingdoms, even loved ones. That these men served as mercenaries had as much to do with feeding mouths as with becoming rich.

All thought of the garden fading, the captain patted Albord on the shoulder. "I'll see what can be done about the lot of you going home. If I do, can I trust you to bring something back to the families of those lost? If I read our host right, one small sack should have enough to split among the survivors and leave them well off."

"Aye, captain! You know I'll be honest."

Kentril had no doubt about that. He also knew which other men from the survivors would be cut from similar cloth. No one joined Captain Dumon's company who did not first undergo thorough scrutiny. If Kentril sent Albord home with coin for those left behind by Benjin, Hargo, and the others, it would reach them.

Grateful, the younger fighter saluted. He started to step away, then hesitated. "Captain, two men still haven't come back from the city."

"I know. Gorst told me three, actually."

"Simon dragged himself in just a little while ago, but he said Jace was headin' back hours before, and no one's seen a sign of Brek."

Having known far too many men like the pair missing, Kentril shrugged off Albord's concern. "They'll pop up, you'll see. They won't want to miss their share, remember."

"Should I send someone out to look?"

"Not now." The captain became a little impatient. He needed to take some time to think about how best to phrase things so that Tsin would readily see his point of view. Kentril had no more time to waste on drunken mercenaries gone astray. "I told Gorst already that if they don't show up in a couple days, maybe then." Hoping he had not sounded too uncaring, Captain Dumon patted Albord's shoulder again. "Try to relax. Enjoy this! Believe me, Albord, it happens all too little for those like us. The jungle we crossed or that winter near the Gulf of Westmarch, that's our usual payoff."

Albord gave him a plowboy's smile, reminding Kentril of the background of almost every low-paid mercenary ever born. "I suppose I can take the food and women a little longer."

"That's the spirit!" the older fighter proclaimed as he

began guiding the other back down the hall. In his mind, Kentril pictured Atanna, his own reason for staying . . . perhaps forever. At least until he had talked the Vizjerei into persuading Juris Khan no longer to seek the righteous path to Heaven, the captain did not want to broach the subject of payment. It was not as if Albord and the others were not being rewarded in other ways.

Besides, Kentril thought, what *harm* could a few more days' waiting do?

Πίπε

The perpetual shadow over Ureh worked in Zayl's favor as he climbed toward Gregus Mazi's mountain sanctum. Even though the former monastery faced away from much of the city below, enough of a line of sight existed that would have made it quite simple in daylight for anyone to spot the cloaked form wending his way up the half-broken path carved into the rock face.

Zayl could appreciate the location the sorcerer had chosen and wondered why he had never noticed the ruins of it earlier. The spell that had taken a spirit form of Ureh and cast it Heavenward had interesting touches to it that he hoped later to investigate.

Below him, the celebrating continued unabated. Zayl frowned. Did the people require no sleep? True, the realm of limbo did not fall under the same laws as the mortal plane, but surely by now exhaustion should have taken many of the inhabitants.

Huge, ominous forms stood guard as he at last reached what passed for a gateway to the monastery. Once they had been archangels with majestic, blazing swords and massive, outstretched wings, but, like their counterparts on the doors of Khan's palace, these had been heavily damaged. One angel missed an entire wing and the right side of its face; the other had no head at all and only stubs where once the magnificent, plumed appendages had risen.

Zayl crawled over rubble, finding it interesting that Gregus Mazi's abode remained so ruined when all else in

Ureh had been restored to new. The necromancer could only assume that the people of the cursed city had taken out their anger at some point on the abode of their absent tormentor. Zayl only hoped that this did not mean that Mazi's sanctum had been ransacked.

He wished again that he knew more about the ways of the realm in which Ureh had been trapped. Khan hinted that a semblance of the passage of time did exist, for had he not talked of researching a method of escape during those centuries of imprisonment? Yet it seemed that no one had needed to eat, for certainly the food could not have lasted so very long.

What remained of the monastery itself did not initially impress Zayl. Thrust out of the very side of the mountain, the unassuming outline indicated only a two-story, block-design structure that could not have held more than two rooms to a level. A single small balcony overlooked all below, and only a low wall pretended to give any protection whatsoever to the place.

Despite some disappointment in what he had found so far, the necromancer continued on. At the base of the building, he found a plain wooden door the likes of which might have decorated a simple country inn. His eyesight far better suited to the dark than most humans, Zayl made out damage on every side of the doorway. Someone had used axes and clubs to batter every inch of the stone frame, almost as if in absolute frustration. Oddly, though, the door itself looked absolutely untouched.

It took only the placing of his hand on the wood to discover why. A complex series of protective spells criss-crossed all over, making the door itself virtually impenetrable not only to physical attack, but even to many forms of magical assault. The stone frame, which had suffered some superficial cracks, also had spells cast over it, but those felt older, as if not laid upon the structure by its last and most infamous tenant. Zayl's estimate of the monastery as a place for a sorcerer to live rose. The monks who had built it had evidently strengthened it through some very powerful prayers if even after all this time most of the wards held.

Looking up, the necromancer found no visible windows. In one place, it appeared as if once there had been a window, but in the past it had been covered over quite thoroughly with stone. Zayl assumed that if he climbed up and investigated it, he would find the former opening as well-shielded as the entrance.

That left only the door as a way inside. The pale spellcaster touched it again, sensing the myriad bindings Gregus Mazi had set into place to ensure the safety of his sanctum. The ancient sorcerer had clearly been very adept at his art.

Zayl pulled Humbart's skull free. "Tell me what you see."

"Besides the door, you mean?"

"You know what I want from you."

He thrust the skull closer to the entrance, letting it survey everything. After a few moments, Humbart said, "There's lines all over, boy. Some good strong magic here and not all by one person. Most of it is, but there's underlying lines that have to be from two, even three. Even some prayer work, too."

One interesting feature concerning the skull that the necromancer had discovered after animating it had been that the spirit of Humbart Wessel could now see the workings of magic in ways no living spellcaster could. Zayl had no references upon which to draw for a reason for this ability and could only assume that the many centuries of having lain near the ruins of Ureh had somehow changed the skull. Over the past few years, the talent had come in quite handy, saving Zayl hours, even days, of painstaking work.

With his other hand, the black-clad figure removed the ivory dagger. Hilt held up, he asked Humbart, "Where do most intersect?"

"Down to the left, boy. Waist level—no!—not there. More to the right—stop!"

Pointing the hilt at the spot the skull had indicated, Zayl muttered under his breath.

The dagger began to glow.

Suddenly, a multicolored pattern reminiscent of a hexagon within a flower burst into existence at the point specified. Still whispering, Zayl thrust the hilt into the exact center, at the same time turning the end of the dagger in a circular motion.

The magical pattern flashed bright, then instantly faded away.

"You've cleared much of it, lad. There's still a little lock picking to do, though."

With Humbart's fleshless head to guide him, Zayl gradually removed the last impediments. Had he been forced to rely on his own skills alone, he doubted that he would have had such quick success. The wards had been skillfully woven together. However, one advantage the necromancer had discovered had been that the most cunning had been set to guard against *demons*, not men. Questioning the skull revealed that the majority of those had been created more recently, which likely pointed to Gregus Mazi as their caster.

"You can walk right in now," Humbart finally announced.

The skull in the crook of one arm and the dagger now held ready for more mundane use, Zayl stepped inside.

A darkened hall greeted him. The necromancer muttered a word, and the blade of the dagger began to glow.

Zayl had thought Mazi's sanctum rather small, but now he saw that he had been sorely mistaken. The empty hall led deep into the mountainside, so deep that he could not even see the end. To his left, a set of winding steps obviously led to the more visible portion of the structure, but Zayl only had interest in where the corridor ahead ended. True, he might have been able to find what he needed in the outer rooms, but the spellcaster's curiosity had been piqued. What secrets had Gregus Mazi left behind?

With the dagger lighting the way, Zayl headed down the hall. The walls had been patiently carved from bedrock, then polished fine. However, the same monks who had no doubt performed the back-breaking work had not then bothered much with adornment. Now and then, the fluttering figure of an armed archangel pointed farther ahead, but other than that, neither the monks nor Mazi had bothered to decorate further.

Zayl paused at the third such image so lovingly carved into the walls, suddenly noticing something about it.

Humbart, still in his arm, grew impatient. "I'm staring at a blank wall inches from where my nose used to be, Zayl, lad. Is there anything more interesting above?"

The cloaked figure raised the skull so that his dead companion could see. "It is untouched."

"And that would mean?"

"Think about it, Humbart. The doors of the palace. The archangels at the gateway leading here. All purposely damaged, as if by those who hated such holy images."

"Aye, and so?"

Moving to the next angel, Zayl saw that it, too, remained in pristine condition. "Why would so corrupted a mage as Gregus Mazi has been claimed to be leave these untouched?"

"Maybe he didn't want to make a mess in his own good home?"

"This means something, Humbart." But what it meant exactly, the necromancer did not know. He pushed on, glancing at some of the other heavenly guides, yet none had more than a slight weathered look to it. No, Mazi had not wreaked any harm on those images within his own abode, and that made no sense to Zayl.

They came at last across the first rooms actually carved into the mountain, rooms the last tenant had clearly not bothered much to use. Little remained of any furnishings. A few very old beds sat lonely in the far corners of some, the wood slowly rotting away. Some had already collapsed.

"Old Gregus never struck me as a sociable sort," Humbart commented quietly. "Looks like that was truth. Can't think he had too many visitors here."

After several more such rooms, Zayl at last came across a set of stone steps leading down. Unable to see the bottom, the necromancer proceeded with even more caution, the dagger ahead of him and a spell upon his lips.

Fortunately, no trap or demon struck. At the end of the stairway, he found a short corridor ending in three closed doors, one in front and the others flanking him. A quick study revealed all to be identical, and when Zayl had the skull look them over, Humbart informed him that none of them had any sort of ward in place.

"I'm reminded of a story about an adventurer," the skull went on while the necromancer considered his choice. "He came across three such doors. Now, he had been told that two doors led to treasure and escape, while the third held certain, horrible death. Well, the lad gave it some thought, listened at the doors, and finally made his choice."

Zayl, just on the point of picking the one to his left, noticed Humbart's sudden silence. "And so what happened?"

"Why, he opened one and got himself eaten alive by a pack of ghouls, of course! As it turns out, none of the doors led to gold or safety, and all of them, in fact, had monstrous, grisly ends waiting for those who—"

"Shut up, Humbart."

Even though the skull had not seen any wards, Zayl did not assume the entranceways were free of risk. Placing his unliving companion back in the pouch, he readied himself for any trap his opening the first door might spring.

A vast chamber full of dust and nothing more greeted him.

"Are you eaten yet?" came Humbart's muffled voice.

The necromancer grimaced. Gregus Mazi might have taken over what had been left of the old monastery, but he had not made use of much of it. Perhaps, Zayl thought, he would have been better off searching through the outer rooms first after all.

Looking at the remaining two doors, he chose the first of the pair. Surely the door faced first by any who came down the steps had to be the one.

Steeling himself again, Zayl pushed it open.

Row upon row of half-rotted tables spread out before him, and a looming archangel with one hand held forward in blessing seemed to reach out from the wall on the far side. Zayl swore under his breath, realizing that he had found where the monks had met for their meals. From the looks of everything, it was yet another chamber not bothered much with by the late Mazi.

With little fanfare, he turned about and headed directly for the one entrance left. Thrusting the glowing dagger before him, Zayl barged in.

An array of glassware and arcane objects greeted him from every direction, even the ceiling.

Zayl paused to drink it all in. Here now, the world of Gregus Mazi began. Here, displayed before the necromancer, was the workplace of a man of intense interest in every aspect of his calling. With one sweep of the illuminated blade, Zayl saw jars filled with herbs of every kind, pickled and preserved creatures the likes of which even the necromancer could not identify, and chemicals by the scores in both powder and liquid form. There were racks of books and scrolls, open parchments with notes, and drawings atop some of the tables, and even artifacts hung by chains from certain parts of the ceiling.

Everything had a polished appearance to it, making it seem as if it had been only yesterday that the sorcerer had been at work here. In point of fact, Zayl realized that for this sanctum, it *had* only been a few days at most. The peculiarities of limbo had once again preserved history.

"Must be very interesting out there . . . I suppose," Humbart called.

Pulling the skull free, the necromancer placed it on the

main table next to where Mazi had been making notes. Holding the dagger near, Zayl looked over the writing.

"What is it?"

"Spell patterns. Theoretical outcomes. This Gregus Mazi was a practical thinker." The necromancer frowned. "Not what I would have expected of him."

"Evil can be very clever, if that's what you mean, lad."

Zayl studied the parchment in more detail. "Yes, but all of these notes concern only how to make the ascension to Heaven possible. It is written as if by someone who truly believes in the quest."

Giving the parchment one more glance, the necromancer turned to study the rest of the chamber again. As he held the dagger ahead of him, Zayl saw that the room stretched farther back than he had initially imagined. In the dim light, he could make out more shelves, more jars . . .

"Here now! You're not going to leave me alone, are you?"

"You will be fine, Humbart."

"Says the one with the legs."

Disregarding the skull's protests, Zayl moved farther into Gregus Mazi's sanctum. From container after container, creatures long dead stared back at him with bulbous, unseeing eyes. A black and crimson spider larger than his head floated in a thick, gooey mixture. There were young sand maggots and even a fetish, one of the sinister, cannibalistic denizens of the jungle. Doll-like in appearance, but with a totem mask face, they hid among the trees and thick foliage, seeking to take down the unwary by numbers. Necromancers destroyed them wherever they found the foul creatures, for nothing but evil came from them.

"Zayl, lad? You still alive there?"

"I'm still here, Humbart."

"Aye, and so am I, but it's not like *I've* so much choice in that respect!"

One specimen in particular caught the necromancer's attention. At first, he thought it a square sample of skin, perhaps even from one of the tentacle beasts in the jungle rivers. Yet, as he peered closely at the gray, hand-sized patch, he saw that on each corner were three tiny but very sharp claws and in the center what might have been a mouth of sorts. Slight bits of fur also seemed evident near the edges of the form.

Curious about this oddity, Zayl took the jar down, placing it on the nearest table.

"What's that you've got there, boy? I heard glass clink."

"Nothing to concern yourself with." The necromancer removed the lid, then, after locating a pair of tongs no doubt used just for such a purpose, fished for the specimen. He pulled the bizarre creature free of the soupy liquid, letting residue drip back into the container as he used the dagger to study it up close.

"I don't like to complain, boy, but are you going to investigate every damned jar—"

Zayl glanced over his shoulder at the barely seen skull. "I will not be long—"

A hiss suddenly arose from the container.

The tongs were pulled from his hand as something massive tried to wrap itself over the top half of his body.

"Zayl! Zayl, lad!"

The necromancer could not answer. A dripping, pulsating form with hide like an alligator covered his face, shoulders, and most of one arm. Zayl cried out as what felt like daggers thrust into his back, tearing through his garments as if they were nothing.

Teeth, jagged teeth, tore at his chest.

Belatedly, he realized that he had also lost the dagger. Zayl tried to speak a spell, but could barely breathe, much less talk.

The force of his monstrous attacker sent both tumbling to the floor. The shock of striking the stone surface almost did Zayl in, but he held on, well aware that to give in to unconsciousness would mean certain, grisly death.

The hissing grew louder, more fearsome, and, so it seemed, did the monstrosity seeking to overwhelm him. Now the necromancer could feel it almost covering his body down to his hips. If the creature managed to enshroud him entirely, Zayl knew well that he would be lost.

With all his might, he struggled to push the moist, unsettling form up. As he did, though, the talons tore at his back, ripping through everything. The agony almost caused him to lose his grip.

From without came the muffled, desperate voice of Humbart Wessel. "Zayl! Lad! I can see a light! I think the blade's by your left! Just a few inches left!"

Using his weight, Zayl sent both his attacker and himself sliding in that direction. He felt something near his shoulder, but then the tapestry-like horror shifted, causing the necromancer to move with it.

Humbart shouted something else, but whatever it was became stifled by the thick, suffocating form atop Zayl.

More desperate now, Zayl threw himself again to the left. This time, he felt the hilt of the dagger under his shoulder blade. Half-smothered, in danger of being bitten, he twisted to reach it with his right hand.

The teeth clamped down on his forearm with such ferocity that the necromancer screamed. Nonetheless, Zayl forced himself to continue reaching for the ivory dagger. His fingers touched the blade, and although he knew it would cause him more suffering, the injured spellcaster seized the weapon tightly by the sharp edges.

Blood dripping from the cuts in his fingers, the necromancer brought the dagger up. At the same time, he muttered the quickest, surest spell of which he could think.

A lance of pure bone thrust up from the dagger, flying unhindered through the thick hide of the beast, tearing flesh, and soaring upward until it struck the ceiling hard.

Zayl's horrific foe fluttered back, a strange, keening sound escaping its bizarre mouth. Ichor spilled over the necromancer as it pulled away.

As he dragged himself back, Zayl gave thanks to the dragon, Trag'Oul. The lance represented one of the talons of the mystical leviathan who served as the closest thing the followers of Rathma had for a god. Among the most effective of a necromancer's battle spells, the bone lance had been summoned twice in the past by Zayl, but never under such dire circumstances.

However, despite its terrible injury, the tapestry creature seemed far from dying. Moving with swift, gliding motions, it rose up to the ceiling, then over to a corner. A slight shower of life fluids spilled onto the floor below it.

"Are you all right, lad?"

"I will live. Thank you, Humbart."

The skull made a peculiar noise, like the rushing of air out of pursed lips. "Thank me when you've finished that abominable rug off!"

Zayl nodded. Raising the dagger toward the heavily breathing creature, he muttered another spell. Trag'Oul had helped him once; perhaps the great dragon would grant him one more boon.

A shower of bony projectiles roughly the size of the dagger formed from the air, shooting upward with astonishing swiftness.

The thing near the ceiling had no chance to move. Without mercy, the needle-sharp projectiles ripped through its hard hide. A rain of blood—or whatever equivalent the monster possessed—splattered the necromancer, the sanctum, and one cursing skull.

Now the creature keened, loud and ragged. It tried to flee, but Zayl had summoned the Den'Trag, the Teeth of the Dragon Trag'Oul, and they struck so hard that they pincushioned the struggling form to the wall and ceiling.

The movements of Zayl's adversary grew weaker, sporadic. The flow of life fluids slowed.

At last, the monster stilled.

"Zayl! Zayl!" called Humbart. "Gods! Wipe this slime off of me! I swear, even without a good, working nose, I can smell the stench!"

"Q-quiet, Humbart," the necromancer gasped. Summoning the aid of Trag'Oul twice had taken much out of him. Had he been more prepared, it would have not been so, but the initial assault by the beast had left him weakened even before the first spell.

As he tried to recoup his strength, Zayl eyed the vast array of specimens Gregus Mazi had collected over his life. The monster had been one small, seemingly dead sample among so many others. Did that mean that each of the sorcerer's collected rarities still had some life left in it? If so, Zayl gave thanks that none of the shelves had been disturbed or their contents accidentally sent shattering on the floor. The necromancer doubted that he would have long survived among a room filled with dozens of strange and dire creatures.

When his legs felt strong enough to trust, Zayl returned to where the skull lay. A thick layer of yellowish ichor covered most of what remained of the late Humbart Wessel. Taking the cleanest edge he could find on his cloak, the necromancer proceeded to wipe the skull as well as possible.

"*Pfaugh!* Sometimes I wish you'd left me to rot where you found me, boy!"

"You had already rotted away, Humbart," Zayl pointed out. Putting the skull on a clear part of the table, he looked around. Something on the wall to his right caught his attention. "Aaah."

"What? Not another of those beasts, is it?"

"No." The pale figure walked to what he had noticed. "Just a cloak, Humbart. Just a cloak."

A cloak once worn by Gregus Mazi.

Yet it was not the garment itself that so intrigued Zayl, but rather, what he could find upon it. Under the light of the dagger, he carefully searched.

There! With the utmost caution, the necromancer plucked two hairs from inside the collar region. Even better than clothing, strands of hair granted almost certain success when summoning a man's shade.

"You finally got what you want?"

"Yes. These will help us call the sorcerer forth."

"Fine! It'll be good to see old Gregus after all this time. Hope he's looking better than I am."

Surveying the chamber, Zayl noticed a wide, open area to the side of the entrance. As he neared, he saw that symbols had been etched into the floor there. How more appropriate—and likely helpful—than to summon the ghost of Gregus Mazi using the very focal point from which he had cast many of his own spells?

Muttering under his breath, the necromancer knelt and began to draw new patterns on the floor with the tip of his blade. As the point slowly drifted over the stone surface, it left in its wake the design Zayl wanted.

In the center of the new pattern, he placed the two hairs. Moving carefully so as not to disturb them, Zayl brought his free hand over, then, with the dagger, reopened one of the cuts he had suffered earlier.

The barely sealed cut bled freely. Three drops of crimson fell upon the hair.

A greenish smoke arose wherever the blood touched the follicles.

The necromancer began chanting. He uttered the name of Gregus Mazi, once, twice, and then a third time. Before him, the unsettling smoke swelled, and as it did, it took on a vaguely humanoid shape.

"I summon thee, Gregus Mazi!" Zayl called in the common tongue. "I conjure thee! Knowledge is needed, knowledge only you can supply! Come to me, Gregus Mazi! Let your shade walk the mortal plane a time more! Let it return to this place of your past! By that which was once a very part of your being, I summon you forth!"

Now the smoke stood nearly as tall as a man, and in it there appeared what might have been a figure clad in robes. Zayl returned to chanting words of the Forgotten Language, the words that only spellcasters knew in this day and age.

But just as success seemed near, just as the figure began to solidify, everything went awry. The billowing smoke abruptly dwindled, shrinking and shrinking before the necromancer's startled eyes. All semblance of a humanoid form vanished. The hairs curled, burning away as if tossed into hungry flames.

"No!" Zayl breathed. He stretched a hand toward his two prizes, but before he could touch them, they shriveled, leaving only ash in their wake.

For several seconds, he knelt there, unable to do anything but stare at his failure. Only when Humbart finally spoke did the necromancer stir and rise.

"So . . . what happened there, lad?"

Still eyeing the pattern and the dust that had once been hair, Zayl shook his head. "I don't—"

He stopped, suddenly looking off into the darkness.

"Zayl?"

"I *do* know why it failed now, Humbart," the necromancer responded, still staring at nothing. "It never had a chance to succeed. From the first, it was doomed, and I never realized it!"

"Would you mind speaking in less mystifying statements, lad?" the skull asked somewhat petulantly. "And explain for us mere former mortals?"

Zayl turned, eyes wide with understanding. "It is very simple, Humbart. There is one and one reason alone that would make this and any other summoning of Gregus Mazi a futile gesture: he still *lives!*"

Ten

If anything, Quov Tsin had grown more unsettling, more unnerving, by the time Captain Dumon next visited him. An empty mug and a small bowl of half-eaten food sat to the side of where he feverishly scribbled notes. His withered features had become more pronounced, as happened only in the dead as the flesh dried away, and he looked even more pale than the necromancer. Now the Vizjerei did not just mumble to himself; he spoke out in a loud, demanding tone.

"Of course, the sign of Broka would be inherently necessary there! Any cretin could see that! Ha!"

Before entering, Kentril questioned Gorst, who leaned against the wall just outside the library. "What sort of state is he in?"

The giant had always been untouched by Tsin's acerbic personality, but now Gorst wore a rare look of concern and uncertainty. "He's bad, Kentril. He drank a little, ate even less. He don't even sleep, I think."

The captain grimaced. Not the mood he had been hoping for, although from the beginning it had been unlikely that the Vizjerei would be any more reasonable than before. Still, Kentril had no choice; he had to try to speak with Tsin now.

"Keep an eye out, all right?"

"You know I will, Kentril."

Straightening, Captain Dumon walked up to the stooped-over sorcerer. Quov Tsin did not look his way, did not even acknowledge that anyone had entered. Taking a quick glance at the spellcaster's efforts, Kentril saw that Tsin had filled more than a dozen large parchment sheets with incomprehensible notes and patterns.

"You're a bigger fool than I thought, Dumon," the Vizjerei abruptly announced in an even more poisonous voice than previously. He still had not looked up at the fighter. *"I went against my better judgment last time in forgiving your interruptions—"*

"Easy, Tsin," Kentril interrupted. "This concerns you greatly."

"Nothing concerns me more than this!"

The mercenary officer nodded sagely. "And that's exactly what I mean. You don't realize just what you might lose."

At last, the diminutive figure looked at him. Bloodshot eyes swept over the captain, Quov Tsin clearly pondering what value the words of the other man might contain. "Explain."

"Knowing you as I do, Tsin, you've got two reasons for doing this. The first is to prove that you actually can. The Vizjerei sorcerers are well known for their reputations as masters of their art, and your reputation exceeds most of your brethren."

"Seek not to mollify me with empty flattery."

Ignoring the dangerous expression on the bearded face, Kentril continued. "The second reason I can appreciate more. We came to Ureh for glory and riches, Tsin. My men and I want gold and jewels—"

"Paltry notions!"

"Aye, but you came for riches of a different sort, didn't you? You came for the accumulated magical knowledge gathered in this kingdom over the many centuries, rare knowledge lost when true Ureh vanished from the mortal plane."

Tsin began tapping on the table with one hand. His gaze briefly shifted to the magical staff, then back to the mercenary, as if measuring options.

Kentril defiantly met the baleful gaze of the Vizjerei. "Lord Khan has offered you all that you can carry off if you succeed, hasn't he? That would mean books and scrolls worth a kingdom each, I imagine."

"More than you can imagine, actually, cretin. If you could understand one iota of what I've discovered here so far, it would leave you astounded!"

"A shame, then, that so much else will be lost again."

The spellcaster blinked. "What's that?"

Resting his knuckles on the table, Captain Dumon leaned forward and in conspiratorial tones whispered, "What could you accomplish if given a year, even two, to further study this collection?"

Avarice gleamed bright in the sorcerer's bloodshot eyes. "I could become the most powerful, most adept, of my kind."

"Juris Khan intends to open the way to Heaven again."

"He lacks the assistance he had the first time," Tsin commented, "but I must admit from listening to him that I think he has some notion of how to get around that. I'd not bet against him that once he is free, he will succeed with his holy dream in short order."

"And with him goes this entire library."

Kentril saw then that he had Quov Tsin. More than the mercenaries, the Vizjerei had known that the riches of the fabled realm would only return when the city once more breathed life. Tsin had not even attempted to inspect the library before the coming of the shadow because he had known that there would be nothing. The Vizjerei had pinned all his hopes on the legend, and now that same legend threatened to take from him much of that for which he had worked so hard.

"So much lost again," the wrinkled spellcaster muttered. "So much lost and for no good reason . . ."

"Of course, you could fail to find a solution to Khan's own curse, but then he might eventually suspect and send you away. If you tried to steal all this—"

Tsin snorted. "Don't even blather on in that direction, Dumon. Even if I would stoop so low, there are wards in this library that only our good host can unravel, or else why do you think I stay in here save when I must heed personal needs?"

"So there's no hope, then."

The robed figure stood straight. "Quite obviously, you *do* have a suggestion, my good captain. Kindly tell me what it is right now."

"A clever mage like yourself could find excellent reasons why it would be to Lord Khan's benefit to make Ureh a permanent part of the real world."

Quov Tsin stared silently at Kentril, so much so that the captain began to question the worth of his notion. What if Tsin could not convince the ruler? What if it only served to make Juris Khan angry at the adventurers? He might demand that all of them be escorted out of the kingdom. The Vizjerei might be skilled, but against a squadron of trained warriors such as now guarded the palace, he would quickly lose.

"You have—the core—of a possibility, I must admit," the sorcerer grumbled, seating himself again. "And, curiously, you may have come at just the right moment."

Now it was Kentril's turn to wonder what the other meant. "What do you mean, 'the right moment'?"

With a sweep of one thin arm, Tsin indicated the mountain of notes he had compiled. "Look there, Captain Dumon, and gaze in wonder! Stare at what only I, Quov Tsin, could have wrought in such short notice. I have done it!"

"Done it? Done—"

"Aaah! I see by your gaping mouth that you've realized what I mean. Yes, Dumon, I think I can release our good host from Gregus Mazi's foul but quite masterful spell!"

Conflicting thoughts rushed through Kentril's mind as he absorbed Tsin's announcement. On the one hand, they would have the gratitude of Ureh's monarch, but on the other hand, that would mean time would be at even more of a premium should Khan decide to go on with his holy mission.

"You've got to convince him to end this quest, Tsin!"

A cunning expression spread across the wrinkled countenance. "Yes, and for something far more worthy than your dalliance with his daughter. It'll take me two more days' work, I suspect, to be positive of my calculations and phrasings, but I am almost completely certain that I walk the right path, so much so that I'll begin the effort to turn his mind to our thinking within hours. First, however, I shall need time to clear my thoughts and prepare myself for an audience with him."

"Should I come with you?"

This brought another snort from the sorcerer. "By all means, no! He sees you, Dumon, and he'll think that this is all for your sake. The lust of one paid fighter does not balance well against the glorious sanctuary of Heaven!"

Nor does the greed of one very ambitious mage, Kentril could not help thinking . . . but Quov Tsin did have a clever tongue when he needed it and knew well how to deal with those of breeding. Surely he would be able to do far better than a base-born mercenary.

"Well? Why do you still stand here, Dumon? Do you want me to succeed or not? Go, so that I can organize everything."

Nodding quickly, Kentril immediately left the Vizjerei to his own devices. He knew that he could trust Tsin to attack this with the same obsessiveness with which he had attacked all that concerned the shadowed kingdom. With the endurance and determination of a predator, the sorcerer would somehow convince Juris Khan.

And then Captain Dumon could press his own suit for Atanna.

"You're still alive," Gorst commented as Kentril left the library. "I think the magic man's beginning to like you."

"Heaven forbid that should ever happen. We came to an understanding, that's all."

"He going to try to keep you from losing her?"

Kentril's brow furrowed.

The giant gave him a Gorst grin. "Only thing'd make you go to him is her. Only thing he's interested in is magic. Ureh vanishes, you both lose."

Even Kentril sometimes let Gorst's barbaric appearance cause him to forget why he had made the ebony-maned fighter his second in command—and his friend. "That sums it up."

"He'll do it, Kentril. He'll convince Juris Khan."

The captain grunted. "You see any sign of Zayl lately?"

"Not for a long time."

Kentril did not trust the necromancer on his own. Someone of Zayl's ilk could bring out the distrust in the most trustful of people. While he harbored no dislike for the easterner and actually found Zayl's presence more tolerable than Tsin's, Kentril worried about the other spell-caster wandering among the locals. Perhaps it was time to make certain that nothing else happened to endanger his hopes.

"I'm going for a walk, Gorst."

"Down into the city?"

"That's right. If Zayl shows up, tell him I want to talk with him."

The decision to hunt for the necromancer did not sit well at all with Kentril. He would have preferred his original plan, which had entailed telling Atanna of his success with Tsin, thereby ensuring some reward from her. Now, instead of the beauteous company of Khan's alluring daughter, he sought that of the dour, formal Zayl.

No one challenged the captain as he left the abode of Juris Khan. In fact, the armored guards stood straighter, and some even saluted him as he passed. Truly their master had given the mercenaries the run of the kingdom.

That made him think about his own men, including the pair who had not so far returned. There had been no reports of unseemly behavior, but Kentril wanted nothing to undo the good will they had gained.

The moment he touched foot at the bottom of the long, winding steps leading down from the palace and entered the city proper, Kentril found himself surrounded by merrymakers. Under the ever-present lamps and torches, women in bright, exotic garments of silk danced to the music of guitars, horns, and drums. Children laughed and ran between celebrating throngs. A table of local men hard at work on flagons of ale waved for the captain to come over, but with a smile and a shake of his head, Kentril excused himself.

There had to be people asleep somewhere in Ureh, but Captain Dumon would be damned if he could find any evidence of that. Several of those out now must have slumbered when he had, or else they surely could not have been up and about at this moment.

Some distance ahead, he spotted Orlif and Simon playing a game of dice with some of the locals. Kentril started toward them, then decided that it was unlikely that they would know where Zayl was. Both men had probably just returned to the city after some recuperation in the palace.

Leaving the duo to their entertainment, the captain wandered deeper into Ureh. Wherever he went, merriment seemed to be in full swing. The citizens of the legendary kingdom celebrated with such exuberance that Kentril found it somewhat difficult to believe that this had been the most revered, the most pious of realms. Still, he supposed that they deserved such harmless pleasure after suffering as they had.

"Are you one of the heroes?" asked a melodious voice.

Turning around, Kentril found himself facing not one but two enticingly clad young women. One wore a fanciful golden outfit that reminded him of the harems an older mercenary had described to him, while the other, blessed with the curves men desire most, smiled under long, dark lashes. Either would have at one time been a prize greater than

Kentril could have ever imagined, but now, although he still found them most interesting to look at, they offered nothing he wanted. Atanna held sway over him.

"He must be," said the one with the curves. She smiled. "My name is Zorea."

"And I'm Nefriti," added the one in gold, bouncing prettily.

"My ladies," Kentril returned, bowing.

This action caused both of the women to blush and laugh lightly. "A true gentleman!" exclaimed black-tressed Zorea. She let her fingers caress his right arm. "And so strong!"

"Will you celebrate with us?" asked Nefriti, pursing her full lips as she took his left arm.

"It would honor us to honor you," said her companion. "Ureh wishes to offer you all the reward you deserve."

He carefully and politely pulled away from them. "I thank you for your kind offer, my ladies, but I'm in search of someone at the moment."

Zorea brightened. "One of your friends? I saw two strangers playing dice with some of the men."

"Yes, I saw them. I'm looking for someone else." It occurred to him that Zayl would certainly stand out among the people here. Perhaps this unexpected encounter would turn out to be of some use to him after all. "Maybe you've seen him after all? Tall, pale of skin, with eyes more like yours than mine. He would've been dressed mostly in garments of black."

"We've seen him!" chirped Nefriti. "Haven't we, Zorea?"

"Oh, yes!" she responded, her reaction almost identical to that of her friend. "We even know where he is."

"We'll take you there!"

The captain allowed himself to be guided on by the pair. He would not have thought this celebrating of much interest to the necromancer, but perhaps he had misjudged Zayl.

With great perseverance and more than a little strength, the two women pulled him along through the throngs. Zorea and Nefriti each held a hand—out of fear of becoming separated, so they claimed. The women clearly knew where they were going, expertly turning here and there and moving among the other celebrators with ease.

The crowds gradually began to thin, and as they did, Captain Dumon's suspicions arose. He had believed the women when they said that they knew Zayl's whereabouts, but the situation now resembled one far too familiar to any seasoned fighter in a strange land. The area toward which they headed looked fairly deserted. More than one mercenary had ended his career with a dagger in his back thanks to such charming decoys. A holy city Ureh might be, but Gregus Mazi had already proven that even the most devout of lands had their personal demons.

Before they could lead him any farther astray, Kentril stopped in his tracks. "You know, my ladies, I almost feel certain that my friend has left wherever you saw him last and now heads back to the palace to meet me."

"No!" gasped Nefriti. "He's just ahead."

"Not far at all," insisted Zorea, sounding like a twin of the first girl.

Kentril gently but firmly twisted free of both. "I thank the two of you for trying. The people of this kingdom have been most kind."

"No!" insisted Zorea. "This way."

Nefriti nodded. "Yes, this way."

They gripped his arms anew and with such force it brought a slight sound of startlement from the captain. He tried again to pull free, only to discover that the two women had surprisingly powerful holds.

"Let me go!" He managed to get away from Zorea, but Nefriti held on as if she were a leech.

"You must go this way. Please!" she demanded.

Kept in place by the one, Kentril risked being snared again by the second. Not trusting that a third partner—this one probably a male wielding a well-worn knife—might not materialize at any moment, the mercenary dropped any sense of honor and swung at the oncoming Zorea.

He could just as well have struck one of the nearby walls. His fist hit her chin hard, but it proved to be Kentril who suffered from the blow. Every bone in his hand, in his arm, jarred. Pain shot through him, and he almost felt as if he had broken one or more fingers.

Zorea's grasping hands came within inches of him, but at the last Captain Dumon turned to the side, leaving her ripping at only the air. At the same time, he used his free hand to draw his sword as best he could.

Reacting to his weapon, Nefriti flung Kentril back. Caught off guard by her astounding strength, he could not keep himself from colliding with the nearest wall.

As the back of his head struck, the world around Kentril changed. First he saw everything in duplicate, even down to two Zoreas and two Nefritis glaring at him. Then an even more horrific transformation took place.

A nightmare surrounded the captain. Gone suddenly were the sea of torches and the crowds of happy revelers. The magnificent buildings had not only crumbled back to ruin, but they bore a dark stain about them, a sense of foreboding and despair together. Somewhere in the distance, what sounded like the cries of thousands of men, women, and children in agony tore at his ears. Above, a horrific light with no obvious origin spread its monstrous crimson touch over everything.

And everywhere he turned, Kentril Dumon confronted what he could only imagine were the souls of the damned.

They strained for him, hungered for him, pleaded with him, even as they sought to make him one of them. All looked as if a great beast had sucked them dry, leaving only husks who wished to do the same to the fighter. Eyes sunken in, skin dry as dead leaves, they moved as if they had just burst free of their tombs. In tattered clothing, they strained toward Kentril, mouths gaping in anticipation.

"No!" he shouted without thought. "Get away from me!"

The blade free, he swung to and fro, forcing back the tide but finding no immediate escape. A sense of doom filled Kentril as he quickly realized that sooner or later, he would tire enough for them to overwhelm him.

"Captain! Captain Dumon!"

Ignoring the calling of his name, Kentril swung wildly at the fiends. Suddenly, they seemed fewer in number and dwindling more so by the second. Hope resurrected, the captain took a step forward, thinking that perhaps he might yet cut a path to escape.

"Captain Dumon! Look at me! Listen to me!"

Someone seized his shoulders from behind. Tearing free, Kentril spun about, determined that if they now came at him from all sides, he would wreak what havoc he could before they claimed his life and soul.

"Captain, it's Zayl! Zayl!"

Slowly, the necromancer's concerned visage came into focus. Kentril stared at the spellcaster, both fearful and grateful to see the man.

"Zayl! Do something! Don't let them get us!"

"Us?" Zayl looked confused. "Who, captain?"

"*Them*, of cour—"

Kentril stopped dead in his tracks. The horrifying mob had vanished. The cries had ceased. In fact, all Ureh again looked as it should have, the buildings, the people, and the sky all normal. The inhabitants themselves watched the mercenary with expressions mixing concern and sympathy.

However, of the two women who had led him into this he could see no sign.

The necromancer quickly pulled him away from the watching crowd. With Zayl leading, they headed back in the direction of the palace. Neither man said anything until they had gone some distance from the area of the incident.

Guiding Kentril to a narrow side street, Zayl muttered,

"Tell me what happened back there, captain. I heard your voice and came running to find you standing there in the midst of everyone, slashing with your sword and screaming as if the hosts of Hell sought your blood."

"Not my blood," murmured the fighter. Kentril glanced at his hand, saw that he still gripped the sword's hilt so tightly his knuckles were white. "My life . . . my eternal soul."

"Tell me about it. Everything. Describe it in detail, if you can."

Taking a deep breath, Captain Dumon did as requested. He told Zayl about the two females and how they had tried to trick him into a deserted area, then how, after a curiously difficult struggle with them, the entire world had gone monstrously mad.

The necromancer listened closely, saying nothing, revealing nothing with his eyes. Yet, despite the silence, Kentril did not feel that Zayl thought the mercenary insane. Rather, the tall, pale figure listened as if he took every single word with the utmost seriousness. That, in turn, enabled Kentril to relax more as he told his tale and thus allowed him to recall even more specifics.

Only when he had finished did Zayl finally question him, and to Kentril's surprise, the necromancer asked first not about the demonic horde, but rather about the two women.

"You described the one wearing a revealing golden outfit much like what might be found in Lut Gholein. You also gave ample detail of her friend's rather generous charms, captain. More than enough detail, in fact, to make me most curious."

"I'm not the first man to fall prey to a woman's honeyed words, Zayl, and they both made it sound credible that they could lead me to where you were."

Kentril's companion nodded. "And I am not trying to insult you. Rather, I would commend your memory. I did meet those two as they claimed, Captain Dumon. I met them when they were celebrating with one of your men, the one called Brek."

"Brek?" Kentril's episode of madness became a secondary concern. One of his soldiers had been in the company of a pair of conniving wenches who had clearly tried to do away with the captain. "As far as I know, he never came back from the city. Neither Gorst nor Albord, both of whom keep track of the others, has seen him since he initially stepped out with the rest."

"A point to be investigated . . . one of many, I think."

"What does that mean?" Kentril cautiously asked.

"Captain Dumon, it was no mistake that I came upon you. I needed to find you in order to discuss a disturbing encounter of my own."

"And what's that?"

The necromancer frowned. "I will not go into my own story now, but I have reason to believe that what we have been told concerning Gregus Mazi might not be the entire truth."

"Entire?" blurted a voice from Zayl's side. "It's all a blessed lie!"

Kentril, in the act of finally sheathing his sword, suddenly drew it anew. "What in the name of Heaven was that?"

"An unruly and far too vocal companion." To the pouch, Zayl added, "I am warning you for the last time, Humbart. Cease these careless interruptions, or I will remove the spell animating you."

"Hmmph . . ." came the reply.

Suddenly, every bizarre and vile rumor that Kentril had heard concerning the mysterious followers of Rathma seemed to come true. He backed away from Zayl, disregarding the fact that the necromancer had only been of aid to him so far.

"Captain, that is not necessary."

"Keep back from me, spellcaster! What is that in there? A familiar?"

Zayl glanced with annoyance at the pouch. "Much too familiar at times. Humbart forgets his place and the danger he presents to me every time he feels the need to voice his opinion."

"Hum—Humbart *Wessel?*"

"What remains of me, lad! Listen! As one old soldier to another—"

"Silence!" The necromancer rapped hard on the side of the pouch. To Kentril, he said, "Captain, I have lived near the ruins of Ureh most of my life. I watched and waited for it to appear as we know it now, but never did the right conjunction of shadow and light bring it back. Yet that does not mean that I did not have any success in my quest in the meantime." He reached into the bag. "One day, I found this."

The empty eye sockets of a battered skull stared unblinking at Kentril. The jaw bone was missing, and some of the upper teeth had been broken. Near the back of the cranium, a great crack indicated a likely blow, either intentional or accidental, he could not say.

"The final remains of Humbart Wessel," Zayl quietly announced. "Soldier, mercenary, adventurer—"

"And the last man to see Gregus Mazi before he vanished into the shadowed city to try to complete his foul plan."

From the direction of the skull, a hollow and exasperated voice retorted, "Old Gregus would've never harmed another soul!"

Kentril barely held onto his sword. He had known that Zayl's kind could raise the spirits of the dead, but a talking skull was just a bit too much even for the hardened soldier. "What're you up to, necromancer? What's your plan?"

With a frustrated sigh, Zayl answered, "My plan is to find out the truth, Captain Dumon, as it relates to the balance of the mortal plane. In attempting that, I went in search of something to use to summon the spirit of Gregus

Mazi so that I could perhaps find some way to help break his spells."

"And did you?"

The sound of revelry passed nearby. Quickly putting the skull back into the pouch, Zayl waited until the merriment faded away. Then, beckoning Kentril to look toward Nymyr, he continued, "In the mountainside sanctum once used by the sorcerer, I retrieved that which I could use to call him back. I cast a spell that I have cast a hundred times and more, all without failure." His countenance grew grim. "This time, though, no shade from beyond answered."

The captain found this entirely unimportant. "So you failed at last. One dead man escaped your power."

"He escaped because he was not dead in the first place."

Zayl let his words sink in. Kentril frowned, not certain he understood and, if he did, not certain that he wanted to know such news. "But Juris Khan told us plainly that he and Mazi fought, and after Mazi trapped him, Khan still managed to destroy the villain before any further harm could be done to Ureh."

The shadowy spellcaster nodded sagely. "Yes, Juris Khan did say that."

"Then Gregus Mazi is dead."

"He is not. I know this. The only reason for my failure is his continued life."

Sheathing his sword at last, Kentril turned toward the palace. Sudden fear for Atanna had replaced his uncertainty about his own sanity and even his distrust of the necromancer. "We've got to warn them! There's no telling where Mazi might be."

Zayl, however, clamped a slim but strong hand onto the mercenary's shoulder. Leaning near, he whispered, "There is . . . and I have performed that spell. Gregus Mazi is still in Ureh, captain." His gaze also shifted to the grand structure atop the hill. "And I fear that he is in the palace itself."

ELEVEN

If Zayl had told Kentril that Diablo himself resided in the palace where Atanna lived, the veteran soldier could not have been more horrified. Gregus Mazi, the man who had cursed a kingdom and lusted after Khan's daughter, not only lived but lurked near enough to do her harm. Never in his life had Kentril wanted so much to slay a person, not even after so many campaigns. During those, he had been performing a duty for which he had been paid, nothing more. Here, though, the task had a personal nature beyond any he had ever confronted.

"Where in the palace?" he demanded of Zayl as the duo worked their way to the hill. "Where?"

"Below it, actually. As for a precise location, that cannot be ascertained. There are forces in play the likes of which I have never come across. Spells I cast that should work to delve deeper are twisted and turned, rendering them useless. If I get closer, perhaps that will change."

"They've got to be warned," Kentril insisted. "They have to know the danger's right below them."

At the base of the ancient steps, the necromancer forced his companion to halt. "Captain Dumon, have you noticed anything amiss in the palace so far?"

"Only that some of my men haven't returned."

"But neither Lord Khan nor his daughter seems at all at risk."

The soldier did not like the way Zayl spoke. "What of that?"

"You have fought in many battles, in many wars.

Do you announce to the enemy your intentions, or do you instead try to trick him, to leave him unsuspecting?"

Kentril's eyes narrowed. "Are you trying to tell me we should say nothing to them?"

"Not until we at least discover more—or until we sense some danger to them."

"And what would you suggest, necromancer?"

Zayl glanced around, making certain that no one stood near enough to hear. "We find out what lies beneath first."

A part of Kentril thought Zayl's suggestion foolish, that the right thing to do would be to alert Atanna of Gregus Mazi's return. Another part, though, feared that the corrupted sorcerer would also find out. Surely Mazi watched Khan and his daughter closely to make certain that they did not know of his hidden presence. Alerted, he would most likely strike and strike to destroy.

But the odds were good that the villain also watched his old master's guests. If they simply went in hunt of him, he would surely lay traps designed to kill all.

"We won't tell them just yet," Kentril finally agreed. "But we'll need some sort of distraction that would capture his interest so much that he won't pay any mind to searchers."

"He's got a point there," came Humbart's muffled voice.

Zayl tapped the pouch, then nodded agreement.

They kept silent about their goals as they reentered the palace some time later. Neither had yet thought up a manner by which the attention of the hidden spellcaster might be diverted, but both knew that they could not wait long. Surely Gregus Mazi had some imminent mischief in mind.

Thinking of that, Kentril sought out Albord. He found the younger mercenary just preparing to set out with two others for the city, which fit in directly with the captain's plan. Pulling Albord aside, Kentril whispered, "Don't ask why, but I have orders for you."

Although his body revealed no reaction to his commander's surprising words, the blond fighter's eyes let Kentril know that Albord understood the seriousness. "Aye, captain?"

"I need to cut short the men's celebrations for the time being. I want you three to go down and collect the others you find. I want everyone up here and accounted for. Anyone who can't be found, let me know. Above all else, don't split up, and don't let any of the locals know what you're up to . . . and if anyone offers to help you find someone missing, refuse that help."

This at last brought some reaction. "Just how serious is this, captain?"

Kentril recalled his own encounter, when the city had been transformed into a nightmare straight out of Hell. He had finally come to the conclusion that the two women had used some exotic potion that had not only weakened him but also caused his horrific hallucinations. It had been said that some assassins used such potions on their nails and that only a touch might be needed to affect a victim. "Serious enough. Beware especially of two women, one in gold and both far too eager for your company."

As he sent Albord and the others off, Zayl rejoined him. "What did you tell him?"

"Enough to be wary. It won't look out of the question that I would be checking up on my men, necromancer. Mercenaries have a tendency to wear out their welcome quickly in times of peace, and having them all called in will just seem like a simple, honest precaution."

"Do we tell Master Tsin as well?"

Kentril shrugged. "I don't know. I do want to tell Gorst right away, though, and he's near the sorcerer."

They quickly hurried to the library but found, to their mutual surprise, that it was empty. The table where the Vizjerei had sat for so long still lay all but hidden under a cluttered pile of books and scrolls, but Tsin and the mountain of notes he had made had vanished.

The captain noticed one other thing missing: Gorst. The giant might have simply followed Tsin in order to keep track of him, but the considerable pile of parchment missing coupled with the difficulty the short spellcaster would have had trying to carry all of it around made it obvious that Tsin had commandeered Gorst into helping him with something.

Barely had Kentril and Zayl turned back when from down the corridor Atanna appeared. She saw the two, and her expression, already bright, seemed to the fighter to positively glow.

"Kentril! You've done it! You've done it!"

Utterly ignoring the necromancer, she threw her arms around the captain and kissed him passionately. Kentril momentarily forgot the sinister danger below as he accepted Atanna's gratitude. That he knew not what she thanked him for he did not care.

Gradually, he became aware of a bemused Zayl watching him from behind Lord Khan's daughter. At first annoyed by this intrusion, Kentril finally recalled what he and his companion had been trying to accomplish. With gentle force, Kentril pushed away Atanna, reconciling himself with at least being able to gaze at her up close.

"And for what am I being thanked so well?"

"As if you didn't know!" She almost kissed him again, but noticed his reluctance. A playful smile spreading across her perfect features, she allowed Zayl to join in the conversation. "You might find this of interest, too, sir."

"I suspect I might, my lady."

Atanna graciously accepted his courtesy. "At this moment," she informed both, "the Vizjerei sorcerer Quov Tsin has an audience with my father."

"Already?" interrupted Kentril. He had not thought Tsin would begin trying to persuade Lord Khan for some time yet. Surely the Vizjerei's greed had much to do with this sudden development. Kentril only hoped that by rushing in, old Tsin had not ruined everything.

"The good sorcerer has told Father that he thinks in a

day or two he can help remove Gregus's curse! It will take hours of preparation and at least as much spellwork, but he feels certain it will succeed!"

Her eyes widened in hope and anticipation. Kentril prayed that Tsin would not let Juris Khan down, if only for Atanna's sake. "I'm pleased to hear that, but—"

"And more important for some," the red-haired princess added, her gaze especially fixed on Captain Dumon now. "Master Tsin has already accomplished one miracle. He has convinced Father that Ureh should be a part of the world again, that the quest for Heaven is one we should undertake in the manner of any other mortal, through the trials of life itself."

Kentril hesitated to respond, hoping he had correctly understood her. "Juris Khan won't try to recast the spell? He won't try a second time to claim the sanctuary of Heaven?"

"No! Thanks to the Vizjerei, Father now believes that we've a role here. He thinks that we may be needed to help guide the rest of the world toward the proper path. Father even wonders now if this was meant to be from the beginning!"

It all sounded too fantastic to Captain Dumon, but in Atanna's face he read only truth. Lord Khan had changed his mind. Tsin had actually succeeded, and far sooner than Kentril could have ever imagined possible.

"My congratulations on this news, my lady," Zayl politely said.

"Thank you," she replied, giving the necromancer a momentary smile before returning her full attention to Kentril. "Father is so thrilled, he would like to honor you and Master Tsin shortly with a private dinner. You, too, if you wish, Master Zayl."

The pale figure shook his head. "My kind are not known for their social behavior, and besides, I have really done nothing to deserve such recognition. However, I certainly agree that Captain Dumon and the sorcerer should be so honored."

"As you wish." Atanna seemed to forget the necromancer from there on. "Kentril, I hope you'll say yes."

What else could he say? "Of course. The honor's mine."

"Splendid! It's all settled, then. A servant will be at your quarters before long to help you dress."

"Dress?" The mercenary did not like the sound of that.

"Of course," interjected Zayl innocently. "One must always be properly attired for a state dinner, captain."

Before Kentril could protest, Atanna kissed him once more, then hurried away. Both men watched her alluring form swiftly vanish down the hall.

"A unique woman, Captain Dumon."

"Very much."

The necromancer swept closer. "This dinner could also be to our benefit. With Lord Khan and his daughter occupied with you and the Vizjerei, I can try surreptitiously to investigate our likely route to below. There must be some detailed outline of the palace's design and possibly even mention of the caverns Khan hinted of even deeper."

Kentril continued to eye the direction down which Atanna had disappeared. "I still don't like not at least telling her."

"Remember that Gregus Mazi once desired Khan's daughter. He has not touched her so far, but if he realizes she has been alerted, he may decide to steal her away. Her ignorance is her safety."

"All *right*," the captain snapped. He glared at the tall, slim figure beside him. "Just make certain that you don't get caught. That would be hard to explain."

"If I am, I shall make it known to all that I acted on my own. She will have no reason to lose her trust in you, captain."

With a slight bow, Zayl departed. Kentril frowned, still not quite certain about this pact he had made with the necromancer, then headed to his quarters to see what could be done about making himself presentable for this no doubt elegant dinner.

He would have rather been fighting a pitched battle.

A crisp black dress uniform with gold ornamentation had been laid out on his bed, a uniform with long, sleek pants and a jacket with sharp tails. Epaulets decorated the jacket's shoulders, and the stylized image of a crown and sword had been sewn onto the left breast. The gleaming black leather boots rose knee-high, completing a rather dashing image.

Kentril felt foolish in the outfit. He was a soldier, a mercenary. The uniform should have been worn by a commander, a general, not someone of his lowly station. Still, he could not appear at a formal dinner with Lord Khan and Atanna dressed in his tired, oft-mended garments.

That the uniform fit perfectly did not entirely surprise the captain. Atanna would not have bothered to have it set aside for him if she had not known it would serve perfectly. He wondered whether it had once belonged to someone else, or if she had somehow simply conjured it up.

Although he knew the way to his destination, Kentril found two armed guards outside his door waiting to escort him. With much ceremony, they marched down the halls with him, leading the fighter at last to where Khan waited.

"Welcome, my friend!" the fatherly figure called from his chair. "I am so pleased that you've agreed to join us."

Because of the robed monarch's inability to move, a heavy sculpted table had been brought in for the dinner. Decorated with filigree and lovingly carved by some expert hand, it likely cost as much as Kentril made in ten years—if he was lucky. Atop it, a golden cloth had been set, and on top of that, gleaming plates, pristine silverware, and tall, magnificent candelabras.

Three chairs had been placed at the table. Juris Khan himself could not be moved off the dais, but a smaller yet no less richly adorned table had been positioned near him.

The larger table had been turned so that the lord of Ureh sat at its head.

Quov Tsin already sat on what would have been the left of their host, but Kentril saw no sign of Atanna. However, as he approached, she suddenly emerged from the side of the room, hand held out toward him.

He stared unashamedly at her, both because he could not see how he had missed her entrance and because nothing else in the richly decorated chamber could match the vision she presented.

Her billowing emerald gown complemented her lush, crimson tresses, which had been artfully draped down over her shoulders and breast. The sleeves stretched all the way to the backs of her hands and even fit over the three lower fingers of each, almost like a partial glove. Other than her hair, her shoulders were bare, and the gown itself plunged just enough to entice but not to flaunt her perfect form shamelessly.

He took the hand she offered and kissed the back. Atanna then took his hand in hers and led him to the table.

"You shall sit there, at the end," she murmured. "I shall be on your left, very near."

Kentril almost went to his appointed place, then recalled how polished officers acted in the presence of ladies of the court. He steered her toward her own chair, then held it out for her. Smiling prettily, Atanna accepted this gracious gesture.

"About time," Tsin muttered as Kentril seated himself. Judging by the empty goblet in front of him, the Vizjerei had already had at least one cup of wine. He had come clad, of course, in the robes that he always wore. As a sorcerer, Tsin was not expected to dress in anything other than the garments of his calling, and, in truth, the rune-inscribed robes did not seem out of place here.

"You look splendid!" Juris Khan informed the captain. "Does he not look splendid, my dear?"

"Yes, Father." Atanna blushed.

"A wise and portentous choice, daughter! Truly, Captain Dumon, the uniform is appropriate for you."

"I thank you, my lord." Kentril did not know what else to say.

"I'm so gratified that both of you could come on such short notice. I owe each of you much already, and it appears I'll owe so much more before very long!"

"We are honored, Lord Khan," Quov Tsin responded, raising his empty glass in salute. A liveried servant appeared from nowhere and filled it from a dark green bottle, which perhaps had been what the Vizjerei had desired all along.

Kentril nodded in appreciation of his host's words, although he did not feel as if he had done so much to deserve the praise. Yes, he had helped set the Key to Light in place, but any strong arm could have done that. More to the point, it would be Tsin who would release Ureh's ruler from Gregus Mazi's curse. Captain Dumon could understand the sorcerer being given his due, but for himself, he felt grateful just to be able to sit near Atanna.

Snapping his fingers, Juris Khan had the first portion of their dinner brought out by several uniformed servants so similar in appearance that Kentril had to study each golden figure in turn in order to ascertain that they were not all identical. The servants treated him with as much honor as they did their master, which only further embarrassed him. He was a hired soldier, a man of rank only because he had survived when so many other brave but poor men had not.

As the dinner went on, the veteran fighter feasted on fruits and vegetables the likes of which he had never seen and thick, well-cooked meats dripping with their own juices. The wine he drank had such full flavor that Kentril had to take care for fear he would imbibe too much. Everything he tasted had been made to perfection. The dinner seemed more a dream than a reality.

Throughout it all, he also feasted on the glorious sight of

Atanna, so much so that it was not until late into the meal that a question that had bothered him earlier came again to mind. He stared at what little remained of the contents of his plate, finally asking with the utmost caution, "My lord, where does all the food come from?"

Tsin glanced at him as if having just heard an unruly child interrupt. Juris Khan, however, not only took his question in stride, but made it sound so very wise. "Yes, well you should ask. You wonder, no doubt, because I've indicated that although we were trapped between Heaven and the mortal plane, we were aware of our fate. In some ways, time did indeed pass, but in others, it did not. Even I can't fully explain it, I'm sorry to say. We only knew that years went by in the true world, but we did not age, we did not much sleep, and, most important, we did not *hunger* at all."

"Not at all?" Kentril uttered with some surprise.

"Well, perhaps we did . . . but only for our *salvation*. And as we did not age, so, too, did our food not age. Thus, we are still plentifully stocked and shall be for some time." Atanna's father smiled benevolently at both guests. "And by then, I hope our situation will be already much improved."

Kentril nodded, grateful for the answer but inwardly still embarrassed for having asked it in the first place.

"My lord," piped up the Vizjerei, "during the time you were explaining the obvious to the captain here, some further considerations formulated in my head."

Khan found much interest in this. "Considerations dealing with my condition?"

"Aye. I will definitely have need of your daughter's abilities as well as your own, just as I earlier proposed. You see . . ."

As Tsin began a lengthy and, for the mundane captain, incomprehensible explanation, Kentril gladly returned his attention to his hostess. Atanna noticed him gazing at her again and smiled over the goblet she had just started raising to her lips.

Eyes and mind on the heavenly view before him, Captain Dumon grew careless with the knife and fork he had been using. The blade slipped from the bit of meat he had been carving and jabbed the side of the hand that had been holding the other utensil.

Drops of blood splattered on the dish.

Pain shot through Kentril.

The lavish, brightly lit chamber became a chamber of *horrors* instead.

Blood—fresh blood—seemed to flow over tarnished, scratched walls, and the ceiling, which now existed only as a jagged hole, revealed a sky as turbulent and tortured as the rest of his surroundings. Crimson and black clouds did battle, monstrous bolts of lightning marking where they collided. Swirling maelstroms formed, seeming ready to swallow the bleeding world below.

Bones that looked suspiciously human lay scattered everywhere upon the stained and cracked floor, and something not a rat scurried over one before disappearing into a small fissure running along the side of the room. A fierce wind coursed through, howling as it went. An intense heat that somehow still chilled Kentril to his very soul swept along in its wake.

Moans and cries suddenly assailed his ears. He rose at last from the rotting table, seeing on the broken, dust-ridden plate before him not the freshly cooked meal he had been eating, but instead a moldy, maggot-infested piece of greenish meat.

The moans and cries continued to increase in intensity, so much so that the captain had to cover his ears. He stumbled back, falling against one wall—and only then finding the source of the mournful pleas.

From each of the walls, hundreds of mouths began to cry out for help. Those nearest him seemed to scream the loudest. Pulling away in horror, Kentril stumbled back to the table . . . and into, of all things, a very *annoyed* Quov Tsin.

"What do you think you're doing, cretin? You're making a fool of yourself in front of our host!" The Vizjerei pointed in the direction of the dais.

But when Kentril looked there, he did not see the good and fatherly Juris Khan. The chair remained fixed in place, true, and of all things it looked most untouched by the horrors around, but in it did not sit the lord of Ureh.

Before Captain Dumon's fearful eyes arose—

"Kentril! Speak to me! It's Atanna! Kentril!"

And as if it had all been a dream, the grand chamber immediately became whole and bright and *alive* once more.

Atanna held his bleeding hand tight, her eyes wide and concerned. Staring into those eyes gave the mercenary something on which to focus, to use as an anchor for his suddenly questionable sanity.

"Captain Dumon, are you unwell?"

With great reluctance, Kentril looked to Juris Khan. He breathed a sigh of relief upon seeing the robed, masterful monarch standing tall, absolute concern written over the elderly visage. Gone was the image of—of what? Kentril could not even recall exactly what he had seen, only that it had been like nothing he had ever come across in all his life. The sheer act of trying to remember even the slightest image caused him to shiver.

Khan's daughter brought a goblet to his mouth. "Drink this, my darling."

For her and her alone he drank it. The wine calmed him, pushed away all but the vestiges of his nightmare.

Atanna led him back to his chair. As he sat, Kentril mumbled, "I'm sorry . . . sorry, everyone."

"There is no need for one who is ill to apologize," Khan kindly remarked.

One hand still on the captain's shoulder, Atanna said, "I think I know what happened, Father. We walked in the garden earlier, and something bit him."

"I see. Yes, the jungle insects sometimes make their way

here, and some are said to carry disease that causes delusions and more. One must've bitten you, Captain Dumon."

Having fought in many vile lands, where weather and wildlife made a more fearsome foe than the opposing soldiers, Kentril could well believe their conclusions. Yet the monstrous clarity of his hallucination still stuck with the fighter. What within him could dredge up such horrors? As a man who had seen and shed blood, he had dreamt about the dark side of war, but never had his imagination created such a picture.

Still, Atanna's explanation would also give reason for his earlier episode in the city. Had that been the first sign of the sickness? He had assumed that Zorea or the other woman had drugged him, but such a drug should have worn off by now.

Lord Khan seated himself again. "Well, whatever the cause, I am sure that under my daughter's ministrations, you will recover fine. I want you to be able to accept my gifts with full clarity of mind so that I may not force upon you anything you do not wish."

"Gifts?"

"Aye, good captain—although if you accept, you'll be captain no more." The robed figure leaned toward his two guests. "In the struggle against Gregus Mazi, lives were lost. Important ones. Good ones. Good friends. A vacuum thus exists in Ureh, and if we're to become part of the mortal world again, that vacuum must be filled. You two can help in that."

Kentril felt Atanna's fingers tighten on his shoulder, and when he looked up, she gave him an expression of pride and pleasure.

"Master Tsin, you and I've already discussed this in part, so you have some advantage over Captain Dumon. Nonetheless, the decision is no less a significant one for you, and so I state my offer again, with more conciseness this time. All those who wielded and governed the magic arts of my kingdom have perished save my daughter and

myself. I ask of you if you will bring honor again to that
which Gregus tainted. I ask you to take up the mantle of
royal sorcerer, the magical knowledge of my realm yours if
you will sit ever at my left hand."

The Vizjerei rose slowly, a satisfied smile across his
wrinkled countenance. Kentril could only imagine the
spellcaster's pleasure. He had more than gained long-term
access to the books and scrolls of the library; for all practical purposes, Juris Khan had given the diminutive figure
everything the Vizjerei could have wanted.

"My Lord Khan," Quov Tsin graciously replied, "nothing would please me more."

"I am gratified." Now the stately monarch turned toward
Kentril, who felt his stomach tie in knots. "Captain Kentril
Dumon, through your efforts to help us and the recommen-
dations of one who has come to know you better than I, I've
learned of a man of ability, determination, honor, and loyalty.
I can think of no better qualities in a soldier—nay, in a
leader!" Khan steepled his fingers. "We are an old realm in a
new world, one you know much better. There's need for
such a man as you to guide us, to protect us from elements
that may desire our downfall in this different time. I need
you as a commander of my warriors, a protector of my people, a general, as that uniform calls for."

Despite his recent spell, Kentril pushed himself back to
his feet. "My gracious Lord Khan—"

But his host politely cut him off. "And in Ureh, you
should know that such a rank comes hand in hand with a
title. The commander of our defenders is not only a soldier
but a *prince* of the land as well."

He left the captain momentarily speechless. Atanna, her
hand now on his arm, squeezed tightly.

"And as a member of the nobility, all rights therein are
yours. You will be granted an estate, be able to raise servants of your own, marry other members of nobility—"

At the last, Atanna's hand squeezed particularly tightly.
When Kentril briefly let his gaze fly to her, he saw the

answer for why Juris Khan would especially offer him this wondrous posting. Despite their liaison so far, the soldier had always known inside that he truly had no hope for a lasting love. Atanna was a princess, born and raised to marry someone equal to or higher than her lofty station. Kings, sultans, emperors, and princes could have easily asked for her hand, but not a lowly officer.

Now her father had eradicated that one impediment with a single gesture.

"—and so forth," finished Juris Khan. He smiled as a father would smile at his son . . . perhaps a foreshadowing of events. "What say you, good captain?"

What could Kentril say? Only a fool or a madman could refuse, and despite his recent episodes, he did not feel himself either of those. "I-I am honored to accept, my lord."

"Then all that I've offered is most definitely yours. You and Master Tsin have made me very happy! Master Tsin assures me of complete success in freeing me, and if that holds true, three days hence, as marked by the sun seen beyond our borders, I shall before the entire court officially acknowledge your new stations." Khan nearly fell back into his chair, as if both physically and emotionally exhausted by his grand gesture. "You've the gratitude of all Ureh . . . but the gratitude of my humble self the most."

Atanna returned to her seat, and she blushed even more whenever her eyes and Kentril's met. The talk began to turn again to Quov Tsin's plan to free Lord Khan from his chair, eventually even drawing Atanna in because of her necessary role. Left alone now, Captain Dumon turned to his own thoughts.

And those thoughts concerned his subterfuge. Even after all Juris Khan had granted him, after all Atanna had promised him with her eyes and lips, he had said nothing concerning the possibility that Gregus Mazi still lived and might yet turn his black arts again on them. At this moment, Kentril knew, Zayl crept about the palace, seeking behind the backs of their hosts the plans of its design.

True, the pair had only the best of intentions in mind, but still the captain felt as if each second he failed to speak he betrayed Atanna and her father further.

Despite his regrets, though, Kentril chose to say nothing. If Zayl proved to be wrong, no harm would be done. Yet if the necromancer had divined correctly, there would be only him and Kentril to deal with the threat. Khan could do nothing while so impaired, and not for a moment would Captain Dumon even consider letting Atanna face the corrupted spellcaster. Tsin already had too much with which to deal. No, if Gregus Mazi did indeed live, Kentril would have to see to it himself that the corrupted sorcerer paid the ultimate price for his past crimes.

Atanna caught his gaze once more. She smiled and blushed, completely ignorant of the darkening thoughts behind the captain's own smile. No, no matter what happened, Gregus Mazi could not be allowed ever again to touch her . . . not even if it cost Kentril Dumon his own life in the process.

TWELVE

Zayl met him some hours after the dinner, the necromancer's expression giving no sense of success or failure as he slipped into the captain's chambers. Only when Zayl had held up his ivory dagger and turned one complete circle did the pale figure finally announce the results of his search.

"An easier task than I had anticipated. Clearly marked and filed in the library among other papers. In his own abode, our host apparently did not think he had to be cautious about such information."

"No," responded Kentril somewhat bitterly. "He probably believes that he can trust everyone."

Zayl presented to him a tracing of the chart someone had made showing how to reach the caverns beneath and what routes the system of tunnels took. "You can see that it is good we have this. The system is complex, almost mazelike. One could get lost down there and never find the way back."

"Where do you think Mazi might be?"

"That is something I shall try to divine just before we depart, captain. I did not leave the sorcerer's former sanctum empty-handed. I have a few more samples of his hair. I will try to use them to find his location. It may not be exact, but should be enough for me to hazard an expert guess."

Kentril tried not to think of the two of them wandering through the caverns seeking the insidious spellcaster. "Will he be able to detect what you're doing?"

"There is always the chance of that, but I have taken

the utmost precaution each time and will do so again. The methods of my kind are much more subtle than those likely learned by such as Mazi or Tsin. That has been in great part for the sake of simple survival, for we know how most others view us. We have even learned by necessity how to move among other practitioners of the magic arts without them ever knowing we were present. You may rest assured, Gregus Mazi will not notice."

The ability to fool Tsin did not impress Kentril as much as Zayl perhaps thought it did, but the time to turn back had long passed. "How long do we have?"

"Such a spell as the Vizjerei must cast will require many hours, even a day, but we must start out as soon as they begin preparations." The necromancer glanced again at the tracing. "Which makes it all the better that we have this. Do not lose it, captain." Zayl stepped back as if preparing to leave, then suddenly asked, "How went the dinner?"

"Well." Now did not seem the time to tell the necromancer all that had happened.

Zayl waited for him to elaborate, but when Kentril remained quiet, the cloaked figure finally departed.

Kentril fell back onto his bed. He had nearly managed to fall asleep when a single tap on the door made him sit up straight, one hand already on the dagger habit caused him to keep at his side. A moment later, Gorst and Albord stepped in, both looking perturbed.

"What is it, Gorst?" Kentril asked, hand relaxing only slightly.

"Albord's got something to say."

The younger mercenary clearly felt ill at ease. "Captain, there's something I don't like."

"What's that?"

"No one's still seen hide nor hair of Brek, and now besides him there's two more missing."

Not what Kentril wanted to hear at any time, but even more so with the coming events. "Who?"

"Simon. Mordecai. I asked the others, and no one knows when they were last seen."

"Everyone else accounted for?"

Gorst nodded. "Kept 'em in. They're a little cranky about it, but it ain't too bad bein' stuck in here, eh, Kentril?"

The captain was certain that his face flushed, but he could hardly worry about that now. Counting Albord, that made only seven men left besides Kentril and Gorst. "Three missing now. I don't like that. Someone resents our being here." Inwardly, he wondered if the disappearances had anything to do with Gregus Mazi. Did the sorcerer work to eliminate his former master's new allies?

"What do we do?" asked Albord.

"We keep this to ourselves. No one leaves the palace until I say so. There's not enough of us to go hunting the others. We'll have to consider the worst, I'm afraid." Kentril rubbed his chin in thought. "Albord, you've got charge of them. I've something in mind I need Gorst for. Can you handle it?"

The younger mercenary snapped to attention. "I'll see it done, captain!"

"Good lad. And if any of the three do return, question them carefully as to their whereabouts. We need to find out all we can."

Not once did he mention saying anything to Lord Khan, and not once did Albord or Gorst suggest it. Whatever choice their captain made they would accept.

Kentril dismissed Albord, but had his second stay. "Gorst, there's something I need you to help with, but since there's a strong element of risk, I'll only accept you as a volunteer. If you don't want to go, I'll understand."

The familiar grin faded. "What is it, Kentril?"

Captain Dumon told him, starting with Zayl's astonishing revelation and what the necromancer and he had decided to do. Gorst listened quietly through it all, the dark, round eyes of the giant never once leaving his commander.

"I'll come," he responded as soon as Kentril had finished.

"Gorst, this could be more dangerous than any battle-field."

The giant smiled. "So?"

Despite some guilt at having included his friend in this possibly suicidal quest, Kentril also felt much relieved. Having Gorst at his back made coming events seem a little more reasonable, a little more normal. This would just be another battle situation, a special mission behind enemy lines. True, the foe wielded sorcery, but they had the talents of Zayl for that. If the necromancer could keep Gregus Mazi at bay, the two fighters would move in to strike the mortal blow. A three-pronged assault on a single enemy, a nearly perfect battle plan.

Kentril snorted at his own naive notion. It all sounded so simple when thought of in such terms, but he doubted that would turn out to be the case once reality hit. One thing he had learned early on in his career, when the battle began in earnest, *all* the magnificent plans for victory went up in smoke.

Waiting for the moment itself proved to be the worst of ordeals. To the captain, each minute felt like an hour, and each hour a day. If not for those interludes when Atanna could break away from the preparations Tsin required, Kentril suspected that he would have gone mad.

Lord Khan's daughter and he spoke little when they were together, and what talk did take place concerned more hints of the future. Half-veiled promises filled the captain's head as the enchantress herself filled his arms.

"Not long now," Atanna whispered more than once, "but so much longer than I want to wait . . ."

Fueled by such honeyed words, Kentril silently swore that when the time came, he would take Gregus Mazi's head himself and present it to Atanna and her father as proof of his worthiness. Surely then Lord Khan would see him as a respected suitor.

And then at long last came the time. A different Atanna met Captain Dumon as he pretended to be cleaning his gear. She wore a chaste white robe much akin to that of Juris Khan, and her luxurious hair had been tied tightly back in a tail. The solemn expression alone informed Kentril of why she had come dressed so.

"It's to begin?" he asked, his question having double meaning to him.

"Master Tsin says that the forces are in correct alignment and the patterns matched to their purposes. It will still take us hours, but I must be there for all of it. I came to ask for your confidence, your belief in our success."

He kissed her. "You'll succeed—and I'll be there in spirit."

"Thank you." She gave him a hopeful smile, then rushed off.

Kentril's own smile reversed as he understood that his quest had also now begun. Gathering his gear, he waited a few minutes to be safe, then marched out of his chambers to seek Gorst and the necromancer.

The giant met him in the hall, their encounter quite casual in the eyes of any guard seeing them. They spoke of stretching their legs, taking a run to keep their muscles strong, the typical routines of veteran fighters. Acting completely at ease, the pair made their way through the many halls of the palace, finally exiting the building altogether.

Far beyond the protective wall surrounding the palace lay what the necromancer had revealed as the best of entrances to the caverns that honeycombed Nymyr. This had been the very opening that Khan's brave volunteers had utilized to carry the Key to Shadow to its resting place deep below. According to Zayl, the passage through which they would enter the system had no natural origin; someone had carved into the rock until they had met up with one of the natural caverns inside. The necromancer suspected that perhaps the ancient monks had taken up the task, either as a place to hide should the monastery be overwhelmed or possibly as some part of their holy rituals.

Kentril had not cared at the time of explanation about the history of the cave, only that it existed and gave them a direct route to the underworld. However, when he initially saw the craggy mouth, his heart suddenly beat as it had not since his first battle. Only by quickly taking deep breaths was Kentril able to approach without revealing to Gorst his inexplicable fear.

"I don't see Zayl," the captain muttered.

"I am here," replied one of the shadows near the narrow opening.

A section of rocky mountainside suddenly fell away as the cloak of the necromancer dropped, revealing the waiting figure. "I thought it might be best to mask myself in illusion until you arrived."

Gritting his teeth, Kentril pretended not to have been startled by the spellcaster's astounding appearance. "How's it look inside?"

"Carved to let one man pass at a time. Your friend will have to bow his head and may find a few parts a bit tight."

"Don't worry about Gorst. He'll make his own path if necessary."

Turning from the two mercenaries, Zayl led the way inside. As Kentril entered, he experienced a slight sensation of the walls closing in on him, but fortunately, the feeling quickly passed.

Zayl muttered something. A moment later, a peculiar, pale light filled the shaft. In the necromancer's left hand, Kentril saw the ivory dagger gleam.

"This should go on for about five, six hundred yards," Zayl commented. "After that, the caverns should begin to open up."

Gorst was indeed forced to keep his head bent much of the way, but only once did he have to squeeze through in order to continue on. As for Kentril, he might as well have been taking a walk through a darkened hall in the palace.

Even the floor had been smoothed, making footing almost perfect.

Their good luck appeared to end almost where the caverns should have opened up before them. Rounding a turn, the trio at first saw not the widening mouth that they had expected but instead, a wall of rubble.

"I had not counted on this," responded the necromancer. "And according to the drawing, there is no other path."

Kentril went up to investigate the wall of rock and dirt, pulling at a few good-sized stones.

The vast pile suddenly rolled toward him, burying his legs up to the tops of his boots in a matter of only seconds. Gorst pulled him back before he could become any more trapped. The trio stepped back quickly and waited for the dust to settle.

"I think . . . I see something," Zayl declared after a brief coughing fit.

Sure enough, the dagger revealed a hole near the top. Borrowing the necromancer's enchanted blade, Kentril quickly but carefully crawled up to investigate. "It opens wide just ahead. If we can crawl through safely for a few yards, we should be clear."

Gorst and Kentril worked to make the opening bigger while Zayl held the light for them. Once that had been accomplished, the necromancer worked his way through, followed by the giant, then Kentril.

And on the other side of the collapse, they at last stood before the true beginning of the cavern complex.

The chamber stretched hundreds of feet up and across. Jagged limestone teeth thrust down from the ceiling, some of them three, four times the size of Gorst. Others burst from the floor of the vast cave, several more than a yard thick and twice that in height.

Water trickled over the walls, carving niches, creating myriad shapes everywhere, and, in the process, revealing bright, glittering crystals embedded in the rock face. In the light of the dagger, the cavern *glistened*.

Kentril looked down, and any wonder over the beauty of the chamber died as he saw what faced them. Roughly twenty yards ahead, the floor dropped off abruptly, a veritable cliff that ended in a chilling, black abyss.

"Down there?" Gorst cheerfully asked.

Zayl nodded as he reached into the confines of his voluminous cloak. Kentril marveled that despite their crawling, the spellcaster looked unsullied.

From the cloak, Zayl suddenly pulled forth a short, almost laughable length of rope. However, as the necromancer began tugging on the ends, it *grew*. Only a foot long in the beginning, under his effort it stretched to twice, then three times more what it had been.

"Gorst," the pale figure called, "help me with this." Handing the dagger again to Kentril, Zayl gave one end of the small rope to the larger mercenary. As the two pulled, Kentril saw that it stretched even farther.

Five feet, six, eight, and more. Gorst and the necromancer pulled and pulled, and each time they did, the rope gave way. In but the space of a few breaths, the party ended up with a sizable length, more than enough to begin their descent.

Zayl wordlessly took back the dagger. The two soldiers secured the astonishing rope around one of the broader stalagmites, then tested it. The necromancer, meanwhile, leaned over the edge, studying the dark depths.

"If the original drawing is correct, we should have more than enough room on which to land."

The captain did not like the sound of that. "And if it's not?"

"Then we shall find ourselves dangling over a thousand-foot drop."

Fortunately, the calculations of the nameless person who had originally charted the caverns proved to be accurate not only with this initial descent, but with those that followed. Moving with more confidence, the trio journeyed farther and farther down into the system, guided all the while by Zayl's glowing blade.

At last, they came to an area where the passages leveled off. The necromancer paused to consult the tracing, not desiring to head off toward a dead end or a pit. Kentril and Gorst, meanwhile, drew their weapons just in case.

"Are we on the right trail still?" the captain asked of Zayl.

"I believe so. The spell I cast before leaving for the cave did not give me as exact a location as I had hoped, but it did pinpoint matters enough for me to believe we are very near. Be wary."

Slowly they wended their way through a series of twisting passages punctuated on occasion by small and unprepossessing chambers. Only once did they have any cause to halt, that being when Gorst came across a tattered water sack that they all assumed had been left by the party carrying Juris Khan's creation. Zayl inspected it for any clues, but found none.

Then Kentril noticed that the area ahead of them seemed slightly brighter than Zayl's dagger should have been able to make it. He touched the necromancer on the arm, indicating that he should cover the enchanted blade.

Despite the momentary loss of the weapon's light, the passage ahead remained illuminated.

Sword at the ready, the captain proceeded, Zayl and Gorst ready to back him up at the slightest sign of danger. With each step, the glow ahead increased a bit. It never truly grew bright, and even what illumination there was had a dark quality to it, but Kentril could definitely see better the nearer he drew.

And suddenly the party entered a wide, rounded chamber in the midst of which, atop a reworked stalagmite, gleamed the source of the illumination . . . the *Key to Shadow*.

Those who had risked themselves to bring it down here had carefully chipped away at the cavern growth, creating a stone hand of sorts in the very center of whose craggy palm the mighty black crystal pulsated quietly.

Seeing no sign of danger, Kentril moved to investigate better Lord Khan's creation. Dagger thrust forward, Zayl stepped up next to him, also eager to see the magical gemstone.

A face of utter horror suddenly greeted both men from a stalactite just beyond the crystal.

Both mercenaries swore loudly, and even Zayl muttered something under his breath. They stared in disquiet at the figure carved into the growth. A man of limestone and other minerals, he hung as if violently tied to the very stalactite from which he had been sculpted. Arms and legs had been pulled back as far as they could humanly go, seemingly bound together from behind. The expression of agony and dismay had been shaped so exquisitely that Kentril expected the trapped figure to finish his silent cry at any moment. The artisan had managed to touch both the macabre and the human at the same time, making the sculpture even more arresting.

"What is that thing?"

"Some sort of guardian, perhaps. Like the gargoyles and archangels we have seen."

"Why didn't he raise the alarm when we entered?"

The necromancer shrugged.

Kentril stepped up to the horrific sculpture. With great care, he stretched forth his sword and tapped the figure on the chest.

Nothing happened. The eyes shut in pain did not open to condemn him; the mouth did not move to bite the foolish interloper's head off. The statue remained just that, a statue.

Feeling a little foolish, the captain turned back to the others. "Well, if Gregus Mazi isn't around here, we'd better—"

A chill ran up his spine, and he saw both of his companions' gazes suddenly widen—and focus not on Kentril, but rather *behind* him.

Captain Dumon spun around.

The eyes—the eyes that had stayed closed even after his

somewhat arrogant inspection—now did indeed glare madly at him.

The already open mouth let loose with a terrible, haunting cry.

All three men covered their ears as the harsh, painful sound overwhelmed all else. Over and over, the sentinel cried, the mad scream echoing throughout the chamber and well beyond.

For more than a minute, the horrific sound continued. Then, finally, the cry gradually lessened, enough so that at last the party could lower their hands.

And that was when they could finally hear the flapping of oncoming wings.

A flock of batlike forms darted into the chamber, shrieking wildly as they attacked. In the uncertain illumination, Kentril saw small, gray, demonic shapes no more than knee-high and looking vaguely like reptilian men. Talons akin to those of predatory birds slashed at the trio whenever one of the creatures passed overhead, and toothy maws sought bites of their flesh.

"*Alae Nefastus!*" shouted the necromancer. "Winged Fiends! Lesser demons but dangerous in quantity!"

And in quantity they had come. Kentril quickly ran one through the torso, watching with grim satisfaction as it fell twitching to the floor. Unfortunately, in its place came six new and very eager ones. Nearby, Gorst battered two with the flat of his ax, only to have another dig deep into his shoulder. The giant shouted in surprise and pain, even his muscular hide no match for the demon's razor-sharp nails.

They filled the chamber, their savage cries almost as terrible as the warning by the sentinel. The captain managed to slay two more yet still felt as if he accomplished nothing. Nevertheless, he continued fighting, the only other recourse not at all attractive.

One of the fiends dove past him, seeking instead Zayl. Opening his vast cloak, the necromancer trapped the small demon within.

A brief, muffled squeal escaped the creature . . . then a pile of brown ash dropped near the spellcaster's boot. Zayl released the cloak and focused on the other attackers.

"They must serve Gregus Mazi!" Kentril called. "That thing that screamed was meant to alert him!"

Zayl did not answer. Instead, the necromancer now shouted incomprehensible words at another group of fluttering terrors. At the same time, he drew a circle in their direction with the tip of the dagger.

The winged imps he had targeted, five in all, suddenly turned away and, to Kentril's surprise, began attacking their fellows. Two unsuspecting fiends perished under shredding talons before others began to assault in great numbers the traitors in their midst. In moments, the five ensorcelled demons had fallen, but not before taking two more with them.

An imp raked the captain across the cheek, splattering Kentril with his own blood. The wound stung so greatly it made his eyes water, yet he managed to catch the offending demon as it flew away, impaling it.

Unfortunately, even another death seemed not to deter the massive flock.

"There're too many!" grunted Gorst.

"Captain Dumon! If you and Gorst can fend them off me for a moment or two longer, I may be able to rid ourselves of this trouble!"

Seeing no other option, Kentril battled his way back to the necromancer, Gorst doing the same from the other side.

As the pair shielded Zayl, the cloaked mage again spoke in the unknown language. With the dagger he draw another glowing image, this one resembling to the mercenary officer an exploding star.

A haze suddenly filled the chamber, a noxious-smelling but otherwise seemingly harmless fog that rapidly spread to every corner, every crack, leaving no place untouched.

Yet if the haze did nothing to the trio save to irritate their nostrils and obscure their vision some, its effect on the winged demons proved anything but harmless. One by one, then by greater and greater numbers, the taloned fiends suddenly lost control. They collided with one another, crashed into the walls, even simply dropped to the floor of the chamber.

Once on the ground, the savage imps shook as if in the throes of madness. Gradually, their hisses and squawks became more feeble. Finally, they began to still, first a few, then more and more.

Soon all lay dead.

"*Zerata!*" called the necromancer.

The haze instantly faded away, leaving no trace.

Zayl suddenly staggered forward and would have dropped if not for Gorst's quick reflexes. The spellcaster leaned against the giant for a few seconds, then seemed to recover.

"Forgive me. The last took much out of me, for I had to say and control it perfectly, otherwise the effect would have been different."

"What do you mean?" Kentril asked.

"We would be lying there with the imps."

Gorst kicked at a few bodies, making certain that none pretended, then took a peek down the passage from which they had come. "Don't hear anything more."

"There were quite a few attacking us." Zayl joined the other mercenary near the passage. "It is quite possible that we destroyed the entire flock."

The giant nodded, then asked, "So where's their master?"

That had been a question on Kentril's mind as well. Were these creatures all that Gregus Mazi had been able to send after them? Why had he not attacked with some spell while the three had been distracted? Even the most basic tactician understood the value of such a maneuver.

Another thing bothered him. Turning back to the Key to Shadow, he stared at the artifact, wondering why Mazi had not simply removed the black crystal and shattered it on the floor. While it was perhaps possible that such a deed would have required far more effort than it appeared, Juris Khan had given every indication that his former friend had been a sorcerer of tremendous skill and cunning. Gregus Mazi should have been able to reduce the crystal to shards . . .

So why had he not destroyed the gemstone?

Any hesitation likely had nothing to do with the Key's monetary value, although Kentril knew of several dukes and other nobles back in the Western Kingdoms who would have paid him enough for the stone for the mercenary to retire in wealth. One could scarcely believe that it had been created from magic, so real did it look. Still, he had heard of few stones so perfect. Each facet seemed almost a mirror. In some, the captain could see himself reflected back. In others, he could make out the vague forms of his companions or even some of the dead imps. Captain Dumon could even make out details of the macabre sentinel's face . . .

Kentril spun around, gaze fixed on the eyes of the horrific figure. Of all the features of the monstrous sculpture, they showed the most precision, the most care.

They were the most human.

"There's no need to worry about looking for Gregus Mazi," Kentril called to the others. He tried to will the eyes to look his way, but they did not move. "I think I've found him."

Thirteen

"I think you must be correct, captain," Zayl quietly answered after studying the figure in detail. "Now that I have had a chance to cast a few spells of detection, I can swear that there is life in it."

"But how?" Kentril wanted desperately to know. "How could this be? How can this have happened to Mazi?"

The necromancer did not look at all pleased. "I can only assume that Juris Khan has not been forthcoming in his tales."

"That can't be! Lord Khan would never do anything like this. You know that."

"I am as deeply troubled as you by this discovery . . . and just as confused. I suppose it is quite possible that Lord Khan is also unaware of the true fate of his former friend, and, therefore, one must assume Khan's daughter is unaware also."

"Of course she is!" the captain snapped.

Gorst shook his head. "Can you do anything? Can you make him human again?"

"Alas, I fear not. This is far more complex than the curse upon our host. What I have been able to determine is that Gregus Mazi is more than just sealed to the stalactite. He is, in essence, a very part of the mountain. Such a spell cannot be reversed, I'm afraid."

"But he's still alive, you said," persisted the giant.

Zayl shrugged, to Kentril quite clearly disturbed more than he tried to show. "Yes, otherwise my spell to summon his shade would have worked the first time. If it is any

comfort, I suspect that if his mind survived after the transformation, then it has long since fallen into total madness. I
daresay he suffers no longer."

"I want to see," demanded a voice. "Take me out so I can
get a good look at him."

From the pouch, Zayl produced Humbart Wessel's skull.
Gorst looked on with some slight unease but overall more
interest. Kentril realized that he had forgotten to tell his
second of the necromancer's unique companion.

Holding the skull up high, Zayl let it examine the ghoulish display. Humbart said nothing save to direct the spellcaster to point the empty eye sockets this way or that.

"Aye, 'tis him," he remarked rather sadly. " 'Tis old
Gregus come to a more ill end than myself."

"Did you sense anything?" the necromancer asked.
"Any hint of who might have done this?"

"This is powerful sorcery, lad. I can't tell. Believe me,
I'm sorry. You're right on one thing, though; this can't be
changed. There's no way to make him human again."

Kentril tried hard not to think of what it must have been
like for the man. Had he suffered much? Had it been as
Zayl had suggested, that perhaps Gregus Mazi had been
cursed to this form with his mind still functioning? All
those centuries trapped like that, unable to move, unable
to do anything?

"But why?" the captain finally asked. "Why do this? It
looks like more than punishment. You saw what happened, Zayl. He let out a scream that alerted those winged
beasts!"

"Yes . . . apparently he is part of some method of warning." The necromancer turned toward the Key to Shadow.
"I am wondering if perhaps he did so because we were too
near this."

"That makes no sense! We'd be the last ones to want to
touch the crystal! Ureh needs that in place, too, or else it
won't matter that we set its counterpart atop Nymyr."

Zayl reached for the artifact as if to pick it up, at the

same time watching to see how the monstrous figure would react.

The all-too-human eyes suddenly widened, almost glaring at the presumptuous necromancer. However, this time, no scream alerted guardians, perhaps because there might not have been any left.

As Zayl withdrew his hand, they saw the eyes of the sentinel relax, then close again. The mouth remained open in mid-scream.

"He does guard it. Interesting. I recall that when you walked up to him, I shifted position slightly, which would have placed me about as near to the crystal as I was just now. That must have been what caused him to react."

"So what do we do now?" asked Gorst.

Kentril sheathed his blade. "There doesn't seem much at all for us to do. We might as well make our way back. There's no telling how far along Tsin might already be with the spell."

Zayl looked to the ceiling. "I still sense great forces at work, but you are correct. He may be done soon . . . and, as you said, there remains nothing of value for us to do here. We will retire to the palace and discuss this among ourselves in more detail."

"Hold on there!" called Humbart Wessel's skull. "You can't leave him like that."

"Now, Humbart—"

But the skull would not be silenced. "Are you good men or the kind of villain you thought old Gregus to be? Captain Dumon, what would you do if one of your fellows lay trapped and bleeding badly on the field of battle and you couldn't take him with you? Would you leave him for the enemy to do with as they pleased?"

"No, of course not . . ." The veteran officer understood exactly what the ghostly voice meant. You never left a comrade behind to be tortured by the foe. You either let him take his own course of action, or with your sword you did it for him. Kentril had been forced to such action more than once, and while he had never taken any pleasure in it, he had known that he had been doing his duty. "No . . . Humbart's right."

Drawing his weapon again, he approached the ensorcelled Gregus Mazi and, with much trepidation, started tapping at the torso in search of a soft enough spot. Unfortunately, his initial hunt revealed nothing but hardened minerals. The spell had been very thorough.

"Allow me to do it, captain. I think my blade will better serve." Zayl came forward with the ivory dagger, but Kentril stepped in front of him.

"Give the weapon to me, necromancer. I know where best to strike to kill a man quickly and cleanly. This has to be done right."

Bowing to the soldier's experience, the cloaked spellcaster turned over the dagger to Kentril. The captain studied the rune-inscribed blade for a moment, then turned his attention once more to Gregus Mazi.

As he raised the dagger to strike, the eyes of the limestone-encrusted sentinel suddenly opened, focusing upon Kentril with an intensity that made the fighter's hand shake.

On a hunch, he moved the dagger slightly to the side.

The eyes followed the weapon with especially keen interest.

There and then, Captain Dumon realized that the mind of the sorcerer remained intact. Insanity had not granted Gregus Mazi any escape from his tortured existence.

For just a short moment, Kentril hesitated, wondering if perhaps there might be some way yet to free the man, but then the eyes above his own answered that question, pleading for the soldier to do what he must.

"Heaven help you," the captain muttered.

With a prayer on his lips, Kentril thrust the dagger into the chest area with expert precision.

Not one drop of blood emerged from the wound. Instead, a brief gust of hot wind smelling of sulfur burst forth, almost as if Kentril had opened a way to some volcanic realm deep within the mountain. It startled the mercenary so much that he stepped back a pace, withdrawing the blade as he retreated.

He expected another hellish cry such as had brought the imps to attack, but instead only a tremendous sigh emerged from the frozen mouth. In that short-lived sigh, the captain heard more than just a death; he heard Gregus Mazi's relief at being at last released from his terrible prison. The eyes gave him an almost grateful look before quickly glazing over and closing for a final time.

"His curse is ended," whispered Zayl after a time. "He has left this terrible place." The necromancer gently took the dagger back from Kentril. "I suggest we do the same."

"Rest well, Gregus," the skull muttered.

Much subdued, the trio completed their ascension through the caverns in silence. They had gone in search of an evil sorcerer and found a fellow human being in torment. Nothing they had assumed had proven to be fact, and that bothered all of them, Kentril most of all.

Exiting through the shaft by which they had first entered the mountain, the fighters separated from Zayl, who advised that it might not be wise for the three of them to return together.

"I will spend some more time out here, then return as if from the city. We need to meet again later, captain. I feel we both have questions we wish answered."

Kentril nodded, then, with Gorst trailing, headed back to the palace. Although the unsettling events in the caverns remained an important part of his thoughts, Kentril could not help but think more and more about the outcome of Tsin's work as he neared Lord Khan's abode. Had that, too, gone awry? Was nothing to be as he had assumed it would be?

To his further apprehension, he and Gorst discovered the gates—the entire entrance, in fact—utterly unmanned. Worse, as they entered the ancient edifice, both quickly noticed that not a sound echoed throughout the vast palace, almost as if the deathly quiet of the abandoned ruins had swept once more over the kingdom. Down an ominously empty hall Kentril and the giant cautiously journeyed, searching in vain for some hint of life.

At last, they came across the massive doors to Juris Khan's sanctum. Kentril glanced at his friend, then reached forward . . .

The doors swung open of their own accord, revealing a reverent crowd kneeling before the dais occupied by the robed lord's tall, regal chair.

A chair now empty . . . for Juris Khan stood among his flock, reaching down now and then to touch guard, peasant, and courtier alike upon the back of the head, giving them his blessing. Near his side, Atanna followed, her expression enraptured. Utter silence filled the room, the silence of awe and respect.

Yet it seemed that even the wonder of her father's freedom could not withstand the pleasure Atanna manifested when she saw Kentril at the door. She immediately touched Lord Khan on the arm, indicating to him who stood at the entrance.

"Kentril Dumon!" the elder monarch called cheerfully. "Let you and your good man come forth and be part of the celebration, for surely you are as much a reason for this glorious moment as the masterful sorcerer!"

He indicated with one hand a very self-satisfied Quov Tsin. The Vizjerei stood far to the left side of the dais, fairly preening as courtiers both male and female moved to pay their humble respects. Tsin caught Kentril's gaze and gave the captain a triumphant look that contained not one iota of humility.

Urged on by Atanna, Captain Dumon strode toward the regal pair. The kneeling throng gave way for him with as much respect as they showed for their master. Never in his life had Kentril felt so awed by the simple fact that others honored him so much. He recalled all that Juris Khan had offered him and for the first time actually believed it could come to pass without trouble.

"My good Kentril!" Lord Khan gave him a strong, comradely hug with one arm while pulling his daughter near with the other. "This is a day of rejoicing as great as when the archangel first presented to me the hope of our salvation. Truly, the rebirth of Ureh as a beacon of light in the world is near at hand."

"I'm very happy for you, my lord."

The weathered yet noble face twisted into an expression of bemusement. "How certain I am of that. But look! Here is another more eager to express our gratitude and able to do so far better than I. If you'll excuse me, my son, I must show myself to the people beyond the palace walls. They must know that the end of our great curse is near at hand!"

Armored guards hurried to flank their master. The gathered throng rose as one behind Lord Khan, following him as he headed out the chamber for the first time. Atanna guided Kentril to the side so that they would not be swept away by the human flood. Gorst, grinning, let the pair be, the giant instead breaking his way through the crowd as he headed toward Quov Tsin.

"All my hopes," she breathed. "All my dreams . . . they come true at last, Kentril . . . and there is no one but you to thank for that!"

"I think you might thank Tsin some. He broke the spell on your father, after all."

Atanna would not hear his protests. "The Vizjerei master provided the mechanics of my father's freedom, but I know that you urged him on, you enabled him to convince my father that we would be served best and would serve best by not seeking the pathway to Heaven again." She leaned up and kissed him. "My thanks for all that."

"I'm just glad it went well."

"That it did, but all the while I worked with them, I couldn't help thinking of you . . . so much so I feared a couple of times that I might accidentally ruin the spell!"

Her eyes twinkled as she looked at him. "Much better to see you before me than only as imagination!" A brief frown graced her exquisite visage. "Why, Kentril, you're dusty, and your cheek is bloody! What's happened to you?"

In all the excitement, he had forgotten about his appearance. Kentril had not decided yet what to say about Gregus Mazi, so in the end he could only reply, "As a soldier, I'm used to training. I took a run outside, then a small climb." He shrugged. "I lost my hold once and slid down a few yards."

"How dreadful! You mustn't let that happen again. I won't have it. I won't lose you now!"

Although her reaction caused him to regret his lie, Kentril did not change his story. "I'm sorry to worry you."

But her mood had already begun to lighten. "Never mind. I've just realized that you must come with me to the grand balcony. You've never been there yet. That's where Father's gone now."

"Then we shouldn't bother—"

"No! You must be there!" She pulled him in the direction Juris Khan and his court had gone.

Because of its lofty location, the palace of Ureh's rulers had, of course, many balconies, but none so vast as the grand one upon which they found Atanna's father already standing. Kentril estimated it to be wide enough to hold more than a hundred people. With its gleaming white marble floor and stylishly crafted stone rail, it likely served also as a place where guests congregated during state functions. He even imagined that during the height of Ureh's power, it had acted as a place for elegant outdoor dining.

At the moment, however, it served a more important purpose. To the captain's astonishment, Lord Khan did not face his court, but rather leaned forward over the rail, calling down to the city below.

And evidently they could hear him well despite the distance, for cheers arose at some remark he made, cheers that lasted for quite some time.

Six guards stood in attendance near the white-robed figure, each bearing a torch that the captain assumed somehow enabled those in the city to see their master. Another half dozen soldiers stood watch, making certain that no one attempted something so foolish as to push Juris Khan over the edge. Kentril thought the precaution unnecessary; clearly everyone both nearby and below worshipped the elder leader.

"This is where Harkin Khan made the Speech of the Saints," Atanna told him. "This is where my grandfather, Zular Khan, married my grandmother and presented her to the people. This is where my father spoke the words of the archangel for all to hear."

"How can anyone possibly hear him all the way up here? Or even see him, for that matter?"

"Come look!"

Kentril had no intention of becoming part of the event, but Atanna proved quite determined. She pulled him forward, but far to the right of where Lord Khan continued to speak. As they reached the rail, Kentril noticed a pair of gleaming metal spheres with rounded openings pointed in the direction of the masses below.

"What are those?"

The scarlet-tressed woman pointed out an identical duo on her father's left. "They amplify and project the voice of whoever speaks from where Father stands. At the same time, an image several times larger can be seen clearly by the crowds below. They are very, very old, and the spellwork used to create them has been lost to us, yet still they function."

"Incredible!" Kentril remarked, feeling the word highly inadequate but unable to summon anything stronger.

Suddenly putting her finger to his lips, Atanna whispered, "Hush! You'll want to hear this."

At first, all Captain Dumon heard were more of the same promises of the future that Juris Khan had been announcing to his flock. He spoke of the ending of Ureh's trials, of once more the sun touching their flesh without burning it away. He talked of the new role the Light among Lights would play in the world, guiding it toward goodness and peace . . .

And then he began talking about Kentril.

The veteran mercenary shook his head, hoping that his host would stop. Khan, however, spoke at length about the captain's role—much of that role an exaggeration as far as Kentril could recall. To hear Ureh's ruler describe him, Kentril Dumon was a paladin extraordinary, a defender of the weak and challenger of evil wherever it lurked. The people below began to cheer loudly every time Lord Khan spoke his name, and several of those on the balcony twisted their heads to see this righteous paragon.

Then, to his even greater fear, Atanna's father gestured for Kentril to join him.

He would have refused, but Atanna gave him no choice, guiding him to where Juris Khan awaited. The benevolent lord again placed one arm around the fighter's shoulder, his other extended to his audience in the city.

"Kentril Dumon of Westmarch, officer at large, skilled commander . . . hero of Ureh." More cheering. "Shortly to take up a new mantle . . . general of this holy realm's defenders!"

This brought renewed cheering plus jubilant applause from the court. Kentril wanted nothing more than to melt into the background, but with Atanna tightly attached to his other side, he could not move.

"General Kentril Dumon!" Khan called. "Commander of the Realm, Protector of the Kingdom, Prince of the *Blood*!" The fatherly monarch smiled at Kentril. "And soon . . . I hope . . . member of my own house!"

And the cheers erupted with such fervor that it seemed

certain Nymyr would collapse from the sheer vibration. Kentril stood confused for a moment about what the last meant, but then Juris Khan placed the mercenary's hands atop Atanna's and eyed both with much favor.

Only then did the captain realize that his host had just given his blessing for the two to marry.

Atanna kissed him. Still dazzled, he followed her from the balcony, uncertain yet whether it had all been a dream. Hope filled him, true, but so did much uncertainty. Did he really dare to take on all that Ureh offered? General, prince, and royal consort?

"I must return to my father," Atanna whispered quickly. "I'll see you soon." She kissed him, then, with a last lingering glance, hurried back to the grand balcony.

"Well," said a voice near his ear. "My sincerest congratulations, captain—pardon me—my lord."

Kentril turned to find Zayl emerging from a shadowed corner. The necromancer nodded, then looked past him. "Quite a display."

"I never asked for anything—"

"But it is pleasing to receive it, is it not? At the very least, the affections of the glorious Atanna must put a thrill in your heart."

Not certain whether or not the cloaked figure mocked him, Kentril scowled. "What do you want?"

"Only to ask you how you found things when you entered. I became curious, I must admit, and decided to return to the palace earlier than I had said. To my surprise, there were no guards at the entrance, no people in the halls. I heard the noise from this direction and came just in time to hear you named heir to the throne."

"I'm not *heir*," the captain retorted. "I'll be royal consort if I marry her, not—" Kentril hesitated. In some lands, those who married a princess or the equivalent became ruler when the crown was finally passed. Had Juris Khan just made him future ruler of Ureh?

Zayl took one look at Kentril's questioning expression

and, with a hint of a smile, replied, "No, I do not know how the line of succession works in Ureh. You may be right . . . or you may not be right. Now, come! We likely have but moments together before she returns to see to your dressing properly for your new roles."

"What do you want to know?"

"Did you say anything about Gregus Mazi?"

Captain Dumon felt insulted. "I keep my word."

"I thought as much, but I had to ask." The necromancer's eyes narrowed to slits. "Tell me as best you can what has happened to you since you entered." When Kentril had related to him everything as detailed as the fighter could, Zayl frowned. "An interesting but uninformative tableau."

"What did you expect me to tell you?"

"I do not know . . . just that I felt that something should have given a hint to our next course of action." The necromancer sighed. "I will return to my quarters and meditate on it. If you should recall some significant moment that you forgot to mention, please come to me at once."

While he doubted very much that he had forgotten anything of value, Kentril promised Zayl that he would do as the spellcaster desired. As Zayl departed, Kentril suddenly thought again of his present condition, realizing that he had stood among the nobles and before the people of Ureh dressed in dusty, worn garments. Although it was already too late to rectify that situation, he could at least present a better image when next anyone, especially Atanna and Juris Khan, saw him. Surely now would be the time to don the regal dress uniform he had worn at the private dinner. At the very least, it would serve him until he could procure other appropriate clothing.

He started for his quarters, only to see down the hall Gorst and Tsin. The Vizjerei seemed quite disturbed by something the giant was saying, and when Tsin noticed

Kentril, he glared at the captain as if the latter had just burned down Ureh's treasure trove of magical tomes.

An uneasy feeling coursed through Kentril, and the glance Gorst gave him over his shoulder only strengthened that uneasiness. He picked up his pace, praying that he had read their faces wrong.

"I told him," Gorst said as his commanding officer neared. "I had to."

"By the seven-eyed demon Septumos, Captain Dumon! What were you thinking? Why was I not informed? Is everything this cretin said about the caverns and Gregus Mazi truth? I find it hard to believe—"

"If Gorst told you, then it's true," Kentril replied, cutting off the sorcerer's tirade. He had no time for this. What had the other mercenary been thinking? Gorst usually had a level head. Why would he include Tsin without first discussing it with his captain?

The Vizjerei shook his head in disbelief. "I should have been down there! Gregus Mazi! So many things he could've explained!"

"There wasn't much of anything that he could explain." Kentril eyed Gorst, who did not look at all ashamed. "You did tell him how we found Mazi, didn't you?"

Gorst nodded. "Everything. I had to, after what Master Tsin said."

"And what was that you said, Tsin?"

Drawing himself up, the robed sorcerer muttered, "I still don't know if this brute here has a point, but—"

"*What* did you say that set Gorst off, Tsin?"

For once he had made the Vizjerei uncomfortable. "The one trait that makes this one here more tolerable than the rest of you is his proper respect for all things magical. Because of that, I tolerated his questions about the work involved in casting my great spell. He wanted to hear about the difficulty and how I overcame it. He also—" Tsin broke off as Kentril stepped closer, hand on the hilt of his sword. "I'm coming to it! I told Gorst about the patterns and incantations I'd created to undo the clever binding of the curse and how all proceeded as smoothly as I'd expected it would."

If the bragging did not cease quickly, Captain Dumon suspected he would soon try to throttle the spellcaster regardless of the consequences. "Everything went well. You expected that. Not one hitch. I assumed—"

"Then you assumed wrong, cretin," the bearded figure snapped. "There *was* one point when I feared that all my hard work would come to naught, when something outside my control nearly ruined a carefully prepared work of art!" Quov Tsin tapped his staff on the floor. "I expected trouble only from the girl, a skilled wielder of power but one far too distracted by daydreams . . ." At this, he frowned hard at Kentril, an obvious hint to the captain being the cause of those distractions. "What I did not expect was someone as well-versed, as well-trained, as our *host* nearly to turn it all into disaster!"

"What did he do?" Kentril asked, suddenly unconcerned with such mundane things as dress uniforms and marrying the daughters of lords.

Tsin snorted. "Like a first-year apprentice, he did the unthinkable! We had come to the threshold, the point where there could be not the slightest fraction of an error. I had the girl drawing together the proper forces, while I, guiding them by words and gesture, worked to reverse that which had turned flesh, wood, and stone to one. Had it been more than simply his legs, the complexity might have been too great even for me, but, fortunately, that was not the case. I—"

"*Tsin—*"

"All right, all right! He *moved*, cretin! Juris Khan, whose task was to focus his power, his will, from within in order to foment changes to the spell structure of his own body, *moved!*"

The Vizjerei leaned back, as if what he had said explained everything. Kentril, however, knew that there had to be more. Gorst did not overreact.

"He did more'n just move," the giant interjected, now as impatient as his captain with the sorcerer. "Tsin says he almost leapt up, Kentril! Leapt up as if someone lit a fire underneath him. And from how Tsin describes it, I'd say it happened right about the time you put the dagger through Gregus Mazi's *chest*."

Fourteen

Gorst's unsettling suggestion remained with Captain Dumon long after the three had separated. Kentril did not yet know what to make of the notion that somehow Juris Khan had reacted to Mazi's death, but the implications did not bode well. That Tsin had been unable to offer any other idea that sufficiently explained the reaction did not help, either.

Despite that, the Vizjerei had not completely accepted Gorst's concerns that their host hid some secret from them, and neither could Kentril. However, the captain had to admit to himself that a tremendous part of his own reluctance had to do with the honors Lord Khan had bestowed upon him, especially the upcoming marriage to his daughter. As for Quov Tsin, his reasons for reluctance were even more obvious; the vast collection of Ureh's magical library lay open to him for as long as he had the good graces of the elder ruler.

Sleeping on it did little good for Kentril, for even his dreams turned to the troubling development. In truth, he welcomed the unexpected knock on his chamber doors, for the noise stirred him from a dream in which Juris Khan proved to be Gregus Mazi in disguise and Atanna the willing lover of the masked villain.

Although he hoped that it would be Khan's wondrous daughter at the door, Captain Dumon instead found himself facing a rather pensive Albord. Kentril's first fear was that some of the other men had gone missing, but the younger mercenary quickly erased that fear. Unfortunately, in its place he presented one that in some ways disturbed his commander even more.

"Captain, the men want to leave."

"No one goes into the city until I say so."

Albord shook his head. "Captain . . . they want to leave *Ureh*. They want to go home . . . and I think they should be able to."

This time, Kentril could think of no good reason to hold them back. He had a life offered to him here, but the others wanted only to return to the Western Kingdoms. They might have even had their rewards by now if not for his own hesitation.

"All right, give me a few days, and I'll see that our host makes sure each—"

Now Albord looked even more uncomfortable. "Captain, Jodas and Orlif have already talked to him."

Kentril almost seized the white-haired mercenary by the throat, but fought back the impulse before he could betray himself. "When? When did they do it?"

"Just a little while ago. I only found out myself after they came to me. They said they told his lordship that they had to go, and would he be still granting them that which he'd promised."

"And Khan said he would?"

"To listen to them, he hugged each like a brother and promised that every man would have a full sack!"

There existed no doubt in Kentril's mind that the fatherly ruler had done just that, yet another example of graciousness that made it difficult to fathom what tie existed between the saintly monarch and the mysterious Mazi. The captain leaned on a nearby chair, trying to organize his thoughts. What could he do, though, but accept their departure as wisely and kindly as Juris Khan had? After all, by rights, they could do as they pleased now. Their contract to Tsin had ended long ago.

"Can't say as I blame them," he finally responded.

"And they're probably safer out of Ureh, at least for now. So how long before you all leave?"

"They want to go when next it's day beyond Nymyr, captain. I'd say that's basically tomorrow." Albord straightened. "I'm not going with them, sir."

"You're not?"

The plowboy face lit up. "Captain, I thought about it a lot after the last time I mentioned leaving. Under you, I've learned more than I ever would've back in my village. I've got family there like everyone else has somewhere, but they knew I might not return for a long time, if ever. I'd like to stay on awhile longer after all." He grinned. "Leastwise, I can always go home sayin' I served under a prince!"

The words brought some relief to Kentril. "You sure you don't want to go with them?"

"My mind's staying made up this time, sir."

"All right. I'll see they're sent off right. They've done well . . . you've *all* done well."

A grin as great as any Gorst had ever given spread across Albord's youthful visage. "Appreciate that, captain—my *lord*. I'll be happy to volunteer to escort them to the outer gates of the kingdom, though."

The task seemed simple and safe enough, even with the yet-unexplained disappearances of the three other men. Kentril still suspected that, like him, each had been lured to a more deserted area, then knifed. The odds were their bodies would never be found. Still, so long as Albord kept in the open where the crowds could see him, he would be safe.

"I'll be glad to give you that pleasure, lad . . . and thanks for the loyalty."

Giving his commanding officer a sharp salute, Albord left. Kentril started back to his bed, but his thoughts would now not leave his men. He could not help wondering if even one of the vanished trio could have been saved if he had let the men go home sooner. To die on the field of battle was one thing for a mercenary, to end up tossed into an alley with a dagger in your spine was another. For that matter, Kentril did not even know if the men had actually been slain; it was possible that they still lived as prisoners or—

Prisoners?

Captain Dumon bolted upright. He knew of one way to tell . . .

Kentril found the necromancer in one of the rooms farthest away from the others, a special request, it appeared, from Zayl himself. The spellcaster did not respond to his quiet knock, but something made the fighter certain that he would find Zayl within. Kentril knocked again, this time quietly calling out the other's name.

"Enter," came the unmistakable hollow voice of Humbart Wessel.

Slipping inside, Kentril discovered the necromancer seated on the floor, his legs folded in, his hands on his knees, and his eyes staring straight at the ivory dagger that hung suspended in the air before him. Zayl's vast cloak lay on the bed. Atop a small wooden table to the side, the skull had been set so it faced the doorway.

"Hallo, lad!" it cheerfully greeted him. "He does this two to three times a day, if he can. Mind completely disappears from this world . . ."

"How long does he stay like this?" whispered the captain.

The necromancer's left hand suddenly moved. At the same time, the dagger dropped toward the floor, only to be caught by the hand.

"As long as need be," Zayl remarked, quickly unfolding his legs, then rising in one smooth action.

The skull chuckled. "Just in case, though, he leaves me pointed at the door. Anyone comes in, I give the alarm."

Zayl gave Humbart a dark look. "And I am still waiting to hear it."

" 'Tis only our good comrade Kentril Dumon, boy! I recognized his voice right away."

"While I have nothing against you, captain, what Humbart fails to remember is that you might not be alone . . . or you might not even be you. There are spells of illusion that can fool almost anyone, even the overconfident dead." The slim, pale man retrieved his cloak. "Now, what is it I can do for you?"

"I came because . . . because an idea occurred to me based on your own experiences."

"And that would pertain to—?"

The captain found his gaze drifting to the skull. "Three of my men have never returned from the city. The rest, by the way, are making plans to leave come the morrow. Before that happens, though, I may need them to plan a rescue."

He had Zayl's full attention now. "A rescue? You have reason to believe that the missing ones still live?"

"That's where you come in. I remembered all of a sudden that you said the reason for your earlier failure had to do with Gregus Mazi actually still being alive. You then used a different spell to locate his general surroundings—"

"And you wish me to attempt to do the same for those of your command now lost." The necromancer frowned in thought. "I can see no reason why it should not work—and perhaps it might yet shed some light on this shadowed land. Yes, captain, I would be glad to try."

"How soon can you start?"

Zayl reached for the skull, placing it in the pouch hidden by his cloak. "I cannot do anything until we find some personal item or, better yet, a hair or clipping from any of the three. Would it be prudent at this time to visit the quarters they used?"

Doubting that anyone would question the company's captain wanting to investigate the missing men's belongings for some clue to their disappearance, Kentril readily nodded. That seemed all the necromancer needed to sat-isfy himself. With a wave of his hand, he indicated for the captain to lead on.

In that most rare of circumstances for a mercenary, the kindness of their host had enabled each man of the hired company to have rooms of his own. Some, like Kentril, had become so used to cramped quarters or sleeping without a roof at all that they had barely made use of more than the bed. Others, meanwhile, had taken advantage of the situa-tion to the point where the few items they had lay scat-tered everywhere. Kentril felt certain that they would find something useful in the rooms of all three.

Which made it all the more startling when, upon enter-ing the first set of rooms, they found no trace of habitation at all.

When Kentril had first stepped into his own chambers, he had not been able to imagine anyone else ever having entered them before. From the silky, gold-threaded draperies to the wide, plush, canopied bed, everything in sight had looked absolutely new. Both the bed frame and the elegant furniture had been meticulously carved from the finest oak, a wood that the captain could not recall hav-ing seen anywhere in eastern Kehjistan, then stained a dark, rich reddish brown. Besides the bed, the main room in his quarters came equipped with a sturdy bronze-handled cabinet, four chairs, and a pair of tables—the wide one possibly used for dining and the other a small twin near the doorway. The filigreed walls had also been accented by a series of small but detailed tapestries that seemed to outline the early history of Ureh.

Beyond the main room, the smaller of the two lesser chambers gave the occupant a place for personal care, including rarely seen plumbing, a true mark of the wealth wielded by Lord Khan and his predecessors. The remain-ing room consisted of a pair of leather chairs, a tiny but no less elegant table, and a shelf filled with books. Out of mild curiosity, Captain Dumon had picked over the collection in his own chambers, but he knew that most of his men could not even decipher letters, much less read.

Brek's rooms had been chosen first, and one quick survey of them led the captain to decide quickly that someone else had straightened up after the mercenary's disappearance. Brek had not been the most organized of fighters and certainly not one of the cleanest; there should have been food, empty bottles, and more lying about. Even the bearded warrior's pack, which he would have left in the palace during his sojourns down to the city, had vanished.

"This is most troubling," Zayl quietly remarked.

A quick hunt through the rooms of the other two brought the same unsettling results. All had been arranged as if they had never been occupied by the hardened mercenaries. Even Kentril, who kept his quarters neater than most of his kind, could not match the cleanliness.

He sought out Gorst, whom he found playing cards with Albord and two other men. The fighters rose as he entered the giant's quarters, but Kentril quickly ordered them at ease.

"Who's been in Brek's rooms? Anyone?" When all four shook their heads, he focused on Albord, whose own quarters sat next to those of the missing man. "You've heard nothing through the wall?"

"Not since the last time Brek himself was in there . . ."

Letting them return to their game, Captain Dumon rejoined the necromancer. It did not please Kentril to see that the generally calm Zayl looked quite irked by what they had discovered.

"The palace has many servants," the latter solemnly proposed. "They move with a silence and swiftness worthy of my brethren, but it is very possible that they removed the belongings for some custodial reason."

"Or they didn't expect the boys to return," countered Humbart from the pouch.

Kentril felt defeated . . . and even more anxious than ever. "Is there nothing you can do, then?"

Holding up the dagger, Zayl muttered under his breath. The enchanted blade flared bright. The necromancer held the dagger before him, letting it sweep across the room.

"What're you up to?"

"I am trying to see if any useful trace at all was left behind. A single hair hidden under a chair, a scrap of cloth accidentally covered by a blanket . . ." No sooner had he explained, however, then the necromancer lowered the blade in mild disgust. "None of which I can find in this particular place. I am sorry, captain."

"Maybe we can—"

Before Kentril could finish, the door swung open, and Atanna appeared. "Why, here you are!"

She swept toward the fighter, Zayl seemingly nonexistent. Kentril accepted a swift kiss from her, then discovered himself being conducted out of the room.

"And you've changed back into that horrid, old outfit!" She *tsk*ed at him, sounding more like a mother hen than the desirable enchantress at which he stared. "You must dress before it's too late! Father already expects us there!"

"Where?" Kentril could recall no urgent matter.

"Why, for a formal introduction to the court, of course. You must be known to everyone before you officially take up the roles Father's promised you. It would be bad form otherwise."

"But—" Despite his uncertainties, despite the surmounting questions concerning Lord Khan, Captain Dumon found himself once again defenseless against the charms of the crimson-tressed princess. Atanna had come to him clad in a white-and-green gown fit perfectly to her well-curved form and designed, as it seemed with everything she wore, to utterly bewitch him.

"Now, you mustn't argue," she returned, guiding him to his own rooms. "I'll wait for you, but you must hurry! This is very important for your future here, Kentril"—her eyes seemed to shine like jewels—"and for *ours* as well."

And against that last point, his final defenses fell.

Away went any concerns about the secrets of Gregus Mazi, about any subterfuge by Juris Khan . . . and any doubt that he would be Atanna's slave forever.

Despite some faint amusement concerning how completely overwhelmed the good captain had proven to be in the presence of Juris Khan's glorious daughter, Zayl otherwise worried about the man. Kentril Dumon surely had to feel caught between trust and betrayal, love and lies. Not trained as followers of Rathma were in the cultivation and control of emotions, the mercenary risked making a fatal misstep. Zayl hoped that would not be the case, for he knew that the captain remained his best ally. The giant Gorst could be trusted, yes, but lacked some of Kentril Dumon's battle-honed wits. As for Quov Tsin, if the Vizjerei ever proved Zayl's only hope, then surely they were all very much doomed.

But doomed to what? The key, he suspected, had something to do with the three missing men. More and more, the necromancer distrusted the notion that they had simply perished at the hands of common street thugs. No, he felt that there had to be something darker, something more ominous going on.

A check of the rooms inhabited by the other two missing mercenaries revealed the same lack of clues. Zayl considered mesmerizing one of the servants into revealing what had happened to the men's effects, but not only did that seem likely to earn him the watchful eye of their host, he could also not *find* any of the attendants. As the necromancer had remarked to Captain Dumon, they indeed moved as if trained by Zayl's own people, a curious thing to think about liveried servants. Yet another confounding piece of a puzzle whose image he had yet to divine.

"One hair, one piece of nail," he murmured as he finished his second search of the last set of rooms. "Not so much to ask, but apparently too much to hope for."

One single strand, one follicle, and he could have done

as he had in the sanctum of Gregus Mazi. Zayl did not like being thwarted by such minuscule things; surely the forces that sought to keep the mortal world in balance did not intend such frustration. Zayl only wished that he could have—

The necromancer froze in the act of putting away the dagger, his mind suddenly aflame with a realization that he had been ignoring an entire path open to him all this time. Captain Dumon had actually brought it up, but, focused on the mercenary officer's actual reason for coming to him, Zayl had lost sight of it. The possible answer to all their questions shouted to be heard, and the spellcaster had been blithely deaf to it.

When first Zayl had sought the shade of Gregus Mazi, the latter had not been dead.

But now the sorcerer was . . . put down mercifully by the necromancer's party after discovering his horrific plight.

"I am a fool!" he uttered.

"Are you looking for argument?" came Humbart's voice.

He looked down at the pouch. "Gregus Mazi is dead!"

"Aye, and it's nothing to cheer, you hear me, lad?"

But Zayl did not answer him, already departing the emptied chamber for his own. He would set up the patterns, arrange the spell—

No! His room would never do. During the course of their search, the captain had told Zayl of Juris Khan's disturbing reaction during Tsin's spellwork. The necromancer suddenly wondered if seeking the ghost of the sorcerer would be a wise thing to do in the very sanctum of the one who had claimed, either erroneously or falsely, to have slain him.

At the very least, it would pay to perform the spell elsewhere, and Zayl could think of no better location than the mouth of the cave leading to where they had found what had remained of the unfortunate mage.

It took the necromancer little time to retrieve what he

needed from his quarters and even less time to exit the palace by secret means. Zayl had memorized the layout to the edifice well, suspicious, somehow, that it would prove opportune later. Part of a calling held in mistrust and apprehension among most folk, he had done so out of habit. One never knew when an overzealous official might decide to make his mark by capturing and disposing of the "evil" summoner of the dead.

In some ways, escaping to the shaft filled Zayl with more assurance. Born to the jungle lands, he was distracted by the confining qualities of any building, even one so massive as the palace. Now, outside, he felt as if he could breathe again. His wits seemed to grow sharper, so much so that the necromancer had to ask himself again why he had not thought to attempt a new summoning of Gregus Mazi once the latter had actually perished. So much time wasted . . .

With the dagger to light his way, Zayl headed several yards into the shaft. Finding a fairly open part of the corridor, the necromancer squatted down and began to draw patterns in the dirt floor with the glowing blade. The spell Zayl planned would be virtually identical to the one he had cast in Gregus Mazi's sanctum, the only difference being some added symbols to increase the odds of success.

From out of the pouch he took Humbart's skull, three small candles, and a single strand of hair. Putting the skull to the side, Zayl arranged the candles, then placed the hair in the center. After pricking his finger and letting the necessary number of drops of blood fall onto the one hair, the necromancer lit each of the candles with the tip of his blade, then proceeded with the incantation.

A slight breeze arose in the shaft. Zayl quickly paused in his efforts, moving so as to block the wind before it could blow the hair away. Satisfied, he started his work anew.

Suddenly, the wind came at the display from the other side. Zayl frowned, recalling no such turbulent currents during his previous visit. He sniffed the air, seeking the scent of magic, but found none.

"Trouble?" asked the skull.

"A minor nuisance." Taking some rocks, the spellcaster built a small wall to protect everything.

Once more, he began muttering. This time, no wind interrupted. Zayl focused his gaze on the hair, thinking of the dead sorcerer.

As before, smoke arose above the hair where the blood touched it, the smoke then taking on a vaguely humanoid shape. As the necromancer advanced in his spell, the smoke swelled tremendously, growing as tall as a man and taking on more and more the characteristics of one. Zayl could make out a robed form, a man in a sorcerer's garb. The figure seemed to be reaching out, at the same time trying to speak.

"Gregus Mazi, I summon thee!" Zayl called. "Gregus Mazi, I conjure thee! I call upon thee to walk the mortal plane for a time more, to come to me and share your knowledge!"

And in the smoke, there formed an imposing, black-haired figure more like Kentril Dumon than either the necromancer or the Vizjerei. Broad of shoulder, determined of face, Gregus Mazi looked not at all like the viper he had been portrayed as and more like a legendary protector.

"Bit younger than when I saw him," Humbart remarked.

"Quiet!" Zayl had not yet bound the spirit to him, and until he did, any interruption risked breaking the summoning.

He muttered more, then with the dagger drew a double loop in the air. Mazi's flickering ghost solidified, becoming so distinct that ignorant onlookers might have believed that they could actually touch him. In truth, had Zayl worked hard, he could have created an even more substantial specter, but the necromancer had no need of such and respected the dead mage too much even to try to bind him so.

Soon, very soon, the spell would be complete. Then only Zayl would be able to dismiss the shade without the most extreme effort.

And as he became more a part of the mortal world, Gregus Mazi tried once more to speak. His mouth opened, but no sound escaped him. He continued to try to reach for the other spellcaster, but moved as if caught in some thick fluid. Only the eyes managed to express anything definite, and in them Zayl saw an urgent need to communicate a message, perhaps the very information he and the captain had sought.

"Gregus Mazi, let air once more fill your lungs! Let speech be yours as I permit it! Let the words you wish to speak be heard!"

The dead sorcerer moaned. With grim determination, he thrust a finger toward Zayl and at last forced a single word from his gaping mouth.

"*Diablooooo!*"

And as he spoke, Mazi's appearance transformed. His sorcerer's robe, briefly a resplendent blue and gold and covered with holy wards, *burst* into flames. The finger that pointed in warning shriveled rapidly, becoming skeletal. Likewise, the strong, determined visage melted away, leaving until the end the staring, warning eyes . . .

"Zayl, lad! Look out!"

Craggy, monstrous hands of rock suddenly thrust forth from the walls, catching the necromancer from both in front and behind. They forced the air from Zayl's lungs, and it was all he could do to keep from being immediately crushed to a pulp.

In his struggles, he kicked apart the display. Now bound to the necromancer, the monstrous ghost of Gregus Mazi should have remained fixed where it was, but instead it instantly faded away, the single word of warning still on its lipless mouth.

Zayl still had the dagger, but with his arms clamped awkwardly to his body, he could not raise it. With the vestiges of breath left to him, the desperate spellcaster shouted out words of power.

"Beraka! Dianos Tempri! Berak—"

He could not force anything more out. A rumbling shook the cave, and somewhere distant Zayl heard Humbart Wessel's voice calling to him.

The necromancer blacked out.

Fifteen

Juris Khan did not shirk when it came to rewarding the mercenaries who had chosen to depart. Kentril marveled at the riches he rained upon the men—gold coins, glittering diamonds, scarlet rubies, and so much more. The only limit to what the men received had to do with how much they themselves could carry, for the lord of Ureh had no horses or other animals to give them. That did not seem to bother Jodas and the rest, though; they found the bounty they had received more than sufficient.

"Come back to us again once Ureh stands among the mighty kingdoms of the world, and I shall make amends," Lord Khan informed them. "All of you are ever welcome here!"

The soldiers' host had arranged a ceremony in the grand chamber where once he had been imprisoned. A legion of courtiers clad in their finest flanked Kentril and the rest, clapping enthusiastically at various points during their master's speech. Kentril had met many of the nobles at least twice now, but still could not recall any names. Other than Atanna and her father, those in the palace seemed almost of a single kind, voices constantly in echo of the great Lord Khan. That did not entirely surprise the captain, of course, for powerful rulers often ended up surrounded by such, and in a realm as blessed as Ureh, what reason would anyone have to do otherwise? Juris Khan had seen them through the worst that anyone could possibly imagine.

Kentril himself bid the men farewell once the ceremony

had ended. He reminded the six of the safest route possible through the jungle and emphasized the importance of avoiding the deeper waterways. "Once you reach Kurast, the way should be clear. Just try not to let anyone see everything you bring with you."

"We'll be careful, cap'n," Orlif bellowed.

Gorst clapped each man on the back, sending most staggering, and like a dutiful parent told them to remember everything the captain had taught them.

At a signal from Albord, the six saluted their commander, then headed out. Kentril and Gorst followed the party to the outer gate, wishing each man the best again.

Although the breaking up of a company always affected Captain Dumon more than he revealed, watching his surviving men depart now nearly shattered the mask of strength he generally wore at such times. Bad enough that so many would not be returning home, but the dark shadow cloaking the kingdom made him feel as if the six left in the dead of night. Both the men and their escort carried torches just so that they could see the steep steps. While Kentril knew that just beyond Nymyr the sun had only an hour before risen, he could not help worrying about nighttime predators or enemy warriors hiding in the dark. Even knowing such vile dangers existed mostly in his mind, it was all the captain could do not to go chasing after the others.

"Think they'll be okay?" Gorst asked suddenly.

"Why do you ask?"

The giant shrugged. "Dunno. I guess I always feel bad when others go."

Chuckling at this reflection of his own concerns, Kentril responded, "They're together, armed, and know where they're going. You and I made it back from the mountains of northern Entsteig with only one sword between us." He watched the torches, now the only visible sign of the party, descend into the city. "They'll do just fine."

When even the torches could not be singled out among

all the other fires illuminating Ureh, the duo headed back to the palace. Lord Khan had given some hint of planning to speak with Quov Tsin about the work needed to settle the kingdom completely in the real world and remove the last vestiges of the vile spell. However, what interested Kentril more had been the knowledge that Atanna awaited him within. More than ever, he longed for her lips, her eyes, her arms. The departure of the others signified to him the end of his life as a mercenary and the beginning of something astounding. If not for the concerns he and Zayl had regarding the truth about Gregus Mazi, Kentril would have considered himself at that moment the luckiest man alive.

Thinking of the necromancer, he asked Gorst, "Have you seen Zayl lately?"

"Not since you tried to find out about Brek and the others."

When the captain had finally managed to ask Juris Khan what had happened to the quarters of the missing trio, the elder monarch had expressed complete puzzlement and a promise to have the matter investigated by one of his staff. He had spoken with such honest tones that Kentril could not disbelieve him. In fact, Kentril had even wanted to find Zayl afterward in order to tell the spellcaster of his certainty that Lord Khan could have had nothing to do with the clearing out of the mercenaries' belongings. Unfortunately, even then he could not find the necromancer.

"Keep an eye out for him. Tell him I need to see him as soon as possible."

Gorst hesitated, a rare thing for the generally sure-minded giant. "Think he's gone the way of Brek?"

Kentril had not considered that. "Check his room. See if his gear is still there." The Rathmian had few personal articles, but surely he would have left something behind. "If you discover his room just like theirs, come running."

"Aye, Kentril."

Now it was Captain Dumon who paused, his gaze turning to the flickering torches and lamps of eternally darkened Ureh. By now, Albord and the men would be well on their way to the city's outer gate. In an hour, two at most, Jodas, Orlif, and the other four would greet the sunlight.

"Kentril?"

"Hmm? Sorry, Gorst. Just wondering."

"Wondering what?"

The veteran mercenary gave his second a rueful smile. "Just wondering if I'll regret us not having left with them."

The gathered crowd cheered and waved as Albord and the others marched through the city. It looked to the young officer as if every citizen had come to see his fellows off. Never in his short career had he imagined such acknowledgment from others. Captain Dumon had warned him from his first day that a mercenary's life was generally a harsh, unappreciated one, but this moment made every past indignity more than worth it.

"Sure you don't want to come with us, Alby?" Jodas called. "Another good arm's always welcome!"

"I'm sticking here, thanks." Albord had few regrets about staying behind, despite his earlier desire to see his family. How better to return in, say, a year and show them what he had reaped as one of Captain Dumon's aides. Lord Khan had already announced as a certainty the captain's elevation to the nobility, his command of the military forces of the holy kingdom, and the upcoming marriage to the monarch's own daughter—possibly the greatest prize of all in Albord's mind.

"Well, maybe we'll come visit you again," the other mercenary returned with a short laugh. He hefted the sack containing his reward. "After all, this can't last forever!"

The rest laughed with him. They all had a king's ransom. Each man could live in wealth for the rest of his life and still have much left over. True, mercenaries were gambling men, but Albord doubted that the worst of them would go broke before a few years had passed.

"These jokers know the way to their own city gates?" Orlif grunted, referring to the six armored guards making up their farewell escort. Solemn and silent, they marched in unison even Captain Dumon's strict training had never managed to perfect among his men. "Seems like forever to reach it, and this load ain't goin' to get any lighter!"

"If those heavy sacks are slowing you down," Albord jested, "I'll be glad to watch 'em for you until you get back from Westmarch!"

Again, the men all laughed. Albord felt a hint of withdrawal; he would miss them, but his odds were much better with his captain. He had always sensed a greatness, and now that had been more than proven.

"There it is at last," one of the others cried. "Only an hour past there, lads, and we'll be smilin' in the sun! Won't that be a welcome sight?"

To Albord, the gates stood so very tall. When the party had first come to investigate the ruins, the gates had still been shut, almost as if yet trying to protect Ureh's secrets. Rusted relics then, the recreated gates now looked far more imposing. At least twelve feet high and so very, very thick, they could have barred an army trying to force its way inside. As with the doors of the palace, winged archangels brandishing fiery swords acted as centerpieces for each of the pair, and as with the other doors, those figures had been battered brutally by some force. Albord vaguely wondered again how the damage had occurred. Had some vassal of the sinister Gregus Mazi he had heard about taken to trying to destroy the symbols of Heavenly power?

The honor guard stopped at the gates, turning to face the departing soldiers. Their solemn, almost expressionless faces made Albord nearly reach for his sword, only at the last the white-haired fighter realizing how foolish that would have looked.

Then a strange silence fell over the crowd, a silence

made all the more obvious by the distant sounds of continual celebration, the same sounds that had gone on without pause ever since Captain Dumon had set the magical gem in place atop the peak. Albord looked around, discovered that all the faces had turned to him, waiting.

Jodas and the other found nothing wrong with the scene and, in fact, eyed him impatiently. "Time to say our goodbyes, Alby. Got to be goin' . . ."

Caught up again in the moment, the departing mercenaries shared handshakes and back slaps with the young officer. Albord had to struggle to keep tears from showing and found it amusing to discover that Jodas and Orlif, among others, clearly suffered from the same affliction.

"Be better if you go off before we step out," Jodas suggested as the honor guard started to open the gates. "Good luck and all that, you know."

Many mercenary companies had a variety of superstitions, one of those among men from Westmarch being that if you didn't actually see your comrades walk out the gates, then there stood a good chance you would be seeing them again soon. Seeing them step through meant the definite possibility of never reuniting—and the likelihood that some had perished elsewhere afterward. Mercenaries lived too chancy a life not to take to heart whatever beliefs might help them survive. In fact, that had been in great part why their captain and second-in-command had remained at the palace in the first place.

Giving the six one last wave, Albord marched off. Still uncertain about his control of his emotions, he did not look back and suspected that the others imitated his ways. The continual noises of celebration began to get on his nerves, for he felt no reason for cheer at the moment. Even the thought of his own future in Ureh did not assuage him at the moment.

Louder and louder the merrymakers grew, the most adamant sounds coming now from behind him, where he had left his comrades. Albord quickened his pace; once he returned to the palace, surely his nerves would settle and he would recall all the good reasons he had chosen not to leave with Jodas and the rest.

But at that moment, a voice just barely audible over the raucous cries caught his attention. Albord paused, trying to understand what he had just heard. The voice had sounded like Orlif's—and the man had been calling the white-haired fighter's name.

Albord took a step toward Juris Khan's abode, but the sudden uncertainty made him pause. What harm would it do to go back and check? If he had heard Orlif, then surely they wanted something of him. If he had been mistaken about even hearing the man, there would be no trouble or danger of bad luck, for by this time surely the six had long vanished through the gates.

He turned back. It would take him but a minute or two to discover whether or not he had heard Orlif. At least, then, Albord could be satisfied that he had done all he could.

The shouts of merriment had risen so high now that they actually hurt his ears. Did these people never rest? Had they nothing more to do than celebrate? True, they had much reason for their happiness, but even a mercenary liked peace and quiet on occasion. The sooner Albord returned to the palace, the better. At least there he could find some escape from the carefree madness spread among the populace—

A short-lived scream cut through the air.

Drawing his sword, the young fighter raced the rest of the way to the gates. Perhaps he had been wrong, but he swore to himself that the scream had sounded as if torn from the throat of *Jodas*. Albord rounded the final corner—

And came across a tableau of terror that stopped him dead in his tracks.

A sea of horrific, shambling corpses—husks of bodies, to be precise—swarmed together like the hungry, vicious fish he had seen once in the jungle rivers. Clad in tattered, soiled garments, they madly fought one another as they all sought to claim some prize in their midst. Their gaping mouths, rounded and full of sharp teeth, opened and closed repeatedly. A few to the side could be seen feeding, their gnarled, skeletal hands gnawing on some bloody bit of meat.

From within the ever-growing mass, a human figure struggled his way to the top.

Orlif, his face ripped, his arms drenched with his own blood, cut with his sword, trying to reach freedom. From where he stood in shock, Albord could see that most of the mercenary's other hand had been either torn or bitten off.

Orlif saw him, and what Albord caught in that pleading gaze made him more terrified than he ever could have thought possible.

Then suddenly something tugged at the older fighter from within the hungering mass of fiends. Orlif let out one hopeless cry—and was dragged back down among them.

"No!" The shout escaped Albord before he could stop himself.

Empty eye sockets stared unerringly at the stunned soldier. Ghoulish shapes began to turn his direction.

Sense at last returned . . . and Albord turned and ran as fast as he could.

Throughout the monstrous, grisly scene, the music, laughter, and cheers had continued unabated. Albord looked this way and that as he ran, but of the merrymakers themselves he saw no sign. It was as if a city of ghosts celebrated around him.

Then, from an alleyway, one of the grotesque, shambling forms reached for him. Albord leapt aside, slashing with his sword as he hurried on. The sharp edge cut through one of the wrists, sending the clawed, cadaverous hand flopping to the ground. However, undeterred by the loss of its appendage, the ghoulish fiend followed after the mercenary.

The palace. If he could reach the palace, Albord felt

certain that he would be safe. Captain Dumon would be there, and he would know what to do.

As he ran, the city itself began to change, with each second growing as twisted and deathly as its foul inhabitants. Buildings rapidly decayed or crumbled, and what seemed like thick blood slowly poured over rooftops onto cracked walls and parched earth. The sky took on a sickly color, and the smell of rotting, burnt flesh assailed the young fighter's nose.

In the distance, though, the palace of Juris Khan looked untouched. Albord focused on the one bit of sanity in a world now gone mad. Each step took him closer and closer to salvation.

Then, to his horror, he found the way blocked. A horde of desiccated, hungry corpses moved slowly and purposely toward him from the very street that would have led him directly to the stone steps. Rounded, toothy mouths opened and closed in anticipation of a new feast. The stench they exuded turned the frantic fighter's stomach, and it was all he could do to keep from falling to his knees and throwing up.

Albord looked left, finding an open side street. Without hesitation, he raced into it, hoping that it would open up onto a path leading to the steps.

Something in the shadows caught his arm. Albord found himself face-to-face with one of the ghouls, a mockery of feminine form, a dry husk clad in the shreds of what had once been a very feminine, very revealing golden outfit. Strands of hair draped around the horrific visage, and the mouth opened wide in anticipation.

"Come, handsome soldier," it rasped in a voice straight out of the grave. "Come play with Nefriti . . ."

"Let go of me, hellspawn!" With wild abandon, Albord struck at the demon, dealing only superficial damage. He finally cut into one arm, but then, recalling how not even that had slowed another of the creatures, he went for the neck.

The blade bit through the crusted skin and the dry bone as if through parchment.

The head of the demon dropped to the street, rolling several feet away. It spun for a moment, then stopped with the soulless face pointed in his direction.

"Nefriti hungers for your kiss," the head mocked. "Come kiss Nefriti . . ." The mouth opened and closed.

To his further dismay, the body continued to struggle with him. Albord managed to cut himself free, then for good measure ran the torso through. As the body finally began to collapse, the desperate mercenary fled.

The side street led to a major avenue that was, thankfully, deserted. Albord paused to catch his breath and decide on the best direction. Atop the hill, the palace, larger now, seemed to encourage him on. If he could get around the unholy throng, then the way would be clear.

With visions of Orlif to urge him forward, the young officer stumbled his way toward the hill. Now he knew what had happened to the three men who had earlier vanished. Surely this somehow had to be the work of the sorcerer their host had mentioned, the vile, corrupted Gregus Mazi. The Lord of Ureh had claimed to have destroyed the villain, but Albord had seen enough of sorcerers to know that they could create perfect illusions. No doubt Mazi had tricked his former master into believing his death and now sought his revenge.

Captain Dumon and the others had to be warned . . .

Laughter and music continued to assail his ears. Now the tones took on a mad quality, as if those who celebrated did so in an asylum. Albord wanted to cover his ears, but feared that to do so would slow him down, even if only by a fraction of a second. The sounds tore at his very soul, filled him with as much horror as the demonic horde behind him.

His pace picked up as he came within sight of the base of the hill. Only a short distance more . . .

His boot snagged on something.

Albord tripped, falling forward. He struck the stone avenue hard, sending waves of sharp pain through his entire body. For a few moments, he blacked out.

Forcing himself to consciousness, Albord saw his blade a few feet away. He reached for it, then pulled himself up.

Only then did he sense that he was no longer alone.

They came from the alleyways, the ruined buildings, and the streets. They moved as one, with one vile purpose. They plodded toward him, reaching, reaching . . .

Albord spun around, only to find every possible avenue of escape filled with gaping, hungering corpses. He glanced longingly toward the steps, toward the palace, and knew that despite his close proximity to the former, he stood no chance of making the final few yards.

Curiously, the voice of Captain Dumon suddenly filled his head. *Whenever possible, take the battle to the enemy. Better to fight and die quickly than to wait for the inevitable.* Captain Dumon had taught him that early on. The company commander had also taught Albord the facts about a mercenary's life, how for the vast majority death would prove almost a certainty.

Gripping his sword tight and raising it high over his head, Albord roared and charged.

As he collided with the foremost horrors, his blade bit well into dried flesh, crisp bone. Grasping limbs flew, and cadaverous bodies crumbled. Farther on, the palace continued to beckon, encouraging him to do his best.

They caught his free arm, then his legs. Grotesque faces filled his view. The sword was wrenched from his hand. Still, Albord struggled forward another foot, two . . .

At last, they brought him down, monstrous faces leering at him, hideous mouths eagerly working.

Albord screamed.

In the vast, silent library, Quov Tsin pored over the books left by centuries of predecessors, marveling at the work they had gathered for him. As much as he had savored the praises he had received from the courtiers of Juris Khan, the wizened Vizjerei loved his calling more.

Yet now he could not concentrate as well as usual . . . and for that he had to thank the fool mercenaries. Captain Dumon and the giant, Gorst, had left him with small but irritating doubts abut the veracity of their host's stories. Tsin did not like having doubts; Lord Khan had given him the entire library and made him high sorcerer for the most fabled of kingdoms. With such power, the Vizjerei could become known as the greatest of his kind!

"Damn you, Dumon!" Tsin muttered as he turned a page. "Damn you for not leaving things lie . . ."

"Is something amiss, Master Tsin?"

The sorcerer jumped. He glared at the newcomer, only to see that the fatherly Juris Khan himself towered above him.

"Nothing—nothing of consequence, my lord."

Khan smiled beatifically. "I'm so glad to hear that. You've done so much for the kingdom—and myself specifically—that it would disturb me if you were not happy."

Standing up, Quov Tsin surreptitiously studied his good host. How could the suspicions of the captain possibly have any merit? The man before him truly fit every aspect of the legend that the sorcerer had studied so closely over the decades. Surely he, Tsin, could better read the situation than a lovestruck, low-caste brute like Kentril Dumon! "I am most pleased by your gracious reward, my Lord Khan, and know that I live to serve you in whatever capacity as sorcerer you need."

"For that I'm very grateful, Vizjerei. It's the reason, in fact, I've come to see you alone."

Tsin's already narrow eyes narrowed further, almost becoming slits. "My lord desires my aid?"

"Yes, Master Tsin . . . in fact, I cannot hope to save Ureh without you."

The bold statement caught the diminutive spellcaster's imagination. *I cannot hope to save Ureh without you.* A flush of pride washed over Quov Tsin. Here at last was a ruler who appreciated his fine skills! More and more, the murky anxieties of the mercenary captain seemed but smoke. "I am at your beck and call, Lord Khan . . ."

The taller man put a companionable arm around the shoulder of the sorcerer. "Then, if you can tear yourself away from the books for a time, I need to show you something."

He more than had Tsin's interest. "Of course."

Juris Khan led him from the library. As they walked, the monarch of Ureh explained some of the historical aspects of the holy kingdom, telling how this ancestor or that one had helped gradually raise the realm to its ultimate glory. Knowing that his host simply sought to pass the time until they reached their ultimate destination, Quov Tsin all but ignored the other's words, instead noting such little things as how each guard stood at his most attentive when they passed or the way the servants looked in complete awe when Lord Khan simply acknowledged them with a nod of his head. The tall elder man ruled absolutely, and yet his people loved and honored him. Against that, Kentril Dumon's fears meant nothing.

Tsin quickly realized that he was being led to a part of the palace to which he had never been before. Near the grand hall, Juris Khan opened an unobtrusive door that the sorcerer could not understand having missed earlier. Within, a narrow stairway led down a passage only barely lit by a source undefinable. Deeper and deeper Tsin and his new lord descended into the underlayers of the vast edifice. The Vizjerei had expected that the holy palace had levels below ground, but he was astounded by just how far down they went.

No candles, torches, or oil lamps could be seen throughout the journey, yet the mysterious dim illumination prevented the two from having to travel entirely in the dark. Curiously, the dank, almost sinister aspects of his surroundings did not disturb Tsin, but rather heightened his anticipation. Surely what Lord Khan led him toward could only be a place of great importance.

And then he felt the forces in play, forces raw and chaotic. Even before they reached the thick iron door, Tsin already had some idea of what awaited him.

The savage, beaked head of a gargoyle acted as holder for the massive ring used as a door handle. Quov Tsin marveled at the intricate work of the head, so very lifelike that he expected the creature to snap at Juris Khan as the robed monarch reached for the ring.

"Tezarka . . ." whispered Khan as he touched the handle.

With a slight groan, the door slowly opened—to reveal the sanctum of a sorcerer extreme.

"My private chamber . . . a place of power."

Shaped as a hexagon, the room stretched wide in every direction. The Vizjerei could have fit his own humble sanctum in this place a dozen times over. Shelf upon shelf of powders, herbs, and various rare items lined every wall, while books of arcana lay open upon three vast wooden tables. Jars with specimens that even the well-versed Tsin could not identify had been arranged on another set of tables to his right. Runes had been etched into various places around the chamber, wards against possible spells gone awry. From the center of the ceiling, a vast crystal illuminated all, its source of power that which Quov Tsin could feel permeating the entire place.

But most arresting of all proved to be the vast stone platform in the center of the room.

It stood at least as tall as the Vizjerei, and etched in the rectangular base were intricate runes, many of which even Tsin did not recognize. The platform, too, had been covered with such markings and, in addition, bore the symbol of the sun.

Without thinking, the gnarled Vizjerei stepped forward to inspect the platform. Running his bony fingers over the upper edge, he sensed the inherent forces that had been called up in the past . . . and still waited to be called upon again.

"This is . . . very ancient," he finally commented.

"Carved before the concept of holy Ureh had even been birthed in the minds of my ancestors. Built before any of the eastern realms, much less the western ones, existed. Created by the precursors of the Rathmians, my own people, and your worthy Vizjerei brotherhood, good Tsin. There are times when I question if those who hollowed out this sanctum were even human but perhaps instead heavenly servants sent to prepare the way . . ."

"So much power . . ." More than any of Quov Tsin's kind had ever wielded, even during those centuries when they had made pacts with supposedly subdued demons.

"It is here that you and I will undo the last of Gregus's curse, my good friend. It is here that I plan to restore Ureh fully to the mortal plane."

And Tsin could well believe that possible. Such primal forces proved tricky enough to manipulate, but if Lord Khan could do as he hoped, it would make all that the sorcerer had seen before seem like the spellwork of apprentices. Here existed a place of true mastery . . .

"I could do nothing," explained his host, "nothing at all while I was trapped. Yet I considered and considered well what would happen once someone of skill could free me. Thanks to the treachery of Gregus Mazi, all sorcerers were lost to me, save my dear Atanna." His expression shifted. "But, of course, as talented as she is, she is not you, Master Tsin."

The spellcaster accepted readily this obvious statement. Atanna did indeed have skill—enough so that if she had not already fallen for Kentril Dumon, Tsin might have approached her in the future himself for breeding purposes— but to manipulate such forces required great care, exceptional experience. In truth, without the Vizjerei, Tsin felt certain that any attempt by Lord Khan alone would have ended in abject failure.

"In this chamber," Juris Khan whispered, having somehow come up behind the short sorcerer, "with skills such as the two of us combined wield, there is no limit to what we can accomplish, my friend. Even beyond Ureh rising once more among the great kingdoms. The secrets of the world, and those beyond, could be open to us, if we are only willing to chance matters."

Quov Tsin could see all of it, all the glory, the power. He ran his hands across the runes, drinking in the forces each held. The wrinkled Vizjerei imagined all of them at play, all his to command, to wield . . .

Then he caught sight of a strange pattern at the very center of the platform, a curious, disquieting marking almost like a stain that someone had not quite been able to remove.

"What is that?" he asked.

Juris Khan barely looked at the marking. The tone of his voice when he responded completely dismissed the spot as unimportant.

"Blood, of course."

Sixteen

Zayl . . .

He tried to move, but could not.

Zayl . . .

He tried to breathe, but could not.

Zayl . . .

If not for his training, he would have already been dead, his lungs completely deprived of air.

Zayl, you bloody young fool! You can't die on me now, damn it!

The necromancer tried to talk, but although he knew his mouth was open, no sound escaped it. He tried to open his eyes and at first they resisted. Only with arduous effort did he manage finally to raise the lids enough to see.

And only then did Zayl discover that he had been made like Gregus Mazi.

Even with eyes well-suited for the dark, Zayl could only just make out enough detail to know his terrible fate. He hung from a stalactite high above the first massive chamber that he and the two mercenaries had come across on their previous journey. Like the unfortunate Mazi's, Zayl's arms and legs had been pinned back tightly. Unlike the sorcerer, though, Zayl clearly lacked any purpose for being there. The power that had placed him there desired no sentinel, but rather merely wished the necromancer very, very dead.

Zayl *would* die, too—and soon. Already he could feel his body changing, becoming the same as the stalactite. Strange forces leeched into his body, altering his structure.

Given time, he would become more a part of the mountain than even Gregus Mazi.

But before that happened, he would suffocate.

"Zayl, boy! You've got to still be able to hear me!"

Humbart Wessel's hollow voice echoed through the vast cavern, seeming to come from every direction. Straining, the necromancer managed just to make out the passage through which he and his companion had earlier entered. Somewhere within, the skull no doubt still rested, in many ways as trapped as he.

His hopes, which had briefly risen, plummeted. What could the bodiless Humbart do for him?

Zayl's thoughts grew murkier. An immense exhaustion filled him.

"If you're hearing me, I'm right where you left me, remember? You've a sharp mind! You see it in your head?"

What did the skull hope to accomplish? Zayl only wanted to go to sleep. Why did Humbart have to bother him?

"I think you're still listening, lad, or at least I hope so! Don't like the thought of sitting in this dank place the rest of eternity, so hear me out!"

Humbart's voice irritated the necromancer. He wanted to tell the undead mercenary to go away, but without legs, Humbart could hardly do that.

"Your dagger, Zayl! You need your dagger to help yourself!"

His dagger! Zayl's eyes widened. Did he still have his dagger?

His companion answered that quickly. "I can see it, lad! It's just a few feet ahead of me!"

And a thousand miles away, for all the good it would do. If the necromancer could have at least seen it, he could have summoned it to him. Zayl, however, had never mastered indirect summoning of objects, especially not under such dire circumstances. He had to see what he desired.

The urge to sink into oblivion grew strong again.

"Listen to me!" insisted the skull. "It's pointed toward me, with just a little bit of rock covering the tip. There's another rock shaped like a giant's tooth propping up the hilt area . . ."

Despite his desire to sleep, Zayl listened. In his mind, a picture of the dagger began to form. He even saw Humbart's skull, the empty eye sockets staring hopefully at the blade.

But why bother?

"You see it, don't you, lad? Damn it! If you're still alive and can hear, you've got to see it!"

And finally Zayl understood. Humbart had been with Zayl long enough to know the skills of the one who had animated him. He knew that the necromancer needed to see the dagger, so the skull sought to create a perfect picture for him.

It would never work—or would it? It would require what remained of the air trapped in his body, the minute particles here and there that enabled Zayl to last four, five times longer without breathing than a normal man. Zayl would have to squeeze his lungs completely empty in order to draw enough strength for this one spell.

Meanwhile, Humbart went on with his descriptions, the skull either very optimistic about his companion's chances or merely not wanting to think yet about the alternative. If the latter, Zayl could hardly blame him, for thanks to the spell the necromancer had used, Humbart, too, would suffer. If someone did not find the skull, then unless the rest of the passage collapsed and shattered him, the former mercenary would be trapped in Nymyr forever, his spirit unable to move on.

"That's about it, Zayl, lad!" the skull shouted, Humbart's voice slightly more subdued. "You should have a good image now . . . that is, if you've heard anything at all."

Focusing on the dagger, Zayl quickly pieced together the image as the other had described it. He saw the rocks and how the blade lay upon them. He saw again Humbart's skull staring at the partially buried tip. The necromancer visualized each variation in the rocky walls, filling out his picture.

With every last iota of strength, Zayl fixed on the enchanted dagger, *demanding* in his mind and heart that it come to him.

"Zayl!"

Something gleaming flew out into the cavern as if shot from a crossbow. The trapped necromancer immediately focused on it. The object suddenly veered toward him, a beacon of light in the deathly dark.

The ivory dagger flew unerringly toward him. For just a brief moment, Zayl recalled what they had been forced to do for Gregus Mazi. Should he now will the dagger to come point-first? Should Zayl wish the blade to sink deep into his still-human flesh?

But the situation with Mazi had been different. Not only had the sorcerer been set into place with a purpose, but the spell had been given centuries to do its foul work.

Not so with Zayl. The transformation had barely begun. With the dagger to guide his work, he could still save himself—

The blade suddenly dropped. Struggling, the necromancer brought it back toward him. His concentration had slipped, and, worse, he felt his will ebbing.

Come to me, he called in his mind. *Come to me.*

It did, moving with such swiftness that at first it seemed it would yet slay him. Only at the last moment did the dagger suddenly veer, darting around Zayl and the stalactite and forcing itself into the necromancer's encrusted hand.

The moment the hilt touched, Zayl found he could move his fingers. Gripping the blade, he channeled his strength into it. His lungs screamed, his heart pounded madly, but the imprisoned spellcaster would not give in.

As if struck by lightning, the shell around him shattered.

Weakened, Zayl plunged earthward. Had he been above

the uppermost floor of the cavern, he likely would have died, but the stalactite upon which he had been bound had hung over the vast drop. That and that alone enabled him to recover enough to save himself.

As he fell past the ledge, Zayl managed to utter a spell. A gust of wind suddenly lifted him upward. With tremendous effort, Zayl managed to take hold of the cavern wall before him. His success proved timely, for the spell suddenly faltered, nearly sending him falling into the abyss.

Zayl managed to drag himself slowly to the upper floor of the cavern. Exhausted beyond belief, he lay there for some time, his breathing ragged and every inch of his body feeling as if someone had dropped Nymyr on top of him.

"Zayl?" came a tentative voice.

"I—I am—alive," he croaked back.

"You sure?" returned Humbart's skull. "You don't sound like it."

"Give—give me—time."

"It ain't like I'm going anywhere," mumbled the necromancer's companion.

Gradually, Zayl's breathing normalized. His body continued to ache, but at last he could at least move.

Under the glow of the dagger, Zayl discovered he had not escaped unscathed. His clothing had been reduced to shreds, and his skin had scars everywhere from where the spell had caused the stalactite and his body to begin to merge. Zayl had no doubt that his face, too, bore such marks, but he thanked the Great Dragon that his life had been spared.

On unstable legs, the necromancer finally returned to the passage in which the attack had taken place. The rock slide that he and Captain Dumon had discovered had all but vanished, almost as if it had been blasted away by some tremendous force. Zayl held the dagger before him just in case he might be assaulted anew, but could sense no danger.

Several yards in, he came across the skull.

"Ah, lad! Aren't you a sight for sore eyes—or just a sore sight, from the look of you!"

"I am not ready to join you in the afterlife, Humbart." Exhausted again, the spellcaster sat down on a large rock. "Tell me exactly what happened to me."

"After the two beastly hands clamped tight on you, you dropped the blade. I worried then that they might flatten you like a bug, but instead those rocky mitts began moving along the walls, heading toward the cavern. They ran you right through the collapse, sending more rock tumbling to me—you know I almost got cracked like an egg?"

Zayl could appreciate the skull's apprehensions, but he wanted to hear the rest. "Go on."

"That's it. You vanished from sight, there was a flash of some ungodly light, then I started shouting my head off."

"And I thank you. You saved me."

The skull somehow made a snorting sound. "Well, I had to! Who else is going to carry me out of this place?"

Zayl frowned as he looked past Humbart. What the skull could not see, apparently could not guess, was that farther ahead a ton of debris now sealed the entrance quite thoroughly. The necromancer doubted that he could either dig or magic his way through. That meant finding an alternative route of escape.

"Come, Humbart." He picked up the skull and started back into the cavern.

"You're going the wrong way, lad."

"No, I'm not."

A moment of silence, then, "Oh."

The pair entered the vast chamber. Holding up the dagger, Zayl surveyed his surroundings in every direction.

"We go that way," he finally said, indicating the mouth of a passage up near the very top of the chamber.

"That way? And by what route?"

Humbart had asked an excellent question. At first glance, there seemed no humanly possible manner by which to reach his goal. Zayl searched through the ragged remains of his cloak, but found that the rope he had earlier used had vanished. Still, according to the charts he had memorized, the gap above represented his best hope of finding a way out of Nymyr's gargantuan belly.

Staring at the slick surface leading up to the passage, Zayl took a deep breath and replied, "I climb, of course."

"Climb?" The skull sounded positively aghast. "Climb that? Zayl, lad, do you think—" The rest of his protest became muffled as the spellcaster stuffed him back into his pouch.

The necromancer needed no discouragement, his trust in his skills already quite limited. If he slipped on his way up, Zayl very much doubted that he had enough will to cast a spell sufficient to keep every bone in his body from shattering on the harsh surface below. Regardless of that risk, though, he had to try.

What Zayl had not told Humbart, what he had only come to realize from his own predicament, was that whatever secret existed in Ureh planned soon to reveal itself . . . and that could not, in any way, be a good thing.

Gorst came to see Kentril, the giant not at all in a good mood.

"Albord's not back."

Still trying to find some comfortable fit in the dress uniform, Kentril paused from adjusting the jacket to eye his second-in-command. "It's nearly the dinner hour. You check his room?"

"Aye, Kentril. His things are still there."

"Maybe he decided to stay in the city for a little while after the others left. Maybe their going made him a little homesick." The captain himself had felt so after bidding his men farewell. Even the pleasure of Atanna's company had failed to eradicate the feeling completely.

"Could be," Gorst grunted, not sounding any more convinced by Kentril's words than the captain himself had been.

For once, Kentril wished that he did not have to meet Atanna. Albord's absence did not sit well with him. "Scout the palace as surreptitiously as possible. Make sure that you've searched anywhere Albord might've gone. If I get a chance, I'll try to do some of the same."

"Aye."

"Any hint of Zayl?"

"His stuff's in his rooms, but he's still missing, too."

And that, in some ways, seemed to bode even more ill than the young mercenary's disappearance. Zayl did not seem the type just to go wandering off, not after the concerns the necromancer had expressed.

"Gorst?"

"Yeah, Kentril?"

"Go armed."

The giant nodded, patting the sword dangling at his side. "Always do. You taught me that."

Carrying an ax around would have drawn some suspicion, but a sheathed sword did not raise many eyebrows. Nor would the fact that the massive fighter wandered the halls of the palace seem too out of place. Clearly, as a foreigner, Gorst would be curious about the grand edifice, and, besides, for a giant of a man, the other mercenary had the stealth of a cat.

Gorst started to leave, then hesitated. "Kentril, if I don't find Albord in the palace at all, should I maybe go take a peek in the city?"

Captain Dumon thought it over, weighing options and lives. Finally, hoping that Albord would forgive him, he answered, "No. If it comes to the point of searching the city, we go together, or we don't go at all."

Alone again, Kentril tried to finish dressing, but this latest news refused to sit well with him. Now both the necromancer and Albord had gone missing. The captain gave thanks that at least Jodas and the others had left when they had. If not, how long before all of them would have disappeared?

Disappeared?
Albord had been last seen escorting the rest . . .

"No . . ." Forgetting his garments, forgetting even Atanna, Kentril burst from his rooms and ran to the nearest palace window that gave him some glimpse of the torchlit city. He stared down at the shadowed buildings, listened to the celebrating throngs, and tried to convince himself that the horrific thought he had just conjured up could not have happened. Surely the six who had chosen to leave had exited the outer gates and even now journeyed through the sunlit jungle. Surely they, at least, had reached relative safety . . .

Yet some churning feeling within would not let the captain accept what seemed a most reasonable possibility.

"Atanna." She would tell him what was going on. She would show him one way or the other whether his fears had merit.

He strode through the regal halls, ignoring the salutes of the helmeted guards he passed. Kentril had only one focus—Juris Khan's daughter—and for once he did not seek her for pleasure.

One of the almost faceless servants confronted him as he neared the grand hall. Before the pasty-faced man could say anything, Kentril seized him by the tailored collar and demanded, "Where's your mistress? Where's Atanna?"

"Why, I'm right here."

Startled, Kentril released the servant and turned. The beautiful crimson-haired princess wore a robe similar to the one in which she had been clad when aiding in the release of her father from his curse. Far behind her, Kentril vaguely noted a door he had never seen before.

"What is it you want, my love?"

He had the greatest urge to take her in his arms, to forget his problems, but despite how simple it would have been to do so, Captain Dumon could not forget his men. At least three had definitely gone missing and possibly seven more, excluding the necromancer.

"Where were you?"

"Helping my father," she responded offhandedly. Her lips pursed in concern. "You look troubled, Kentril. Have I offended you somehow?"

Again he had to fight the desire to drown himself in her. "I want to talk to you"—Kentril recalled the servant—"in private."

"We're quite alone," she said with a teasing smile,

Glancing over his shoulder, the captain discovered the liveried figure nowhere to be found. Truly they were swift of feet and as silent as the night.

Atanna suddenly stood at his side, her arm entwined with his. "Let's take a walk, shall we?"

She led him toward the balcony where Lord Khan had made his appearance after being freed by Quov Tsin. Kentril wanted to question her even as they walked, but Atanna put a finger to his lips and shushed as if he were a child. Gazing into those entrancing eyes, Kentril could do nothing but obey.

The air outside had a slight chill to it that caused the mercenary officer to shiver. How he looked forward to when Ureh could withstand the sun and the shadow of the mountain would only mean the aging of the day.

"I so enjoy it out here," his companion murmured. "I know we only sit upon a hill, but it feels like a mountain as tall as Nymyr!"

It could have been so easy to follow her lead, to let the mood take him. Kentril refused, though. He had lives to consider. "Atanna, I need to talk with you."

"Silly! You already are!"

Now he grew slightly angry. "Don't play games! This is important! At least three of my men are officially missing, and now another seems to be nowhere to be found. I'm even growing concerned about the six who left, not to mention Zayl. Too many people are unaccounted for, and that, in my book, means something terrible's going on."

She gave him an almost petulant frown. "Surely you're not saying that I did anything to them?"

"No, of course not. But something's amiss here, and I don't know what to think. Nothing is as it should be, not even Gregus Mazi—"

"*Gregus Mazi?*" Her gaze hardened. "What about that viper?"

Kentril decided he had to tell her. Surely Atanna did not know the truth. He gripped her by the shoulders. "Atanna, your father didn't slay him."

"What do you mean? Father said—"

"Listen to me!" He leaned close, letting her see in his eyes that he spoke only the truth. "Atanna, I found him . . . Gregus Mazi, that is. He'd been cursed, turned into a part of the caverns below, and used as some sort of hellish sentinel."

"What were you doing down there? How did you know where to look for him?"

Kentril glanced briefly over his shoulder in order to make certain that no one spied upon them, then answered, "Zayl found out. He'd been to Mazi's sanctum and there tried to summon the sorcerer's shade in order to question him about—"

Turning back to the view of darkened Ureh, Atanna muttered, "The necromancer . . . of course, he would be able to do it."

Frustrated, Kentril spun her to face him again. "Listen to me! You know your father best. Has he acted at all different? Is there anything about him that might be of question to you?"

"My father is exactly the way I expect him to be."

"But something's not right here, Atanna, and because of the two of us, I've ignored it much too long. Men who depended on me may be dead, and whatever took them could still be lurking in Ureh. If your father—"

She put a hand to his cheek, caressing him and making it hard for Kentril to concentrate. "Nothing can touch us here.

This is the palace of Juris Khan. I have you, and you have me, and that's all that matters, isn't it?"

How simple it would have been to agree. Her very touch thrilled him, made all else inconsequential.

"No!" As he shouted, he grabbed her wrist. "Atanna! You've got to take this seriously! I can't stay here and pretend nothing happened! At the very least, I have to go searching for Albord and the others! They—"

"You can't leave! I have you now, and I won't let you go!"

Kentril gaped, caught unprepared for the vehemence with which the young woman spoke. Her eyes held a fury he thought not possible.

She took a step toward him, and to his surprise the hardened fighter backed up.

"I asked Father for you, and he said I could have you! All I wanted was you. I didn't want the others. Just you, don't you see?"

The fury had abated, but in its place Kentril discovered an unsettling look, a look that seemed to cut through him, see him inside and out. Without thinking, he took another step back.

Her face softened. "It was so lonely there . . . so lonely save for him and the few others . . . and when they were gone, I yearned for something more."

Every hair on Kentril suddenly tingled. As Atanna proceeded toward him, the wind seemed to catch her hair and robe, making the former flow wild and sensual and the latter pull hard against her curved form. Her smile promised everything as she eyed him under her lashes.

"I want you with all my heart, my soul, and my body, Kentril," she cooed. "Don't you want me, too?"

He did. He wanted her. He wanted to give himself to her in whatever manner she desired. The captain wanted to serve her, protect her . . .

But as Juris Khan's daughter reached out for him, something made Kentril throw himself forward.

The mercenary collided hard with Atanna. She let out a startled gasp, then fell backward, completely off-balance.

And dropped over the *rail*.

"Atanna!" Straining, Kentril tried to reach her, but already she had slipped completely out of sight. He stumbled to the rail, peering down in horror for some sign. Unfortunately, the deep shadow made it impossible to see anything. Kentril listened, but heard neither a scream nor the sounds of discovery.

He fell back, his heart seeming ready to explode. It had never been his intention to *kill* her! All Kentril had wanted was to break whatever hold she had upon him. He knew that she had been a wielder of sorcery like her father and that in her fear of losing him she must have thought that it would be all right to cast a glamour over him, make him love her more. If she had only understood—

Her father. Whatever concerns Kentril had once had about Lord Khan, they paled now in comparison to this situation. How could he face Ureh's master and tell him that his only daughter had plummeted to her death after having been pushed by the man she had loved? How?

Deep down, Captain Dumon knew that his mind still did not function properly. Contrary thoughts vied with one another, seeking domination. While a part of him worried over Atanna's death and its consequences, another part still battled the question of the disappearances and the truth about Gregus Mazi.

One way or another, he had to face Juris Khan. What Kentril had done could not be ignored. He had to face Khan.

He recalled the door he had seen far behind Atanna, the one from which it seemed most likely she had come. She had claimed to have just come from helping her father, which suggested that the elder monarch could be found wherever the door led.

Without hesitation, the mercenary ran from the balcony. The hallway echoed with the sounds of his booted feet, but nothing else. Of the servants and the guards, there existed no sign. Had they heard what had happened and gone to find their mistress's remains? Why had none of them come to the balcony to investigate what had happened?

Such matters faded in importance as he came upon the door. Throwing it open, Kentril saw that it descended deep into the lower levels of the palace. No torches or lamps lit the way, but some illumination enabled him to see a fair distance down.

Veteran reflexes almost made the captain reach for his sword, but then he recalled what had just happened. How would it look to come to explain Atanna's fall while wielding a weapon?

As he started to descend, Kentril thought about going back to find Gorst, but then decided that his friend should be no part of this. This had to be between Juris Khan and Kentril.

With great trepidation, the scarred mercenary followed the steps to their end. At the bottom, a gargoyle head with a ring in its mouth savagely greeted him from an ancient iron door. With nowhere else to go, Kentril tugged on the ring.

A cold yet soft breeze swirled briefly around him.

Tezarka . . .

Startled, he let go of the ring, then turned in a circle. Kentril could have sworn that he had heard Atanna's voice, but, of course, he had made that forever impossible. Any hint of her presence could only arise from his overriding guilt.

Reminded of why he had come down to this place, Kentril decided to try the ring once more. He already knew that it would not work, but at least—

With a slow groan, the iron door gave way.

Kentril stepped inside.

"Aaah, Dumon! What excellent timing!"

In the center of the chamber within, near a tall stone platform covered in mystic symbols, a smiling Quov Tsin reached an almost friendly hand toward the mercenary.

The silver runes of the Vizjerei's *Turinnash* blazed brightly, and the diminutive figure seemed almost years younger, so enthused was his expression.

Baffled, Kentril slowly walked toward him. "Tsin? What're you doing down here?"

"Preparing for a sorcerous feat such as I could have only imagined! Preparing to delve into powers no other Vizjerei has touched in centuries, if ever!"

Kentril looked around, but saw no one else in the vast room. Even though he had interacted with sorcerers in the past, even visited them in their own sanctums, this place filled him with an inexplicable dread. "Where's Lord Khan?"

"Returning shortly. You might as well wait. He wants you here, too."

But Kentril paid him no mind. "I've got to find him . . . explain to him what happened to his daughter . . ."

Tsin frowned. "His daughter? What about his daughter? She left but a short time ago."

"I think the good captain fears that terrible harm's come to my darling Atanna," a voice behind the fighter boomed.

Startled, Kentril stumbled away from the door. Through the entrance stepped Juris Khan, looking stronger, more fit, despite his elder years, than Captain Dumon had so far seen him.

Lord Khan smiled benevolently at the dismayed figure. "She surprised you. She caused you to react instinctively. Atanna can be a creature of moods, good captain. You only reacted as was warranted."

"But—" Kentril could hardly believe that his host could speak so pleasantly about such a terrible accident. While it relieved him that the robed monarch did not hold him responsible, that did not change the fact that the man's child had fallen to the rocky landscape below. "But Atanna's *dead*!"

At this comment, Juris Khan chuckled. "Dead? I should say not! You're not dead, dear, are you?"

And from behind him stepped his daughter.

Captain Dumon let out a strangled cry and fell back against the massive platform.

"I didn't mean to make you upset before," she purred, the door through which she had just walked closing of its own accord. As Atanna moved closer, she wobbled some, for clearly one leg had snapped in the middle and the foot of the other twisted to the side. Her left arm bent at an impossible angle behind her, and the right, which reached out to Kentril, ended in a hand so badly mangled it could not even be identified as such. Dirt stained her torn robe, but, oddly, not a single drop of blood.

Her head bent completely to the side, barely held on by tendons from the neck.

"You see?" offered Juris Khan. "Broken a little, perhaps, but certainly not *dead*."

Seventeen

Gorst had been through nearly every level of the palace and had discovered a few significant things. Most important of them was that almost all of the servants and guards had vanished; only those he would have expected to see in the vicinity of his and Kentril's quarters seemed to be still active. When he secretly visited other floors, the halls remained empty, silent. Even the many courtiers who had clustered around the grand hall during Lord Khan's announcements could not be found. It was as if only a skeleton crew manned the vast edifice.

The giant had not yet concluded his hunt, but had already seen enough that he knew he had better report to his captain. Kentril would understand what this all meant. Gorst admired his commander and friend immensely and trusted his judgment—except perhaps sometimes with Khan's daughter. Then it seemed that the captain on occasion lost track of matters. Of course, if she had focused her beauty on *Gorst*, the giant suspected he probably would have been even more befuddled. Battle was one thing; women were four, five, six complex things all at once.

He slipped past two watchful but unsuspecting guards near his own rooms, then, pretending to come from a side hall, nonchalantly walked into sight. Although he did not see their eyes move, Gorst sensed them suddenly take in his presence. They were good, but not good enough.

Reaching Kentril's apartment, he rapped twice on the door. When no one answered, he repeated the action, this time much harder.

Still no response. While it seemed very likely that the captain could be found with Atanna, Gorst nonetheless felt his unease grow. He could not imagine what he would do if now Kentril, too, had vanished. While he could certainly think for himself, Gorst worked best when given orders.

The giant had started to turn back to his own rooms when a hint of black at the back end of the hall caught his attention. He glanced in that direction, but saw nothing. Still . . . one did not survive long as a mercenary by ignoring such things.

Reaching the location without alerting the guards proved simple enough, but trying to find the source of the momentary patch of black afterward turned out to be much harder. Gorst soon began to wonder if he had imagined it. He could find no trace whatsoever in the hall, and unless it had somehow managed to melt into the wall—

And then the giant's sharp eyes noticed part of a door frame *ripple*.

Curious, Gorst reached out and gently touched the area in question.

The left side of the frame suddenly lost all but a vague semblance of normalcy, rippling so madly it almost seemed as if he stared at it through flowing water. A second later, even that vestige of reality faded away—and suddenly the battered, torn body of the necromancer, Zayl, fell toward Gorst.

The startled giant barely caught him in time. Zayl groaned slightly, clutching at him with what little strength remained.

"Get me—" the slim, pale figure gasped. "Get me— inside—room!"

Making certain that no one saw them, Gorst carried the spellcaster into the rooms set aside for him. He quickly lowered Zayl onto the bed, then anxiously looked for something to give the injured man.

"Open the pouch, damn it . . ."

At first, Gorst thought that the necromancer had spoken,

but a quick check revealed Zayl's eyes were closed, the spellcaster's breathing slow but steady. The giant finally recalled Zayl's disturbing companion and where best to find him.

It had probably been fortunate that the skull had spoken, for when Gorst reached for the pouch, he saw that, like the spellcaster's clothing, it, too, had been ripped in several places. Hints of its grisly contents could be seen through the tears, and if not for some luck, Gorst suspected the contents would have spilled out long ago.

Gingerly removing the skull, he placed it on the nearest table.

"My thanks, lad. Didn't think there for a while that we'd make it back in one piece."

Gorst tried to remind himself that he spoke with a fellow mercenary, not simply the skull of a man dead for centuries. "What happened?"

"Young fellow there tried to conjure up the spirit of old Gregus," Humbart Wessel explained. "Only, when Gregus did show up, he wasn't old, and he wasn't by far in a good mood! He tried to warn us, but right when he spoke, the very walls grabbed for poor Zayl . . ."

Humbart went on to tell of a most horrifying fate that the necromancer had only barely escaped with the skull's assistance, then the arduous climb out of the caverns and the exhausting return to the palace. The tale would have struck Gorst as half fanciful if not for all else that had gone on.

"Let no one tell you," the skull concluded, "that this young one's not as fit as a fighter for all his being a spellcaster, lad! Zayl'd be a good, sturdy man to have on your side in battle any time."

"Is there anything we can do for him?"

"Well . . . see if you can find a small red pouch among the things he left here."

Picking through Zayl's meager belongings, Gorst found the pouch in question. He held it up.

"Aye, that's the one. Now, if there's no curses or wards on it, open it up."

The giant obeyed, only after undoing the strings realizing just what Humbart had said. Fortunately, nothing sought to strike him down or reduce him to dust.

"There a small vial with a yellowish liquid in it?"

There was, right next to what looked like a dried eyeball. Swallowing, Gorst pulled out the vial, then immediately sealed the bag.

"Pour it down his gullet. I saw him use that kind of stuff once after a thorned hulk almost beat him into the ground— 'course, Zayl did manage to blast him to splinters in the end."

When opened, the thick, ugly liquid proved to have an odor well-matched to its appearance. Wrinkling his squat nose, Gorst went to the unconscious figure and, slipping his other hand under the back of Zayl's head in order to lift the latter up slightly, the mercenary carefully poured the contents into the other's mouth.

Zayl coughed once, then swallowed everything. Suddenly, the necromancer's entire body jerked wildly. Dismayed and startled, Gorst pulled back.

"Thought you said it'd help him!"

The skull did not reply.

The jerking abruptly ceased . . . and Zayl began to cough again. As he did, the peculiar wounds over every visible part of his body began to heal, then even fade away. The giant watched in amazement as, in but seconds, what little color the spellcaster had ever had returned and the last of the injuries utterly vanished.

Still weak but clearly recovering, Zayl eyed the soldier. "My thanks."

"And don't I get any credit?" grumbled Humbart Wessel. "Isn't like it's my fault that I haven't any hands, or I'd have fed you the stuff myself!"

"I definitely thank you, too, Humbart." The necromancer tried to rise, but could not. "It appears I need a few minutes longer. Perhaps it would be best if you brought Captain Dumon to see me. There is much we need to discuss."

"Can't find Kentril," Gorst admitted. "Can't find anyone but you so far."

The silver, almond-shaped eyes that did and did not remind the giant so much of Quov Tsin's narrowed in suspicion. "No one?"

"Albord's gone missing. That worried Kentril enough so he sent me looking around the palace. Couldn't find Tsin, couldn't even find hardly a soul anywhere besides on this floor. Seems the whole place is all but empty . . ."

"Yes, that is making more and more sense, I am afraid."

This brought a snort of disapproval from the skull. "Now, you said that once or twice while climbing out of Nymyr, and you still haven't explained to me just what you mean."

Zayl frowned. "And that is because I do not yet completely understand it myself."

Gorst knew he understood less than either, but one thing of which he felt certain was that his captain had gone missing, and that meant only one course of action as far as he was concerned.

"I need to find Kentril."

"It might be best—"

"Come with me or not," the giant said, determination hardening, "I'm going after my captain."

The necromancer forced himself up. "Give me just a short time, Gorst, and I will be more than happy to help you search. I think it might be best if we left Ureh and its shadowed past. The holy kingdom seems to me anything but."

Despite his impatience, Gorst agreed to wait. He knew that magic was involved and knew that against such he had little hope. He could wield an ax or sword well against any blood-and-flesh foe, but against magic he felt pretty much defenseless. Having Zayl with him would help even the odds. Gorst had already seen how skilled the man was.

It took the necromancer some minutes to recover his strength sufficiently and a few more minutes to do anything about his ruined garments. Gorst expected him to magic up some new clothes, but instead Zayl went to his pack and removed an outfit nearly identical to that which had been torn to shreds. Only the cloak could not be replaced.

"We shall have to find you a new pouch," Zayl commented to the skull. "I fear I do not have another large enough in which to place you, Humbart."

"Well, I'm not staying behind! If you don't—"

Gorst did not want to have to wait for them to finish arguing. "I've got a bag big enough. It can tie to your belt just like your old one."

Zayl nodded. "Then it is time to go find the captain and be rid of this place."

It seemed to Zayl that he had underestimated the giant. Gorst appeared far more clever, far more adept, than the necromancer had assumed. The information he provided Zayl concerning the layout of the palace not only matched the drawing that the spellcaster had studied, but corrected some errors caused by expansion and even evidently sheer mistake on the part of the one who had drawn the diagram.

The mercenary had used simple tricks to evade the notice of the armored guards, but Zayl felt that even such would slow their efforts too much. Thanks to the potion that Gorst had fed him—and whose contents the necromancer knew he had best never explain to the fighter—Zayl felt almost as good as new. His wounds had vanished, and the only remnant of his almost catastrophic finish consisted of a slight twinge in one arm. Still, the necromancer felt confident that he could now not only mask himself from the sight of the soldiers, but do the same for the giant as well. They would save much time by walking right past rather than inching their way along the sides.

While Gorst obviously did not entirely agree, he did not argue when Zayl began casting. Using the dagger to draw the fiery symbols in the air, Zayl strengthened his normal spell, then touched the mercenary with the tip of the blade.

"Nothing's happened," complained the giant.

"We are both tied to the spell. We can see each other, but no one else can see us. The same applies for most basic sounds, but I would not recommend shouting or sneezing as we pass. Abrupt and loud noises might penetrate the glamour."

Still a little reluctant, Gorst followed him out into the hall. Farther on, the sentries continued their motionless, tireless stare across the corridor. Zayl could not help but admire their training, so akin to his own. Each of the eight men stood tall and straight. Armed alternately with sword or ax, they almost could have been mistaken for very life-like statues. Their nearly identical faces and expressions only served to emphasize that look and, in addition, had made Zayl early on wonder if they were perhaps all related.

He and Gorst slowly walked along, shoulder to shoulder, step by step. They passed the first pair, then the second, without any notice whatsoever. The mercenary seemed to relax, and even Zayl, who knew the power of his spell, felt some relief.

Then something about the next guard's countenance made the necromancer pause despite the urgency of the situation. Gorst gave him a worried, insistent look, but Zayl ignored it. He stared cautiously at the armored figure, wondering what about the man's face so bothered him. Unable to ascertain what it might be, he glanced at the opposing sentry, studying him.

It suddenly occurred to him what it was that he found so disturbing and yet so difficult to identify.

Neither guard had blinked. Zayl had waited far beyond

reasonable human limit, and yet neither had reacted like a normal man. No matter how well-trained these guards might be, surely they had to blink at some point.

And yet they did not.

Zayl wanted to tell Gorst, but feared risking his spell. Once they were far past, he could tell the other of his disquieting discovery. For now, it behooved them to—

The unblinking eyes of one of the guards suddenly shifted in his direction, meeting the necromancer's widening gaze.

"They see us!" Zayl shouted.

Everyone moved at once. Gorst had his sword out and ready to confront any of the four they had already crept by. The one who had met Zayl's eyes leapt forward, ax swinging, face completely expressionless. The other three moved in behind him, similar blank looks on each.

Dagger before him, Zayl muttered. A black sphere briefly materialized, then shot directly into the chest of the first attacker. The armored sentry hesitated, then continued as if unhindered.

The results did not please the necromancer. Never before had he cast a spell of weakening and seen it completely fail. These guards were more than simply men— and, because of that, possibly more than he and Gorst could handle.

If he worried about such things, the gigantic mercenary did not show it. In fact, where Zayl's magical assault had failed, Gorst's considerable skill and strength made up for it. The first to reach the wild-maned fighter moved in with the obvious intention of quickly decapitating Gorst with his ax. Seemingly outfought already, Gorst waved his blade wildly about, leaving himself wide open.

However, as the ax neared, the giant did an amazing thing. He let the head and upper part of the shaft come within inches of his throat, then, with one meaty hand, stopped the ax in mid-flight and finally ripped it from the hands of its wielder.

Although disarmed, the guard charged forward. Keeping the handle foremost, Gorst slammed the sentry hard in the stomach. Metal bent in, and a gasp of air escaped the giant's otherwise emotionless foe. Not satisfied with forcing his enemy to double over, Gorst swung hard, using the flat of the ax to strike the guard solidly in the face.

A face that *shattered*.

The fragments fell away. Within the helm, utter darkness reigned. To his credit, the mercenary did not even wait for the pieces to hit the floor. Quickly twisting the ax around, he did as his adversary had intended for him, slicing off helmet, neck brace, and whatever might have held them in place.

The now-completely headless figure collapsed with a clatter onto the marble floor.

"They're not alive!" Gorst shouted needlessly.

"But they can be stopped," Zayl returned. Now that he knew better what they confronted, the necromancer felt more confident. Small wonder his spell had failed; he had based his work on the type of enemy he assumed he faced. These were not men, no. They resembled golems of a sort, and as a necromancer he had become well-versed in dealing with their like.

For the followers of Rathma, animating a construct—a figure of clay, stone, or some other substance—had been an art hand-in-hand with their dealings with raising the dead. In many ways, animating a golem required many of the opposite elements needed to summon a spirit or revive a corpse. With the latter, one brought back what had once been life. With the former, one imbued that which had never known life with a semblance of it.

Dodging the sword of his nearest opponent, Zayl ran through the spell for creating a golem, then reversed it. Hoping he would not misstep, he shouted the words not only in the latter order, but completely backward as well— everything to create the opposite effect.

The guard dropped his sword . . . and his hand . . . and his arms and legs and head and body. Armor scattered over the floor, and the face the golem had worn cracked into a thousand pieces as it struck the hard surface.

A second one nearly caught the necromancer while he stood admiring his work. The ax came within inches of Zayl's chest. Only barely did Zayl manage to spout out the altered spell again before the monstrous sentry could try a second strike.

Something different happened, though. The guard lost his ax, and his actions became uncoordinated, but he did not crumble as the first had. In fact, Zayl could see him slowly recovering, his movements returning to fluidity.

The golem had adapted to his spell.

Behind him, Gorst grunted as he lifted another adversary up into the air using the spiked head of the ax. Had the guard truly been human, he would have been impaled to death, but the golem only struggled, trying hard to reach the giant with his sword.

With massive effort, Gorst used the ax to throw the one construct into another. The force of his toss caused the one beneath to shatter when the pair hit the floor. However, the first rose again, a gaping hole in his armor where his chest should have been. He seized the ax left behind by his fellow and moved in to match weapons with the mercenary.

Zayl, meanwhile, found himself hard-pressed against his three foes. Reacting instinctively, he summoned the Talon of Trag'Oul, which had served him so well in Gregus Mazi's sanctum.

The bone spear shot through the foremost golem, the one he had already slowed. The damage caused by both spells proved too much for the animated guard to overcome. The torso collapsed in on itself, then, as if a house of cards had been knocked over, the entire golem dropped in pieces.

Knowing he could no longer use the Talon, Zayl immediately summoned the Den'Trag, the Teeth of Trag'Oul.

The combination had perfectly finished the carpet beast and surely would serve as well here.

But when the shower of swift, deadly shafts struck the pair, most *bounced* off.

The necromancer could scarcely believe what he saw; he had heard no tale of the Teeth ever failing. True, some of his missiles did pincushion the two golems and had even managed to disarm the one who had wielded the ax, but other than causing some slowness of movement, the projectiles had succeeded in doing little else.

It occurred to him then that the similarities between the Teeth and the Talon had enabled the golems to adapt to the former as well. Zayl cursed his stupidity, then sought some other spell not at all akin to any of those he had cast. He had to think fast, too, for although the animated sentries clearly respected the power of his dagger, its short length meant that they still had the advantage of reach.

As the one who had been disarmed bent to seize the ax again, the necromancer's remaining opponent thrust hard with his sword. The tip of the long blade came within an inch of Zayl's throat. He backed away, colliding with Gorst, who had been pressed back by his own remaining foes.

An idea occurred to Zayl, one he hoped would not prove wrong, or else he would be sacrificing both their lives needlessly. "Gorst! We need to switch opponents!"

"Switch? Why?"

"Just trust me! When I give the word!"

To his credit, the mercenary did not protest. Still back-to-back, Zayl could feel the giant's body tense as he prepared to follow the spellcaster's lead.

"Drive them back three paces, then turn to your left!"

Zayl himself dove forward, his sudden shift in tactics causing the golems to step away. However, the necromancer cast no spell, but rather simply did exactly as he had ordered Gorst. Spinning around, he abandoned his foes for those the giant had fought. At the same time, Gorst turned to confront Zayl's original pair.

Pointing the dagger at his two new adversaries, the necromancer unleashed the Teeth of the Dragon again.

The needle-sharp projectiles tore through the golems, completely puncturing the armor and shattering the guards into a hundred pieces that flew in every direction.

Zayl let out an uncustomary yell of triumph. As he had suspected, since these had not yet faced him in battle, they had not adapted themselves to his particular spells. By switching opponents, he had outwitted their creator's handiwork.

But that left Gorst with the pair that the necromancer had originally faced. Concerned that they might prove too much for the mercenary, Zayl whirled about, already putting together a spell that he hoped would at least slow the sentries down.

He need not have worried. Gorst had the situation well in hand—and one of the golems in hand, too. His weapon abandoned, the giant had one of his foes upside down over his head. Without hesitation, he thrust the golem toward the floor as hard as he could, and where Gorst was concerned, that proved hard indeed.

Helmet and false face crumpled into an unrecognizable jumble. The massive fighter tossed the rest of the body away, then turned on the final golem. Undaunted, the construct tried to cut a deadly arc with his sword. However, Gorst, moving far more swiftly than his form warranted, seized the wrist of the sword arm and tugged.

As the guard fell toward him, the mercenary slammed his fist through the emotionless mask with such force that his hand dented the inside of the back of the helmet.

Seemingly determined not to take any risks, Gorst ripped the helmet off, then he kicked with his foot at the creature's chest.

The last golem fell back onto the floor and broke, limbs clattering in various directions, bits of armor spinning about.

"Now what?" asked Gorst as he retrieved one of the axes.

"As you said, we find Captain Dumon."

They hurried down the hall again, the silence and emptiness of the palace doing nothing to ease Zayl's concerns. Surely the commotion caused by the battle should have sent more guards running to aid the others. Where were all those who had once inhabited this place?

More to the point, where was Captain Dumon? In a place so huge, with so many hidden passages, how could they possibly—

What a fool he had been! Zayl halted, Gorst nearly running him down in the process.

"Do you have anything of the captain's on you? Anything at all? If not, we'll have to return to his chambers."

The giant brooded over the question for a moment, then his face brightened. "Got this!"

He dug into a pocket and removed a small, rusted medallion with the picture of some bearded western monarch upon it. In badly worn script around the edges had been inscribed *For Honor, For Duty, For King and Kingdom.*

"Kentril got it from his father. Carried it with him for years. Used to say it brought him good luck. He gave it to me after I almost got my head chopped off about a year ago. Said I needed it more than he did."

Not exactly what Zayl had hoped for, but if Gorst's aura had not yet overwhelmed the older one set into the medallion by Captain Dumon, then it could still be of use in tracking the missing mercenary down. Unfortunately, their lack of time also demanded that the necromancer make use of a far less accurate spell, one with the potential to be more affected by outside influences such as the recent change in ownership.

Zayl had to try, though. Holding the medallion in his right hand, he dangled the tip of the blade over the center, all the while muttering under his breath.

Immediately, he began to feel a tug—but toward the

watching Gorst. Irritated, Zayl focused on Kentril Dumon, picturing him as best he could.

Now the pulling came from another direction, an area near the grand chamber but in an area of which the necromancer knew little. Muttering a few more words, the necromancer tightened the focus his spell to make certain, then nodded to Gorst.

"Did you find him?"

Holding the rusted memento before him, Zayl checked the direction a third time. The invisible force continued to pull him toward the same path. "He is most definitely that way."

Ax gripped tightly, Gorst trailed close as Zayl followed the guidance of the bewitched medallion. As they proceeded, though, the spellcaster noticed an unnerving peculiarity about the lit torches and oil lamps nearby. The flames flickered rather oddly, and Zayl thought that the light actually looked *darker*, as if something drained it of its natural fury.

Their path led them to a secluded door, through which they entered without hesitation. Before them the pair found a passage descending below the main palace, a passage that neither could recall from the drawings. Gorst did not like the dim illumination that came from everywhere and nowhere, and even the necromancer felt a chill up and down his spine, but down they went, certain more than ever that there they would find the captain.

At the bottom, the duo came upon an immense iron door. The head of a fearsome gargoyle with features like those of the ones they had seen outside thrust out from the right side, a large ring in its mouth.

Gorst put an ear to the door, a moment later shaking his head. "Can't make out a sound." He tugged on the ring. "It's too strong for me. I'll just ruin the handle trying."

"Let me see what I can do." Slipping around the giant again, Zayl leaned close with the dagger. He sensed great forces in play not only around the door but beyond.

"Zayl," came the skull's voice, "I think—"

"Not now, Humbart. Can you not see—"

He broke off as the ring suddenly slipped from the gargoyle's beaky maw. A shriek echoed through the passage. The necromancer lurched back as the beak snapped at him, falling against Gorst.

A full-sized, winged, and taloned gargoyle leapt out of the door at them.

Eighteen

"Atanna—" Kentril bit back the rest of what he had been going to say. This could not be Atanna, not this horrifying marionette.

Her head still tipped completely to one side, she gave him a macabre smile. "My darling Kentril . . ."

Juris Khan put his arm around her. With an expression akin to that on the face of any loving father, he said to her, "Now, my dear, you should go to your beloved looking your best, don't you think so?"

He gently put the arms in place, then ran his hand over the maimed limb. As Lord Khan's fingers pulled away, Kentril saw that Atanna's own hand had been restored.

Muttering words the likes of which the mercenary had never heard, the robed monarch took a step back. A fiery corona surrounded his daughter from head to toe. Atanna rose several inches into the air, and as she did, her legs twisted, reshaped, becoming once more normal limbs. The gouges in her face and form quickly dwindled, finally disappearing. Even her dress restored itself, all signs of damage vanishing.

"*Olbystus!*" called out Juris Khan.

Slowly, Atanna descended to the floor again. The shimmering corona faded away. Before Kentril stood an almost completely restored woman.

Almost . . . because her head yet hung to the side.

With a gentle smile, Atanna's father put her head back in place. Muscles, veins, tendons, and flesh instantly fused. The terrible wound sealed itself, all trace soon gone.

Juris Khan briefly adjusted her hair. "There! So much better."

"Am I pretty again, Kentril?" she innocently asked.

He could say nothing, could think nothing. In desperation, he looked to Quov Tsin, who seemed to be taking everything in with an eagerness that did not bode well at all.

"It's as you *said*," the diminutive Vizjerei almost cooed to their host. "The power to do almost anything, even to preserve life itself!"

"A gift of Heaven," their host returned. "A gift that can be shared."

"Heaven?" blurted the captain. "This is hellish!"

Khan gave him a paternal look. "Hell? But this is Ureh, my good captain! No beast or servant of the Prime Three can touch this holy kingdom—is that not so, Master Tsin?"

The Vizjerei sniffed. "Don't be so mundane, Dumon! Can't you even imagine the power of Heaven? Do you think Hell could preserve life so?"

"Preserve it? You call that *life?* She's *dead,* Tsin! Just look at her!"

"Why, Kentril, how could you possibly say that?" Pouting, Atanna stepped close. Her eyes glittered in that magical way they always had, and he could feel the warmth of her body even though she still stood a few scant inches away. Each breath rose and sank in fascinating display, enough so that even Captain Dumon had to start questioning his own fears. "Do I truly, *truly,* look dead to you?"

"Open your eyes and mind, captain," Quov Tsin urged, coming toward the pair. "You've always struck me as a little brighter than most of your earthy kind. You know the stories, the legends of the Light among Lights! You know how the archangels granted great miracles to the people, revealed to them things we can only just imagine!"

"But—but this?"

"Kentril is correct to be skeptical," commented Juris

Khan. He extended his hands to take in the entire chamber. "Do not the archangels tell us to be wary of evil in the guise of goodness? Does not the world have tales about cunning demons seeking to corrupt humans at every turn? My good captain, the history of Ureh at the time when we sought the pathway to Heaven's sanctuary very much backs your suspicious nature. It is because of the subtle guile of Diablo and the many lesser demons that I prayed for a miracle, for a way to secure my kingdom completely from their evil. To my good fortune, the archangel did grant me that miracle, but in the meantime we more than once had to deal with cunning traitors and plots sinister barely recognizable as such. Yes, I applaud your skepticism, however misplaced it might be at this moment."

Tsin turned the veteran soldier so that the platform filled Kentril's gaze. The mercenary's eyes widened as he noted the glowing, pulsating runes. The urge to get as far away from the artifact as he could filled Kentril. Unfortunately, not only did the Vizjerei hold his arm, but Atanna stood right behind him.

"The archangel who had spoken to Lord Khan could not undo what had been done," the short sorcerer explained. "But he revealed to our host a possible escape should the proper elements come into play. They have."

Now Khan stepped around the platform, eyeing Kentril from the opposing side. "I had originally thought to make use of your fortuitous arrival to fulfill my original intention, to see Ureh at last rise to Heaven. However, your good Master Tsin rightly convinced me of our need to stay on the mortal plane, and, as it turns out, this works out so perfectly with what I've calculated that I cannot but believe that the archangel truly meant this route instead."

For lack of anything better to say, Captain Dumon muttered, "I don't understand."

"It's very simple, Dumon, you cretin! The archangel pointed out powers not bound by Heaven or Hell, powers of nature, of the world itself. What better than these to help bind Ureh to our plane again? The natural tendencies of such forces are to create a balance, to set everything into harmony. Ureh will become truly real again, its people once more able to go out in the sun, to go out and interact with other kingdoms, other realms."

At the moment, Kentril did not see that as quite the wondrous notion that Tsin clearly did. In fact, he regretted even having set the one stone in place. Ureh had not proven to be what he had expected—and his future not what he had thought it to be.

"What about Gregus Mazi?" the captain demanded, shaking off both Atanna and the Vizjerei. He could not forget the horrible sight he had seen.

"Lord Khan explained that simple matter to me, Dumon. You didn't find Gregus Mazi, but rather one of his acolytes. He tried also to destroy the Key to Shadow, but a protective spell cursed him so. The cretin brought it on himself. He now guards against others with equally vile notions, protecting Ureh's hopes . . ."

There were too many holes in the story, too many gaping holes, but for Quov Tsin, who had not been there, Khan's explanation seemed to make perfect sense. Not so for Kentril Dumon, however. He knew very well that Juris Khan had added another lie to the many already piled up. Everything that the captain and his companions had assumed about the holy kingdom had been wrong. They had come to find a legend and instead had unveiled a nightmare.

"And what about my men, Tsin? What about Albord and the rest—and even the necromancer, Zayl? A lot of good men have gone missing, and I've not yet heard a reasonable explanation for their disappearances."

Juris Khan came from around the platform. He seemed even taller, more foreboding, than previously. "The taint left by Gregus has touched some of my people, I admit. However, once Ureh is settled among mankind again, those who've done these terrible deeds shall be taken to account."

While a part of him wished desperately to believe the elder man, Kentril had heard too much he could not accept. "Tsin, you can stay here if you like, but I think I'll be going . . ."

Atanna was suddenly there at his side again. The captain felt torn between desire and revulsion. Here stood the woman of his dreams . . . the same one he had seen fall to her death, then return in most grotesque fashion.

"Oh, but you can't go, Kentril, darling, not yet!"

Spoken with honey yet still not sweet enough not to make him even more wary. Again pulling away from her, the veteran soldier readied his blade. "I'm going through that door. Tsin, you'd be smart to go with me."

"Don't be a bigger fool than I take you for already, Dumon. I'm not going anywhere, and you certainly can't. We need you most of all right now!"

"Need me? For what?"

The Vizjerei shook his head at such ignorance. "You're critical to the spell, of course, cretin!"

He looked from face to face to face—and turned to run. Against one spellcaster, Kentril Dumon might have defended himself. Against two, he might have even entertained some hope of victory.

Against three, only a madman stayed and fought.

But as Kentril ran toward the door, he abruptly discovered himself running toward the *platform* instead. With one fluid movement, the captain spun around, only to see the platform again.

"Do stop wasting our time with such games, Dumon!" snapped Tsin. "It isn't as if we plan to kill you."

Unable to make any progress toward escape, Kentril paused to listen. "No?"

"The amount of blood needed will hardly even make you dizzy, I promise."

Blood. . . .

"Damn you!" Still gripping the sword, Kentril lunged.

The weapon disappeared from his hand, reappearing but a second later in that of Juris Khan.

With an almost casual air, Atanna's father tossed Kentril's last hope aside. "My dear captain. You continue to misunderstand everything. Yes, we require you to lie down upon the platform, but this is hardly a human sacrifice. Let me explain . . ." An almost saintly look spread across his lined visage. "We deal with powers that are part and sum that which keeps the natural order in balance. In that natural order, life is most paramount, and in life, *blood* is the strongest representation. To bind the power, then, we need blood. The platform acts as a focus, which is why the blood must be drawn there."

A soft but cold hand touched his cheek. Jumping, Kentril once more faced the creature he had thought he loved.

"And they only need a few drops for that. The rest they draw, my love, is for *us*."

The caress both teased him and made his flesh crawl. "Us?"

"Of course, Kentril, darling! When the entire spell is complete, not only will Ureh be once more in the real world, but you shall never have to fear death again. Isn't that wonderful?"

Never fear death again . . .

They would make him like *her*.

He tried to flee again, but his body refused to obey his demands. Kentril could breathe, he could even blink his eyes, but his legs and arms remained frozen.

"Really, Dumon! The embarrassment you cause us both. You can certainly spare a few drops to save a city and the offer Lord Khan gives you—if it could be done more than once, I'd do it to myself."

To his minor satisfaction, the mercenary commander discovered his mouth worked. "You're welcome to it, Tsin!"

"I, regrettably, must assist in the spell. Besides, our good host assures me that when the conjunction of forces is correct again, he shall grant the favor. For now, you are the fortunate one!"

Kentril's legs began to move, but not by his choice. Next to the platform, Quov Tsin made walking motions with two fingers. As he did, the fighter's legs mimicked his actions.

"Damn it, Tsin! Don't you realize that something's wrong here?"

As he neared the Vizjerei, though, the captain noticed a faint, glazed look in the sorcerer's eyes. Up close, Tsin had the appearance of a man *entranced*.

"Up, please," the Vizjerei commanded.

Unable to resist, Kentril climbed atop the platform, spreading out as if his limbs had been bound by invisible cuffs.

Juris Khan loomed over him. In his hand, the monarch wielded a slim but serpentine dagger. "Have no qualms, Kentril Dumon. Ureh shall be eternally grateful to you."

As he raised the blade above his head and uttered words of power, the captain caught sight of Atanna smiling expectantly at him.

Soon they would be together again . . . and he would be just like *her*.

The winged gargoyle leapt out of the door, its entire body seeming to sprout from the iron itself. The beaked maw opened and roared, and the metallic talons slashed at the pair.

To his credit, Gorst placed himself in front of Zayl and began trying to slay the creature with his ax. Unfortunately, the ax bounced off the body of the beast with a loud clang, chipping the weapon's head in the process.

"What do we do?" asked the giant. The gargoyle stretched a good eight to ten feet from end of beak to tip of hind quarters. Zayl knew that even Gorst dared not get too close; the unliving sentinel would tear him to ribbons.

"Let me try a spell." The gargoyle seemed much like a golem, only in animal form. Perhaps, the necromancer thought, it could be dealt with in much the same manner.

He did as he had done before, reversing both words and spell, trying to transmute false life back into an inanimate object.

For a moment, the monster paused. It shook its head as if trying to clear its thoughts, then continued to advance unchecked.

Beaten for the moment, Zayl and Gorst withdrew, winding their way back up the steps. The gargoyle continued to follow until it reached the midway point between the top and bottom of the stairway. There it suddenly froze, iron gaze fixed upon the pair above.

"So . . . first and foremost, it protects the door," Zayl muttered, wondering what he could do with that bit of information.

Gorst leaned on the ax, glaring back at the beast. "We gotta get down there. Kentril's there for sure, and I don't like that."

The necromancer had to agree with him. For what reason Captain Dumon might be down there, he could not say, but surely it had to involve something dire. The longer the gargoyle kept the two of them at bay, the greater the likelihood that the captain would be murdered . . . or even worse.

"What goes on out there?" demanded a voice at his belt.

In all that had happened, Zayl had forgotten about Humbart. Of course, the skull could do little, but unless the necromancer responded, he knew that Humbart would only continue to rant.

"We face a gargoyle blocking the door through which we believe Captain Dumon can be found," he informed the contents of the bag. "Unless you have something to offer, I would suggest you keep still."

True to form, the skull paid him no mind. "You try one of your golem spells?"

"Yes, and it failed."

"What about—?"

Zayl sighed, exasperated as usual with his bodiless companion despite the good Humbart had done for him in the past. "This is hardly the time! I—"

"Only one question, lad! What about the Iron Maiden?"

"Iron Maiden?" grumbled Gorst, likely knowing the term only from the torture device.

"Another spell involving reversal. Why it should even be brought up I—" The pale necromancer hesitated. "But it could work, I think. It will involve risk, but if I am careful, I should be all right."

The giant shook his head. "If it's dangerous, use me."

"Gorst—"

The massive fighter would not hear him. "If it doesn't work with me, you can try something else. If it doesn't with you, what am I going to do?"

He had a point there, one that Zayl disliked immensely. Servants of Rathma saw themselves as the front line in the battle to keep the mortal world in balance. They did not generally gamble the lives of others in their place.

"Very well, but do not risk yourself needlessly."

"What do I do?" Gorst asked.

Already casting the spell, Zayl replied, "You must engage the gargoyle in combat."

"That all?"

From the skull came another response. "You could also try praying a bit, lad!"

Gorst grunted. Zayl finished the spell, explaining, "If it works as planned, whatever blow it strikes against you will damage it instead. If you feel the slightest pain, retreat quickly."

The giant said nothing more, not even commenting on the

fact that if the gargoyle got one good strike at him, he would not have the chance to retreat. Hefting his weapon, the mercenary descended toward the metallic beast.

Nearly within range, Gorst suddenly paused. "If I strike him, does it hurt me?"

"No, you may attack at will."

The massive figure gave him a happy grin. "Good."

Nearly motionless while the two had stood atop the steps, the winged gargoyle suddenly stirred to savage life as the human approached. It snapped and slashed at Gorst even though the fighter had yet to get near enough. Despite his confidence in his spellwork, Zayl could not help feeling much concern for his companion. One never knew what spells might also surround the beast. He readied himself to protect Gorst the moment anything turned awry.

Barely a yard from the guardian, the giant suddenly raised the ax over his head and let out a war cry. The gargoyle roared in turn, leaping forward.

Metal clashed against metal. Despite the spell set upon him by the necromancer, Gorst fought as if his skills alone would save him.

Twice, three times, the head of the ax met the claws and savage beak of the gargoyle. The razor-sharp nails came within inches of the mercenary, but Gorst avoided them as he would have any attack.

With his prodigious strength, he dented the head of his adversary, but the toll of hitting the iron hide of the beast proved too much. The blade chipped and dulled, and each swing came slower and slower.

The gargoyle finally got one paw under Gorst's defenses. The fighter tried to retreat, but stumbled over the step behind him.

"What's happening?" Humbart called.

Zayl said nothing, poised to cast a spell even though he knew that it would not save the mercenary from terrible injury.

The claws tore at Gorst's right leg.

A horrible, metallic screeching sound rippled through the passage.

Gorst's monstrous foe suddenly tumbled to the side, its right rear leg shredded open. Seemingly unconcerned, the gargoyle pushed forward, trying with its beak to snap at the human's unprotected midsection.

Again the metallic shriek echoed throughout the area. Now the gargoyle did back away, although in rather haphazard fashion. In the area of its belly, a gaping hole now existed. A live animal would have already been dead or dying from such wounds, but the magic animating the winged terror kept it going, albeit without as much skill and fluidity of movement as in the beginning.

"It's working!" shouted Gorst. "I'm going in closer!"

Even seeing that his spell worked perfectly, Zayl did not relax. He also moved nearer to the struggle, watching for any possible threat or an opening of which he could make use.

Swinging the ax hard, the giant actually indented the gargoyle's left shoulder. Unimpeded by such a wound, the beast struck again, reaching for Gorst's right forearm.

The results were as expected. Instead of mangling soft, human flesh and ripping apart muscle and bone, the animated guardian only tore its own front right leg asunder. Suddenly stricken with two badly mauled limbs on the same side, the gargoyle teetered, falling against the wall. Yet still it did not give in.

"This is takin' too long!" bellowed the mercenary. "I'm gonna try something!"

He threw down his ax and leaned forward, presenting his face and throat for the beast.

"Gorst! No!" Even though the spell had so far protected the fighter, Zayl wanted to take no chances.

The metallic guardian, however, reacted too swiftly for the necromancer. With its good front limb, the winged creature slashed hard, aiming for the entire target. Claws that could have ripped away Gorst's face to the very bone came closer and closer . . .

With a savage squeal of wrenching iron, the gargoyle's own muzzle and throat tore off.

Little remained of the monstrous visage save a bit of eye. A ragged hole reminiscent of the damaged golems greeted the staring humans.

The gargoyle took an awkward step forward, choosing to stand on the ruined front limb. This time, it toppled completely to the side and seemed unable to right itself.

With almost childlike interest, Gorst leaned down and bared his chest to the one good forelimb. He then reached out and tapped the ruined guardian on the paw.

The paw instinctively attacked.

A great gouge appeared in the gargoyle's chest.

The metallic beast screeched once . . . then stilled.

"Nice spell," Gorst commented, rising. "How long does it last?"

"This battle is done," replied the necromancer. "It is gone now."

"Too bad. Can you cast it on me again?"

Zayl shook his head. "Not with any trust to its success. Besides, I suspect that such a spell will not help you down there."

The giant seized his battered ax again, not at all bothered by the other's answer. "Guess I'll just have to fight like normal, huh?"

With the gargoyle destroyed, the handle to the door had also been lost, but Zayl suspected that it did not serve as the true mechanism for entry. Such a place would not depend upon so mundane a device. The true key to opening the door had to involve magic—but how to discover that key?

He pulled the skull free. "Humbart, what do you see?"

"A red force blankets the whole thing. There's dark,

greenish lines zigzagging over it from top to bottom, and in the center I see a kind of blue-yellow spot—"

That had to be what Zayl sought. "Guide the tip of the blade to it."

The skull did, urging the necromancer's hand left and right, up and down, as needed. "Right on the mark there, lad!"

A slight tingle coursed through Zayl as he touched the point of his weapon to the spot. Immediately, he began a spell of searching and unbinding. Without the unique properties of the skull, Zayl knew that he would have never been able to pinpoint the area so precisely, so cleverly had the wards been set in place.

His mind untied and unfolded the myriad patterns creating the lock, slowly teasing out the secret to its opening. Unbidden from his mouth came words even he had never heard before, old, old words of dark imagining. The necromancer considered pulling free, but that would have left him with no other options, and Captain Dumon most certainly in some dire strait.

Then, at last, a single word came to him, the final key and, if he had been privy to the knowledge of the original caster, the only one truly needed.

"*Tezarka . . .*" Zayl whispered.

With a slow moan, the door began to open.

The necromancer leapt back, joining a wary Gorst in preparation of the attack surely to come. The iron door opened wider, revealing light from within. A flood of varied and powerful forces emanated from within, enough to awe even Zayl.

Yet nothing burst forth to attack them. No guards, no golems, nothing.

Glancing at each other, Zayl and Gorst cautiously entered.

The vast, angled room immediately snared their attention, for here clearly stood the most private sanctum of a powerful spellcaster. The weighty tomes, the gathered specimens, powders, and artifacts—Zayl had never seen such a collection. He stared, for the moment caught up in the sight. Even Gregus Mazi's abode had not touched him so.

It took Gorst to break the spell over him, Gorst, who asked the question that had to be asked.

"Why is it empty?"

Nineteen

They had left him unable to move but at least able to talk, and Kentril saw no reason to remain silent. "Tsin, Snap out of it! Can't you see how wrong everything about this is? You're under a spell yourself, damn it!"

"Do relax, Dumon," chided the Vizjerei. "Such an ungrateful cretin you are! Immortality, riches, power . . . I thought that was what a mercenary dreamed of."

It was no use. Quov Tsin could not see past whatever had been cast upon him. Lord Khan had preyed upon the sorcerer's greed, just as the captain himself had when first instigating Tsin to persuade their host to make Ureh part of the mortal world again.

Or *had* their host needed any convincing? It had been Atanna who had first broached the subject with Kentril, telling him that they could be together if her father did not decide to try once more to follow the path to Heaven. The mercenary realized that he had been *duped*; Juris Khan had no doubt sent his daughter to fill the gullible captain's head with such notions, knowing that Kentril would do his utmost to sway the Vizjerei.

Both he and Tsin had been played like puppets or, worse, fish on a line. Bait had been set to catch each, then the lord of Ureh had reeled them in with ease.

"It's quite ironic," commented the elder monarch. "I had only just sent my darling daughter to find you when you apparently came looking for her. I had meant to wait longer to cast this spell . . . but my children were so eager, so hungry, that I was forced to move the spell to this night."

Kentril looked to Tsin to see if he heard any of what their host had just confessed, but the short, balding sorcerer seemed quite contented preparing for the task at hand. The Vizjerei had begun to go around the edge of the platform, using mumbled spells to cause various runes to glow brighter. Whatever hold Juris Khan had over the sorcerer looked to be very complete, indeed.

"I had promised them your men when first we noticed your arrival, but I needed one of you for this precious work. I also needed another wielder of sorcery to aid in my effort, the others having been necessarily sacrificed to my sacred mission long ago."

"Gregus Mazi never tried to destroy Ureh, did he?"

The regal lord looked offended. "He did worse than that! He dared claim that I knew not what I did, claimed that *I*, Juris Khan, loving lord of all my subjects, *damned* rather than saved my people! Can you believe such audacity?"

Captain Dumon could believe that and much more about his captor. He saw now what he and the rest had so blindly missed. Ureh's master had gone completely insane, his desire for good somehow twisted into all of this.

"I admit, there were times when my beliefs faltered, but whenever that happened, the archangel would appear to me, bolster my will, and once more set me on the proper course. Without his guidance, it's possible I wouldn't have pressed on to the end."

This archangel Juris Khan constantly spoke of had to have been a product of his own mind—and yet, here stood the man who had nearly succeeded in reaching the sanctuary of Heaven! How could the archangel have been delusion, then? Only with the efforts of such a one could any mortal possibly have hoped to accomplish so incredible a feat.

"He warned me of the insidious efforts of the dark powers to influence those around me, that I could not trust any but myself. Even those who worked in concert to bring success to our goal might have become tainted . . ." Khan wore an expression of intense pride. "And so I cleverly planned to make certain that none of them would have the opportunity to betray me at the moment of our destiny!"

When the priests and spellcasters had gathered to do their part, they had not realized that their master had something else in mind in addition to their work. Devised in secret, Ureh's monarch had instituted a second spell, one so enmeshed in the principal effort that none of his underlings would take notice of it. Each would unknowingly assist in ensuring that there would be no attempt to usurp the holy quest.

Juris Khan had laid within the master spell a means by which to slay each and every one of those who aided him.

Their fates had been decided the moment they had begun. The spell that had sought to cast Ureh to Heaven had not only drawn from the innate magical powers of the world, but had also done so with equal force from the casters themselves.

"It had all been so well-planned, down to the most delicate of details," Kentril's captor went on. "I could feel Ureh's soul being lifted from its earthly shell . . . and the life forces of the corrupted ones being leeched from their treacherous selves."

But he had underestimated one among them, the one he most should have watched. Gregus Mazi, trusted confidant and nearly son to the elder ruler, a sorcerer knowledgeable and skilled. Along with the priest Tobio, Mazi had been the one who had most contributed to the breakthrough needed to make the great spell possible in the first place.

"I saw it in his eyes. I saw the moment when he comprehended what the spell sought to do to him. He didn't realize that I had done the altering, but he knew nonetheless the result. At the most crucial moment, at the most critical juncture, Gregus tore himself free from the matrix we had all created. With his remaining power he cast himself *out* of Ureh . . ."

The instinctive reaction had done more than save Mazi; it had also created an imbalance that had ripped the soul of Ureh free from the mortal plane, but, instead of sending the realm to Heaven, had left it in a shadowed, timeless limbo. With the aid of the rest of the kingdom's sorcerers and priests, Juris Khan might have been able to correct the matter and complete the quest for holy sanctuary, but his spell had done to them what it had failed to do to Gregus Mazi.

The one exception proved to be Tobio, whom providence had saved virtually unscathed. Lord Khan had decided that this had meant the priest had been chosen to live, and it pleased the monarch to know that one old friend of his had remained true. With Tobio, Khan had immediately worked to find freedom from their endless prison, but all plans had failed. The people had begun to panic, to fear that they would be trapped forever.

Juris Khan raised the dagger over Kentril as he talked, drawing invisible patterns. "And then, when our hour was darkest," he added with a grateful smile, "the archangel came to me in my dreams again. As you already know, he could not alter what had happened, but he could, at least, guide and—more important—assist me in fulfilling my people's destiny. The Heavenly One showed me how to open a door of sorts, let his power flood into me, let his wishes and mine mingle . . . and from there touch my children."

However, when he found out about this new gift, Tobio had proven to be a most jealous priest—at least in Khan's eyes. He had confronted his old friend, had claimed him to be not the recipient of holy powers but *tainted* by infernal ones. The priest had even had the audacity to attempt to restrain his lord, but Juris Khan had easily overwhelmed the misguided clergyman. With saddened heart, he cast Tobio into the ancient dungeons below, hoping that someday the priest would shake off the sinful thoughts and return to the fold.

Unhindered now, Lord Khan had acted upon the archangel's dictates, creating spells that would help preserve his precious children while he sought a more permanent remedy. The archangel showed him how to keep the people calm, how to open up each to the subtle ministrations of other angels, one for each person. He had Ureh's trusting ruler bring into the fold his own daughter, reveal to her the glory of the archangel and the gifts she would gain by helping her father and her people.

Pulling back the dagger from over Captain Dumon's chest, Juris Khan extended one arm to Atanna. The crimson-tressed princess came to her father, letting him envelop her in that arm. Atanna gave Kentril a loving, knowing smile, one filled with the certainty of the right-eousness of her sire's cause.

"She was scared, my good captain, scared because she did not understand the blessing he wished to give her." The weathered but noble face beamed down at his loving offspring. "I had to be forceful. I had to *insist* . . . despite her unwillingness. It took much perseverance, even on the part of the archangel, but at last she opened herself up to him."

Atanna wore an enraptured expression. "It was so *child-ish*, my love! I actually feared what Father wanted! When the archangel entered me, I actually *screamed*, can you believe it? It all seems so silly now!"

To the captive mercenary, who had seen what such a blessing had created of Atanna and her father, it hardly seemed silly at all. Whatever their angelic benefactor had sought to accomplish, it had resulted in an abomination of everything holy.

"I believe I'm nearly ready, my lord," Quov Tsin suddenly announced. "There are but a few minor patterns to cast."

"I'm gratified, master sorcerer. Without your effort, this could not come to be."

Kentril chose to use the distraction as a chance again to test the mobility of his body. Unfortunately, even despite the Vizjerei's numerous tasks and Lord Khan's horrific reminiscences, the sorcery keeping the captain prisoner had not faltered in the least.

Atanna came to his side again, rubbing what would have been a soothing hand on his forehead if not for the fact that she used the same appendage that had earlier been mangled to pulp. The rich emerald eyes gleamed but did not blink. "You'll feel so silly yourself when this is all over, darling Kentril. You'll wonder just as I did why I made so much of a fuss."

He could not meet her gaze, not while the memory of how she had looked when she entered the chamber still burned harshly in his mind. Instead, the captain glanced past her at Juris Khan, who seemed to have finished with his tale and now intended to do the same to Kentril. "What did happen to Gregus Mazi?"

The pleasant smile on the robed monarch's kindly face became not at all pleasant. "I told you of the Keys, their making, and our earlier attempt to lock the shadow in place just as you eventually did for us. I also told you how Gregus came again to do the unthinkable, to betray us again. In all this, I did not lie, good captain. What I omitted, though, was that he had help . . . in the form of the misguided Tobio."

Gregus Mazi had secretly returned to Ureh and had learned of the crystals just as Lord Khan had previously said, but in the process he had also come across the still-imprisoned priest. Seizing on Tobio's madness and pretending to believe it, the sorcerer had informed his new ally that they had to remove or destroy the two Keys so that the holy kingdom could not remain on the mortal plane. It was decided that their chances would be double if each went in search of separate stone. Then, if only one of them succeeded, Ureh would again be cast into limbo.

But although he had entered the city unnoticed, Gregus Mazi did not escape his former master's attention when he sought out the Key to Shadow. The sorcerer had almost succeeded in stealing away the crystal, but Lord Khan had managed to catch him in the midst of the act.

They did battle, but the traitorous spellcaster did not know of the powerful gifts the archangel had given. Mazi fell swiftly, and in order to make certain there would be no repeat of such betrayal, Khan transformed him into the sentinel Kentril and the others had discovered. Before that happened, however, the lord of Ureh had wrung from his former friend the fact that Tobio had already started for the other crystal.

"You see, my dear captain, the Key to Light had indeed been set in place by brave martyrs. However, when I learned from Gregus that Tobio had gone to destroy my hopes for our eventual release, I admit I grew furious. Summoning the powers granted to me by the archangel, I transported myself to the shadowed side of the peak, there to find the misguided priest seeking to wrest the Key to Light from its anointed place." Khan paused, eyes momentarily closed in what appeared to be a moment of renewed mourning. When he opened them again, he told his prisoner, "I still cry for poor Tobio, corrupted by Gregus. His death I could not help. I gave him one good opportunity to see the errors of his way, to break free of the madness and come back with me to Ureh . . ."

Suddenly, Kentril recalled the grisly discovery he had found all but buried in the cold, hard soil atop sinister Nymyr. "But he didn't, did he?"

"Alas, no. Instead, foolish Tobio tore the Key free and stepped back into the first rays of the day. I admit I reacted without thought, only aware that he had stolen my children's freedom."

The weathered bone Captain Dumon had found had

belonged to the determined priest, not one of the so-called volunteers. Uncorrupted, Tobio had been able to step into the sunlight, but it had not saved him from Juris Khan's wrath. Fortunately, the crystal had fallen to where even the lord of Ureh could not reach it. The madness that had consumed the shadowed kingdom had been kept in check.

That is, until Kentril and his men had come along.

"Even if the good Tobio had failed, I admit I would've still required the aid of a worthy sorcerer such as our friend Quov Tsin here," concluded Atanna's father, "but that would've been so much easier with the kingdom set in place, not resurrecting only once a day or two every few years." The smile returned. "But come! Time is fast approaching, and I've likely bored you with so much talk of the past. Now we must prepare for the future, when my people—my children—enlightened by the angels and no longer fearful of the sun, can go out into the world of men and spread the archangel's word to others."

But Kentril had seen those "children," the ghoulish creatures that now filled the city. The ghostly forms he and the others had first witnessed had been illusions to mask an even greater horror. Khan had played on the sympathies of the mercenary officer—and because of it, Captain Dumon had sent most of his men to terrible, monstrous deaths.

The vision he had seen twice had been no delusion caused by a thief's drug, no bite from a savage insect. It had been the truth, the reality of Ureh. The holy kingdom, the Light among Lights, had been transformed into something diabolic—*demonic*. All this time, Juris Khan had been manipulating him, preparing the way so that his horrific subjects could spread beyond the confines of the shadow, spread throughout the mortal lands . . .

Yet all the time his captor spoke of the wondrous archangel, the Heavenly figure who had come to guide him and his flock to the ultimate sanctuary. Again, Kentril wondered how everything had turned out so horribly.

When had the archangel's word become twisted or usurped?

Or had there ever been an archangel in the first place?

Lord Khan had already taken his place, Atanna and Quov Tsin following suit. The towering monarch raised the dagger and opened his mouth—

"My lord!" blurted Kentril. "One last question, to ease my mind and enable me to accept this glory you offer! May—may I see what this wondrous archangel looked like?"

The Vizjerei, obviously eager to continue, only snorted at this abrupt question, but Juris Khan accepted it with pleasure, clearly believing that the fighter sought to understand. "Why, bless you, Kentril Dumon! If it makes all the difference, I can *try* to show you. You must know, of course, that I draw from memory, and so what you see, however magnificent, is but a dim, human representation of a being perfect in all manner. In truth, even I never saw him fully, for what mortal could stand the blinding glory of one of Heaven's guardians?"

Giving the blade to his daughter, he held his hands up high and muttered a spell. Kentril tensed more, although he could not be certain exactly why. Lord Khan would only be summoning a representation of the archangel, not the true being. The mercenary could hardly expect any aid from an illusion.

"Behold!" Juris Khan called, indicating an area well above the platform. "Behold a warrior of Truth, a guardian of the Bastion of Light, a sentinel of Goodness watching over all! Behold the Archangel Mirakodus, the golden-haired defender of mankind! Behold Mirakodus, he who has protected Ureh from the evils seeking its soul!"

And as his words echoed throughout the chamber, a figure formed for all of them to see. Atanna let out a raptured gasp, and even the jaded Tsin fell to one knee in homage. Juris Khan himself had tears in his eyes, and he mouthed silent thanks to the image of the one he had called his people's greatest protector.

Kentril stared in awe, too. Clad in glorious armor of the brightest platinum, intricate runes and sculptured glyphs decorating his breast plate, the tall, angelic form glowed as brightly as the sun. One arm held in it a flaming sword; the other reached out to the onlooker, as if beckoning him to come nearer. From the archangel's shoulders radiated a display of crackling, writhing tendrils of pure magical energy that in their continual frenzy created the illusion of massive, fiery wings.

The carved images that the mercenary had grown up around had always depicted the angels as hooded, faceless beings, but not so this one. The hood had been thrown back, revealing a visage of perfection surrounded by cascading golden hair. Captain Dumon at first felt some guilt for even gazing upon the heavenly features of Mirakodus, as if somehow the mercenary had not yet proven himself worthy to do such a thing. The broad jaw, the heroic cheekbones, the impossibly commanding visage—Kentril could never quite make out the specifics of any feature, but the overall impression left him momentarily speechless. No human being could ever hope to match such beauty, such perfection. Lord Khan had only managed to catch an earthly indication of Mirakodus, but even that proved enough to overwhelm the senses.

And then Kentril looked into the eyes and felt his awe suddenly supplanted by an entirely different sensation.

The eyes drew him in, snared him. He could not identify their color, only that they were dark, darker than even the most perfect black. Like a horrific vortex, Kentril Dumon felt as if Mirakodus drew in his very soul, pulled it into some bottomless pit. The urge to scream arose, yet at the same time the vision the mercenary beheld kept him in silent fear. An unreasonable panic such as Kentril had never suffered shook him. He wanted to rip his gaze away, but the eyes would not permit him that escape.

The captain felt himself dragged deeper and deeper into the archangel's eyes, deeper and deeper into a horror impossible to define yet in some way innately familiar. His skin tore from his flesh, and his bones danced free. Kentril felt the death of the grave and the unending torment of the damned soul.

Something within, some desperate push for sanity, for hope, at last enabled the fighter to tear his eyes from the figure above. As his mind slowly pieced itself together, Kentril tried to come to grips with what he had witnessed. Outwardly a messenger, a guardian of Heaven, but within, recognized perhaps even by the subconscious of Juris Khan, a thing that could not in any manner be associated with the archangels or their realm. Behind the facade that no one else seemed to see past, Captain Dumon had recognized a monstrous force, a thing of pure evil.

And in his mind, Kentril could only imagine one creature, one being, who could invoke such fear, such terror. The name thrust itself unbidden from the hardy fighter as he sought futilely to push himself away from Lord Khan's illusion.

"Diablo . . ."

"Yes," his captor said with an enthralled smile, seemingly ignorant of what Kentril had cried. "Mirakodus in as much his glory as an earthly mind can comprehend!" The image suddenly vanished as Juris Khan clasped his hands together in outright pleasure, his smile now turned toward the still dumbfounded soldier. "And now that I've shown you the wonderful truth, shall we begin?"

Zayl studied the chamber he and Gorst had so desperately sought to reach, the chamber where the necromancer had felt with complete certainty that Captain Dumon would be found. He stepped toward the center, all but unmindful of the massive, rune-covered platform as he tried to fathom what had gone wrong.

"Where is he?" asked the huge mercenary, eyes shifting

warily from one part of the chamber to another. "You said he'd be in here."

"He should be." Zayl consulted the spell again, but the result came up the same. Everything pointed to this being the captain's whereabouts.

Yet, quite clearly, it was not.

He put away the medallion, trying to see what the dagger itself might reveal. Unfortunately, a full sweep indicated nothing.

Gorst wandered around, peering at every corner no matter how unlikely. "Think there's another door somewhere?"

"Possible, but not likely."

"Could he be below or above us?"

An astute question from the giant, but the necromancer had worked to focus his search spell in order to avoid that error. According to his results, their companion *should* have been right before them.

Shutting his eyes briefly, Zayl let his senses expand beyond his body. He suddenly became much more aware of the fearsome and wild powers at play and the fact that they most gathered near the stone platform just before him.

"You notice something?" Gorst asked hopefully.

"Nothing that clears up the question of what went wrong. I feel certain that he is supposed to be here."

The gargantuan fighter mulled this over for several seconds, then suggested, "Maybe Humbart could help."

A suggestion Zayl should have thought of himself. The skull had proven without a doubt its value, yet the necromancer ever hesitated. Zayl's instructors had always taught him the importance of independence, but when a tool such as Humbart Wessel worked, why not make the best of it?

He pulled the last bit of mortal remains of the older mercenary from the new pouch and showed Humbart the chamber. The skull made small, thoughtful sounds, but did not otherwise speak as his wielder let him view everything.

"I can't see hide or hair of him," Humbart announced when they had finished. "A real puzzle, that!"

"You see nothing?"

"Oh, I see a lot! I see a damned hodgepodge of colors and lines and other shapes and forms all swirling madcap about that big block of stone there. I see just about every rune on that thing glowing like lightning. I see enough signs of raw, earthly, and unearthly energy wrapping itself about that thing to make me wish I had feet again so I could hightail it out of here. But I don't see Captain Kentril Dumon *anywhere!*"

The necromancer grimaced. "Then my spell went awry after all. Despite my best efforts, it sent us in the wrong direction."

"It happens to everyone, lad. Maybe if you tried again?"

"I have tried enough. The results would be the same, I promise you."

This did not please Gorst at all. "But we can't give up on him!" the behemoth roared, slamming a fist on the nearest table and nearly upsetting an entire shelf of specimens nearby. "I can't!"

"Easy, boy!" snapped Humbart.

Fearing that the giant's growing rage might end up recreating Zayl's own near disaster in Gregus Mazi's sanctum, the spellcaster quickly said, "No one is giving up, Gorst! We need simply to think this through. Something is wrong here, something that I must consider carefully."

Somewhat mollified, the mercenary quieted. Zayl only hoped that he could live up to his words. He studied the various parts of the sanctum again, trying to find anything amiss. He stared at the shelves, the tables, the stone platform, the jars full of—

"Humbart, tell me once more what you see when you stare at the platform."

The skull did, recounting the furious forces and the glaringly bright and vivid runes. He told of the swirling energy, wild and monstrous, gathered over it. Humbart Wessel described a virtual maelstrom of sorcerous powers at play above and as a part of the stone structure.

"I don't see any of that," Gorst commented when the skull had finished.

Nor did the necromancer, and that interested him very much. He could sense them, yes, but not see them as Humbart did.

And from the skull's vivid description, it sounded as if the forces at play grew more alive, more violent, with each passing moment. They had to be building up to something, something Zayl could only imagine very terrifying.

Returning Humbart to the pouch, the necromancer stepped to the platform. Although he saw no life in the various runes, the feeling that they had been brought into play remained with him, so much so that when Zayl ran his fingers over several, he could swear he felt them pulsating.

"What is it?" Gorst asked.

"I do not know . . . but I must try something." Inspecting the runes, Zayl touched three he recognized for their power. He muttered a spell under his breath, creating ties between himself and those runes. Raw forces charged through his system, causing the necromancer to gasp.

The giant started toward him, but Zayl shook his head. Still struggling to keep the forces in balance, the spellcaster drew forth his dagger. The blade gleamed bright, and as he held the weapon over the platform, a rainbow of colors arose from various markings etched in the stone, creating an almost blinding display of power.

"Let the truth be known!" Zayl shouted to the ceiling. "Let the mask fall away! Let the world be shown as it is, our eyes uncovered at last! *Hezar ky Brogdinas! Hezar ke Nurati! Hezar ky—*"

Suddenly the necromancer felt a sense of displacement

so great that he could not maintain his link. He fell back, his eyes seeming to lose all focus. He saw the entire chamber doubled—and yet also very different. While one version held Zayl and Gorst, the other revealed a different, barely visible scene with three figures standing very near him.

As Zayl stepped farther back, Gorst came forward. "I see him! I see—"

He got no farther. The room—all sense of reality—shifted again for the pair. The giant fell to one knee, and it was all the necromancer could do not to do the same.

The other version of their surroundings began to fade. Zayl struggled forward again, determined not to lose it. The vaguely seen figures did not even notice what happened around them. They appeared engrossed in something concerning the platform. One of them looked like Juris Khan, and another had hair the color of his daughter's. The shortest of the three put Zayl in mind of the Vizjerei, although what Quov Tsin would be doing here he could not say.

Planting his hands on two of the runes, Zayl barked out his spell anew. He summoned the forces to him. Something else sought to draw them away, but the necromancer persisted, certain that if he did not, it would result in disaster.

Again everything shifted. The two variations moved closer into sync.

A fourth form coalesced on the platform, the arms and legs spread as if bound.

The startling addition almost caused Zayl to lose his concentration a second time. Everything began to fade again, but he managed to keep it from disappearing altogether. For a third time, Zayl shouted the words of power while he demanded that the forces inherent in the runes obey his dictates.

The figure trapped on the platform came into focus. Zayl recognized Kentril Dumon, who did not yet see him. In fact, the captain stared wide-eyed at something above him, his expression so intense that the necromancer had to look himself.

Juris Khan loomed over them, eyes wide with anticipation. His hand had just begun a swift plunge toward Captain Dumon's chest—and in that hand a wicked blade sought the mercenary's heart.

Twenty

A simple spell had left Kentril unable to protest any longer, Juris Khan proclaiming that he needed the silence in order to cast the spell accurately. He actually apologized to his captive, assuring the captain that when all had been accomplished, he would make it up to him.

Atanna had come before the spellwork to stroke his forehead and kiss him gently on the lips. Now her mouth felt cold, dead, and the eyes looked glassy, a parody of life. Had someone long ago told the mercenary that the offer of a beautiful princess and immortality would someday revolt him, he would have surely laughed.

Now Kentril could only pray for a miracle.

Quov Tsin continued to ignore the obvious, continued to aid in this abominable plan. The Vizjerei began the first part of the spell, summoning forth forces locked in the runes and intertwining them with the raw powers emanating all around. Beside him, a blissful smile on her face, Atanna murmured words in what sounded like a backward version of the common tongue. She had her arms spread apart, the palm of one hand facing Tsin, the other facing her father.

Lord Khan himself presided over the prone Kentril, the sinister dagger held high and seemingly ready at any moment to strike. The monarch of blessed Ureh spoke in a combination of understandable and unintelligible phrases, both of which lent further fear to the prisoner.

"Blood is the river of life!" the elder man shouted to the ceiling at one point. "And we drink gratefully from the river!

Blood is the sustenance of the heart . . . and the heart is the key to the soul! The soul is the guide to Heaven . . . and the guide to mortality . . ."

The dagger edged nearer, then receded as Khan started speaking in one of the cryptic languages again. Kentril wanted to faint, but knew that he if fell prey to such an escape, he might never wake up. Whether that would be preferable to the monstrous existence offered to him, the captain could not yet say. If he stayed conscious, at least some hope existed, however meager, that he would still find a way to free himself before it was too late.

But no avenue of escape presented itself to him. As Kentril watched wide-eyed, Juris Khan finally leaned forward and raised the dagger high above his captive's heart. The look in the elder man's eyes told the mercenary that this time, the blade would be plunged into its target.

Swirling tendrils of pure energy arose around Kentril, causing every fiber of his being to go completely taut. Quov Tsin guided the tendrils, from which Lord Khan then seemed to draw strength.

"Great servant of Heaven above, Archangel Mirakodus, hear this humble one! Blood, the harbinger of the soul, opens the path to the true world! Let your power guide! Let at last the might of Heaven undo what has been done! Undo the shadow's binding! Let the sun serve not to give death to your children! Let Ureh return to the mortal plane, and from Ureh let your children go forth and bring to their fellow men and women the truth you so dearly wish all to know!"

It all sounded so mad, but Kentril could do or say nothing to prevent the sacrifice.

"Blessed Mirakodus, with this blood, I, Juris Khan, do humbly beg this boon!"

The dagger came down—

A hand suddenly appeared out of nowhere and clutched Captain Dumon's right arm. Kentril paid it little mind, expecting that Tsin had simply wanted to make certain that the mercenary did not somehow manage to shift position. Shutting his eyes, Kentril waited for the agony, the emptiness of death . . .

"Captain, you must move quickly! I fear we may have little time!"

His eyes flew open. "Zayl?"

Sure enough, the necromancer leaned over him, one slim hand clutching the right arm. Farther back, Gorst watched them, his expression caught midway between relief and mistrust.

Of the other three, he could see no sign. All else in the chamber looked exactly as it should, but Khan, Atanna, and the Vizjerei had all *vanished.*

"What—?" he began, only belatedly realizing that the power of speech had been returned to him.

The necromancer cut him off. "Hurry! He may realize at any moment that I have usurped his spell. I must get us away from here before then!"

Zayl took his dagger and quickly passed it over each limb. As he did, Kentril felt the ability to move return. He needed no more urging from the spellcaster to leap free of the sacrificial platform.

"I am going to try something," Zayl informed him and Gorst. "With so many sources to draw power from, it may work. It may be our only chance!"

Not liking the thought of just standing around and hoping that the necromancer could save them, Kentril asked, "Can we do anything?"

"Indeed you can! Gorst, give the captain a weapon. The two of you must watch out for me in case our esteemed host realizes what I am now doing."

Kentril took the sword the other mercenary offered him, realizing at the same time that Zayl fully expected Juris Khan to return from wherever he had been sent at any moment. The two wary soldiers kept guard while the necromancer swiftly drew a complex pattern over the runes.

"This should do it," Zayl suddenly remarked. Without

explanation, he pointed the dagger first at himself, then at each of his companions.

A sense of extreme lightness touched Kentril, almost as if he had lost every bit of weight. The mercenary officer almost expected to begin to float away, much as a cloud might. He opened his mouth to ask what the spellcaster planned—

The chamber vanished.

A wind-tossed mountain ridge materialized around him. Kentril reacted to this abrupt change of venue by planting himself against the rock face as quickly as he could.

Zayl had transported them to the most precarious edge of Nymyr.

The wind howled ominously, and thunder rumbled. Kentril looked up, saw that the sky had transformed. The nightmarish colors of his earlier visions had returned. He quickly glanced down at Ureh, to see now only a few sinister lights below. Captain Dumon could only imagine the scene within the city, the demonic denizens of the once-holy realm now stripped of any pretense of humanity.

"This was not where I planned to send us," muttered Zayl, his expression quite frustrated. "With the power I usurped from the runes, I should have easily been able to transport us to somewhere beyond the confines of this cursed shadow."

Kentril recalled the image of the false archangel. "Maybe that's not allowed. Maybe there is no escape from Ureh."

The necromancer eyed him closely. "Captain, what was Juris Khan doing when I appeared?"

"He said he had to cast a spell to ensure that Ureh would remain on the mortal plane, a spell that would allow his children to go forth into the world." With a deep breath, Kentril quickly went into what details seemed relevant. He described the monarch's clear madness, Tsin's entranced betrayal, the horrific incident involving Atanna, and the discovery that Lord Khan's archangel had been anything but Heaven-sent.

"This begins to add up, although not in any way I find comforting," Zayl remarked when Kentril had finished. "I think I understand. My friends, I think that Juris Khan did not nearly send his people to the sanctuary of Heaven . . . but instead all but condemned them to *Hell*."

The news did not surprise Captain Dumon nearly as much as it once might have. Such an answer would explain much of what they had confronted and certainly explained how he had felt simply staring into the eyes of Khan's interpretation of the mysterious archangel.

Zayl peered around carefully, almost as if he expected other ears to be listening on the godforsaken ridge. "This is my thought. In the days when Ureh stood above all others as a symbol of purity, that which spellcasters and priests knowledgeable called the Sin War took place. Little is known about its true form, but the powers of darkness were most active then, and such a place as the holy kingdom suffered many insidious attacks. Some of the legends you know hint of this, but hardly explain the full depth of the danger present to the mortal world back then."

"Demons attacked Ureh?" Gorst asked, his brow furrowing deeply at such a monstrous notion.

"Not as an army, but rather as forces seeking to corrupt those within. Generations of rulers worked endlessly to keep the corruption out, to protect the innocents from the Prime Evils . . ." The necromancer suddenly knelt and began drawing symbols on the ridge with his dagger. "Forgive me. I must work while I explain, or else we are all lost . . ."

"What're you doing?"

"Providing us with some protection from the eyes of our host, I hope, captain."

He drew a vast circle, then in the center put in place a

series of runes. Although the necromancer appeared quite untouched by the harsh wind, both mercenaries had to continue to press against the mountainside to garner even some minute bit of security.

"Your tale fills many of the gaps in my own," Zayl went on. "I fear that while Juris Khan so carefully guarded his flock, he did not himself remain wary enough of the wolf. I believe that, as you indicated, something taking the semblance of a warrior of Heaven seduced the good ruler into believing that what he did would be best for Ureh. I believe, as you do, that this may very well have been *Diablo* himself!"

"But surely it can't be!" Kentril protested, not wanting to believe that he had seen the truth. "That would be just too outrageous!"

"Hardly. Ureh was the greatest prize of all. It would demand the effort of the greatest of demons. Yes, captain, I think that Diablo came in the form you saw, corrupted Lord Khan without him realizing that fact, and twisted everything good the man desired into worse and worse evil. Instead of Heaven, he would have sent them to Hell, and only the timely action of Gregus Mazi prevented that. However, even limbo could not save them forever . . ."

Diablo, so the spellcaster suspected, had managed at last to touch once more the mind of his pawn. Slowly, he had made Juris Khan give both his people and his daughter to the demon lord. Ureh had become a corrupt nightmare, where the few who had perhaps resisted had become sacrifices or worse.

But the Lord of Terror had not been satisfied yet. Perhaps it had initially occurred to him when Ureh had first momentarily returned to the mortal world. Perhaps then Diablo had seen the opportunity for a true gateway through which his evil hordes could spread out into the world, unchecked by any barrier whatsoever.

"But Diablo required blood, untainted blood, to do this. Unfortunately, in his madness, Juris Khan had slain all other available spellcasters. He needed someone to aid him, someone of knowledge and skill. By either chance or fate, your party provided him with both."

"But you rescued me. We've stopped him."

Zayl arose, his solemn gaze meeting the captain's own. "Have we? The spell seemed quite advanced when I finally reached you."

"But he never drew any blood from me."

The necromancer nodded, but clearly took no comfort from that fact. "He still has Master Tsin."

Kentril gaped. Tsin had become Lord Khan's puppet, but, like the mercenaries, he had not been touched by either the original spell upon Ureh or its subsequent corruption. "But is that possible? Won't they need him for the rest of the work?"

"The Vizjerei has aided them in binding the forces that they need. It would be risky still, but I would not put it past our host and his true master if they grow desperate. Tsin's blood will do, if necessary."

Then, even though he had been rescued, Kentril and his companions had still failed. They had left behind them a demon-corrupted kingdom that would soon no longer be trapped under the shroud created by the mountain's shadow.

And when that happened, the horrors that had been visited upon Kentril would be delivered unto the rest of the world.

"No . . ."

"No, indeed," agreed the pale figure. "But I believe there is still a chance to prevent this horrific thing from coming to pass, a chance to send Ureh to its long-overdue and proper rest."

"But how? If Tsin's blood is already spilled, doesn't that mean that the city's already a part of our world again?"

"In order to work, the spell must be tied into the two Keys. It is my suspicion that they must still be in place when the sun touches the one atop this peak. Only then will the spell of blood tie itself to darkness and light and grant those within Ureh the ability to step freely beyond the shadow."

Gorst put the matter into simpler terms. "If the stones're in place, the demons can go free. If they're not, then Ureh turns back into ruins."

"Correct . . . but if the latter occurs, this time it will be permanent."

That made their path quite clear to Kentril. "Then use your sorcery to transport us to one of the Keys. We smash it, and all's done."

"Alas, captain, that would be unwise. I tried to use the power of the runes to send us to your original encampment, just beyond the shadow, but"—he spread his hands—"you can see where we ended up."

"So what do we do, then?"

Zayl toyed with the knife. "I have not entirely given up on using the vestiges of the power I usurped from the runes to transport us at least part of the way. I believe I can send you and Gorst near enough to the Key to Light to give you a chance. In the meantime, I will descend toward the Key to Shadow. One of us may succeed. That is all we need to do to stop this horror from expanding beyond Ureh."

That plan had been tried before, though, and for Gregus Mazi and the priest Tobio, it had failed miserably. Kentril pointed that out.

The necromancer, however, had an answer ready. With a grim smile, he explained, "I shall make myself much more noticeable. I suspect that Juris Khan will believe me the greater threat because of my skills. Besides that, he will have every reason to believe we all travel together."

"Illusion?" It hardly seemed likely to Kentril that Khan would fall for so simple a spell.

"Hardly. Captain . . . may I have a bit of your blood?"

After nearly having had it spilled already, the mercenary was surprised by the question. Still, he felt he could trust Zayl, especially under the circumstances. The man had saved his life.

Kentril thrust his hand forward, palm up.

Nodding, the necromancer reached forward with his blade, at the same time saying, "You, too, Gorst."

The giant obeyed with less trepidation, likely because of Kentril's own decision. Zayl pricked the forefinger of each, then had the pair turn their palms down.

Spots of blood stained the ridge. The ebony-clad spell-caster waited until each fighter had lost three drops, then ordered the two to step back.

He whispered for several seconds, waving one hand over the stained areas. Then, to both mercenaries' astonishment, Zayl pricked his own finger, carefully letting three drops fall upon each set.

"Under other circumstances, I would cast this in an entirely different way," he commented. "But this will have to do."

Again, he muttered under his breath. Kentril could see the strain in the necromancer's face and understood then that what Zayl sought to accomplish opposed everything he had been taught.

Suddenly, the ground before the captain began to rise up. A few inches at first, then more and more, in less than a minute the mound of rock and earth growing to half the size of a man and getting larger by the second. The taller the mound grew, the more it also took a defined shape. Arms sprouted from the sides, and from the arms grew individual fingers, then entire hands.

As the first mound rose, a second did the same next to it. This one outpaced even the first, quickly rising to become as tall as Gorst. In fact, the more Kentril studied it, the more it outwardly resembled a carving of the giant. Legs formed, and the outline of a torso developed. Even the thick mane of hair began to sprout forth.

And before the astounded eyes of the fighters, their very twins came into being.

The new Kentril and Gorst stood as still as the rock from which they had been born. Only the eyes blinked, but they did so at a uniform pace, not randomly like living people.

"A variation on the golem spells," Zayl told his friends. "Not an experiment to be tried first under such conditions, but at least it worked."

Gazing at his own face, Kentril asked, "Can they talk?"

"They have no true minds of their own. They can perform basic functions, such as walk and, to a point, fight, but that is it. Enough, though, I think, to keep the eyes of Juris Khan upon me until you reach the Key to Light."

"Zayl, you're setting yourself up to be a decoy—and not the type that usually survives the hunt!"

The necromancer's expression remained guarded. "I present us with our best odds, captain."

He obviously would not be talked out of it, and, in fact, Kentril could think of no good reason to turn down his plan. In truth, Zayl had more of a chance against Khan than either of the nonmagical fighters.

"We have taken enough chance here," Zayl went on. "I must send you away before he finally discovers where we are. I believe only because we did not end up where I expected did we avoid instant pursuit."

Once more, the necromancer focused his powers on the two. Kentril stood close to Gorst and tried to prepare himself for the sorcerous journey. That Zayl's last attempt had gone awry did not ease his mind about this second try. For all they knew, the mercenaries might end up dangling from the top tower of Khan's palace.

"May the Dragon watch over you," the spellcaster quietly called.

Zayl and the ridge vanished.

Juris Khan stared at the place where Kentril Dumon had been, stared at it in both pious anger and disappointment. The dark one had to be at fault for this, the foul necromancer he had been forced to accept as a guest in order to maintain appearances. It had disturbed him even to allow such a dealer in the magic of corpses to enter his beloved city, but he had forced himself to smile whenever Zayl had been near.

And now this was how the necromancer had repaid him.

"What in blazes?" spouted Quov Tsin. "What happened?"

"A misunderstanding," Khan returned. "A foolish misunderstanding."

Atanna had a look of intense disappointment on her face, something that only deepened the monarch of Ureh's fury at the unclean Zayl. "My Kentril!" she cried. "Father! My Kentril!"

He put a calming hand on her soft shoulder. "Calm yourself, my beloved daughter. The good captain will be returned to us. We may have to perform a different rite on him to make him ready for you, but rest assured, it'll happen."

"But what of Dumon?" the Vizjerei demanded. "Where did he go?"

"It appears I underestimated this Zayl. Not only did he see past the magical variation of this chamber I had long ago cast, but he used it to his advantage, reaching out from the other reality into this one and taking the captain with him."

"What of the spell, though? What of that?"

Lord Khan gazed thoughtfully at the sorcerer, but directed his words to his daughter. "Yes, what of that?

Atanna, my darling, has our work been completely ruined?"

"Of course not, Father! I would never let you down like that. How could you even ask such a thing?"

"Of course, of course! My sincerest apologies, Atanna." He chuckled. The tall robed figure stepped within an arm's length of Quov Tsin. "And to you, too, Master Tsin."

The diminutive sorcerer squinted. "Apologies? For what, my lord?"

"For what I must do now." With shocking strength, Juris Khan seized the short Vizjerei and flung him atop the platform.

"My lord—"

"Know that your sacrifice will allow my children to spread across every land and open the way of Heaven to this benighted world!"

Tsin's mouth opened in preparation of a spell. Every rune upon his robe flared bright. The elderly sorcerer even sought to stave off Khan with his stick-thin arms.

None of his defenses, either magical or mundane, aided him against the power wielded by Juris Khan. With a prayer to the great archangel Mirakodus, Lord Khan drove the dagger into the Vizjerei's bony chest.

Tsin's eyes bulged. He gasped for breath but found none. His hands slid from the robes of the monarch, at last falling limply.

Blood spilled from the deep wound, racing over the garments and at last falling upon the platform.

A crackle of lightning shot up from the body of Quov Tsin, forcing Lord Khan back. More bolts quickly followed, creating an epic battle of forces in play directly over the corpse.

The master of the holy city fell to one knee in supplication. "Great Mirakodus, hear my humble plea! Let the world of mortal men be ours once again!"

A tremor shook the entire palace, but did not at all frighten Juris Khan. A sense of displacement swept over him, and momentarily he saw a hundred different variations of his surroundings. At last, however, they all began to merge, finally coalescing once more into the version with which he was most familiar.

The spell had succeeded. The soul and body of Ureh had been united again. The Light among Lights once more shone brightly on the mortal plane . . .

And all he needed to make it perfect was for the sun, only a scant time away from rising, to let its glory touch the Key atop Nymyr. That would seal the spell in place, remove the last impediment—

But no . . . there existed one more impediment, for surely the necromancer would attempt to stop him. Surely the corrupted one would persuade his friends to try to steal or destroy the stones, just as Gregus had convinced poor Tobio.

Zayl had to be removed. Without him, Kentril would return to the fold. The giant Gorst seemed an innocent, but if he could not be turned back to the light, then Lord Khan would have to remove him also.

"*Shakarak!*" A fiery ball materialized before him. Khan muttered another word of power, and the center of the burning sphere suddenly grew transparent.

The face of Zayl appeared.

"*Shakarog!*" The image backed away, revealing more and more of the pale necromancer and his surroundings. Juris Khan looked upon the corrupted figure with loathing. Hardly any color in his flesh and clad in clothes almost entirely as black as his heart. Truly an instrument of Hell, not Heaven. The archangel would have immediately commanded him destroyed for the good of all.

A second figure appeared behind Zayl.

Captain Kentril Dumon.

"So," he whispered to himself, "unlike Gregus and Tobio, these choose to travel together, the better to concentrate their efforts. A pity that it'll avail them nothing."

Atanna stepped up beside him, one delicate hand stretched out toward the mercenary captain.

"Kentril . . ." she cooed.

"I shall bring him back for you, my darling." He did not add that he would do so only if it did not prove necessary to slay the man. The spell that would have given his daughter the perfect mate could no longer be cast, and although Lord Khan had promised her that Captain Dumon would yet be hers, more and more he realized how difficult that might be.

Still, he would try . . . but first he had to distract her, lest she wish to come with him. It would not do for her to see the captain slain, should that prove necessary.

"Atanna, my darling, I see no sign of the large one, the one called Gorst. I need you to keep watch on the Key to Light, make certain that he doesn't climb up and try to take it before sunrise. Understood?"

Fortunately, she had not heard what he had said about the group traveling together, nor did she see, as he briefly had, that the giant followed behind his fellow mercenary. "But I want to go to Kentril—"

"He would only become more confused, possibly even injure himself because of that. You know how torn he was. The necromancer will surely have turned his mind wrong for the moment."

Atanna obviously still wished to go, but she nodded her head nonetheless. "All right, Father . . ."

"Wonderful!" He gave her a hug, then kissed her forehead. "Now, be off with you. Soon we'll have this all sorted out, and the good Captain Dumon will be yours again."

"As you wish." She smiled, kissed him on the cheek, and vanished.

Any pleasantry vanished with his daughter. Grimly, Juris Khan glared at the figures wending their way down toward the Key to Shadow. They had condemned themselves with this sinful action, just as Gregus had. He would smite them down, even Atanna's beloved, if necessary. Their wicked deeds could not go unpunished.

Still, fairness dictated that he pray for the sinners even as he prepared to slay them. Just as he had done with Gregus and Tobio, Lord Khan whispered a few words, then ended with the phrase that always most brought him comfort.

"May the Archangel Mirakodus take up your souls."

And with a satisfied smile, he went to send the three to their final rewards.

Twenty-one

With the last of the power he had drawn from Juris Khan's sanctum, Zayl had managed to send himself and the golems to the very cavern in which he had so recently been imprisoned. The necromancer had dared not attempt another, similar spell, such magic risky at best and, under the circumstances, more foolhardy than helpful. From here on, it had to be with the aid of spells he knew well, no matter how that might limit him in the long run.

In truth, the necromancer did not expect to reach his goal unhindered—or possibly to reach it at all. Captain Dumon had suspected the truth; Zayl fully intended to sacrifice himself if it meant that the two mercenaries would manage to reach their own goal. Only one Key had to be removed before the sun rose, and the one atop Nymyr would serve as well as any.

Zayl had done everything he could to draw the attention of their foe, leaving a trail of sorcerous residue any competent wielder of power would notice, much less trace. That alone might not perhaps have sufficed, but the necromancer's companions surely erased any chance that Khan might turn his gaze elsewhere. Surely with his might, the ruler of Ureh would seek out his prey, beginning with the so-simply-detected spellwork of Zayl, then, through the arts, divining that the Rathmian did not travel alone.

The other two followed docilely along, almost like puppies trailing their mother. They wore determined expressions, but only because Zayl desired such from them. It would not do for Juris Khan to arrive only to see that the two fighters stared like empty-minded zombies. That would give away the truth much sooner than Zayl hoped. Every second extra granted to the captain and his comrade meant greater hope of success.

With the aid of a makeshift version of his original magical strand of rope, they quickly descended deep into the mountain's belly. The necromancer led each segment, showing the golems how it had to be done. Tied to his blood, they could repeat his actions exactly. The only danger other than their adversary remained any need for independent action. If they had to act for themselves, they risked falling and shattering.

"Are you sure of this?" asked Humbart as they drew nearer and nearer to their goal. "Maybe he went after them instead."

That had occurred to Zayl early on, but the pale spellcaster had not wanted to speak of such a disastrous turn of events. "He would surely come after me first, for fear that with my skills I would be the most logical threat."

"Aye, but logic might not have much to do with it, eh?"

"We shall hope for the best, Humbart."

The skull did not reply to that, answer enough in many ways.

Yet the deeper they descended, the more the concern grew. Had Lord Khan ignored the obvious and instead discovered the trail of the mercenaries? Had he recognized the necromancer's ploy with the golems from the very start? Question after question, uncertainty after uncertainty, plagued Zayl as they had never done in his entire life.

At last, they reached the level at which the enchanted crystal could be found. Keeping his dagger ready at all times, Zayl guided the golems along. The constructs had weapons identical to those of the men they had been designed to emulate, although these weapons had actually been forged from the same rock used to mold the bodies. How strong those would prove in combat, the spellcaster could not say.

Again, all he hoped for was enough of a delay to give the others time to fulfill their own mission.

Nearer and nearer they drew, and still nothing impeded their progress. The slight frown that had early on creased Zayl's mouth deepened with each step. Already he noticed ahead the peculiar illumination radiating from the Key to Shadow's lair. So close, and still no sign that Juris Khan had pursued him. Would it be the necromancer who succeeded and the mercenaries who paid the ultimate sacrifice?

He paused. After a moment's thought, Zayl indicated that the Gorst golem should take the lead.

The massive figure stepped forward, ax in hand in much the same manner as the true Gorst would have held it. Every movement spoke of the fighter, a sign of how well the necromancer's quick spell had worked.

The false Gorst stepped into the very edge of the Key's unsettling light. He readied his weapon.

Nothing happened. The golem turned to Zayl, awaiting orders.

A howling form materialized over the construct, falling upon him.

The necromancer had never seen such demonic figures before, but he recognized well Captain Dumon's description of the ghoulish creatures that had been all that remained of Ureh's once-pious inhabitants. The dry husk of a body, the gaping, rounded mouth filled with edged teeth, the soulless black holes where the eyes should have been—even versed as Zayl was in the arts of dealing with the dead and undead, the corrupted humans of the fabled kingdom left him shuddering.

As the golem struggled with his monstrous foe, a second and third materialized around him. Zayl started forward, only to have another fiend leap out of the rocky wall and attack.

Under strands of loose hair, a face out of nightmare stared hungrily at the necromancer. The tattered remnants

of a once seductive emerald dress barely clothed the shriveled, cadaverous form.

"Kiss me," it croaked. *"Come enjoy my caresses . . ."*

Again, Zayl shuddered in open fear. Acting more on
reflex than anything, he thrust.

To his surprise, the blade sank readily into the ghoul's
throat.

The dagger flashed brightly as it dug into the dry flesh.
The abomination let out a gasp that almost sounded
relieved. For good measure, Zayl twisted the magical
weapon, uttering a few quick words.

The throat wound flared. As the necromancer
removed the blade, the flaring intensified, quickly overwhelming the macabre figure. The creature fell against
the wall, curling into a fetal position. In but the blink of
an eye, the entire body lay bathed in the furious brightness, the already shriveled form shrinking ever more in
on itself.

Zayl watched a moment longer in order to assure himself that soon there would be nothing at all remaining. He
then turned to face those already attacking the first golem
and found that not only had their numbers trebled, but
now they attacked from both ends.

He had been surrounded.

The golems did their best to hold the horrific band at bay,
both fighting with the mechanical skill that they had inher-
ited from the true mercenaries. The false Gorst chopped off
the arm of one ghoul, while his counterpart ran another
through the chest. Unfortunately, although both warriors
were the products of sorcery, their weapons lacked the magical abilities inherent in the spellcaster's blade. True, with
enough effort and time, they might be able to hack their foes
to pieces, but the numbers and circumstances did not offer
that as a likely hope.

That left matters to Zayl's skills.

In such tight quarters, he dared not use either the Talons
or the Teeth of Trag'Oul, especially with Juris Khan no

doubt lurking near, preparing to strike. Still, perhaps something similar . . .

Glancing quickly over his shoulder, Zayl cast the spell.

From both walls, the ceiling, and even the floor erupted thick bars of ivory, bars of actual *bone*. One of the demonic attackers collided with the barrier as it arose. Under a silent command from Zayl, the Kentril golem fell back just in time, barely avoiding being caught with the oncoming fiends.

Composed of the bones of a thousand different long-dead creatures, the wall very efficiently barred the ghouls' way. The gaping mouths snapped open and closed, and twisted, dried fingers madly but vainly sought the necromancer. With demonic fury, they struggled to get past his work, but, at least for the time being, the defensive wall held.

Yet for how long he could not say. Quickly turning back to those swarming around the Gorst golem, Zayl cast another spell. With the dagger, he drew a pair of curving lines in the air, at the same time reciting.

Two of the monstrous attackers had slipped past the construct, but they managed to come only a few feet toward the necromancer before the spell affected them. With almost human screams, they abruptly cringed, then swiftly backed away. Beyond them, those that had continued to fight the golem likewise suddenly cowered in outright fear.

One turned, fleeing into the darkened passage beyond. That caused the rest of the ranks to break, creating a scene both horrific and saddening. Each of these horrors had once been human, and in some ways Zayl regretted everything he had just been forced to do to them. They had not been at fault. Rather, they had been betrayed by the one they had most trusted, most revered.

Lord Juris Khan.

With the golems keeping guard, Zayl pushed on to the chamber of the Key. Whether or not he or his companions survived, at least one of the crystals had to be removed or shattered. If it proved necessary that this be the one, the necromancer would not falter.

And there it stood, exactly as he had seen it last. Beyond it, the dead form of Gregus Mazi still hung above, *his* nightmare, at least, at an end.

Keeping vigilant, Zayl started toward the Key. The rotting bodies of the winged fiends he and the others had slain previously lay all about, but no new danger reared its ugly head. Closer and closer the necromancer got to the dark crystal. His fingers came within inches—

A crackling sound drove him back, Zayl's first clue that the ceiling had begun to collapse. He looked up, saw no sign of any fissure or falling bits of rock, yet the harsh crackling sound continued.

Something farther back in the chamber moved.

The necromancer's eyes widened.

With movements akin to those of a marionette, Gregus Mazi tore himself free of his centuries-old prison.

But as Zayl stared into the eyes, he knew that Mazi himself had not stirred to life. The sorcerer had indeed perished earlier . . . but now his corpse moved at the will of the mad Juris Khan.

Body glittering from the many crystalline deposits covering it, the undead figure stretched out a crusted hand toward Zayl, who immediately stepped farther out of reach.

The hand suddenly shot forth, growing larger and longer as it neared.

The necromancer reacted too slowly. The elongated fingers wrapped completely around him, squeezing him tight much as the stone ones had done in the tunnel.

However, in contrast to that nearly fatal struggle, Zayl did not this time have to rely on himself alone. The golems, attuned to his will, strode into the chamber, weapons raised for battle.

The stalactite man thrust forward with his other hand, seeking to do with the false Kentril as he had done with Zayl. Commanded by the necromancer, the golem countered the assault with a swing of his blade. A good chunk of the outstretched hand dropped to the floor . . . but so did a part of the construct's blade.

"Surrender to your fates," Gregus Mazi uttered. *"Repent your sins, and the archangel may yet accept you . . ."*

The mouth might have belonged to the resurrected sorcerer, but the voice and words truly could only be those of Ureh's mad monarch.

"Kentril Dumon, my good captain," the macabre figure continued, the blank eyes fixing on the false mercenary, *"throw off the shackles of doubt and deceit forced on you by this corrupted soul! Immortality with Atanna awaits you . . ."*

Despite his predicament, Zayl's hopes rose. In those few lines, Lord Khan had revealed that he believed the construct to be the true captain. That meant that he had not noticed the two mercenaries climbing Nymyr. Even if Zayl perished, the chance still existed that Captain Dumon and Gorst could put an end to the threat posed by this city of the damned.

The Kentril golem did not answer, of course, that ability well beyond the necromancer's skills. Instead, he struck again at the reaching hand, chipping off one of its fingers but losing more of the sword as well.

Apparently seeing through the eyes of his undead puppet, Khan had not so far noticed anything odd about the golem, not even the peculiarity of the sword. The longer Zayl could distract him, the better.

"Captain Dumon listens only to me, my lord," the spellcaster retorted, putting as much condescension in his voice as possible. "So long as I live, his will is mine!"

"Then for the sake of his soul—and yours, even—you must die, necromancer!"

But although he expected to do just that, Zayl had no intention of falling prey to his adversary so easily. Juris Khan's interest in the captain had bought him necessary seconds in which to plan. The spell risked his own life, but if it succeeded, then Khan himself would have to take the stage.

He pictured a starburst in his mind, then overlaid it upon the crystalline form once inhabited by Gregus Mazi. With what air still existed in his lungs, Zayl shouted out a single word of power.

Gregus Mazi exploded.

The force of the explosion sent Zayl flying backward into the Kentril golem. A torrent of rocky missiles assailed the necromancer and his two puppets. The entire chamber shook, and the stalactite that had held Mazi for so long plummeted to the floor, impaling the earth there.

Zayl struck his head hard, becoming momentarily dazed. Rocks continued to pelt him, forcing the necromancer to cover his face with his arm. He had cast a variation of a spell that caused the corpse of one who had died violently to unleash in an awful explosion the anguish sealed in the body during its last terrible moments of life. Unfortunately, although Zayl had tried hard to focus the direction of that explosion, the size of the chamber had made it impossible for him to avoid some backlash.

With effort, the stunned necromancer rose to his feet. Neither golem moved to assist him, not having been told to do so. Zayl looked them over quickly, assessing the situation. Up close, he could see the damage that they, unprotected by any wards, had taken. Portions of each face had been completely obliterated, and chunks of rock had been broken off from the torso and limbs. Several vicious cracks now spread across both figures, hinting of further instability.

"There are no depths of evil to which you'll hesitate to go, are there, necromancer?"

Zayl quickly turned to the Key to Shadow—and, behind it, the sanctimonious face of Juris Khan.

The robed monarch gazed down fondly at the crystal, even placing his hands upon it as one might a favored child. Illuminated by the peculiar dark light, Lord Khan looked as monstrous as the creatures his people had become.

"To take a man's body, to destroy the house in which his soul had resided so crassly, so without care . . . truly your corruption is irrevocable!"

It proved tempting to remind the robed figure that he had seen no fault in seizing control of Gregus Mazi's corpse for himself, but Zayl suspected that Juris Khan would have a ready rationalization for anything he did. In his own mind, however the lord of Ureh acted, he did so with the blessing of this not-so-Heavenly archangel of which he always spoke.

"I'm afraid," Zayl's former host went on, "that, for your soul, there is only the pits of Hell." His eyes began to shift to the Kentril golem. "But for the good captain and his friend, perhaps there might still be some hope . . ."

In the dim light, Khan had obviously not yet noticed the flaws and breaks in the two figures. Realizing that he still had a chance to stall the other a little longer, Zayl immediately leapt forward, brandishing the gleaming dagger.

"If I am going to the pits of Hell, then I shall take you with me!" he shouted.

Juris Khan reacted exactly as he had hoped, turning away from the constructs and focusing all his attention on the necromancer.

A wave of black light erupted from the Key, striking at Zayl.

He barely raised a magical shield in time. Still, the force with which the dark light hit sent the spellcaster flying against the wall. Zayl let out a scream as the pain of the collision jarred every bone in his body.

"Captain Dumon," the robed figure called out, "step away from him. Come to me. Atanna awaits you."

The golem, of course, did not move.

Leaning forward, face contorted with effort, Lord Khan repeated himself. "Step away from him. Come to me! Atanna—"

And as Zayl struggled once more to his feet, his head pounding and his legs almost ready to buckle again,

Atanna's father realized the trick that had been played on him.

"Homunculi!" Khan shouted. Raising one hand, he pointed at the one resembling Captain Dumon.

The golem trembled. It took one step forward, only to leave the bottom half of its leg behind. The lack of balance quickly assailed the necromancer's creation, and it tipped forward. However, even before it could crash to the floor, the arms, the other leg, even the head, broke off, scattering in different directions.

Lord Khan formed a fist.

The golem lost any last semblance to the form of a man. A pile of fine dirt and crushed rock spilled over the chamber floor, the only remnants of Zayl's cleverly made puppet.

Zayl had not thought it possible for his adversary's countenance to grow any more grim, but the expression Juris Khan wore now caused even the stalwart spellcaster to regret standing so near.

"The mountaintop . . ." Lord Khan stared at Zayl with utter loathing. "They're climbing to the top of Nymyr!"

"M-maybe you should go after them. I shall w-watch the Key to Shadow for you."

"Do not taunt me! By the archangel, you *are* a thing of evil!"

The necromancer felt his strength returning, albeit slowly. If he could hold on to Khan's attention a little longer, then the mercenaries would succeed. "The only evil is the one you yourself let into Ureh, Lord Khan! You have succeeded in doing what demons and duped summoners failed to do for centuries. *You* brought eternal damnation to the holy kingdom. *You* corrupted your beloved people!"

"*How . . . dare . . . you?*"

Again, the wave of black light burst out of the crystal, but this time Zayl was better prepared for it. The attack pushed him against the wall, even made it hard for the struggling spellcaster to breathe, but it did not batter him as before.

Under his guidance, the remaining golem suddenly charged forward, swinging the stone ax at both Juris Khan and the stone.

Lord Khan redirected his power at the oncoming figure, beating at the false Gorst and sending fragments flying everywhere. The stone giant stumbled, but pressed on, driven toward his goal by the will of Zayl.

Forced to deal with two foes at once, Khan's effort against the necromancer himself flagged ever so slightly. It proved all Zayl needed not only to brace himself better, but to counterattack.

He did not seek out the elder monarch, however, but rather the Key to Shadow. Zayl did not know if he had any hope of destroying the artifact. If he managed even to damage it, so much the better. His greatest concern continued to be the success of Captain Dumon and Gorst. A servant of Rathma devoted his life to the struggle to maintain the balance; if Zayl had to give his now, it would only be his duty.

He sent forth the Teeth of Trag'Oul, hoping that one of the missiles would hit its mark.

Juris Khan waved his hand, and a shield of gleaming silver protected the Key from the horrendous rain of projectiles. The bony missiles went clattering in a hundred other directions, some of them even turning back upon the necromancer.

Gritting his teeth, Zayl dismissed the projectiles. As he did, his last golem finally crumbled, the Teeth finishing what Khan had begun.

"Spawn of Diablo!" The towering lord stepped in front of the protected crystal, seeming to grow even larger in the process. His eyes burned as red as those of any demon, an irony considering his opinion of the necromancer. Corrupted so thoroughly by the darkest of the Prime Evils, Juris Khan could not even see his own damnation. "Enslaver of souls! Accept your eternal punishment!"

"Would that punishment involve having to listen to

more of your preaching, my lord?" Zayl taunted. His best weapon so far had not been any of his spells or even his golems. Words seemed to affect Juris Khan more than all else, especially those that placed him in anything other than the pious light he shone upon himself.

But this time, Ureh's master did not react as the spellcaster had supposed he would. Instead, Lord Khan shook his head in mock pity and replied, "Misguided fool. The evil that corrupts you makes you underestimate the powers of light. I know what you try, and I know why you try it!"

"I try it in order to keep you from continuing to assail my ears with your incessant sermonizing."

Again, Juris Khan did not rise to the bait. He chuckled quietly, looking down upon Zayl as if the necromancer were little more than a flea-bitten hound. "The last, desperate weapon of a defeated scoundrel. Your puppets served you better, Master Zayl, for they, at least, fooled me for a short time."

"They only needed to draw you here," countered the necromancer, "where I waited."

"And you think that you'll keep me here, occupy my time while your companions seek to reach the other Key. Did you believe I'd leave it unattended? Atanna watches over it; she will see when the mercenaries come, and she will do what is right."

Zayl allowed himself a slight smile. "Even against Kentril Dumon?"

Now, at last, he had caught Juris Khan's attention. "Atanna will see to it that he doesn't remove or damage the crystal. That is all she needs to do."

"She wants the captain, my lord. She wants him badly. Your daughter may be persuaded by her desire—her love, even?—to hesitate. That may be all he needs."

"Atanna knows her duty," the elder man countered, but his expression hinted otherwise. "She'll not betray the work of the archangel!"

As he spoke, Khan's hands suddenly crackled with energy.

Zayl saw that the time for talk had passed; now, if he hoped to give the captain and Gorst any chance of success, the necromancer had to fight with all his might.

"It is time to confess your sins and ask absolution, necromancer," Juris Khan boomed, his face lit up madly by the powers he summoned. "And fear not for Atanna's heart. She is, after all, her father's daughter . . . and she will do what must be done even if it means utterly destroying *Kentril Dumon!*"

The high winds and fierce chill did not in any way touch the crimson-haired enchantress as she searched the darkened mountainside for the giant, Gorst. From her momentary perch atop a narrow, precarious ledge, she surveyed the rock face with eyes that saw in the dark almost as well as a cat's, seeking out the telltale signs of movement.

Only one other thought distracted her, burrowed into her mind with the savage intensity of a hungry leech. She knew that her father had promised not to harm her darling Kentril, but accidents did happen. In his misguided belief that the necromancer spoke truly, Kentril might sacrifice himself for the dour, pale figure. That would very much upset Atanna.

Seeing nothing out of the ordinary, she transported herself to another location. Atanna hoped to stay clear of the near-top of the mountain peak, even the night sky no protection. Only the black shadow, the comforting shadow, shielded her from a horrific fate that even the archangel's gift could not prevent.

Her concerns vanished in an instant as she immediately noticed a distant form below. It had to be the giant. Atanna prepared to move closer, the better to ensure that her strike would prove fatal the first time. For the sake of her Kentril, she would make his friend's death a swift one—

A second, smaller figure moved into sight.

"No!" she gasped. It could not be Zayl, whom she had seen in her father's vision, but neither could it be *Kentril.*

He had been with the necromancer. How could he be here?

She would have to stop them. She would have to keep them from reaching the Key to Light. A simple spell would destroy the part of the mountain on which they climbed . . . and would *kill* Kentril.

Atanna could not do that. There had to be another way to stop them. Yet any attempt to block their path by destroying part of the mountain would also likely slay them.

"I cannot do it," she muttered. Yet to stand idly by would mean betrayal not only of her father, but also of the glorious archangel, Mirakodus.

Thinking of the archangel brought both love and fear to Atanna. She thought of his wondrous gifts yet also recalled with fear what had happened when he had entered her mind and soul. Atanna never wanted to go through that again. The memory still scarred her soul.

She prayed for an answer, and almost instantly her prayer seemed granted as an idea blossomed. Atanna could not raise a hand against her beloved, but neither could she betray all her father had sought. Therefore, she would have to place a challenge before her Kentril, a challenge that would prove whether or not he had truly been worthy from the start. Surely her father and the archangel would see the fairness of that. Surely they would understand what she did.

And if Kentril did indeed die . . . well, Atanna felt that he, too, would simply have to understand.

Twenty-two

It had occurred too late to Kentril that he and Gorst would be at a great disadvantage when they attempted to climb Nymyr. When last they had done so, it had been with torches to guide them through the dark. The captain had only recalled that fact just as Zayl's spell had taken effect, but by then, the chamber and the necromancer had already faded away.

To his surprise, however, Zayl had evidently considered the problem, too, and dealt with it. Upon materializing on the mountainside, Kentril immediately noticed that the utter darkness of the shadow had given way to a deep gray, which enabled the mercenary to see at least some distance in every direction. Gorst, too, had gained this ability. The spellcaster clearly could not have altered the essence of the shadow itself, which meant that he had instead granted his companions a crude form of night vision.

Unfortunately, that gift had also shown them that Zayl had not been able to send them as near to the Key as they all might have wished. The two fighters had been left with quite a climb.

"We're probably gonna need some rope along the way," Gorst muttered.

Another thing Kentril had not gotten to mention prior to the necromancer's spell, and this time one that Zayl had also failed to anticipate. Kentril eyed the path above, trying to find a better route, but the ridge upon which they had been set offered only one direction.

"We'll just have to try, anyway," he finally replied.

Gorst nodded and said no more. If his captain intended to try to make the ascent without equipment, then so would he.

With the utmost caution, they began to wend their way up. Kentril had no way to estimate the hour, but if they suffered few mishaps, he suspected that they could reach the top with some time to spare. Of course, that also depended on whether or not Zayl could keep Juris Khan occupied long enough.

He tried not to think of the necromancer's potential sacrifice. The odds seemed very low that Zayl would survive. Kentril had witnessed the power of their treacherous host too often to believe that. Zayl would do what he could to keep Khan at bay, but sooner or later Ureh's mad monarch would kill the Rathmian.

Kentril could only hope it would be later . . . otherwise, they had all lost.

Up and up they climbed, and still no attack came. The captain had little time to think of much else, but as they drew nearer to the top of the peak, his thoughts went back to Atanna. Despite what she had proven to be, Kentril found some of his earlier memories too precious simply to discard. Perhaps if things had been different, if he had not learned the truth beforehand, he might even have willingly accepted her father's offer of immortality—but then he would have had to live with the results.

Pausing, he took a deep breath and tried to clear his head. It made no sense to keep thinking of Atanna. He had seen the last of her, the last of—

A robed figure stood atop a tiny ledge farther up. Even as distant as the figure was, Kentril could tell that he did not stare at Lord Khan.

"Atanna!" he shouted.

The wind blew dust in his face. Turning away, the mercenary brushed his eyes clear.

When he looked back, the figure had disappeared.

"What was it?" Gorst called from behind. "You see something?"

"I thought I saw—" But Kentril stopped. If it had been Atanna, surely she would have either come closer or destroyed him from the ledge. She would not have simply gone away. That made no sense whatsoever.

"Nothing," he finally answered. "Just my imagination."

They pushed on. Despite constant fears that they would eventually reach some spot that could not be overcome without equipment, the mercenaries' route continued to offer some avenue. Had Zayl somehow managed to send the pair to the easiest area upon which to climb? If so, then he had managed more with what power he had drained from the runes than he had given the fighters to expect.

"We're almost there," Kentril dared finally mutter to his friend. "Almost . . ."

Gorst grunted. *Almost* still meant quite a climb to go.

Reaching up, Captain Dumon seized hold of a promising outcropping, only to have the part he had taken crumble in his hand. Momentarily out of balance, he leaned toward the rock face. At the same time, his gaze went from upward to deep down.

Far below, something that resembled a swarm of ants moved with incredible swiftness up the side of the mountain.

The captain gaped. "Gorst! Can you see that?"

The giant stretched. "I see it. What is it, Kentril?"

"I don't—" So quickly did the shapes move that even in the short time in which the pair had talked of them, they now could be seen with a bit more clarity. They were large, each easily the size of a man and, in general, built like men. They had a grayish tone to them, although he saw bits and pieces of other colors on their backs, their arms, their legs.

Kentril swallowed. "It's Ureh's people. They're coming after us."

He pictured the hundreds of gaping mouths, the withered, cadaverous shells of what had once been human. He imagined those talonlike nails and the hungry faces. The captain could well imagine what had happened to Albord and all the others and understood that now the same fate rushed toward them.

"We have to get to the top, and quick!" But they could only move as fast as their surroundings permitted, and although the pair struggled mightily, it seemed that the voracious horde moved at more than ten times the pace.

The top beckoned yet was still too far up. Exhausted, Kentril and Gorst finally had to pause on a small ridge barely wide enough to accommodate both of them.

Gazing down at their pursuers, Kentril swore. "They climb as if born to the mountain. At this rate, they'll catch us just below our goal."

Gorst nodded. "We can't make it . . . but you can."

Kentril eyed the other. "What does that mean?"

With absolute calm, the giant began freeing his ax, which had hung on his back. "This is the best spot around. I'll hold 'em off here. You go on."

"Don't be a fool, Gorst! If anyone goes up there, it'll be you. I'll hold them off."

The other mercenary shook his head. He stretched one long arm out, the ax extended well beyond it. The weapon would have taken his friend both hands to wield. "You see? I got twice the reach you do, Kentril. We need that. I'm the best choice to stay, and you know it—besides, I owe you for the last time we climbed up here."

"Gorst . . ." Captain Dumon knew better than to continue to argue. Of all the men he had ever met, Gorst had to be the most stubborn. They could have argued until Ureh's abominations overwhelmed them, and still the wild-maned warrior would have stood his ground.

Taking one last glance down, Kentril nodded. "All right—but if you find a chance to save yourself, do it. Don't worry about me."

"I'll do what I can. You better get going."

Kentril put a hand on his friend's shoulder. "May your arm be steady."

"May your weapon be sharp," Gorst returned, finishing the old mercenary litany.

Steeling himself, the captain started up the final leg of the mountain. He pulled himself toward the top, trying not to think of what the giant would face and hoping somehow that they would both get out of the chaos alive. If he could make it to the top before the creatures reached Gorst, perhaps Kentril could yet save him. All he had to do was destroy the Key . . .

The encouraging thought pushed him to renewed effort. Closer and closer he came to the plateau. Rising above it, Kentril could make out the crystal's resting place. Such an irony that he now had to undo what he and his men had struggled so hard to accomplish earlier.

A hissing sound arose below him.

Cursing, Kentril pushed harder. The edge lay just a few yards up. Only a little longer.

Gorst let out a battle cry.

Despite knowing better, the captain had to look.

The giant stood at the edge of his small perch, swinging away with his ax at the first of the demonic creatures to reach him. With little room to maneuver, the abomination could not avoid the attack. The ax bit hard into its head, cutting deep.

The creature let out a horrific sound, then toppled backward off the ledge.

Wasting not a moment, the giant shifted his grip and used the very top of the ax to shove a second adversary off.

Despite those two rapid successes, though, a hundred more moved up, each trying to beat the rest to the lone defender.

Nearly frantic now, Kentril struggled to reach the plateau. However, each yard seemed a mile, and he felt as if he were climbing through molasses.

A very human roar of pain from below shook him to the core and made the fighter look down again.

The ghoulish creatures harried Gorst from every direction. Two had managed to get up on the ledge, and another sought a handhold near the giant's feet. A dozen others maneuvered for position around the lone mercenary.

Gorst landed a strong blow against one ghoul still wearing the battered remains of a breast plate and chain mail. The blade severed the upper part of the fiend's torso, but that upper portion still managed to wrap bony fingers around the upper part of the weapon's shaft.

Although he shook the ax as hard as he could, Gorst could not dislodge the determined ghoul. The effort also hampered his struggles against the others. The second demon leapt onto his back and tried to sink its horrific mouth into Gorst's neck.

Spinning around, the giant threw his ax down upon the one seeking a handhold. Both that creature and the one still clinging to the weapon plunged earthward, taking the ax with them.

Now unarmed, Gorst reached back and seized the monster latched onto his back. Unfortunately, it would not be as easily removed as the others, and while Gorst battled with it, four more made their way up to him.

Kentril continued his ascent, but with each step, his gaze flashed back to his friend. When next he glanced, it was to see the giant now hampered by *three* of the horrors, with more only seconds away. Gorst's shoulders were stained with blood, and despite his strength, he clearly had trouble standing.

The captain nearly turned back, thinking for a second that if he joined the other fighter, they could hold off the entire horde. However, common sense quickly pointed out the futility of his thought. Gorst had remained behind to give Kentril time to do what had to be done. To turn back now would be to waste the other mercenary's sacrifice.

Sacrifice . . . Only now did the essence of that word truly sink in.

At that moment, Gorst let out a battle cry so loud it echoed well beyond Nymyr. As if his strength had suddenly been renewed by some magical means, the massive fighter straightened, raising one of his fiendish foes into the air. By this time, at least half a dozen more of Juris Khan's monstrous children had fastened themselves onto him, each ripping at his flesh, tearing away at his life.

Still roaring, Gorst suddenly charged forward.

"*No!*" shouted Kentril, his plea repeated over and over again by the mountains.

The giant leapt off the ledge.

Unable to let go in time, his many attackers fell with him. Gorst's leap, far less athletic than Captain Dumon knew the mercenary capable of, barely enabled the wild-maned fighter to clear his perch. However, Gorst had obviously had that very thing in mind, for as he dropped, he crashed into one climbing abomination after another, creating, in the process, an avalanche of monstrous forms raining down upon the shadowed kingdom.

"Gorst . . ." Kentril could not tear his eyes away from the dwindling figure. Gorst had been with the captain longer than anyone. The giant had seemed invincible, unstoppable . . .

Tears struggled to be free, but Kentril could not let them come. Taking a deep breath, he looked away and began pulling himself up again, Gorst's last victorious charge burned into his imagination. The sun could not be long in rising. Kentril had to make certain that he had not just let his friend, *all* his men, die in vain.

Nearer and nearer he drew to the top . . . and below him, the horde closed the gap more quickly.

Zayl screamed, and not for the first time. He screamed loud and long, but he did not give in. His clothes were in tatters, and every inch of his body seemed to be either covered in blood or pounding in agony, but he did not surrender.

Yet neither had he come an inch closer to the Key to Shadow.

Seemingly untouched by every one of the powerful spells Zayl had tossed at him, Juris Khan approached the battered, half-dead figure. "Your determination, if not your cause, is quite admirable, necromancer. A shame that your corrupted soul shall be lost to Diablo forever."

"... As yours is? ..."

"Even until the end you persist in trying to twist matters, eh?" Lord Khan shook his head in a most paternal manner, something that all of Zayl's good training could not keep from greatly irritating the necromancer.

"Your blessed archangel is Diablo himself, can you not see that?"

But Ureh's monarch could not, so thoroughly had the demon done his work. Zayl even understood how it had happened, for Juris Khan clearly had been greatly full of pride in himself. He had been lord of the holiest of kingdoms, the symbol of piety and goodness, and because of that, he had not been able to comprehend that the most evil and cunning of demons had played him for a fool.

A *powerful* fool, however. He had taken everything that Zayl could thrust at him, taken it and shrugged it off. Little more remained to the necromancer save his dagger, which might have done him some good if he could have distracted his foe somehow. At least then, Zayl could have tried to circumvent Khan's defenses and perhaps wound the other.

What could he do, though? Every attempt had been more than met. There existed only words . . . and Zayl had few left of those, as well.

Still he tried, hoping against hope that Juris Khan would be wrong, that somehow Kentril Dumon and Gorst had made it to the other stone. Yet, if they had, would this battle still be going on?

"And where is your archangel, anyway, my lord? Perhaps if he were here, then we could prove once and for all whether I lie. Surely that is not too much to ask for, is it? Then again, maybe it is . . ."

"I need not ask of Mirakodus that he prove himself to me, unbeliever, for I have seen his gifts at work, and I have faith in his word. If he would choose to speak with us now, it would be by his choice alone, not yours or mine!" Juris Khan loomed over the necromancer. "Make peace with Heaven, thief of the dead, for in but a few moments, your tongue shall still forever, and so, then, shall end your lies!"

Zayl had no reason to doubt him. As the robed monarch approached, Zayl prayed that Trag'Oul would help guide his soul to the next plane of battle, not let Khan's true master seize it and drag it down to Hell.

And, as if hearing his prayer, a voice suddenly boomed, "Juris Khan! Juris Khan! I would speak to you!"

Both men froze. Khan's mouth opened and closed. He glanced at Zayl again, then looked up to the ceiling.

The voice boomed, "Juris Khan! Noble servant! 'Tis I, your benefactor, your archangel . . ."

The weathered face contorted into an expression of reverence and wonder. Lord Khan raised his hands above his head in a beseeching manner and called out, "Mirakodus! Great Mirakodus! You bless your humble attendant with your presence!"

Much quieter, the voice calling itself that of the archangel suddenly muttered to the necromancer, "If you've got anything left to give, lad, do it now!"

Needing no more urging, Zayl dove toward his foe, focusing his will entirely on the dagger he now thrust at the robed figure's chest.

The beatific look upon Juris Khan's countenance vanished in an instant, replaced by one of the darkest anger. He started to reach for Zayl, the monarch's hands blazing with fiery energy.

The dagger struck first.

A blinding flash of light enveloped the chamber as the necromancer's enchanted blade broke through Khan's defenses. With some initial hesitation, the tip sank into the brilliant robe, then continued unimpeded.

Gasping, Juris Khan struck Zayl a blow across the face. Fueled by both power and pain, he sent the necromancer again flying into the rocky wall.

Zayl felt something crack as he hit. Unable to stop his momentum, he bounced twice on the floor, then rolled to a halt at the very feet of his foe.

"You—you—" Khan seemed unable to find any words to fit his fury.

Through watery eyes, the necromancer saw the blood dripping from the other's wound. He had missed the heart, but certainly had come close enough to it to injure his opponent gravely.

"Where—where is your archangel now?" Zayl managed to spout. "He seems—to have—have abandoned you, my lord!"

"Impudent fool!" The insane ruler leaned against the shield he had created for the Key to Shadow. "I need but a few moments—and then I will heal myself!" Khan bared his perfect teeth. "A few moments you yourself do not have!"

A horribly familiar noise arose from the mouth of the chamber. Zayl heard the movement of many eager feet.

He forced himself to turn his gaze toward the entrance.

One of the ghoulish denizens of the holy kingdom thrust its macabre head inside. Two more quickly followed suit.

His strength on the wane, Zayl's bone barrier had finally given way, releasing the hungry fiends.

Juris Khan, his breath still ragged, pointed at the sprawled necromancer. "There he is, my children! There is the one you seek!"

Their rounded mouths opened in anticipation. The deathly gaps where their eyes had once been fixed upon Zayl. The horrific creatures reached for him, and Zayl knew that he did not have anything left with which to fight them.

With his little remaining physical strength, he weakly held the dagger before him, hoping that he would at least stop one before the rest ripped him to bloody shreds. Despite all his teachings, despite all his training, at that moment, the necromancer dearly wanted to live.

"Now there remains but one," Khan pronounced, his voice already much stronger than earlier. His wound clearly bled less, and his visage, while monstrous in its own right, did not show much agony from the near-fatal blow.

Zayl had guessed wrong. The power behind Juris Khan, the false archangel, protected well his valuable puppet. Diablo, if Captain Dumon had guessed correctly, desired Ureh to spread its gift to the world . . . and open the path for Hell's legions.

"Now there remains but one," the almost demonic figure repeated. He straightened in obvious preparation for his departure from the cavern chamber. "And who knows?" Khan continued, smiling piously. "Perhaps not even *one*, eh?"

And as the horde suddenly rushed to tear Zayl apart, Juris Khan *vanished*—to ensure, the doomed spellcaster knew, that his last question would become truth.

Had the sun yet risen? Under the shroudlike cover of the enchanted shadow, Kentril could not be certain, but he hoped and prayed that it had not done so. With Gorst and surely Zayl now also dead, it would be the greatest shame to have come so far and yet fallen short.

He managed to drag himself up onto the small plateau, but discovered that he did not immediately have the strength to stand, much less continue on. Lying on the harsh, cold ground, the captain inhaled, trying to catch his breath. Just a few moments more. That was all he needed. Just a few moments more.

The sudden clatter of rock from just below the edge warned him that even those few moments would not be granted.

Body shrieking, Kentril forced himself back to his feet.

He staggered toward the final climb, knowing that his goal lay only a short distance up but wondering if he could climb so great a height at this point.

There came more clattering. The captain looked back to see a withered, dead hand reaching up.

He turned and ran toward it. A terrifying face came up, the grayish vision granted Kentril by Zayl making it appear even more deathly.

Mustering his courage, the mercenary kicked at it as hard as he could.

With a shriek befitting a damned soul, the ghoulish creature tumbled backward into the air, vanishing below. Kentril leaned over the edge, saw that four more were only a minute or so from reaching the top, with at least a dozen more right behind.

Dragging himself up to the rock formation, Captain Dumon started his last ascent. He had to make it. He *would* make it.

"Come on, you damned recruit!" he muttered at himself as he grabbed hold. "You can climb five times faster than this!"

Foot by foot, inch by inch, Kentril drew closer. From the east, he noticed no hint of the sun, surely a good sign. By now, he had to be near the very upper edge of the shadow, which should have enabled him to make out some light if any existed. That Kentril did not had to mean that the day had not yet dawned.

Then, shattering his rising hopes, he heard once more the all-too-familiar hissing. Kentril immediately looked down, knowing already what he would see.

The first of the demonic horde had reached the plateau.

They scrambled around at first, seeking him out. One looked up, noticed him. That was all the rest needed. The first of them scurried to the rocky tower, eager, no doubt, for Kentril's tasty flesh.

Fortunately, not every part of the outcropping presented a place for the ghoulish hunters to use to climb up.

Some started along the captain's own route, while others tested paths elsewhere, seeking one that would hold them.

Their hunger for his flesh and blood clearly getting the better of them, a pair hurried to the western side, no doubt in the hopes of beating the rest to the quarry.

They did not get far. As Kentril watched in astonishment, the two suddenly flared bright, almost as if on fire. Their screams caused the rest of the monstrous pack to hesitate. The two started back to their companions, but as they moved, pieces of their dried flesh turned to ash, and the bone beneath began to sag as if made of ever-softening wax.

One fell, already a half-melted parody of human dead that became more liquid with each second. The other managed to reach what surely had to be the edge of the shadow, but not soon enough to save it. It, too, collapsed into a stomach-churning heap that proved so disturbing a sight that the rest of the creatures did what they could to avoid even venturing near it.

Kentril suddenly became aware that the ones just below him had started moving again. Cursing his own morbid fascination with the horrific destruction of the pair, he pulled himself up as hard as he could, trying to make up for lost opportunity.

He almost moved too slowly. A hand nearly caught his left foot. Kicking at it, the captain managed to shatter some of the fingers, slowing the ghoul down.

His own hand suddenly caught the uppermost edge. Heart pounding, blood racing, Kentril pulled himself up . . . and caught his first glimpse of the Key to Light's resting place.

It had not, of course, changed much. A thin layer of frost covered everything, including, by this point, the veteran fighter himself. Carefully checking his footing, Kentril headed toward his prize.

Something stirred up by his boot rattled toward the gem.

The bone he had earlier dug free. The last trace of his predecessor, the unfortunate priest, Tobio.

Trying not to think about how he might soon be joining the late clergyman, Captain Dumon approached the Key to Light. As he did, he noticed that its brightness had remained constant but not overwhelming. In fact, it seemed little more illuminating than its counterpart well below the earth.

Does it matter? Kentril chided himself. *Let it glow as bright as the sun or stay as dark as the caverns. Just grab the thing, and be done with it!*

He reached for the crystal—

Atanna's beautiful face suddenly filled his mind, filled it so much he almost imagined he could see it floating before him, covering the entire shadowed heaven.

My darling Kentril . . . the face said. *My sweet Kentril, how I yearn for your arms again . . .*

The captain hesitated, caught between duty and emotion.

Come back to me, Kentril, she went on, eyes glittering and mouth pursed as if hungry for his kisses. *Let us be together again . . . together for all time . . .*

All time? That notion stirred him to action again. He wanted nothing of Juris Khan's gifts, especially that one.

But despite his determination, he could not escape Atanna's siren song. As the captain touched the surprisingly warm gem, she filled his head with new words, more promises.

Darling, sweet, loving Kentril . . . there is so much we can give each other . . . I was so lonely until I saw you . . . and when you showed me the brooch . . . I knew that Heaven had promised you to me . . . come back to me, and all will be well . . . we will be one . . .

"Get out of my head!" Kentril snapped, shutting his eyes as he tried to force the image, the smell, the taste of Atanna from his memory. "Get out of my—"

A hiss barely alerted him in time. From behind came one

of Lord Khan's vile "children," a hairless, gaunt cada-
ver dressed in the soiled garments of a merchant. A
rusted medallion still containing a few valuable gems
dangled from the neck chain half-buried in the ghoul's
shriveled, hollow neck.

"Fine wares today!" it babbled. *"Good pots! Fresh from the
kiln!"*

Whether the monstrosity knew what it said or not,
its words unnerved the seasoned mercenary, yet another
morbid reminder that what faced him had once been a
fellow man.

Kentril swung hard with his left, landing a powerful
punch to the chest. His hand sank in up to the knuckles, the
dried flesh and old bone giving way. However, the blow
only sent the horrific creature back a couple of steps.

Without hesitation, Kentril kicked with one foot. This
time, he caught his adversary's leg, flipping the ghoul
over.

Unable to control its momentum, the creature slid to the
far side, slipping over the edge.

Again, Captain Dumon gripped the crystal. He ripped it
free, then looked to the east. Still no sign of daylight. He
had been early enough at least. Now all he had to do was
destroy the artifact.

But Atanna's voice and face filled his mind once more,
making it difficult to tell what was real and what was
imaginary. Kentril had trouble recalling just what he had
been intending to do.

*Kentril, my darling Kentril . . . my one and only love . . . come
to me . . . forget this foolishness . . .*

She floated before him in a silver, gossamer gown, arms
outstretched toward him, beseeching him. To Kentril, Atanna
far more resembled an angel than even the false Mirakodus
had. How breathtaking she was, how beguiling . . .

He took a step toward her.

A thing smelling of the stench of the grave fell
upon him.

Kentril hit the icy ground hard, the crystal rolling from his grip. Both he and his attacker slid dangerously near the edge. The captain grimaced as the rounded mouth snapped at him, the ghoul's fetid breath almost as deadly a weapon as its teeth.

Managing to get his knee up, Kentril pushed the horror away. He scrambled for the Key, but his foe grabbed his arm and pulled the mercenary back. Beyond the creature, Captain Dumon saw with mounting dismay that three others had made it up and now converged on him.

Unable to pull his sword free, Kentril managed at least to draw his dagger. He stabbed at the hand that held him, chopping at the bone and decayed skin. The fingers loosened their grip enough on his arm so that Kentril could pull himself free. Dropping the dagger, the weary veteran drew his sword as he carefully backed toward his prize.

The larger blade did nothing to daunt the gathering fiends. They moved toward him as quickly as the slick surface enabled them. Kentril thrust at the nearest, then swung wide at two others following. He managed to strike one of the latter, but not enough to do any damage.

At last, he reached the Key to Light. Fending off the cursed citizens of Ureh, the captain scooped it up.

"Stop!" he shouted as best he could, the cold and his own exhaustion having taken their toll. "Stop, or I throw it off now!"

The creatures paused.

Kentril had them . . . but for how long? They would not simply wait until the sun rose and destroyed them. Even now, others could be heard wending their way up the other shadowed sides. It would take only a single lapse in concentration for Kentril to fall prey to one or more of them.

You would not do that, not when you so much wish to live.

A face appeared in his mind, but not Atanna's this time. Instead, Juris Khan seemed to stare at Kentril from within the fighter's skull, to see what the captain tried to hide from himself—that he very much *wanted* to live, wanted some way to escape from what clearly had no escape.

Kentril . . . my good captain . . . you can live and live well . . . love and love well . . . a kingdom can be yours . . .

Captain Dumon saw himself at the head of a magnificent force, his armor as brilliant, as majestic, as that of Lord Khan's archangel. He saw himself standing before cheering throngs, spreading the good will of Ureh to all. Kentril even saw himself sitting upon the very throne occupied by Juris Khan, Atanna at his side and their beautiful children perched near his feet . . .

Then the godlike figure of Khan swelled to life before his eyes, seeming to rise up all the way from the city far below, filling the sky. A gracious smile on his regal visage, the gigantic monarch reached forth a gargantuan hand to Kentril, offering him escape and all else the mercenary had envisioned.

Replace the Key, and come home, my good captain . . . come home, my son . . .

Kentril felt his will slipping away, felt himself ready to accept everything that the gigantic figure offered—even if that wondrous offer in truth masked an awful horror.

Then Kentril thought of Zayl, who surely had to be dead if Juris Khan had come here. He thought of Albord, Jodas, Brek, Orlif, and the rest of his company, victims of a monstrous evil into which the captain had blithely led them.

Most of all, he recalled Gorst, who had just sacrificed his life for his friend, his comrade. Gorst, who had not hesitated to do what had to be done.

Throwing aside his blade, Captain Kentril Dumon clutched the artifact to his body . . . and ran off the edge of the peak.

He closed his eyes as he did, not wanting to see the oncoming rocks below. The wind pushed at his face, his body, as if trying to tear the Key to Light from his death grip. Kentril imagined himself crashing on the mountainside, becoming battered to a pulp, the crystal shattering in the process.

Then the wind, the sense of falling, ceased.

The captain opened his eyes to find himself floating in air.

No . . . not floating. The ethereal hand of the giant Juris Khan held him, its ghostly fingers wrapped around his body. The look on the patriarch's huge face appeared any-thing but kindly now.

Put it back, Kentril Dumon . . . put it back now . . .

Staring at that gigantic visage, the mercenary could not help but think how much Lord Khan now resembled his sinister archangel. The eyes especially held that demonic intensity, and the more Kentril looked, the more the face seemed to shift, to grow less human, more *hellish*.

Put it back, and you may yet live!

But despite Khan's mutating countenance, despite the crushing fingers of the ghostly hand, Kentril would not. Better death, better every bone broken and his life fluids splattered across the earth below than to let *this* spread across the world.

He raised the Key to Light high, trying to throw it down upon the city. Yet his arms would not make the final move, no matter how hard Kentril tried.

The face of Juris Khan had lost all trace of humanity. Now he more than a little resembled the abominations his people had become. His skin shriveled, and his mouth took on a hungry, loathsome cut. The eyes burned with a fiery fury not of Heaven, but of well, well below.

Return the Key, or I shall shred your skin from your pathetic body, remove your heart while it beats, and devour it before your pleading eyes!

Kentril tried not to listen, choosing instead to concentrate on salvaging his mission. Where was the damned sun, anyway? How much longer before it finally rose?

He could no longer breathe, barely even think. A part of the mercenary begged him to take Khan's offer, even if that offer truly could not be trusted. Anything but to suffer longer.

Everything began to go black. At first, Kentril believed that he had started to pass out, but then the captain realized that Zayl's spell had begun to wear off. Kentril could still make out the ever more hideous form of his host, but little else. Ureh had become a dark, undefined shape, even the mountains nearby only murky forms. A bare hint of gray touched the eastern horizon, but other than that—

A hint of *gray*?

No sooner had Captain Dumon noted it than he felt a warmth in his hands. He forced his eyes upward, saw that the faint glow of the Key to Light had increased.

And as he quickly returned his gaze to the pinpoint of grayness far beyond the shadowed kingdom, Kentril knew that the night had finally come to an end.

With renewed determination, he held the crystal toward the gigantic, phantasmal form. Putting every bit of effort he could into resisting Juris Khan's control, Kentril shouted, "*You* put it back!"

He threw the Key.

The huge, ghostly hand reached for the stone, but as it tried to seize the artifact, the latter flared as brightly as the morning sun. The Key to Light completely *burned* its way through the ethereal palm, then sailed on unhindered toward the city below.

Juris Khan roared, a combination of rage and pain.

Fool! bellowed the giant in Kentril's head. *Corrupt soul! You shall be—*

He got no farther, for at that moment the gleaming crystal struck against something.

It shattered—and from within burst forth an intense, blinding light that rushed out in all directions as if seeking to take in everything in its blazing embrace.

The area around the broken artifact erupted with day. Ureh, the mountain Nymyr, the surrounding jungle . . .

nothing escaped the glorious illumination unleashed by the death of Khan's creation.

A wave of pure sun caught the scores of horrific pursuers still perched atop the peak or clinging to its side. The cursed folk of the once-holy city screamed and shrieked as they melted, burning away before Kentril's sickened eyes. By the dozens, those that had not yet made it to the top plummeted earthward, molten blobs that left fiery stains upon Nymyr's ever-more-battered flank.

And as the light coursed over Ureh building by building, those structures withered, crumbled, returning to the decayed, empty shells that Kentril and the others had first discovered. Walls fell in; ceilings collapsed. The effects of centuries of exposure to the elements took their toll once more, but this time in scarcely a minute.

From everywhere, the howls and cries of the damned souls of Ureh filled Kentril's ears, threatened to drive him to madness. He felt more pity than anything else for the creatures that had slaughtered his friends. They had been turned into abominations by the man they had most trusted, infested by demons who used their drained husks as a gate to the mortal world.

Perhaps now they could find eternal rest.

Then . . . Juris Khan, too, began to twist, to mutate. Kentril tumbled through the air, not falling but not exactly floating, either. He caught glimpses of the monstrous shadow figure as the first rays struck, watched as the corrupted lord of the realm was transformed. Juris Khan became even less than a man, more of a beast. Quickly went the face and form that had matched his people in horror. Now the elder ruler truly revealed the evil within him, the evil that could only be of *Diablo.*

And there, rising momentarily above the vanishing giant, a creature of Hell, a tusked, fanged figure of dread roared his anger at Kentril's desperate action. Ichor dripped from a scaly, barely fleshed skull that almost appeared to have been stretched long. Two wicked, scaled horns rose high above bat-winged ears. Over the deathly crevices that were all that formed a nose, the thick-browed orbs of the demon lord glared at the impudent human, the hatred and evil within them matching exactly that which the horrified mercenary had noted in the image of the false archangel Mirakodus.

Diablo thundered his wrath once more—and vanished as swiftly as he had appeared.

With a howl of agony, the vision of Juris Khan completely collapsed. The regal garments darkened and shredded. What skin had been left grew so brittle it fell off in thousands of pieces. Lord Khan put his other hand to his breast as if somehow he could stop the inevitable . . . and then the entire giant crumbled into a jumble of fragmented bones and scraps of cloth.

The last vestiges of Khan's image vanished.

Kentril found himself falling again.

Down and down he dropped, descending so fast he could scarcely breathe. The shattered ruins of the once-resurrected kingdom beckoned him. Kentril shut his eyes, praying that the end would be swift and relatively painless.

Just as he expected to hit, the terrified fighter suddenly halted once again. Captain Dumon's eyes opened wide. About a hundred feet or so below him, the roofless remnants of a rounded structure met his stunned gaze.

No sooner had this registered than Kentril began to drop, but at a slower, almost cautious rate. He looked around, trying to find the cause of this miracle.

The still shadowed palace of Juris Khan greeted him.

Somehow, the light of the crystal had managed to avoid the towering structure, but now true dawn had finally arrived, and the first rays of the day had already begun to eat away at the last of the false darkness. Kentril might not have thought more of the edifice's demise, but then he saw the figure poised at the very edge of the grand balcony, a figure with flowing hair of red.

Even so far apart, their eyes locked. Kentril saw in Atanna's a combination of emotions that left him so startled that at first he did not realize that she continued to lower him toward safety. Only when a brief, sad smile escaped her otherwise solemn expression did he understand *all* she had done.

The light began to pour over the palace. Kentril felt himself drop faster, but not so fast that he risked death. Atanna leaned over the rail, her arm outstretched toward him.

Although he knew that Juris Khan's daughter did not seek his hand, Captain Dumon could not help reaching for her. Atanna gave him another, deeper smile—

The sun touched her.

As it rose up her body, Atanna simply *faded* away.

At that point, the grand hilltop palace of Juris Khan collapsed in upon itself, quickly reduced to dust and ancient rubble. The hill itself seemed almost to deflate.

And without Atanna's spell to maintain his descent, Kentril Dumon dropped like a stone toward the ground.

Twenty-Three

Voices pierced the darkness.

"Maybe it'd be better if you just raise him from the dead and be done with it, lad."

"He lives . . . although how that can be, I cannot possibly say."

Kentril wanted the voices to go away, to leave him to his eternal peace, but they would not.

"I will try something else. Maybe that can stir him."

A snort. "You should be using some of that power for mending yourself!"

"I will survive . . ."

A pinprick of light pierced the empty blackness, irritating the mercenary. Kentril tried to cover his eyes, but pain suddenly coursed through him.

"He moved, Humbart! He reacted!"

"Will wonders never cease!"

The light became insistent, glaring. It burned into his mind, forced him to look at it.

With a moan, Kentril opened his eyes.

Daylight greeted him, but it had not been the source of the glaring illumination. That proved to be the flaring light of an ivory dagger, a dagger held in the left hand of the necromancer Zayl.

The *only* hand remaining to the necromancer.

Zayl's other arm ended in a bound stump just above the wrist. The pale Rathmian looked even more pale save where his face had been scarred red. His clothing hung in pieces, and he looked as if he had not slept in days.

"Welcome back, captain," the spellcaster commented in a tone that for him almost bordered on the convivial.

"Lo! The dead rise!" chuckled the voice of Humbart Wessel. The skull sat perched on a rock next to the kneeling Zayl.

"Zayl..." Kentril managed to gasp. His own voice came out as more of a dry, hacking sound. "You're ... alive ..."

The necromancer nodded. "You are as surprised about that as I am about finding you. How is it that you are down here among the ruins when you had to climb up to the top of Nymyr to stop Juris Khan?"

Kentril forced himself to turn. As he did, his lower chest and left shoulder ached terribly.

"Be careful, captain. You suffered broken ribs and a dislocated shoulder. They can be healed a little better when I myself have recovered more, but it will take time."

Ignoring him, Kentril looked at all that remained of fabled Ureh. Even less seemed to be left standing than when he had first come across the place. The outer wall stood in fragments, and the roof of nearly every building within had collapsed. Ureh now looked less like a haunted legend than like just one more ancient city abandoned to time and the elements.

And of the palace, only the crumbling foundation yet existed.

"Tell me what happened, Captain Dumon," the necromancer urged. "If you do not mind."

Of all people, Zayl certainly deserved the truth. Accepting a flask of water from the spellcaster, Kentril went into as much detail as he could recall, from the initial ascent to the pursuit, Gorst's sacrifice, and finally his own decision to end the shadowed kingdom's threat even at the cost of his own life. As he spoke of Atanna, the weary fighter's throat closed, and his eyes moistened, but he continued his tale until his companion knew everything.

At the end, Zayl nodded sagely. "Perhaps a true archangel watched over you, captain. You timed it very well, especially where I was concerned. Another few seconds, and Khan's demonic children would have torn me to shreds. Only the knife and some skillful playacting by Humbart preserved me for that long."

"What did he do?" Kentril asked, glancing at the skull.

"Only pretended to be himself, their lord and ruler, calling to them to halt because the necromancer was needed for a spell. Did something like that with Khan, too. Maybe I should go on the stage after this!"

That brought a hint of a smile from Zayl. "Since neither our good host nor his corrupted people could see him, the idea bought a few precious seconds both times. Even still, the horde got over its confusion quite quickly"—he raised the bound stump—"as you can see."

"Is it all over, then? Has the danger passed?"

"Yes. Ureh and her people are at rest, and the gateway to Hell is sealed once more. Before I found you, I searched the area for any traces of the corruption. There was none."

Kentril peered up at the sky. By his reckoning, it had to be just after midday . . . but on *what* day? "How long was I unconscious?"

"Two-and-a-half days. I found you just before sunset of the first and have done what I could."

Two-and-a-half days . . . Fighting the pain, the captain pushed himself up to a sitting position. "How are my legs, Zayl?"

"They appear unbroken, but you would know best."

Testing them, Kentril discovered that although they ached, he could at least tolerate moving them. "If I can stand, I want to get out of here. I don't want to sleep within the walls of this place another night."

Zayl frowned. "It might be more prudent to wait another day or—"

"I want to *leave*."

"As you wish. I understand." With some effort, the necromancer rose. He put the skull in the torn pouch at his side, then moved to help the fighter.

As Kentril stood up, something clattered to the ground near his feet. Curious, he cautiously bent to pick it up.

Atanna's face looked back at him from the brooch.

"What is it?" asked Zayl, unable to see from his angle.

The captain quickly folded his fingers over it. "Nothing. Nothing at all. Let's go."

They headed toward the lush jungle. As they slowly walked, the necromancer informed Kentril of his plan for them. "We can make use of your old base camp tonight, then tomorrow I will guide us safely to some of the others of my ilk. They will be able to help heal both of us, and then you can be on your way."

"An outsider won't be a problem?"

Zayl chuckled slightly. "Not one who faced down Diablo himself. This will be a story they will want to hear."

Through the broken wall they stepped, leaving behind the Light among Lights forever. However, once well beyond the former limits of the shadow, Captain Dumon made Zayl come to a halt.

"Give me a moment, please," he requested.

In silence, Kentril looked back at what had become the end of both a dream and a nightmare. The wind howled through the crumbling skeleton of the lost city, sounding like a lament for all those who had perished.

"I am sorry about your friends," the necromancer said as kindly as he could.

Kentril, however, had not been thinking as much about them as about someone else. "It's done with. Best to be forgotten . . . forever."

He turned away once more, and they continued their trek. Yet, as he walked, Captain Kentril Dumon's hand slipped surreptitiously to a pouch on his belt . . . and dropped the brooch inside.

Behind him, the elements renewed their patient task of slowly and inevitably erasing the last memories of the kingdom of shadow.

About the Author

RICHARD A. KNAAK is the *New York Times* and *USA Today* bestselling author of some fifty novels and numerous shorter works. He has written for such well-known series as WORLD OF WARCRAFT, DIABLO, DRAGONLANCE, CONAN, and PATHFINDER and is the creator of the long-running, popular epic fantasy saga THE DRAGONREALM. He has also written comic, manga, and gaming material, and his works have been translated worldwide.